For the Ari in all of us.

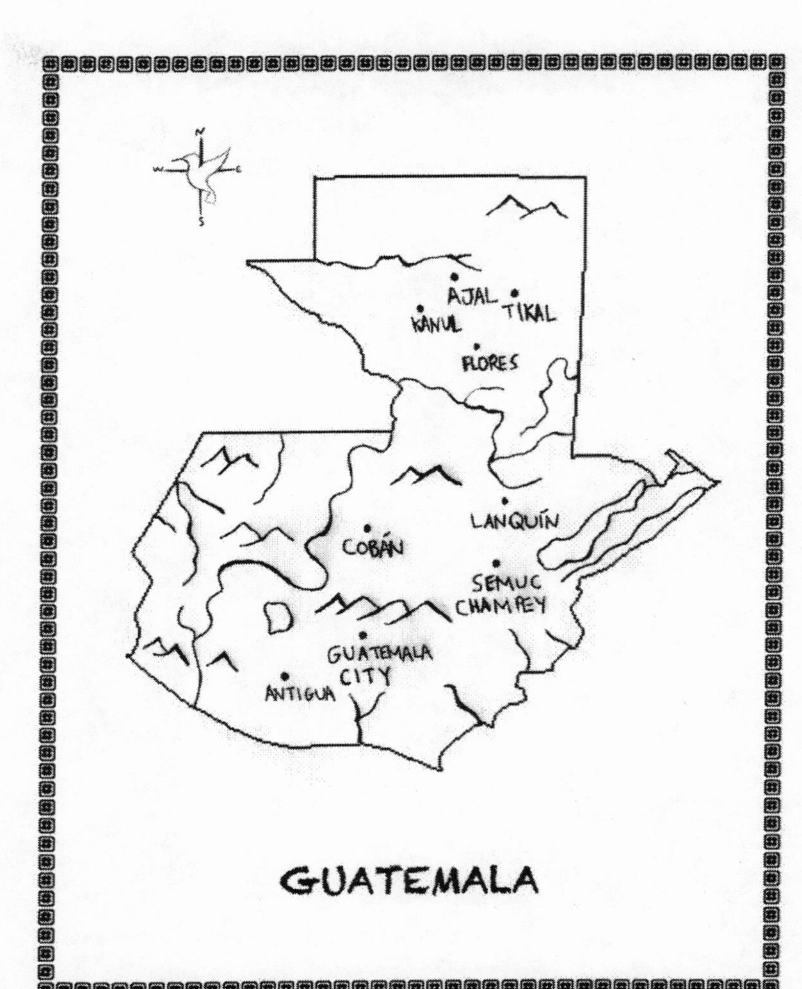
AJAL
TIKAL
KANUL
FLORES
LANQUÍN
COBÁN
SEMUC
CHAMPEY
GUATEMALA
CITY
ANTIGUA
GUATEMALA

Sutton Bishop

ANCIENT PASSAGES BOOK 1

AFRAID TO FALL

SUTTON BISHOP

NliveN, LLC
880 Lennox Drive
Zionsville, IN 46077

Afraid to Fall, Ancient Passages, Book 1

ISBN: 978-0-9898816-4-7
ISBN: 978-0-9898816-5-4 (e-book)

Printed in the USA

For more information, contact: thesuttonbishop@gmail.com

Cover by Ally Hastings, Starcrossed Covers
Edited by Quiethouse Editing and Victory Editing

THE LEGEND

In the beginning, there was the Great God. He was a thoughtful and efficient creator. After making all the other birds, he found he had leftover pieces, so he made a little bird. He called it the colibrí. Weak of legs, the bird would spend almost all its time flying. Because the bird was tiny and vulnerable, the Great God wished to do more, so he bestowed it with extraordinary abilities. He gave the colibrí the capacity to fly sideways, backward, upside down, and hover.

The Great God liked the little bird very much, so he decided to present it with a mate from the last remaining bird parts. To celebrate, he told the couple that they would be married and have the first wedding on the planet.

All the other animals of the forest were invited. The birds sang lovely songs. The spiders made a large spiderweb path and encouraged the female colibrí to use their webs for her future nest. Everything was beautiful, except the tiny colibrís. They were plain and dull. The other birds gifted the bride and groom some of their beautiful feathers, making them festive for their momentous day. The sun came out and announced them married and made it so their feathers would be colorful and shimmer with magic forever.

—Tata
Mayan Shaman
Petén, Guatemala

The tiny *colibrí* (hummingbird) is a common indigenous symbol of safe passage during a long journey, buoyed by hope, and embracing joy and the wonder of the world.

When hovering, a hummingbird's wings beat in a figure-eight pattern, the symbol of infinity—a reminder that we may regret or long for the past, but we need to reflect on it and let it go. What occurred in the past is not nearly as important as what is happening here and now, and we should allow ourselves to experience and savor the present.

MIGRATION

Upon the dawn of the present age, the Great God placed the life-giving Ceiba at the axis mundi of the cosmos, the Earth, the middle world. This was the navel of the world, where creation was birthed.

The massive Ceiba grew and grew. Its roots reached deep into the earth and into Xibalba, the underworld realm of the dead. Its branches stretched up, up, up and supported Heaven, the highest world.

Xibalba, Earth, and Heaven were now connected by the Ceiba.

We, the Maya, believe the souls of the dead follow the Ceiba roots into Xibalba. Our ancestors ascend the same way to visit the living, then pass through the trunk to the tops of the tree and on to Heaven, if that is the journey they seek.

The crown of the Ceiba spreads wide. Its branches grow in the four cardinal directions of East, West, South, and North, spreading life.

—Tata
Mayan Shaman
Petén, Guatemala

THE WADDED-UP LETTER LAY where Ari had tossed it, on her unmade bed. She ran her hands through her riot of coppery red curls, squinting into the blazing sunshine streaming through the large open window. The intimate courtyard, where she had often read or napped in one of the bright woven hammocks during the late afternoons of her two-week stay, was empty except for the ornate fountain. Its cascading water danced, shimmering and sparkling in the early-morning light. A stark contrast to what she felt right now.

Eric had pretty much left her alone for the rest of the semester, yet the letter had been waiting for her at the front desk upon her arrival in Antigua. She had recognized the writing immediately but had avoided opening it. Her heart skittered, and tears pooled in her eyes, threatening to spill over while her breath came in shallow, short cycles. How had Eric found her in Guatemala? Why was he contacting her? She'd ended it. *Breathe*, she told herself. *Calm down.*

She glanced back over at the letter and massaged her temples, which pulsed with pain. Too much beer last night on the terrace. Ari took a long drink of water, accepting that she had stayed up well past when she'd intended, deep in conversation with other travelers and enjoying the mariachi.

Surveying the room, Ari sighed. Clothes she had yet to stuff into her large duffel bag lay scattered around her small room—on the tile floor, the bed, and draped over the top of the desk and the lone chair in the corner. Her bulging toiletry bag hung from the bathroom door.

She stepped back from the window after remembering she wore

nothing other than panties. With resignation, she plopped onto the bed and picked the letter up by a ragged corner as if it were toxic, which in a sense it was. Full of liquid courage late last night, Ari had skimmed it—enough to realize she didn't need to read more. Why read it when she could put it off? She rolled over and stuffed it into the nether reaches of her duffel. Eric was not going to ruin her day.

Out of habit, Ari's fingers migrated to the base of her throat. Her sterling necklace, a delicate chain with a hummingbird, a gift from her father before she'd left for Guatemala, was cool to the touch. Her father had included a message with the gift: "Tenacity and courage, Ari. But above all, safe passage. Your mom and I look forward to your safe return and hearing about your extraordinary adventure at the end of the summer. We love you, Papa."

Ari reached for a tank top and her loose-fitting travel pants. One all-terrain sandal peeked out from beneath her bed; the other was hiding. It was going to be a long day of travel. She'd slip them on after breakfast, as well as a scarf to cover and contain most of her bright locks.

Dressed but shoeless, Ari headed upstairs to the terrace for breakfast—a meal she had skipped most of her life until she arrived in Antigua. She was a convert now. Breakfast here was her favorite meal. Each morning, Ari eagerly looked forward to some new combination of fresh, organic eggs and molé, fried sweet plantains, local cheese, warm handmade tortillas, pureed beans, cream, fruit, and avocado. And of course there was the divine Guatemalan coffee.

The day promised to be another hot and humid one, like every day since she had arrived. A Canadian couple she'd met last night was finishing breakfast at one of the tables.

"Good morning! What are you all doing today?"

"Good morning, Ari!" said the man, putting down his coffee mug and rising. "We're taking a local tour around the city. How are you feeling this morning? Sarah is a little hungover."

"I'm sorry to hear that, Sarah. I hope you feel better. I have a small headache, but I expect breakfast will get rid of it."

Sarah rested her fork on her empty plate and stood. "Thanks. You're headed north this morning, right? How far are you traveling again?"

"I'm going to Guatemala City and then on to Cobán. I'll overnight there and then make another overnight stopover before I get to Flores."

"Ben and I will be thinking of you. You're quite the adventurer, and it sounds so exciting, excavating ancient ruins." She placed her hand on Ari's wrist and gently squeezed. "Be safe."

Ari had forgotten their names since last night, so she was relieved when the couple mentioned them. "Thank you. It was nice to meet you, Sarah and Ben. Enjoy the rest of your vacation here."

Ari sat at another ceramic-topped metal table shaded by an umbrella and turned her attention to the panoramic vista over the terra-cotta tile roof to the west. The majestic peaks of Fuego, Agua, and Pacaya stood in the distance, overlooking Guatemala's first capital. A plume of smoke blanketed the continually active Fuego. She was going to miss the beautiful view of the volcanoes and the charming colonial city and looked forward to coming back someday.

A woman's gentle voice next to her pulled Ari out of her musing. *"Buenos días, señorita."* She mimed pouring coffee with the ceramic pitcher she held. *"Café?"*

"*Sí,*" Ari replied, eager for her morning local coffee. *"Gracias."* Ari smiled to herself as she acknowledged that *good morning* sounded so much more pleasant in Spanish.

"Desayuno Chapin?"

"Sí, por favor." A Guatemalan-style breakfast was simply the best. Ari was confident it would help chase away the pain pounding in her temples. As she sipped the coffee and waited for her meal, Ari's thoughts turned once again to Eric's letter. *Let it go. Focus on the moment.*

The smooth, rich roasted brew cleared the last remains of her sleepy fog. She toasted the view with her steaming ceramic cup, bidding her extraordinary time in Antigua goodbye. She had over three months to spend in Guatemala and so much more to experience ahead of her. Soft wings of excitement beat in Ari's belly. She was truly on her way after breakfast. A huge smile lit her face.

ARI LEANED TO THE RIGHT. The heading above the front window read ANTIGUA GUATE CIUDAD VIEJA, confirming she was boarding the correct bus—the one to Guatemala City's center. She opened her backpack once again as she stood waiting to board the bus, making sure her essentials were at the top: inflatable pillow, rain gear, snacks, full water bottles. *Check*.

The sun was hours from reaching its peak, and yet the air was already terribly sticky. May was the beginning of the rainy season. Ari reflected on her rainy hike up Pacaya two days earlier. She'd arrived back at her hostel tired, damp, and sore yet thankful she had experienced the smoking Pacaya. The views, when briefly uncloaked by the clouds, had been spectacular. She was confident that few could say they had hiked and camped on an active volcano.

Women, children, and men now surrounded her. Through her mirrored sunglasses, she watched a Mayan mother and her children sitting on the grass next to the group of people waiting to get on the bus to Guatemala City. The mother nursed her infant from the safety of a woven sling. Periodically, she spoke to her young daughter. The woman and her daughter wore traditional clothing—decorative brocaded blouses and colorful treadle-loomed skirts were held together by equally colorful and mismatched woven belts. Somehow the vibrant combinations were beautiful. The daughter was bareheaded except for white, red, and green cord braided through her thick black hair. Her mother wore a headdress woven with bright yellow, red, purple, and turquoise striped fabric. Ari found it difficult to stop staring.

She wished she had allowed herself a bigger budget and more room in her luggage for textiles—they were gorgeous. She had shopped a few times in Antigua's central *mercado*, as well as the Nim Po't market within the long hall past Santa Catalina's yellow arch. Indecision had plagued her, so she arrived back at the hostel with a few scarves and a belt. Her friends back home often teased Ari about her frugality. She planned to make some purchases before returning home at the end of the summer.

Squeaky brakes and noisy hydraulics announced the arrival of a bus of many colors, a refitted American-manufactured school bus. Nothing was dull in Guatemala. The *camioneta de pollo*—chicken bus—had once been entirely yellow. Now its exterior was repainted cherry red and sported a turquoise-and-white grill—reminiscent of Guatemala's flag. Yellow, black, turquoise, and green paint covered a good portion of the red exterior. The bus looked like a showgirl on steroids.

Ari once again questioned her choice of transportation. Chicken buses, regularly used by the locals to transport their goods and livestock, were cheap, but their safety record wasn't the best. She smiled to herself, looking forward to sharing her intrepid experience with family and friends.

The group pushed forward, wanting in, unapologetic about invading personal space. Men shouted to each other in Spanish and Mayan tongues. Bags, packages, cages of small animals, and household items were lifted and passed from one person to another and up to the roof rack covering most of the bus's length. Three men nimbly moved about, pushing the items and luggage closer together, making room for more, and hopefully, balancing the top-heavy vehicle. Ari waved her hand above her head.

An earth-brown hand grabbed her duffel, grunting as he hoisted it up. "*Muy pesado!*" a man with merry dark brown eyes said and offered to help.

She acknowledged it was heavy and nodded, her eyes full of apology.

His eyes widened upon noticing the color of her hair. "*Bonita.*"

"*Gracias!*" Ari responded. So many in Guatemala had said something to her about her hair, like this man, saying it was beautiful.

The man tossed her duffel to one of the men on top of the bus, who in turn heaved it to another, whose knees bent when he caught its heavy weight. Grunting, he dropped the duffel onto the pile where it quickly disappeared, covered by a heavy-looking box. Thankfully, there was nothing breakable in her duffel. Maybe the letter would disintegrate. Maybe then she could forget about it. More and more items, including caged chickens, were passed up. The growing pile perched precariously on top of the roof rack, the bus swaying with each addition.

One of the men scrambled off the roof and down the ladder, making his way to the door, yelling and motioning passengers to step back. He opened the door and scrambled into the driver's seat. Women, children, men, and small animals began to pour in quickly behind him, filling the seats.

Ari kept getting pushed aside. The bus appeared full, but the driver motioned her in. He pointed toward the chrome bar, raising his voice above the loud chatter. *"Sostenga!"*

Ari reached up, grabbing hold. A man stood behind her, and another, more massive man, climbed up the steps and moved to stand in front of her. She was pinned in.

Ari had planned on catching some shut-eye, but that was going to be impossible. Now she had to stand the hour-plus ride to Guatemala City, unless someone got off, and then she was going to have to beat these men to a seat. How she wished she had gone to bed early. She looked around at the passengers, praying someone might offer her a seat. Stoic faces met her silent plea.

ARI HELD ON FOR DEAR life to the chrome bar extending from the ceiling. The bar, one of two that ran from the front of the bus to the back and parallel to either side of the aisle, had been added to the old US-manufactured bus when it was refitted with a bigger engine, a six-speed gearbox, a destination board, and longer seats. A metal plate above the steps indicated the Blue Bird bus had been made in Buena Vista, Virginia, in 1990. *I'm sure the people who made this bus never envisioned it looking like this.*

Most of the interior had been painted the same colors as the bus's exterior. However, DRUG-FREE ZONE showed through where the paint had worn above the driver's seat, next to the wide rearview mirror. Christmas lights and a large gold cross hung from the top of the front window. Adhered to the driver's side window was a large transparent decal of Mother Mary. Above it, LE DOY GRACIAS A DIOS POR BENDECIRNOS had been stenciled in red, in a crescent shape and enhanced by yellow hearts. *I thank God for blessing me too.*

Tucked into the driver's window visor was a photo of a woman and four young children. Ari felt some relief wash over her; the driver had deep faith and a lot to lose by being careless. An older man sat in the seat behind the driver. His soiled straw cowboy hat was pulled down over his brow. From his slumping, relaxed posture, he looked to be sleeping. Hopefully a relief driver. Just in case.

Loosening her grip meant Ari would surely land on top of the young child slumbering in his dozing mother's lap to the right of her, risking serious injury to the boy or his mother and incurring mother-wrath as the bus hurtled along its route. If the bus lurched the other way, she might be thrown into the lap of the wizened white-haired man to her left. Back in the US, standing in a moving bus was frowned upon. However, here, on her third bus ride in Guatemala and her first time on a chicken bus, standing-room-only seemed to be the norm, along with sharing a space with a host of animals.

The bus was crammed and uncomfortably warm. Some passengers slept through the cacophony and overcrowded seating, like the mother and child next to her, or ate snacks or midmorning meals from untied cloth, which had been fashioned into bags.

Her stomach growled. A glance at her watch indicated it had been hours since breakfast. Ari ran through what she had in her backpack, a fraction of what she'd packed in her duffel—two oranges, an avocado, and nuts. An orange sounded perfect right now, but it would require cutting, and her Swiss Army knife—a gift from her parents—was in the front pocket of her pants and impossible to get to until she was able to sit.

During her mental calculation, she noted how her fellow bus riders' expressions were calm in the soup of animal and human odors and bus fumes. Ari spread her sandal-and-dirt-covered feet out wider, thankful she had opted to wear socks, seeking to redistribute the shifting weight of her petite frame. Her shoulders and arms ached. She felt the telltale signs of forming blisters on her palms from gripping so hard as her hands slipped during the swaying ride.

Several coppery red tendrils, inherited from her mother, had escaped Ari's braids. One stuck to the damp temple of her freckled olive skin. The other flitted onto her nose, like a fly, as a balmy breeze moved through the open windows, just enough to tickle, and then it was gone. Ari wriggled her nose again, hoping to address the itching without letting go of the bar. No success. She turned her head, attempting to scratch her nose on her arm, and was rewarded with relief and a whiff of her armpit. She had showered that morning before breakfast but must have forgotten to put on deodorant. No doubt her ripeness added to the stench permeating the bus.

Ari rose onto her tippy-toes, straining to give her shoulders and arms a break and to see over the broad man holding on to the bar in front of her. Her calves screamed in defiance. What had she been thinking by hiking to Volcano Pacaya so close to a long bus ride to Cobán? Ari's legs were tight and ached from the strenuous climbing. *I wish I could stretch them.* The trail had been uneven, steep, and at times, slippery. The rough night spent camping had not allowed her body to relax or for her to sleep well.

Her thoughts drifted again to the hike. She had been awestruck by the beauty and the power of her surroundings, and the walking stick she had purchased from a local child before hiking proved useful during the more rugged sections and where the lava was fresher, fragile, and unstable. Pacaya's summit had been exhilarating and the view breathtaking once the rain had cleared the next morning and the noxious gasses blew off in the other direction. But a steep hike over a two-day period and sleeping in a damp tent just days before leading up to riding a series of buses? Not so smart. Ari shook her head. While she was outstanding in the book-smarts department, she often lacked in foresight—something her parents and friends teased her about.

Roasting marshmallows over flowing, scalding lava had been fun, but she had skipped the opportunity to cook a hot dog. Red meat was not part of her diet. Taking a chance on eating one would have likely made her sick, and she had a limited amount of medicine to combat intestinal issues. The other thrill seekers assured her the hot dogs tasted wonderful. *Good for them.*

The brakes screeched as the bus careened and abruptly pulled over, stopping to pick up a family of five on the side of the road. *Where on earth are they going to squeeze in?* Ari's eyes widened as several people moved from their seats and crowded into others. A few seats now had several adults and a pile of kids. She pounced into an open seat and was promptly joined by the man who had been standing in front of her. The seat ahead of her filled with the family of five.

A little girl sat on her mother's lap, facing Ari, eating a tortilla. The fresh-baked scent teased Ari's hungry stomach. She shyly pointed to the wisps of hair stuck to Ari's temples. "*Bonita.*"

Ari smiled back at her, nodding. "*Eres una niña bonita.*"

The little girl giggled her "*gracias*," then fixated on Ari's straight white teeth—the result of braces and exceptional dental care that had cost far more than the average Guatemalan family earned annually.

The man seated next to Ari studied her openly, making her nervous as she remembered the warnings of women being groped on buses. Her parents' concerns flew through her mind. They continued to be overly protective of their only child, even though she was an adult, had her doctorate in anthropology, and taught at the university. Their protectiveness irritated her most of the time, but now she reconsidered.

Ari wedged her backpack between the man and herself, directly challenging his almost-black eyes with her dark brown ones—her father's. He quit staring, his gaze moving to the window, seeming to observe the ever-changing lush terrain.

Ari pulled the Velcro tab of a side pocket and extracted her sanitizer, applying it all over and working it into her hands. Her blisters stung. Once it evaporated, she grabbed an orange out and pulled her knife from her pocket, carefully cutting a section and putting it in her mouth as the bus rocked over the road. Ari offered the man sharing her seat a section, which he accepted with a nod and a smile. The orange was perfectly ripe. She closed her eyes and kept herself from moaning in pleasure, savoring the orange's sweet juicy flesh as it quenched her thirst and stomach.

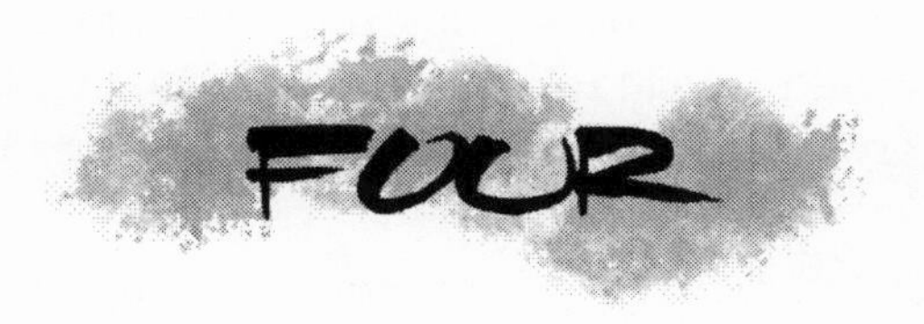

AFTER CLEARING CUSTOMS TWO WEEKS earlier at the airport, Ari's introduction to Guatemala had been armed militia dressed in drab, dark uniforms standing above her in the open mezzanine as she made her way out to find the shuttle she was to take to Antigua. Their serious expressions and machine guns were trained on her and others in the crowd of deplaning visitors and citizens. She had felt like one of those floating toy ducks she used to shoot at the local carnival when she was a child. Only these were real guns, with real bullets.

It was unnerving to know that she crossed the guns' sights and could be picked off more quickly than she could blink. She had inhaled deeply, reminding herself that the militia was not looking for someone like her. And yet someone like her, a redhead, certainly stood out.

Ari had stopped herself from glancing upward and swept the area in front of her, scanning signs for the shuttle. *Bingo.* She moved toward a man wearing dark pants and a light blue polo with the shuttle logo embroidered over his heart. He was roughly her height and held a sign with her name. Her heart slowed to normal as the driver greeted her by name and introduced himself, taking her duffel bag and helping her into the air-conditioned van.

The hour-plus, stop-and-go ride had taken Ari out of the uninspiring sprawling capital. Guatemala City's scenery had quickly morphed as the van drove toward Antigua. Buildings and compounds surrounded by razor wire, homes structured from corrugated metal, and children playing in large mounds of trash gave way to a landscape of beautiful hillsides and ravines punctuated with trees and forest. Relief had flooded her upon arriving at the charming UNESCO city. Colonial Antigua proved to be the perfect balm after her disaster with Eric and the perfect place to begin relaxing and immersing herself in Guatemala.

Antigua had an entirely different vibe than Guatemala City and was far safer. Ari had spent her days exploring the pastel façades, inner courtyards, churches, colonial relics, ruins, and enjoying daily siestas. She eagerly looked forward to traveling north and settling in Petén to work for the summer.

After seeing a documentary on Pompeii in Mr. Cummings's sixth grade social studies class, she was hooked on the past. The next documentary—on the Maya—pretty much solidified her future path. She took every anthropology course available at her large high school and in college, then expanded into forensics after exhausting her university's catalog. Ari's doctorate resulted from fieldwork and research in Italy, Egypt, and North Africa; then the university she currently taught at hired her. Finally, years after being seized by a passion that had never ebbed, she was now in Guatemala, thrilled to be exploring the Maya through their dead in Petén.

The bus driver called back to Ari, his voice urgent, pulling her from her reverie. *Oops.* She was one of the few left on the bus, blocking the man beside her from exiting.

"*Gracias*," she said, exiting the bus. Once out, she saw that her duffel lay in a pile, its strap pinned to the pavement by a crate full of chickens, causing her to wait until their owner claimed them. Ari squinted into the sky through her sunglasses; the sun was at high noon. Her stomach rumbled, not satisfied with the meager snack she had consumed during the trip. Guatemala City's newer modern bus terminal teemed with activity, color, and noise.

It seemed that every stop in Guatemala was a reason for some type of market or hawking of local goods, food, and drinks. This stop was no different. She glanced at her watch to confirm the hour. She had a little time to browse until she boarded the bus to Cobán.

Ari patted her gurgling stomach, willing it to calm down. The spicy scent of grilling meat beckoned, even though she was a vegetarian. How she would love some grilled vegetables or rice or beans, but she had been strongly cautioned against buying any food or drinks from street vendors.

She renewed her tug-of-war with her duffel. It did not budge. Two black-headed young boys ran up and lifted the crate full of chickens. Their squawking faded as the boys disappeared into the crowd, the crate balanced between them. Duffel freed, she slung the straps over her shoulder. Its attached wheels would be of no use on the rutted ground. Ari rocked under its weight, wishing she had packed lighter.

Widening her stance, she adjusted the bulk of it against the backpack hanging off her other shoulder, which was almost as cumbersome as her duffel. It was going to be paramount that she lighten her load considerably when working on-site. The smaller backpack within her duffel would have to do for work; she'd figure it out.

She toddled over to a large tree where space was available in the shade, just enough for one person if she sat on her duffel, and set her bag down as gently as possible between a family with a zillion kids and an elderly couple. Curious faces and gentle smiles greeted her, their eyes lingering on her hair. Getting comfortable with being conspicuous was more difficult than Ari had realized. Not only was she obviously an American but a redheaded one.

Although dappled shade under a tree provided respite from the relentless sun, sweat streaked in rivulets from her hairline. She opened her backpack and extracted the wet bandana packed from one of small packing cubes. It had stayed cool. She placed it on the back of her neck, then pulled the avocado from her pack.

Enormous and delicious, Guatemala's avocados were to die for. She had never eaten one plain until coming to Guatemala—where they were served with every meal. The people of Antigua had earned the nickname *panzas verdes* after surviving the 1773 earthquake's decimation of their city by living off avocados. She might as well become one of the green bellies but for a different reason—she loved the fruit.

She dug in her front pocket and, after extracting her Swiss Army knife, opened the blade. Spanish and Mayan dialects quieted around her. Dark eyes of every age watched her knife. Ari pantomimed how she intended to use the blade. Eyes continued to watch as she sliced the avocado's leathery skin and separated it from the fruit. She cut a wedge and popped it into her mouth. It was perfect. She gave her audience a green-toothed smile. Laughing and nodding, they returned to what they were doing.

She heard her mother's voice in her head. *Ari! No "see food"!* She smiled inwardly, wondering what her mom would think now since Ari had just used *see food* to relieve tension in a place where she knew no one. She had time to find a bathroom and to walk the market before boarding the bus to Cobán.

THE FOUR-HOUR BUS TRIP from Guatemala City to Cobán was uneventful and had far fewer passengers. Ari scored a seat all to herself. Screeching and pumping to a stop, the bus announced its arrival and woke Ari from her nap. In the luxury of space, she stood and stretched before exiting, blowing escaped tendrils of hair away from her mouth and eyes. She climbed the outside ladder and reached to pull her duffel bag from the top of the bus.

"I will retrieve that for you," a deep voice offered behind her. Not American but familiar, similar to her father's Italian accent.

Bingo. She felt the strap. Without turning around, Ari responded, "Thanks, but I have—" Her duffel slid away from her reach and moved downward as other chicken bus passengers scurried to get their baggage. It gathered speed and plummeted toward the paved road, taking other baggage with it. She slipped, falling as well.

"Merda!"

He is Italian. "Merda!" was her dad's go-to expression when he was upset, overwhelmed, or hurt, and as effective as its English translation, which she had a penchant for—*shit.*

Momentum slammed Ari against the man to whom the deep voice belonged. She stopped only when her butt landed hard on the cracking, dusty sidewalk, sending her sprawling on her back. "Ow! Dammit! That hu—" The sight to her right robbed Ari of more words. Instead, the telltale sign of humiliation spread over her chest and face, rivaling the color of a ripe tomato. Her heavy, overstuffed duffel had unzipped itself on impact, spilling some of its contents. Of course some of her personal items had littered the ancient walk.

Mortified, Ari clenched her eyes shut, seeking to block out what had just happened, all too aware of the towering stranger silhouetted by the sun. "Sorry," she mumbled.

A strong hand encircled her forearm and yanked her to her feet, snapping her head up in the process.

Irritation etched thick-lashed emerald-green eyes. "You should have let me help you. What the hell do you have in this thing?"

His gorgeous eyes held Ari's attention, rendering her speechless. Her body certainly responded though. Desire struck like a Mack Truck. It was likely she'd have slid back onto the pavement if he didn't hold on to her.

He waved his free hand. "Hey! That is not a rhetorical question."

His tone, words, and waving hand snapped Ari out of her musing. Agitation bubbled to the surface. Her body tensed, and she spit back, "None of your damn business."

He glared at her once more, as if weighing whether he should say anything else. Slowly a crooked, naughty smile appeared. Letting go of her, he bent over and reached, retrieving—

Oh no, no, no. A fresh surge of embarrassment flooded her.

The stranger held her pink thong by the section that was designated for "between the cheeks" and waved them at her. Amusement coated his words. "Nice. I did not think I would experience anything so, hm"—he shook his dark and shaggy gray-streaked mane, his eyes and voice filling with heat—"so tantalizing in Guatemala."

"Those are mine." Ari seethed. "Give 'em back."

"As you wish." He tossed them at her, his expression turning cool.

She caught them in her hand and deftly shoved them into a front pocket of her pants. "Jerk," she ground out between her teeth.

"You are welcome." Throwing his hands up in surrender, he walked away.

Rubbing her backside, Ari gathered the rest of her belongings and stuffed them into the duffel and rezipped it as best she could. She watched him cross the street and disappear around the corner. *Quit watching him.* Squaring her shoulders, she pulled her duffel along the rutted sidewalk from Cobán's bustling square to her hotel.

Even though she caught some shut-eye, the day's heat, humidity, and proximity to other loud bus passengers had taken their toll during the bus rides from Antigua and Guatemala City. After checking in, she showered, sighing in ecstasy as cool water flowed over her scalp and skin.

Ari surveyed her room while she applied lotion, then slipped into her yellow-print wraparound sundress. The room was small and simple but clean. Mayan art hung on the whitewashed stucco walls. A lamp sat on top of the scarred dark wood desk. She padded across the blue-and-yellow Mayan rug partially covering the tiled floor, bending over to better examine the pattern, that of the double-headed eagle. In Mayan mythology, the symbol represented the Great God with two faces, one face looking to Heaven and the other watching evil. Over time, the symbolism changed, representing the evil bird that came from faraway lands, the Spanish conquistadors, signifying Mayan women should never bear children in its presence because the eagle was cruel and unforgiving, and their children would suffer under its rule. Ari stood. Her fingers moved lightly over the loosely knotted mosquito netting hanging from the ceiling next to her bed. A fan swirled directly over the bed, and the screened window was open.

Opening the thick wood door, she took in her surroundings. Her room shared a terra-cotta tile covered porch with the other rooms on this side of the one-story hotel. Bright woven and mismatched hammocks hung every couple of posts, lining up with the rooms' doors. How she would love to climb into the one in front of her room for a siesta before she left Cobán, but this was a brief layover. She was leaving in the morning.

Looking out farther, she reveled in the beauty of the Guatemalan countryside. A carpet of green undulated into foothills and then into mountains, where she had been told coffee grew. She sat in the wood chair near the door and sipped water from her bottle, absorbing how the peaks and valleys changed hue and intensity as the sun lowered in the sky. The terrain was more verdant than the Antiguan countryside, at least from where she watched. Ari would see more of it tomorrow when she ventured to the hidden paradise Semuc Champey, a two-hour shuttle ride away. She had seen pictures and eagerly looked forward to hiking and swimming there.

Ari padded back into the bathroom and pulled her curly hair into a loose, messy knot at the nape of her neck, smiling deeply enough that her dimples showed. *Perfect.* As she added a little shadow and mascara to perk up her eyes, she thought about the stranger from earlier. Fluttering erupted in her stomach, and her groin twitched. *Omigod, what is wrong with me? Knock it off. Yes, he was gorgeous. Those eyes! But what a jerk.*

She grabbed her room key and purse and headed out to prowl Cobán for a cold beer and something to eat. There was a good chance she'd meet up with one or more fellow PhDs when she passed through the lobby since the team was staying here. If not tonight, surely tomorrow.

Information on all project members had been disseminated two weeks before she left for Guatemala. Ari's had been painfully brief because of her last-minute decision to apply for the project. In retrospect, she was comfortable flying under the radar. She hadn't been herself since discovering Eric's dishonesty and hadn't taken the time to look over her colleagues' materials, neither did she participate in the email exchanges. In fact, she'd never opened them. So here she was, in Cobán without knowledge of how many were involved in the project, what their specialties were, or how to recognize them. On top of that, the reminder of why she'd left the university and town so quickly had been stuffed into the bottom of her duffel before leaving Antigua.

Luca lay back on his pillow in his non-air-conditioned room, lost in the fan rotating above him, its soft breeze pleasant on his still-damp-from-the-shower nakedness. He closed his eyes, hoping to catch a nap before dinner. Traveling for over thirty hours, with stops in three countries and the eight-hour time difference, had wearied his step and his mind. Shuttling to Cobán immediately after landing in Guatemala City had offered little chance of sleep and recovery. Instead, he found himself appreciating Guatemala's rugged scenery and taking photos. It had been years since he was here, and he had forgotten how beautiful it was.

Guatemala's weather was similar to his childhood home in Rome during the summer months. The stone and concrete buildings surrounding the tiny apartment in which he'd lived with his parents held on to the day's scorching heat, baking its residents long after the sun disappeared. There had been no fan in his family's apartment. It was a luxury his parents could not afford, but Mamma had a way of hanging wet sheets in the balcony window and catching the early-evening breeze just right. Luca slept in front of that window during summer nights, after his mamma applied cool, wet cloths to his skin. Comfortable, he would drift off to sleep, feeling deeply loved.

Mamma had such a gentle touch. Would Sofia have touched their child like that? He would never know. Luca's hand drifted to the flat scar snaking from the inside of his right hip bone and ending in his groin. It would always be a reminder. He chided himself softly in Italian, "Enough! It has been eight years. Let it go. Focus on today, for it is the beginning of the future."

Luca raked his fingers through his dark wet hair. It was wavy, long—past his shoulders—and thick. Water droplets scattered across his face and onto his chest. The pillow was soaked. He sat up and reached for the towel on the chair, stuffing it under his head as he lay back.

Sofia had asked him to grow his hair out when they were first dating and he was finishing graduate school. He'd refused, believing his professors would not consider him serious about the field of study he pursued. His hair was almost as long as Sofia's had been when she died.

He had insulated himself from people after the accident, throwing himself deeper and deeper into his research. He spent most nights in his office at the university, showering at the gym after his morning run. It was easier that way. He could avoid their apartment, which was still full of Sofia's things and many memories, some of which were not so pleasant. He could avoid Sofia's sister, her friends, and their mutual ones. He could avoid the aching and sympathy in their eyes and their questions and attempts to engage him in conversations and social events. In time, they'd stopped reaching out to him.

Steeped in research, Luca had let his hair grow. He wore it down when the weather was cool and in a ponytail or a knot when the temperature warmed or when he worked out or trained.

Sofia had disliked facial hair, so Luca had kept his face smooth even though he hated shaving. After she died, grooming had become less important. His salt-and-pepper beard grew bushy, and he trimmed it back every few weeks. Before leaving for Guatemala, Luca planned to shave his face clean and get his hair cut short, but as he mulled over his appearance in the mirror while ridding himself of his beard, he decided to leave his hair long. He liked the look. He would tie it up, which would be adequate when working on-site in the Guatemalan climate.

Luca groaned. Sleep was not coming, but his thoughts were, at an increasing pace. He had only a few days to rest between here and Flores and to become acquainted with most of his team before heading to the project. He rose from the bed and pulled the paperwork from his battered briefcase. After grabbing a dry towel from the bathroom and tossing it onto the wooden chair, which had seen better days, he sat naked and withdrew the accordion folder from his battered leather satchel.

As far as he knew, most of team was gathering for dinner tonight. Luca perused each colleague's file intently. All the files had headshots except one, but that would be simple to figure out. Perhaps it had been lost in transmission. He would be able to remember the corresponding names better after meeting and speaking with each member. The only person not in Cobán tonight was his assistant, who was delayed and was flying into Flores in two days.

Luca tossed the folder on the desk and grabbed the orientation binder. He believed it was thorough; however, he looked it over again. Bored, he rose and stretched. His thoughts strayed to the petite redhead he had been short-tempered with at the bus stop. Would any of them be as interesting as her? He grinned. A sassy American. A hot-pink thong. He felt himself stir. Unconsciously, his palm drifted lower. She was appealing; an unusual combination of fiery hair, umber eyes, freckles, and bronzed skin. Why had he snapped at her? It had to be his fatigue. It would have been enjoyable to run into her again before he left Cobán, see where things went. An undeniable chemistry had sparked between them during those mere minutes; that much he was certain of.

A middle-aged woman stopped Ari as she entered the small lobby area. "Hello, dear. I believe we're working together in Petén. Are you Ariana Antony?"

"I am. I prefer Ari though. And you are?"

"I'm Joan Fisher, from Washington State. It's nice to meet you, Ari. I'm a cartographer. I've never been in Guatemala. I'm so excited about seeing the ruins. I tried to memorize the résumés"—she laughed, shaking her head—"sorry, CVs, and pictures of everyone coming in for this project. You look just like your photo, only younger. Lucky you. Anthropology, right? Forensics is your specialty? I noticed you're a recent tenured associate professor, at twenty-eight? Wow! Good for you!"

Confused, Ari asked, "My photo? Um, I didn't send one in. As it was, I only sent a short bio. You seem to know quite a bit about me."

"I'm a nosy one, dear. I researched you," Joan said, her double chin jiggling under her smile.

Uh-huh. Inwardly, Ari rolled her eyes. She was so tired of people commenting on her youth and tenure. White-haired Joan seemed kind though. "Well, thank you. And yes, I'm fortunate to have been awarded tenure at this point in my career. I started college early, kinda moved quickly through my degrees."

"Dedication, it sounds like to me. Having someone as young and smart as you around will be fun. I'm sure you'll run all of us old-timers ragged."

She just smiled and said, "It's nice to meet you, Joan." She turned to go.

"Where are you headed, Ari?"

"I'm going to go find something to eat and a cold beer."

"A bunch of us, the entire team actually, are headed to dinner, a place known for their molé. Want to join us? Here's more passing through now."

She wavered. It would be nice to be by herself, but she did need to meet her teammates and establish working relationships. She would be spending a lot of time with them over the ensuing months. She turned to where Joan looked—spotting people who were likely her colleagues. They greeted Joan and looked her over with interest.

Joan called to them, "You all go on ahead. We'll be right behind you."

"Well, okay. I haven't met anyone until you, so I guess it's time I meet the people I'm spending the summer with. It won't be a late night, right? I'm exhausted. I rode in buses all day."

"You brave girl! Did you ride a chicken bus?"

She nodded. "It—"

"Come on." Joan began walking toward the door. "Aren't they something else? You know, one went off the road last week, just outside Guatemala City. Injured the passengers and killed the driver."

Ari's stomach lurched. "Really?"

"Yes. So sad. Apparently happens all the time." She patted Ari's hand. "We won't be too late. Most of us are going to Flores tomorrow. We've been here a few days. Seen the town. Seen the markets. Seen Semuc Champey. We're ready to dig in"—Joan laughed at her double entendre—"and begin our research. Are you heading to Flores with us tomorrow?"

"No. I'm going to visit Semuc Champey before immersing myself in the research project. It's on my bucket list. Joan?"

"Yes, honey?" Her eyes were warm, full of motherliness.

"Thanks for including me tonight."

"But of course, dear," said Joan, squeezing Ari's forearm, then prattling enthusiastically as they walked toward dinner.

The team had pushed tables together, expanding the seating area as colleagues arrived. Ari sat toward the back of the small restaurant, a seat away from Joan and next to Keaton, a photogrammetrist who would be assisting Joan with collecting and interpreting the site's geographic data. She wanted to pinch herself. The scope of the team staggered her imagination. In addition to Joan and Keaton, she had met colleagues whose specialties ranged from archaeology and cultural anthropology to biological anthropology and ornithology.

Excitement about working together on the interdisciplinary project bubbled among the group. They became louder and louder as they dined and drank. Their energy was contagious. Ari found herself fully engaged. She was listening intently to Matt—the linguistic anthropologist and epigrapher, when someone else entered the restaurant and was hailed by Joan. "Hey, Luca! Join us!"

Ari turned in her seat and looked, seeking the newcomer. She turned away, disbelief overwhelming her.

"Hello, everyone. I am sorry to be late. I was detained by a phone call." Luca kissed Joan, who had risen to greet him, on both cheeks and then turned his attention to the seat on the other side of him to acknowledge its occupant. He bent over. "Hello," he said into Ari's ear.

She turned, facing him, stunned by his closeness. "Hello," she muttered, her eyes round with the shock of seeing him again.

Amusement sparkled in his eyes and a barely there smile played over his face. There was one chair left—between her and Joan. He rested his hands on its back, claiming it for himself.

Joan's voice was full of surprise. "You two know each other?"

"We've met," Ari said coolly, trying to figure out how she could extract herself from the restaurant as quickly as possible.

Taken aback by the rebuff in Ari's tone, Luca squinted. "Yes. But we did not introduce ourselves." He extended his hand. "I am Luca. Luca Fierro."

The timbre of his voice did funny things to her insides. Ari's eyes widened, and her breathing became shallow. She shook her head and found her hand extending to shake his, hypnotized by his beauty. "Dr. Ariana Antony." Her skin tingled as their hands touched.

His smile was devastating. "We are all doctors here. What is your specialty, Dr. Antony?"

She swallowed, refusing to be baited, and said seriously, "Forensic anthropology."

He smirked, and mischief lit his eyes. "Has someone died?"

Enraptured, Ari returned his smirk. She couldn't help herself. Its effect was disarming and fun. "From what I understand, all of them."

Luca threw his head back, and deep laughter exploded from him.

She joined in. Laughter felt wonderful and cleared out all the fluttering wreaking havoc in her body. When was the last time she'd laughed like this?

He pulled out the chair and sat. His eyes sparkled with mirth. "Can I order you a beer, Dr. Antony?"

"It's Ari."

Leaning toward her, he lowered his voice so that only she could hear, almost purring. His accompanying slow smile grazed her ear. "Can I get you a beer, Ari?"

The mother lode of desire kicked Ari in her core, and her heart beat as though she'd run a 5K. "Okay, thanks."

"Is the local beer fine with you? I understand it is good. Although, I do prefer a nice bottle of red."

"I like red wine, too, but not in Guatemala. Local beer will be great."

He asked the waitstaff for two beers, then smiled at her again. Deep dimples etched his cheeks. Her heart hammered harder. Her lips parted as if to get more oxygen. Ari's senses were threatening to leave her, and that would be a problem.

Luca's eyes searched hers, as if gauging her. He stroked his rough jawline, his eyes crinkling and the corner of his mouth turning up into the sexiest amused grin. Then he shifted slightly to speak to Matt across the table. His fresh soapy fragrance wafted her way.

She took this time to observe him. His thick, wavy hair was pulled back into a ponytail, which was somehow very masculine on him. He hadn't shaved, lending a rough look to his handsome face. The shadows enhanced his mesmerizing eyes, thickly winged brows, and jawline. His worn pale blue button-down shirt was rolled up from his wrists, exposing strong forearms. The memory from the bus stop hurtled forward, slowing the beating of her heart and the heat building in her body.

Luca seemed to sense Ari's change. He crossed his arms and leaned way back in his chair, studying her. A puzzled look crossed his face. "I see. We have a lot of work to do, yes?"

"Is that a rhetorical question?" she asked, mirroring his posture, pushing her weight into her chair so that it tilted onto its back legs. It started to teeter.

Luca's eyes never left her face as his hand shot forward and grabbed her chair, righting it before she fell backward. "You buy the second round." Once again, his eyes took on a mischievous glint.

The voice inside her head warned *danger… danger…* but she overrode it and heard herself saying, "You're assuming I'm staying."

His confident expression challenged her. "It would be rude of you to leave after you accepted my offer of a beer. Would it not, Ari?" He leaned forward and lifted his beer, his green gaze looking deeply into her rich brown eyes. *"Salute."*

She looked at the table as the full impact of Luca's playful sensuality hit her, hoping the restaurant's low lighting hid her flushed face and response to him. She struggled for composure, looking him straight in the eye as was expected in Italian culture, nodding back as she lifted her beer to his. He was right. It would be rude to leave.

Pounding. *Stop it. Please.* Moaning, Ari rolled onto her stomach and pulled the sheet over her head.

More pounding. Someone was at her door. She grabbed her watch. It was six a.m. *Ugh. Why does the hotel staff clean so early?* More pounding.

"I'm not up," she answered. "Come back later."

"Ari, it's Meg. Come on! We're leaving in fifteen. You should get some breakfast."

Plans made last night came racing back. Plans made after her fourth—or was it her fifth?—beer. Meg, from Australia, and one of two botanists on the project had asked if she could go to Semuc Champey with Ari. The women met after dinner last night, mingling and talking over beers. They had moved the timetable up to make the most of the day. Six a.m. came early when she'd gone to bed after one. What on earth had she been thinking?

"Come on, sleepyhead. I'll order your breakfast. You all right with Guatemalan eggs?"

"Perfect! Thanks, Meg. I'll be down shortly," she yelled through the door. Ari flipped back over and kicked off her sheet and stretched and breathed deeply to begin waking up. Sexy green eyes and a teasing smirk flitted through her mind. Her heart beat faster. Heat flushed her body. No. She would not think of him.

The majority of their group had shared their plans to leave early this morning for Flores, undeterred by the late night. Ari assumed that meant Luca as well, even though she had not seen him after their second round of beers.

She had played it smart, drinking as much water as beer. She wasn't hungover, just sleep deprived, which she could make up with a nap later. Ari rushed to get ready and pulled her smaller backpack from her duffel. The letter fell out. She snatched it angrily and compressed it again into a small wad and stuffed it back deep into the larger bag, saving it for the right time to address it properly.

Ari filled her pack quickly and then threw everything else into her duffel. She and Meg planned to spend the day swimming, sunning, and hiking. She had a reservation at a hostel in Lanquín tonight. Last night, Meg had offered to join her. It would be fun. The plan was to drop their duffels off at the hostel before catching a local truck to Semuc Champey.

She glanced around the room. She had barely spent any time here, yet she felt bereft. Her soul begged to be grounded. *Soon*, she promised herself. *Soon.*

THE SPARKLING SAPPHIRE POOLS OF Semuc Champey beckoned. Outcroppings of rock punctuated the thick jungle's growth before disappearing into the water. The muffled thunder of the Cahabón River rushing out under the limestone bridge silenced numerous waterfalls cascading into the clear water around her.

Ari felt she was smack-dab in the middle of a fairy tale. At any moment, she expected to see some creature from the fairy tales read to her as a child. The place was magical, even with people milling about, swimming, tubing, yelling, and singing. How nice it would be to be here by herself, without Meg or anyone else, soaking in the exquisite sunshine dancing on the water's surface and listening to the water and chatter of the birds. She might have been able to lapse into a daydream or lulled by nature's music into a nap on the toasty limestone bank. But first a hike to the *mirador*.

"I hiked most of yesterday in the hills surrounding Cobán with Matt and Keaton. I'm going to stay behind and find us a primo spot to sun our beautiful forms," Meg said, pulling a paperback and sunscreen from her backpack.

Ari glanced ahead to where the trail vanished. "Okay. Can I leave my backpack with you? Hiking will be easier." Her legs were wobbly from bracing herself while standing in the bed of an old pickup for thirty minutes. The wild ride from Lanquín to Semuc Champey had thrown her around as it bounced through potholes and over large rocks.

"Sure! Take some pictures for me, okay?" Meg held a safari hat in her other hand. "I'm going to soak this good, then read and wait for you. Take your time."

Nodding, Ari slung her camera around her neck, stuffed an orange into her front pocket, and hooked a water bottle onto her belt loop.

The forty-five-minute hike to the lookout was challenging. From researching, she knew the steep climb was roughly two-thirds of a mile. The going was slower and more treacherous than normal due to an early-morning flash downpour. Crumbling rock further hindered the path. Eventually the steps turned to wood, giving her a break from those made of stone. Although intact, the steps were uneven and huge for her short legs.

A planked wood deck with railing extended out above, safely overlooking the three-hundred-meter-wide tiered pools nestled in the valley of the rising jungle walls. Ari recovered some of her energy in the dappled shade while she took in the spectacular view. The people below looked like ants. She took a number of pictures and then asked a cute couple to take a few more of her, capturing the pools below her in the background. She peeled and savored her orange before cautiously hiking down, nursing one of her water bottles empty by the time she met Meg, who was absorbed in reading her book. A fine sheen of sweat covered her, rivaling Ari's.

"Hey," Ari said as she sat. "Looks like you're overdue for another dip."

Meg stood and waded in with her hat on and then jumped off the ledge into deeper water. Splashing around and waving, she called, "Come on in! The water's great!"

She waved Meg off, deciding to wait until more of her strength returned before swimming. "Give me a few minutes." There were no lifeguards here. There were few safety precautions anywhere, a stark difference from the US.

Meg pulled herself from the water and sat next to Ari, cooling her with water drops. "The water's perfect."

"I'm so glad I made the decision to do it. Unforgettable." She shared the details of the grueling climb and photos of the view.

"Wow! Looks amazing. You've convinced me. I'm hiking it later. You know, after I'm refreshed from swimming and tubing."

Ari slipped off her sports sandals and socks and waded carefully with them into the calf-deep water covering the submerged smooth limestone rock. Crouching down, she rinsed the mud and broken rock bits from her sandals and socks. Her toes tickled as tiny fish nibbled at them. She smiled; it felt great. She took her time, enjoying the natural pedicure she'd heard so much about. She tossed her socks and sandals back onto the dry rock next to her backpack. Ari hung on to her bikini top as she pulled off her sweat-soaked tee and swished it through the water. *That should get some of the stink out.*

The shallow water felt wonderful. She splashed water up onto her torso and then lay back to submerge herself. Sufficiently cooled off, she waded over to the dry, flat limestone to spread out her socks and tee to bake in the hot sun.

She withdrew another full bottle of water and her shawl from her backpack to use as a makeshift towel and slipped on her sunglasses. As Ari began to recline, she glanced at the view. An athletic hunk of gorgeousness was just breaking the surface of the pool across from her. His tanned, sculpted back was exquisite, the lean muscle of a serious swimmer. Not one iota of extra pounds. He sprayed water in every direction as he shook his long dark hair. Ari continued to stare, entranced. Desire budded low within her. He turned with catlike grace, giving her a view of his rippling six-pack. Her eyes moved upward to his defined pecs and then to his chiseled face. *Omigod. No.* He seemed to look directly at her.

Her eyebrows rose above the top of her sunglasses in shock. She sensed his amusement and threw herself backward too quickly. Pain burst in the back of her head. *Shit.* She wanted to disappear as soon as the pain, nausea, and embarrassment subsided. Ari inhaled deeply and held it for four counts, exhaled slowly for four, and then rested for four. She did it again. And then again. The nausea subsided and the pain diminished, but embarrassment lingered.

"Are you okay?" a deep, softly accented voice asked.

It was him. She fought the waves of desire pulsing through her. *Dammit. I'm falling apart.*

His voice became more urgent. "Are you okay?"

Her nerve endings were going off like firecrackers. She focused on regulating her breathing. To her ears she sounded like she was panting. Ari stammered, "I think so…" She struggled to sit up.

Luca emerged from the water and lowered himself next to her. One large hand braced her arm, holding her steady. His other cupped the back of her damp head. "You have a chicken egg."

Her laughter erupted, easing her embarrassment and the discomfort of having him so close, of touching her. "You mean goose egg."

His smile was gentle, yet beguiling. "Yes. I get your American sayings mixed up sometimes."

Her light-headedness returned.

Luca held her more firmly. "*Cazzarola!* You must have cracked your head hard. You are not okay. I do not have any ice, but I will sit with you until you seem better." He grabbed her bottle, unscrewed the top, ordering, "Drink."

Wow is right, Ari thought, interpreting Luca's Italian. "Thanks. I'm fine," she said, even though her head hurt. "Really. Just go on and swim. Or whatever."

His devastating smile returned. "I am done swimming for now."

She had trouble thinking of how to respond. She felt drunk and dizzy all at once. What a brilliant decision that she had purchased mirrored sunglasses. And of course his gorgeous chest was naked and even more impressive up close.

Luca's dimples deepened as he spoke. "Ari?"

"Oh, yes." She drank deeply from her bottle. "Sorry. I really do feel better. I hiked to the viewpoint. Spectacular but more difficult than I expected. Did you hike up?"

"To the *mirador*? Yes. It was breathtaking."

He seemed to lean in, and she swayed slightly. He grabbed her. "You are off-balance."

You have no idea. "I'm fine. I'll be refreshed if I get in the water."

Luca stood and extended his hand. Like his chest, it was one of lean male strength.

Ari had noticed his hands last night. She'd also noticed the absence of a wedding band. Was he available, or was he like Eric? She was afraid to touch his hand, remembering sparking electricity that had traveled through her body when they'd touched last night and because of what she was feeling now. *With all this water, I might electrocute myself. Omigod, I'm being stupid.* "What?"

"Come on. I will hold on to you, so that you can cool off until you are balanced."

Ari swallowed. She hadn't meant now, but later, after he left. She did not trust her body.

Luca grabbed her hand, pulling her up to stand. "Come on. I will not let go. Trust me."

His words hit home. They reminded her of the letter, why she was in Guatemala.

"Are you swimming in *pantaloncini*? I doubt those will dry if you decide to." Luca's eyes moved appreciatively over the exposed skin her bikini top and cutoffs didn't cover. "Do you have on sunscreen? You are one mass of freckles."

Ari flinched. She hated it when people drew attention to her speckled flesh. After all the teasing she'd endured as a child and teen, she was still sensitive about the freckles that covered most of her body. She pulled her case from the pack's front zip pouch and put her sunglasses inside.

He noticed. "I did not mean to upset you. Your freckles are beautiful. They make an attractive woman all the more alluring."

She fumbled with her shorts at his admission. Confusion rioted with attraction, the mortification of being caught staring, and dawning pride. Ari unbuttoned and unzipped her damp, worn cutoffs. Holding on to her bikini bottom, she carefully extracted herself from her uncooperative shorts. Luca's gaze burned over her intermittently while she struggled, checking her progress yet making her feel undressed. She launched into the water in an effort to cover herself.

The water was deeper where she landed. Her bare feet slipped on the slick limestone and sediment, and she went under and then under again. Ari inhaled water as she struggled for air. She pushed up again, sputtering and coughing.

There was a large splash next to her, and then strong arms surrounded her from behind, lifting her up. Her heart froze in fear and from the realization that these were Luca's arms holding her. Ari's lungs burned with water. Her face burned with humiliation.

Quietly Luca said, "I have you." His lips brushed the outside of her ear. Delightful electricity hummed through her body. "Relax."

She coughed a few more times and then took another deep breath. She nodded, not trusting herself to speak.

He held her easily. He had to be close to a foot taller than her five foot three. Slowly, without letting go, Luca turned her around to face him and asked, "Do you know how to swim?"

His sunglasses were off. Luca's eyes were spectacular. Gold flecks broke up vibrant green. Droplets of water beaded on the edges of his thick black lashes and brows. His skin was tanned to a deep sepia. Scruff, longer than last night, covered his cheeks and chin. His nose was straight and his sensual lips full. His face was one of strength and masculinity.

"Yes. Actually, I swim well. Just… It went down the wrong pipe. This…" She looked around, stuttering. "This… was a combination of poor decisions."

"Poor decisions, huh?" He smiled slowly again, this one tender.

Ari's body went heavy as the full impact of his sensuality hit her.

"I have you. I will not let you fall."

She stumbled out of the water with Luca's help.

"Sit. I will return with my gear." He slipped his sunglasses back on and was gone before she could protest.

She sat on her shawl, wrapping it around her hips before applying more sunscreen on areas she could reach. The fierce rays could burn her quickly, even with her olive complexion and the good base she'd acquired while in Antigua.

The sun indicated that it was only midmorning, but Ari was ravenous. She unzipped her backpack to find the frozen chicken she had requested from the hotel last night thawed, still cold. Nuts, tortillas, an avocado, and hard cheese made up the rest of her meal. She popped a few nuts in her mouth.

"Having lunch already?"

Darn it. She had already forgotten about Meg.

Nodding, Ari held up her finger indicating for Meg to wait until after she had swallowed, then answered, "My light breakfast didn't last through the climb." *And my nerves.* "It's been hours since we left the hotel. Aren't you hungry?" She broke a small section of the cheese off and ate it.

"Not yet. I haven't hiked yet, so I have got reserves. I'm going tubing. I'll probably return ravenous. Back soon. Watch my stuff?"

"Sure, but I'm planning on caving after I eat. How long do you think you might be?"

Meg flipped her wrist to look at her watch. "Thirty? An hour at the most. I'll sun while you cave. Thanks, mate."

"Perfect. Be careful. I heard there are some treacherous rapids where the pools empty out into the Cahabón. You can hear them from here."

Luca walked up behind Meg. "Hello, Meg."

"Hey, Luca! G'day! Didn't realize you were here. I didn't see you on the Lanquín shuttle we rode this morning." Turning to Ari, she mouthed silently, "You didn't say anything. I'll see you two later." Meg looked as if she was about to break into laughter and winked at her.

Ari and Luca watched her go. "You are pink," Luca said, fixing his gaze on Ari's lithe back.

Through her sunglasses, Ari squinted into the sun to where Luca stood above her with a microfiber towel and bag. "I'm okay. I just put more sunscreen on."

He studied her more intently. "I will spread some sunscreen on your back and shoulders."

"Um. That's okay. I can manage. Thanks though, really." Her face flushed with heat, surely making her rose red now.

"You are an octopus? I want to see how you cover your own back." He sounded amused.

She realized her protest was kind of weak. Of course she couldn't coat her back with sunscreen. Ari felt exposed in more ways than one. "You have a point there. Sure, lube me up."

Luca laughed. "Lube you up? I like that." He laughed some more.

Ari felt all of it in her groin. *God, he is gorgeous. And sexy. And probably off-limits.* "Maybe that wasn't such a great image."

A naughty smirk covered his face as he tossed his towel next to her and knelt down. "Where is your sunscreen?"

She handed him the small tube.

He purred in her ear. "I like the image."

Her breath caught. Desire rendered Ari's lower limbs boneless. She was thankful she was not standing because she doubted she could.

Luca's hands were strong, yet his touch was soothing. Did she imagine it, or was he doing more than spreading the sunscreen? He seemed to massage her shoulders and neck and then worked lower.

Her body relaxed under his gentle kneading, even though her nerve endings sparked, and blood rushed to her core, turning it to liquid. She took a deep breath to steel herself. "Are you always so meticulous about applying sunscreen?"

"Your skin enchants me," he said softly. He cleared his throat and spoke louder. "You are a redhead—granted a tawny one. I want to make sure the cream is absorbed. This sun is strong. I suspect you are here for most of the day?"

My skin enchants him. Ari sighed internally and smiled. "Yes."

"Do you have a hat?"

She dug into her backpack, extracting her father's Cubs hat. "Approve?"

"It will do, but your ears, nose, and shoulders will be exposed. You should consider getting another hat with more coverage." His hands moved to just above her strap.

Her voice hitched, and she pulled away. "I can finish up, thanks. Let's eat."

His lunch mirrored hers. Only there was more of it and a wonderful surprise that made her mouth salivate. Watermelon.

"Your sunglasses do not hide your excitement." He unwrapped the fruit, offering it to her. "There is enough. Eat."

"Are you sure?"

"Yes." He chuckled, adding, "You act like a delighted child."

She felt like a delighted child. Luca was gorgeous, thoughtful, and had just told her that her skin enchanted him. His nearness made her giddy. And now he was going to share his watermelon. "I love watermelon. It's practically my favorite fruit—well, along with peaches, strawberries, kiwi, clementines, and crisp fall apples." Catching herself, Ari stammered, "Oh… oh… sorry… More than you want to know, I expect." Ari took the smallest slab of watermelon. She bit delicately and wondered what else he could read about her as she savored its cool wetness. "This is so good. It really hits the spot! How did you keep it cool?"

"I brought a dry bag. I staked it and let it drift in the pool where the water is quiet."

She nodded. The watermelon was perfect. "Smart, so smart." She wanted to annihilate the slab and grab another. Had he noticed her taking in every bit of his sinewy torso earlier after he sat down with her? That thought caused her to take too large of a bite. She choked and juice trickled out of her mouth.

He leaned forward and quickly wiped it from her chin. His gesture was gentle. Heat lingered where his fingers had touched, and he cleared his throat. "I am exploring the caves after I finish my lunch. Would you like to join me?"

Ari's brows knitted together as she considered the turquoise pool before her. She had planned to check the caves out but with a group of tourists. Was it wise to go exploring with him? He had certainly shown himself to be charming and considerate, challenging her previous judgment of him, and he was certainly easy on the eyes.

Her breath quickened. Tingling raced through her body, along with a strong curiosity to see the caves and to spend more time with him. She decided to shelve her previous irritations with him, for now. She was going to be working with him in some capacity through the summer. She might as well face her reaction to him and deal with it.

"I'll take you up on your offer, if you don't mind waiting for Meg. I told her I'd watch her things." Ari busied herself with making a sandwich. She peeled and sliced the avocado with her knife and then added the rest of the cheese and the chicken. "She should be back soon," she said and tore into her sandwich.

"Tell me more about you, Luca. I didn't catch much last night other than you are Italian and like a nice bottle of red." Her brain began to function as she grew more accustomed to his presence.

He leaned forward and grabbed something from one of the front pockets of his backpack. Then he sat back, raking his fingers through his damp waves, quickly sweeping the mass into a thick coil off his neck and securing it to the back of his head. "Like you, I teach. In Italy. Università di Lazio. The program is new for the university. There is a lot of interest. My classes are small and fill before they open."

I bet they do. "What is your class load?"

"Three and one lab. They focus on parasitology and arachnology."

She shivered and took a small bite of her sandwich. "They sound interesting, if rather intense."

He noticed her shivering. "Are you still not feeling well?"

"Much better, thanks. It's just… I'm not a fan of spiders."

"I see. Mo—"

A cheery voice interrupted Ari and Luca's conversation. "Hey, mates!"

"*Ciao*, Meg! Taking a break?"

"My stomach brought me back." She plopped down onto her knees between them, and seeing the rind, she said, "Watermelon! Have any more?"

Ari looked at Luca in question.

"There is a little more. Your friend devoured most of it." His smile twitched. "Can you spare a bite?"

Ari was speechless, totally undone by his teasing and adorable grin. She could barely muster a nod.

He handed the almost-empty wrapper to Meg. "The rest is yours. We are going caving. Do you mind watching our belongings?"

Meg smiled a knowing smile. "You two go ahead. I'm going to read my book while I put my feet in the water. This place is Eden. I want to remember it."

"Are you sure?" Ari asked.

A book in one hand and sunscreen in the other, Meg gave Ari a brilliant smile. "I am." She shooed them. "Go. Have fun. Maybe I'll go after you return."

Luca stood and brushed his hands on his trunks, then strapped on his sandals. He handed Ari her damp sandals. "You will need these. I am ready." A headlamp hung from his hand.

Ari contemplated her half-eaten meal. She was torn by what seemed an order and complying with what might be her wish. *I need to stop comparing him to Eric.* She could eat more now or graze throughout the afternoon, which might be better in this heat. "Okay." She shimmied back into her cutoffs, slipped her sandals on, and followed him across the bridge.

A GROUP OF MAYAN MEN greeted Luca and Ari outside the entrance of the Kam'ba caves. They shared that they were guides and that the only way Luca and Ari could enter the caves was to be accompanied by several of them.

Two women waited closer to the mouth of the cave, war paint applied to their faces, courtesy of the guides. Each held an unlit candle. Ari waved off the war paint, as did Luca. She took a candle and attached her Cubs hat to one of the belt loops of her cutoffs via its snapback while waiting for instruction. The Maya briefly explained and demonstrated how best to navigate the mysterious abyss called the Kam'ba, lit only by candles and Luca's headlamp.

Luca translated the instructions to make sure Ari understood. "We need to be quiet and listen to them. The Kam'ba is full of stalactites and stalagmites. The guides will show us when to watch our heads and where to place our hands and feet. We will walk in rushing water and swim in pools and a cave tunnel. There are ropes in some of the areas. They are slick from the water and the elements. Keep your candle dry."

She nodded. "Thanks for making all of it clear. My Spanish is rusty. You're Italian. How is it you're fluent in Spanish?"

"My mamma is Spanish, so I grew up speaking her native tongue also. And French."

"Nice. I had two years of Spanish in high school and a class in undergrad. I haven't worked in any Spanish-speaking countries yet, so— " *Omigod. I'm babbling again, like an overflowing brook.*

"Do you speak Italian? I have noticed you seem to understand me when I lapse." He offered his hand.

Her struggle to maintain her composure as his hand engulfed hers was successful only when she reminded herself that he was doing it for safety. "My papa is Italian. I don't speak, but I understand a lot of it, the basic everyday conversation." What it might feel like to have Luca's hands gliding over her body flitted through Ari's consciousness. She swayed, and his grip tightened, steadying her before she fell.

"Careful there. As far as Spanish, you will have plenty of opportunity to improve it while you are here this summer. I expect that you will pick up some Q'eqchi' since local Maya will be assisting us during our time in Petén."

Elation washed over Ari. In a few short days, she would be among the Mayan ruins.

Pausing and turning to her before going deeper into the abyss behind one of the guides, Luca asked, "Ready?"

She nodded vigorously and took the lit candle from a guide, staying close to Luca, driving the images of what might be in the cave—spiders, bats, and God knows what else—from her mind and took a deep breath, steeling herself. With a weak smile at Luca, she blurted out, "I'm ready. But one more thing. I only had one class in geology. I don't remember the difference between stalactites and stalagmites. Do you?"

"Yes. I learned an easy way. Stalactite has a *C* for hanging from the ceiling. Stalagmite has a *G* for rising from the ground."

"I can remember that," Ari said, and suddenly she was seeing the first boulders and rock formations. They were beautiful. The air was dank and cooler but still comfortable. She took small, cautious steps on the slick, uneven floor, her sandals providing effective traction.

Their shadows dissolved as they moved deeper into the cave. Ahead was impenetrable darkness. Like the two women who completed their small group, Ari and Luca quieted and concentrated. During the next hour and a half, they walked, crawled, waded, and swam through tunnels and various depths of rushing water and pools—without life jackets, by candlelight and headlamp.

Halfway through, her candle extinguished, making the excursion more dangerous and tortuous. Luca kept his head down, often resting his cheek next to hers to share the beam from his headlight. Its light was far stronger than her candle had been, bathing a wider swath of the cave where he looked. Some sections resembled a forest of stalactites and stalagmites. In other areas, the ceilings and walls had been eroded by centuries of water, rounded smooth. It was surreal.

While she appreciated his generosity, she found his nearness unsettling, the intimacy intoxicating. It took every ounce of discipline for her to concentrate on her careful movements. Gingerly they felt where to put their feet and hands on the craggy and slippery footholds of rocks as they held on to the wet rope above them and climbed the steep, narrow duct-taped ladders, with nippy water splashing over them. He followed her slowly over the unforgiving narrow ledges. One mistake could prove disaster.

Something large and black brushed Ari as it flew by. She started and slipped.

Moving like lightning, Luca pushed her up against the rough wall. "I have you." He held her there until she stopped shaking. "Ready to walk again?"

She nodded, squeaking in answer, "Yes."

"Take your time." He relaxed his hold on the belt loop of her shorts after the ledge descended into shallow water.

Light up ahead revealed the tour was nearing its end. Relief surged through Ari. She had made it through in one piece. Now she could put some space between herself and Luca. Her body and mind couldn't take much more. He was a total turn-on, and she was losing her composure bit by bit. Eric had never had this effect on her. No man had.

The sunshine was blinding after being in the dark abyss. She was soaking wet. Rivulets of water ran from her hair and cutoffs, over her body, serving to keep her cool as the heat and humidity assailed her. Absorbed by the mesmerizing view surrounding her, Ari didn't notice that there was not a path back to the pools.

The guides approached them. Luca listened and then turned to translate for Ari, looking deeply into her eyes. "We are to jump. It is the only way down."

"Are you kidding me? There isn't a path?" Panic began to sink in. "Jump? It's so far down. Is it deep enough?" She began to head back to the cave opening, but Luca's hand stayed her.

He spoke to the guides, who shook their heads. "No path." Luca placed his hands on her shoulders. "You cannot go back the way we came. They do not take tourists out the other way. It is unsafe. It is against the water's flow."

Laughter flew past her as one of the women on their tour careened off the cliff, yelling as she flew. Ari was drawn forward by the splashing below and the woman shouting upward, encouraging her friend to follow her in. The other woman jumped, shouting all the way down until the water swallowed her voice. Ari looked over the ledge; they treaded water, huge smiles on their faces. They waved at her, motioning for her to jump. They looked safe and happy.

"Go ahead. I will jump after you."

She backed away from the ledge. "No."

"Fine. I will jump first, and you can follow me."

She began pacing. "I can do this. I've jumped into quarries before. It's just been a while."

"It's a longer jump than a quarry, Ari."

"No shit."

His eyebrows rose, and a displeased look flickered across his face. "I am looking out for you." Quietly he added, "You did great in there."

Her eyes were downcast in an effort to quell her quaking. "I was terrified at times, especially when that bird or bat flew by me."

"I believe it was a bird." He reached out to steady her. "You are swaying again."

The sensation of his stubbled cheek next to hers and his hand guiding her along, sometimes holding her, still lingered. The unwarranted pull she felt toward Luca was unsettling. She fought the suffocating desire that made it near impossible for her to breathe and couldn't look up because without her sunglasses she felt fully exposed, like he would be able to see everything she was feeling and thinking. After Eric, she was just too vulnerable.

She jerked away, wary. "Please, don't," she pleaded, her brown eyes flashing as she avoided eye contact.

He threw his hands up in the air. His expression looked injured. "I am trying to help."

"Just don't," she said before inhaling deeply and jumping. Ari screamed all the way down, hitting the water sooner than she expected. She popped up and treaded water, her success thrilling, wanting to do it again. Ari used her sidestroke to move toward the shore where the women from their tour stood. She felt as much as heard the loud splash behind her. She picked up her pace.

"I enjoyed that. Very much," he said as he caught up with her, matching her stroke for stroke.

Ari put her head in the water and swam harder, seeking emotional and physical distance.

He pulled up next to her, exiting the water at the same time. "Why the change in attitude? I believed we were making progress."

"I'm here to work on the excavation. Nothing more. You're a good-looking guy, and you find me interesting." Rising, she developed a sudden interest in the tiny fish swimming about her feet. She stepped out of the water and onto the limestone, facing him. "It would be stupid of me to say there isn't attraction between us. I get it. Summer fling."

Luca shook his head at that and scoffed, smirking.

"I'm serious." She continued, "I want to keep our relationship purely professional. The project head requested a forensic anthropologist with archaeological experience and a depth of knowledge about Mayan culture. I was selected because of my expertise. I am going to focus on the excavation and help where my knowledge is needed."

Challenged, Luca kept a straight face, gazing deeply into her eyes. Before turning and walking away, he said, "Sometimes relationships are messy, not quite what you presume. I will see you in Flores."

What the hell does that mean? Ari waited to begin walking back until she could no longer see Luca. When she got to where Meg lay on her towel—hat over her face, snoring, oblivious—his stuff was gone. Ari shook her gently. "Meg."

No response.

She shook her more roughly, her voice louder. "Meg! You're turning red. Where's your sunscreen?"

Meg pointed to her bag, grumbling. "Oh, man… Thanks. That was quick. I need to slather some more on." Pulling sunscreen from her pack, she asked, "How were the caves with Luca?"

A furrow appeared between Ari's eyebrows. "Terrifying. And amazing." She held out her hand so that Meg could give her some sunscreen. Rubbing the lotion onto her exposed nose and ears, she added, "You should check them out." She pulled the brim of her Cubs hat low. Her response to Luca after the tour had caught her off guard. She cast her eyes around. He was nowhere to be seen.

PREPARATION

In the beginning, there was nothing except the sky, and it was empty. Q'uq'umatz and Tepew—the great creators and makers—hovered above the primordial waters, surrounded by light and covered in blue and green feathers.

After much discussion, they decided to create light and lit the dawn so that it would awaken the day. Next they decided there should be something else. "Earth," they commanded. And it rose as the waters divided, complete with hills and valleys and plants and trees.

Then they created big and small animals to live in the trees and forest, including venomous snakes as guardians of the vines. Q'uq'umatz and Tepew asked that the animals sing their praises for creating them, but all they could do was squawk, chatter, roar, and howl.

Displeased, Q'uq'umatz and Tepew set about creating a creature that would be respectful and sing their praises—humans.

To the animals they said, "Hear us. This is your fate. From here on out, your flesh will be consumed and eaten."

—Tata
Mayan Shaman
Petén, Guatemala

LIGHT FROM THE EARLY-EVENING sun bathed Ari's room, mellowing the vibrant hue of the sunflower-yellow walls. The view of Lake Petén Itzá was beautiful. This nice, spacious clean room, with this lovely view, was hers for the duration of the summer project, when she was in Flores during periodic breaks. There was even a pool big enough to swim laps and a restaurant with an intimate bar. She imagined the team would spend a few evenings there discussing the work on-site—discoveries, assumptions, and theories. The small quaint hotel was fully rented out for the team, their little hub away from their homes and work. For the first time since leaving the States, palpable excitement—about what she was undertaking, exploring Mayan ruins and what she might discover—flowed through her unchecked. She was eager to start, feeling like she did as a child on Christmas morning.

She pulled her journal from her duffel and sat down at the scarred wooden desk across from her bed, writing page after page of notes about her impressions and experiences of riding the chicken bus and her time in Cobán, Lanquín, and Semuc Champey. Luca's green eyes permeated her thoughts, causing her heart to race and heat to flush her body. Her pen stilled.

Slouching in her chair, she fiddled with the hummingbird pendant resting between her collarbones. She took a deep breath, willing her heartbeat and body temperature to return to normal. Ari listed all the team members she had met so far, noted their disciplines, their nationalities, and where they taught. She added Luca last, then counted the names, coming up one short. After double-checking, she realized why—she was missing the person who assisted the entire interdisciplinary project. *Oh hell, what is their name? When will I pay more attention?*

She flipped to the next blank page and wrote Luca's name again. She crossed it out and then sat up, pushing the journal in front of her and dropping her pen onto the page. Ari leaned forward, her elbows on the desk, the knuckles of both hands supporting her jaw. She closed her eyes, reflecting on the conversations from yesterday and dinner in Cobán.

She and Luca had shared little personal information, yet there was a familiarity about him. Was it because he was Italian, like her father? She sighed deeply and placed her fingertips on her forehead. No. That wasn't it. Luca intrigued her, the way no man ever had. Something churned in her chest, and a growing ache gnawed between her legs. What scared the shit out of her was what niggled somewhere else. *My head is so fucked-up that I believe I might be feeling something.* Ari laughed out loud, shaking her head in disbelief. *No way.* She knew people could fall for each other fast, like her parents had. They were engaged within weeks of meeting and married within months. They were still happily married.

She picked up her pen again, mulling over how to describe him. She wrote: virile. In retrospect, Eric was certainly not nearly as virile. Not even close. He had been masculine, but it stopped there. Luca oozed sex. And, omigod, those eyes. She was totally sucked in. Her parents had always said that eyes were the windows to the soul. Ari was still in grade school when her mom explained what the saying meant, encouraging her to always look someone in the eye, then she would know what they felt, what their intentions were. "Trust what their eyes are telling you, Ari. And trust your gut." Why hadn't she remembered her mom's wise words with Eric? The truth had always been there. She just hadn't wanted to see it.

Under virile, Ari added strength. She felt safe with him—he had taken care of her when she slipped in the Semuc Champey and in the Kam'ba, yet she was fighting a visceral attraction to him. Just the thought of him sent her body into crazy mode, as if there were thousands of little electrical pulses going off. Her breath became shallow, and her heart started racing. It took all Ari's focus to bring her raging synapses under a modicum of control. Getting upset with him short-circuited her responses. She nodded. Yep, there was that, for a while anyway.

Hell, Luca emanated male strength—physically and emotionally, and just when he could go all macho man, he deflected it with humor or sensitivity. She added those to her Luca list as well. She had witnessed those traits, as well as patience, protectiveness, and nurturing. For not knowing him long or well, she knew a lot. Add it to his gorgeousness, and it was no wonder she was drawn to him, like a hummingbird to sweet nectar. *I don't want to get involved with him. I don't want the complications a relationship with him could bring.* She took a long-drawn breath and flipped a thick curl around a finger.

She thought about Meg—whom she liked a lot. Her gut told her she had met someone who would be a longtime good friend. Being an associate professor was lonely, in spite of loving teaching and research. Ari was by far the youngest in her department, twenty-eight, some twenty years younger than Eric, who was the closest to her age. She was typically treated as such—like regularly being assigned to bring paper products for department pitch-ins because her colleagues assumed she couldn't cook. She couldn't, but that was beside the point. If asked, she would have made a gallant effort, probably succeeding beyond what her coworkers expected. After all, great cooking resulted from following the directions. How difficult could that be? She was never given the chance, although she did bring a festive plate of cocoa-dusted peppermint cookies to the department holiday party. Baking was where she excelled. The men scarfed the cookies up. The women? Nope. They just looked down their academic noses. She never put forth the effort again.

Ari hadn't been blind to the tight expressions of her older female colleagues or the fleeting wolfish glances from male colleagues when she dressed in something that silhouetted her lean, toned physique. She was proud of her body and worked hard to keep it healthy, and she made sure her clothing choices were always appropriate.

Eric had often treated her like a child, something she'd found endearing at first but later, demeaning. That was when the cracks began to expand, but she soldiered on, believing their relationship was somehow special.

What would the other profs have thought about her and Eric? And now, based on what she knew, what would they think of him? Maybe they knew and were okay with it. Who was he really? And who were they?

None of the other profs were what she would consider friends, so why had she taken their jealous comments and obvious exclusions to heart? *I wanted to fit in.*

In her short time in Guatemala, she was making friends, chief among them Meg. They had talked and laughed nonstop late into the night in their shared room at Lanquín's hostel. They summarized the high points of their PhDs—Ari's in anthropology and Meg's just awarded in botany. They filled one another in about their families. Ari—an only child. Meg—an only girl with five older brothers and one younger. They compared where they'd grown up. Ari in a densely populated western suburb of Chicago. Meg on her family's sheep station in Queensland, Australia. As they moved into sharing memories of their childhoods and adolescence in the States and Australia, their conversation was claimed by sleep.

After breakfast, they had boarded the bus to Flores, traveling most of the day. Brief naps punctuated easy conversation and snacks. Meg informed her that the last in their group, someone from South Africa, should be arriving sometime today, after missing a connection that cascaded into a two-day delay. Ari meant to ask about the people responsible for overseeing the interdisciplinary team, but she had grown drowsy again and fallen asleep, waking when Meg jostled her shoulder upon arriving in Flores.

Yawning loudly, Ari had said, "Yesterday was a great day, Meg. Perfect. Spending time with you in Semuc Champey was a blast. And today was nice, when I was awake, I mean…"

"You have no problem sleeping, do you?" Meg asked, laughing.

She fell asleep easily and slept soundly on all transportation. Her parents teased her about it, when she brought a stack of books on vacation, pointing out she might as well pack them with everything else in the trunk; she would be asleep in mere minutes. "I don't. It's a life habit. I've always slept well when traveling. Mom and Papa said going places with me was so easy because I never asked 'Are we there yet?'"

"Lucky you," Meg said wistfully. "We didn't travel a lot because of the station, but I asked constantly when we did. And my brothers got into a lot of trouble. They were a couple of sandwiches short of a picnic—"

"What?"

"Oh, they did a lot of things without thinking," Meg said, sounding amused. "Boys." She shook her head and laughed ruefully. "Sometimes Dad had to stop on the side of the road and give them the what-for. Mum sat in the car with me, wringing her hands in worry. They returned somber or laughing, never crying. I guess it was okay."

The brakes protested as the bus came to a stop. Meg and Ari rose from their seats and ambled outside. While waiting on their bags to appear from the luggage compartments underneath, Ari stretched. "I signed on for this project in part to disappear. I arrived unprepared, but now I'm inspired. I've some catching up to do."

"What are you running from, Ari?"

"Hey! There's Matt. And Joan," she said, pointing and waving.

Meg waved at Joan and Matt, then spun back to Ari. "Sounds like we have an interesting topic to discuss."

"Oh, Meg, I'm sorry. It kinda slipped out. Forget it. Not important."

"You protest too much. Apparently, it is, and we will visit it soon." Meg reached over and hugged her. Noticing Ari's concerned look, she said, "It's okay. Really. And I promise that you will feel much better after talking to me. I'm an expert listener, as you already know, and I can be trusted with what you share. Deal?"

Ari looked into the bright sky-blue eyes of her new friend. Feeling brave, she nodded. "Yes. Thanks, Meg."

The alarm on Ari's phone went off, jarring her from her long reverie. She had dinner downstairs with Meg in an hour and plenty of time to unpack, organize her room, and treat herself to a leisurely shower. The corners of Ari's sun-kissed lips turned upward.

"ARI, OVER HERE!" MEG GESTURED, her blond ponytail bobbing. She sparkled with enthusiasm. Next to her stood a freshly showered Matt.

"Hey! Hi, Matt. Are we it?" Ari said.

Matt laughed, his merry brown eyes matching the color of his unruly mop of dark hair. "Hey, Ari. You look freshly laundered. I saw Miguel, James, Keaton, Sandra, Zhou, Joan, and, oh man… I forgot their names—"

Meg broke in. "No worries, Matty. You'll soon know them well enough." Facing Ari, she said, "I hope you don't mind? I went ahead and asked that the tables be moved closer together so that we can have a Welcome to Petén party of sorts. Aren't the showers cracker?"

Ari cocked her head and frowned. "Huh?"

"Um, that's Aussie for great. Gotcha again."

"You did. I've got to get my Aussie on. And yes, my shower was wonderful." Ari laughed, noticing Meg was talking a mile a minute.

Meg nodded at Ari's khaki skirt. "Adorable."

"It's my favorite, thanks. Washes and dries like a charm."

"My climbing gear works the same, sweat and then dry. Of course, I launder it between." Meg's smile brightened at Matt.

The dark frames of Matt's glasses did not hide his interest in Meg. Ari looked around the room to hide her giggle, decorated with maps and photos of the Petén jungle and Tikal. Colleagues strolled in, mingling, drinks in hand. A few glowed pink, likely due to time around the pool.

She realized they had had extra time to forge relationships. Everyone from Cobán appeared to be present, except Luca.

"Is everyone here?" she asked.

Matt said, "I believe so. I did a quick head count." He raised his beer. "I'm famished. Let's go socialize and eat." He extended his arm out to guide them.

Meg slid her arm loosely through his and moved closer. Ari fell in behind them, noticing they were of similar height and build, one blond and one dark, both lean and wiry.

Ari was relieved that Luca was not present, and if she was being honest, disappointed too.

The voices of her colleagues faded as Ari strolled farther from the gathering. She passed through the empty lobby en route to the stairs, relaxed and sleepy, although she had napped on the bus earlier. Eating more than she usually did at dinner had not helped.

Adrenaline, fueled by small talk, dissipated with each step she took. By the time she was at the top of the stairs, she was definitely more than ready for bed. The door to her room was down the balconied hall, past the right turn, at the dead end.

Persimmon-colored stucco walls held recessed spaces painted bright turquoise between every two rooms and frequently housed sitting areas with carved benches or chairs or an arrangement of planters. The recessed area next to her room was vacant. She planned to inquire about that tomorrow, ask if the hotel had an extra bench, chair, or even better, a hammock. Rings for a hammock were already mounted in the facing walls.

She was rounding the corner when she heard her name spoken softly. She slowed, paused, and shook her head. *Man, I'm really tired. Now I'm hearing voices.*

"Good evening, Ari. Are you ending your day early?" Luca materialized out of the shadow near the other set of stairs, stepping in, facing her closely. His eyes glowed in the moon's subdued light. Forced to look up, she was reminded of how he dwarfed her. His expression was what Nana said when she thought Ari got away with something as a child, reminiscent of the cat that swallowed the canary. The air sparked with electricity. A hint of a smile engaged his eyes. Ari's heart fluttered. She parted her lips.

His smile deepened. His hair was half-down and half pulled into a ponytail. Sexy as hell.

Ari stammered, "I'm going to bed. It's been a long day of travel. I'm ready to settle in."

"That is a pity."

"Why is my turning in for the night a pity?"

"Because I enjoy your company, but I upset you. I want to know you much better. I missed you today."

He wants to know me better. Her breath quickened. *What the hell is wrong with me?* "Why do you say you upset me?"

"Cobán. Semuc Champey."

"I was a bit reactive."

"Pickly."

Ari laughed, thankful for the release of tension. "Prickly, yes. And coming out of nowhere, well, it surprised me."

"English words. Confusing at times." His genuine smile exposed straight white teeth. His eyes twinkled with mischief. It was a handsome face full of character and confidence. "Why are you prickly?"

Her heart skipped a beat. "It's a long story. One I don't care to share right now."

Luca shrugged in acquiescence. "Fine. Are you too tired to take a short walk with me?" His movement stretched the tee skimming his muscled shoulders and chest.

She stared, as if spellbound, eventually becoming aware of the silence. Luca wore a shit-eating grin on his face, totally aware of his effect on her.

Ari's annoyance was diffused by his charm and her curiosity. She struggled for composure, asking, "Where?" *For fuck's sake, what's wrong with me? That is not what I meant to say.*

"There is a lovely promenade that runs next to our hotel, along the lake." His raised eyebrows changed the explanation to a question.

Her hands grew damp, and her heart stuttered again. She was so attracted to him it hurt.

"I am not a bad man. Truly." He reached forward and touched her tenderly on the cheek with his fingers.

Her breath caught from the heat of his fingers, and her nerve endings ignited. Huskiness tinged her voice. "It's late. I think I'd rather stay here."

"You would?" He looked deeply into her eyes. "Hm."

This is safer. I think. Nodding, she said, "Yes. We could…" She stared at his lips, her tongue tracing hers, unable to form any more words, wanting. Just a taste.

"Come with me?" Luca's smile was slow and tender as he took her hand and gently led her into the recessed area.

Her heart was pounding, and she licked her suddenly dry lips. "Yes," she whispered, willingly following.

Sighing, he slowly pulled her to him. Luca angled his head, pressing his forehead to hers. His hands cupped the sides of her neck and his thumbs stroked her jaw as he continued to look into her eyes.

Resting her forehead against Luca's anchored Ari. His feather-soft touches played havoc with her trippy senses. And his eyes… they held her. Made her ache. Made her want more. Something shifted inside Ari and opened.

He inhaled. "You smell wonderful." The tips of his fingers brushed the back of her neck as he tangled his fingers in her hair. "Your hair is beautiful. Soft. Sexy as hell." He drew back, his eyes half-closed and kissed her temple delicately, then paused to gauge her reaction, like a large patient cat.

She leaned into him, yearning. Letting go.

He continued, his lips moved lower, grazing her cheek and neck.

She craned her head back, basking in the sensations exploding through her body, bowing her neck, giving him more skin to kiss. Her lips had a mind of their own and parted, inviting him in. The smoldering heat of his eyes registered before she closed hers. Trembling with desire, Ari surrendered, opening her mouth further to deepen the kiss. She parted her legs, aching to feel more of his rigid length. His hand cupped her breast and thumbed her hard nipple under her tank top.

He broke the kiss to whisper, "Mm… no bra… nice…" Emboldened, he slid his other palm down the back of her naked knee. "I like your skirt," he murmured against her lips and then kissed her deeply again.

Her tongue answered Luca's. His hand moved upward, leisurely, his fingertips tracing lightly along her hamstring, setting her skin tingling in their wake. He brushed the lace of her panties. She moaned softly and reached up, threading her fingers through his hair. It felt so good. She ached for him to quit teasing her.

He moved his lips back to her ear, nipping the lobe. "Damn. Lace—" He groaned, his voice breaking as his fingers languorously stroked the lace, her inner thigh. "Are you wet?"

"Ye—"

Laughter and footsteps snapped them out of their steamy embrace.

"Hey, Ari! Luca! How was the meeting? All set for tomorrow?" Matt asked, his expression perplexed as he glanced back and forth between Luca and Ari hidden partially behind him.

Luca cleared his throat, allowing Ari a smidge more time to pull herself together. "Good evening. Everyone is now here. Natasha has arrived, and our meeting was productive. All of the team will convene after breakfast, as planned. My plan is to be concise so that the team can enjoy the afternoon off since we leave early for Tikal the next morning."

Ari reeled. No. Incredulity quickly chilled any remaining desire. She moved to Luca's side but kept her distance. "Hi, you two. We were having a talk."

Amusement covered Meg's face. "Some talk," she said, giggling.

With a sick feeling in the pit of her stomach, Ari faced Luca, inquiring, "You seem to know an awful lot about the logistics of our project. Just what is your specialty? And what exactly are you doing on the project?"

His steely expression was devoid of his earlier smoldering desire, his tone now all business. "I research and teach as a medical anthropologist. I oversee our time here."

"I don't understand." Confused, she cocked her head and looked from him to Meg, whose face was wreathed in a huge smile.

"Ari, meet our boss."

Ten

Ari compressed and flipped her pillow over for the hundredth time. Unquenched desire had driven her to toss and turn for hours—Luca's kisses and touches and her passionate responses played over and over in her mind. He had awoken a part of her that she'd been unaware of; its existence felt primal. She had fever for him. She had never felt this insatiable gnawing before.

Humiliation and anger kept her awake as well. The startling fact that Luca was her boss bothered her immensely. Her face burned when she remembered how she had abruptly fled to her room, ignoring Luca, Meg, and Matt's pleas—the action of a petulant child. Anger gave way to embarrassment as she reflected.

The blame for not knowing who Luca was fell to her. She hadn't read the CVs. Had she, well, maybe that would that have curbed her interest since his position as her boss would have deemed him entirely off-limits. But now she was in a pickle. She had dropped her defenses and willingly tasted and touched him.

Luca was sex on a stick. Their dance of intimacy had begun, and her entire body electrified with anticipation. He was in her blood, and she was hooked. Another wave of desire rode through her body. She was in deep doo-doo.

Ari sat up and pushed back her thick hair from her face, framing her face with her hands and closing her eyes. *What am I going to do?* She grabbed her watch—2:25. She had to pull herself together, get some sleep. The team meeting was at nine. Her alarm was set to go off in five hours, just enough time for a shower and breakfast. Ari closed her eyes again. She willed the fringes of sleep to appear. After ten minutes, she gave up and threw back the covers and flipped on the overhead light, blinking to adjust her eyes. She took a deep breath for fortification and opened the closet door, pulled out her duffel, and grabbed one of her sandals, just in case. After unzipping the duffel, she turned it upside down and shook it. The crushed letter fell to the floor. She kicked at the letter a few times. Convinced it was free of creepy-crawlers, especially the eight-legged kind, she dropped the sandal next to its mate and picked up the letter.

Smoothing out the wrinkles, she concentrated on Eric's writing—a combination of block and cursive, which made it difficult to read even though she had glossed over his research notes numerous times at his request. Her stomach tightened and ached. Repeated swallowing did nothing to push the burning to her throat. Ari dropped the letter and ran for the bathroom. Stomach roiling, she dropped to her knees just in time to empty the contents of her stomach into the toilet.

Sweating profusely and heart pounding, she rolled to her side, curling up on the cool tile. She hugged her stomach and sucked in air, trying to relax the cramping in her stomach, determined to move past this. She rose after she was sure the nausea had passed and rinsed her mouth with watered-down toothpaste.

Back in her room she chugged half the water in her bottle on the bedside table and plunked down on the tangled sheets with the letter. Her heart still raced as she focused on her task, fingers fidgeting with the hummingbird nestled at the base of her throat. Eric's voice spoke in her head as she read his words.

Dear Ariana,

I miss you. I miss us.

False words. Lying words.

You weren't a fling, well, not like you think. I cared deeply about you. In fact, I still do.

At that, she rolled her eyes, refuting his words, shouting, "Unbelievable! What utter bullshit!" Although her room was at the end of the hall and shared a wall with only one room—Meg's room—she paused and listened, wondering if she might have disturbed her friend. All was quiet.

The memory of discovering Eric's deceit replayed in her head. She saw him clearly in her mind—sitting at a round silver-topped table in the back of the shop, smiling broadly, his arm casually draped around an equally blond woman's shoulders, engaged in a conversation with two towheaded teenaged girls.

Her step faltered when she saw them, just enough that she slammed her toe into the metal trash can next to the door, slicing it open.

Eric, the woman, and the teens looked in the direction of Ari's yelp. His expression turned flinty before turning away and drawing the woman deeper into his embrace and speaking into her ear. Her face flushed as she looked up at Eric with adoration. Bright reflections from the rings on the woman's left hand reflected against the store walls and ceiling as she brushed his face, laughing in response. Wife. Eric was married. Ari stumbled out, trailing blood out of the store, not remembering any of her bike ride back to her apartment.

> *That was quite a fight we had. You have a fiery temper (goes with that interesting hair of yours). I didn't appreciate the foul words you called me. I hope you find it in your heart to apologize to me. You do owe me an apology.*

What an asshole.

Eric had appeared on her doorstep within the hour, incensed, accusing Ari of following him to the shop, of stalking him. He shoved her roughly into her apartment and slammed the storm door shut behind him.

She screamed at him, enraged that her naïveté had allowed this to happen, that she hadn't any idea he was married and a father, and that he had deliberately sucked her into an affair. How had she not seen the real him? He had presented himself as someone else.

Fear exploded in her when his face grew purple and he shoved her again. She seized her cell phone on the entry table next to where she crashed into the wall. Hand shaking, she waved it in his face, threatening to call the police. He had laughed, and she made the call, yelling at him to get the fuck out, to stay the hell away from her.

Like lightning, he had turned on his heel, the door cracking from the impact of his fury on his way out. Ari struggled to calm her panting while she lied to 911, that she had made the call in error. Hurriedly she swept up the glass shards, packed a suitcase, and left for her parents, the blaring country music settling her nerves and helping to staunch the flow of her tears.

As I explained, before you started screaming at me that night in your apartment, the same day you showed up in the ice-cream shop, my wife had planned our family vacation in Banff. She and the girls sprung it on me there as a surprise. At first I fought going because I wanted to spend as much time with you as possible before leaving the country. You and I had discussed making plans, remember? But as luck would have it, my wife stressed I was going to be gone most of the summer working and she and the girls wanted time with me. You understand my wife takes care of the social calendar. I just show up. So, when you acted crazy that night, well, that's why I left. We left on our vacation the next day.

You need to see my side of things. My marriage is not satisfying, but she's a nice person and I have two beautiful girls with her.

I came to see you again, after we returned a week later. Imagine my surprise upon discovering that you had moved, conveniently leaving while I was on vacation with my family. I'm disappointed in you, Ariana. Behavior such as this magnifies your age, despite you having your PhD. It's behavior I would expect from my teenage daughters.

Fuck you, Eric.

I was impressed that you were able to break your lease and move abruptly with no forwarding address. I tried calling, but you had changed your phone number. You ran away from me. I'm not happy that I had to track you down. You are wondering how and why I tracked you down, aren't you?

She nodded. What was his intention? Why bother contacting her?

The semester-end departmental email detailed how you were awarded a last-minute position on the interdisciplinary research project in Guatemala. Well done! And without my approval as dean, I might add. You can be very clever when you want. When I inquired after finding you gone, my secretary was able to dig up your address in Antigua, your new phone number, as well as the research itinerary. The why is pretty simple, Ariana. I miss you. I miss us.

Livid, she asked, "It's all about you, isn't it, Eric?" Her voice grew louder with each word. "Not even one iota of remorse! You are the shit of shits!" Pounding erupted on her shared wall. "Sorry!" she called out.

You and I happened rather fast. You gave me all the signals that you were interested in me. I'm sorry you felt the need to leave immediately after you found out I was married and a father. I thought you knew. In fact, I find it odd you didn't. You're so smart and outstanding at research.

I would have told you. You should have asked.

The night before the ice-cream store visit and their fight at her apartment she had been on cloud nine, buoyed by his words, "I care deeply for you, Ariana." He had manipulated her. Moved by his words, she had let him make love to her. He was somewhat mechanical, and the second time was over just as quickly, leaving her disappointed and her body not sated. The sex wasn't much of an improvement over when she'd lost her virginity to her high school boyfriend in the back of his parents' Ford after the homecoming dance. That had been a fumble-fest.

I haven't told my wife about us because I don't want to leave her and the girls, but I don't want to lose you either. I want to know what you are thinking.

Be your mistress? Are you fucking kidding me? Never. Shame coursed through Ari as she thought about how committed her parents were to each other and how they had modeled a healthy, loving relationship all her life. They would be appalled by her involvement with a married man.

You talked constantly about researching in Central America, specifically the Mayan culture you're so enamored with. Well, now you're there. Your expertise will

> *be extremely useful. I hope the experience is everything you hoped for, and more. You are exceptionally bright, although a bit naïve. That will change as you mature.*

Ari scoffed at that, sitting back and mulling over Eric's words. Always adding a put-down in with the compliment. His special one-two punch. *Prick*. His words blamed her, mocked her. She was so over him and his conceited, all-about-him self.

Ari had first met Eric—her new dean—when she'd attended the department cocktail party at the beginning of the fall semester. He had approached her. Maybe it was due to the second glass of wine she was working on, the one she grabbed from the passing server in order to steel herself against the feelings of inferiority she picked up from her female colleagues. The second glass must have compromised her schmuck radar and allowed him within her normally stout defenses. Or maybe it was due to reading Eric's résumé in the department newsletter, which highlighted his vast travel and publications, particularly in the same areas of anthropological interests she had, specifically the Maya.

Stocky and of average height, Eric was extremely fit for a man his age. Ari relaxed the more they talked, overcoming the initial uncomfortable sensations his eyes evoked. The pale blue color—many would call them ghostly—was the lightest eye color she had ever seen, and it took some getting used to. The alcohol helped. His wheat-hued flat top was peppered with white, and his skin had the undertones of an olive complexion. Ari found the combination interesting.

Eric was a wonderful conversationalist, aside from his ego, which kept making an appearance. She was in awe of his vast anthropological and archaeological experience, hanging on every word, every story.

He had not worn a wedding band, so she believed he was single. In fact, there was no mention of a wife or family when he was featured in the department newsletter as the new dean. The article had focused heavily on his research, publications, travels, and excavation work around the world. That evening, Eric had walked her back to her apartment bordering the university. The night was warm, and the stars popped in the sky. He was the perfect gentleman, leaving when she was safely inside.

She saw him often throughout the semester—in his office, passing on campus, a few times in the union cafeteria, and at departmental meetings and get-togethers. He was professional; however, Ari felt him watching her from a distance. It wasn't until the end-of-semester party, a brittle night with snow spitting in the blustery wind, that Eric walked her home again. He bid her good night with a kiss on the forehead.

She joined her parents on break in Mexico, not giving her fair-haired, blue-eyed dean more than a passing thought. She believed he was too old for her. But as soon as Ari returned, Eric continued to pursue her, and in retrospect, he was calculating, drawing no attention to himself or to them. He was always nice, and his interest disarmed her, offsetting the lack of inclusion by her departmental colleagues.

Their relationship progressed quickly. At the end of January, Eric asked her and a few of their colleagues to dinner. The weather turned to sleet, so he gave Ari a ride to her apartment. No one would think anything of it. He asked her to dinner a week later. This time it was just the two of them at a back table in the tiny dimly lit Japanese restaurant. He told her he would like to see her but wanted to keep it quiet due to the fact that they were colleagues and he was her boss. Many would not approve. She saw the sensibility in his request. He walked her home and sealed the evening with a chaste kiss, which she returned. Thereafter, Eric never again accompanied her anywhere, choosing to meet at her apartment instead, where they enjoyed intimate carryout dinners and conversation. No one knew about them.

She overlooked his autocratic temperament because she was so impressed by his mind and how people listened to him when he spoke. She snuck into several of his lectures and left before they were over, appreciating his mastery at the lectern and how his students hung on his every word, even though he tended to be pompous.

> *I've heard about the fellow heading it up. Italian and machismo. Brilliant. He can be a real son of a bitch. I also hear he chases a lot of skirts, so watch yourself.*

That's rich, Eric. You, the pot, calling the kettle black. Questions about Luca niggled in the back of her mind. Like Eric, he didn't wear a ring. But was he married? Did he have kids? She needed to listen and ask around discreetly. Dammit. Why was this happening again? Why was she attracted to the person she reported to? Granted he is a good decade younger or more than Eric and far more virile.

Luca's physicality made her swoon. His kisses burned hot where Eric's were tepid. And his green eyes, they beckoned her. Her body sizzled whenever his name was mentioned, when she thought of him, or when she was in his presence. Her common sense lagged in the distance. *Bullshit, Ari. He is arresting, disarming. Damnably sexy. Your brain takes a hiatus. All your defenses vanish. You need to find a modicum of control.*

She was in a heap of shit. Her powerful attraction to Luca could screw up her time on the excavation, as well as negatively impact the team of colleagues she had yet to bond with. *Shit, he's whom I report to. What am I going to do? I need to end it before it goes any further.*

> *You have my number. Call me. I want to set you straight, Ariana. You owe me this – and your apology, of course.*
>
> *Eric*

The blood left her brain, making her feel faint. She inhaled deeply. "Leave me alone, you bastard," she whispered angrily, sweating again, her heart racing. Tears ran from her eyes and dripped off her jaw onto her crossed tanned legs.

Her hand pressed the delicate hummingbird to the base of her throat. Closing her eyes, she continued taking deep cleansing breaths, focusing on giving herself a gift—that of forgiveness. She forgave herself for being naïve and for succumbing to Eric's lies. Her tears came harder as she forgave herself for hurting his wife and daughters, the thing that bothered her the most. Ari sat quietly on her bed, calm after she was cried out, recognizing a final step was called for.

She rose and dug through the top drawer of the dresser for matches, striking a match once she was in the bathroom. The letter caught fire immediately. Dropping the flaming letter to the shower floor, she said, "I dodged a bullet. Good riddance, you fucker."

As the paper turned to ash, the sense of weariness was replaced with peace. Ari turned on the shower, watching the ashes circle before disappearing down the drain. Chilled, she shed her clothes and rinsed off the dried sweat. She threw her towel on the back of the chair, flipped off the lights, and climbed into bed. She was asleep in minutes.

Back in his room, Luca started to read through his notes again. *Why? I can discuss the parameters and metrics in my sleep.* He rubbed his hand over the rough planes of his face and then tossed his notes aside and turned off the light, closing his tired eyes.

Ari's eyes, the color of rich earth after a soft morning rain, taunted him. His heart had skipped and sped up when he had seen the hunger in their depths earlier tonight, and when she had licked her full lips, he dove in. *Merda, can she kiss.* Sleep evaded him. However, visions of what he wanted to do to her did not. His body was taut with need. He growled and folded his arms above his head. The fan quietly rotating above pulled him into his thoughts. Sighing, he pulled his focus back to the summer ahead and how he had worked on the project for close to a year, planning and making changes as his team had taken shape, some of the world's best in their specific fields.

Working in Petén this summer might turn out to be his most rewarding project. The breadth and depth of knowledge was impressive, and he suspected having an interdisciplinary team would enrich the discoveries. The sharing of varied specialties would also come in handy when the monotony of excavating set in. And from past excavations, he knew it would become monotonous. Digging in and sifting through the earth day after day became tedious.

The surveys and preliminary work at Kanul, named for the abundance of serpents found on the stone lintels of the main temple, focused on the two sister excavations in the same site—Kaq and Rax. The Kaq excavation had exposed a palace complex, and even though the map of Rax was bare bones, it had already revealed that the settlements were dispersed farther from the palace city than was typical. Joan and Keaton would be exceptional in teasing out more details. The wealth of epigraphic records in the palace complex was promising and would be detailed by Matt. All indications pointed to the fact that there was something extensive in Kanul, possibly human remains and another unknown piece to the puzzle of the Maya.

The team would move between Kaq and Rax as needed, assisted by the local Maya. Luca had reached out to Carlos, a friend of his, when he knew he would be overseeing the project. Carlos grew up in Petén, close to Tikal. He had met him when he was researching and documenting parasitic vectors on the Belize–Guatemala border over a decade ago.

Carlos had taught himself English by escorting English-speaking tourists through the massive sight of Tikal, and the two men used either English or Spanish to communicate. His community had been decimated by Guatemala's civil war. With Carlos's help, Luca had hired other Maya to assist for the summer. Carlos had been in continual contact with Luca since last summer, sharing Mayan folklore and culture kept alive and passed down through the centuries. Luca had a binder of notes, and he was sure Ari would enjoy reading through it and adding more details. Her knowledge of the Maya was encyclopedic, and she was also an expert on the *Popol Vuh*, the Maya's book of community.

He sat up and punched his pillow, then lay back again. Yes, Luca had prepared well, but what he had not planned on was the beautiful, earthy Dr. Ariana Antony. Her curriculum vitae had been the last he had received. Although brief, it was succinct and provided him with the information he required to make an immediate offer to her to fill the last open spot on the project. She had accepted just as quickly, with a promise to get her required medical done and the corresponding paperwork sent in the following week. If she had included a headshot, he likely would have passed on her. She was evocative, her full mouth ripe for kissing. He doubted Ari was aware of her feminine power. There was an innocence to her, even when she was contrary with him. His strong interest in her was unsettling, reminding him of his younger self, the boy who had sailed his small boat on the Tyrrhenian Sea every summer, challenged with keeping his bearings in the sea's ever-changing conditions.

She tasted as sweet as she smelled, like honey, and her small curves, they filled his hands perfectly. Starting things in the hall. What had come over him? He, known for being in control of his emotions and his decisions, had fully given in to his desire. She was surprising and intriguing. Guarded, yet no bra and her choice in panties made him lose his head. He grinned. Lace panties, in the jungle of all places. Add that to the hot-pink thong he had retrieved in Cobán. He grew rock hard at the thought.

Based on Ari's confused expression and angry tone, his chances of moving any further with her were at a standstill. Why was she upset that she reported to him? She had acted stunned when Meg mentioned it. How could she not know? All CVs had been disseminated to the team members, along with photos, as well as the mission statement and a detailed schedule.

Where many had taken advantage to tout their pedigrees, going on and on for pages in their CVs about their research, publications, grants, and more, Ari's had been bare bones, one page of small font, as if not to call attention to herself. In a way, he was happy she had not included a photo. He would have been haunted by it. Her face was not one easily forgotten, and the blanket of freckles covering her tawny flawless skin made her more arresting. And that glorious curly crown of hair… *damn.*

What he did surmise from reading her one-pager was that she was among the youngest of the team, having skipped grades and flown through university and postgraduate school. Her intelligence jumped off the page. In person, she was complex, interesting, and alluring—all the more so because of what he sensed under the surface, a passionate, fiery woman. He had been the recipient of her quick temper at the bus stop in Cobán, responding in-kind while appreciating her unique beauty and the tension between them that was far more than her anger. It was primal lust. Maybe she had not recognized it then, but he had.

She had held back emotionally tonight. Why? Together they were combustion. Their kissing had rapidly escalated to exploration. What would have happened if Meg and Matt had not appeared? *I would like to know.*

His thoughts took him back to when she had been short with him at dinner in Cobán, and after they explored the caves at Semuc Champey she had become guarded and wary, like a jaguar's prey. Her fuse burned fast and hot, and that was a total turn-on. When her guard was down, she sucked him in with genuine displays of compassion, intelligence, and wicked humor. She was the most enticing woman he had ever met.

Luca followed the flat, snaking scar down his ripped abs to his groin and stroked his rigid length, He ached to kiss her again, to explore more of her beautiful body, to make her purr. And she had. Purred. A slow smile lit his features, and he grew harder. Luca's body spasmed with his release.

Something was definitely up with her. He chided himself. *Pazienza.* He was a patient man, and tomorrow was another opportunity to figure out the irresistible puzzle of Dr. Ariana Antony. His course of action decided, he relaxed. Sleep came quickly.

ELEVEN

THE BREEZE MOVING BETWEEN THE colonnaded arches took the edge off the morning's heat. Sunlight reflected off Lake Petén Itzá, bringing an unwelcome glare into the open-air veranda, causing Ari to squint. Ceiling fans rotated at a low speed. Most of the casual groupings of the tables and chairs had been moved closer together in the center front of the room in preparation for orientation. Many were still eating breakfast. She yanked the visor of her Cubs hat lower over her face and made a note to go back to her room and grab her sunglasses during the first break.

The stark light was too much for her puffy eyes. Dealing with Eric's letter and her reactions in the wee hours had drained her emotionally and physically. She had nibbled on pineapple and a tortilla, nervous her raw stomach might rebel.

"I'm so tired!" Meg said as she plopped her leggy self down next to Ari.

"I wondered where you were. I brought you something to eat. A tortilla, some avocado and pineapple, just in case. Not sure when the food is being cleared." She handed Meg the food threatening to fall out of the damp napkin.

"Thanks." Meg swallowed the avocado without chewing. She leaned over as she took a bite of the ripe pineapple and said, "Matt was all right."

"He is all right. Seems really sweet, Meg."

Meg slapped her hand on the table and chuckled. "Ari, for one so smart, you are so naïve. I meant I slept with him. He's amazing!" She gobbled the rest of the pineapple. "I'm famished. This is great. Thanks for thinking of me. Hey, are you going to finish your tortilla?"

She blushed, uncomfortable with Meg's generous sharing. "Oh. Um. That's more than I need to know. But good for you?" She handed Meg the rest of her food.

Meg nodded and gulped down the remaining food, chasing it with a long drink of water. "You look worn out. What or whom were you yelling at last night?" Abruptly she looked behind Ari, and an enormous smile lit her features. She winked at someone.

Ari turned to find the object of Meg's attention. Matt stood there, with a matching smile, his eyes on Meg, nodding. Meg motioned for him to grab a binder for her and join them at their table.

The two of them think they are playing this cool. Right. Unbidden, the thought surfaced of what it would have been like to sleep with Luca. Ari clamped her knees together to stifle her body's immediate response. Annoyance overrode her curiosity. He could have told her. No. She should have known.

Over the room's chatter, a voice called, "I believe we are all here. For those of you who missed breakfast—and there do seem to be a few—extra tortillas, beans, and fruit are next to the coffee in the back. Let's begin. Did everyone pick up a binder from the table next to the door?"

Nodding heads and yeses answered him.

Luca's deep timbre sent shock waves through Ari. She closed her eyes and felt his lips playing on hers again. Shaking her head, she opened her eyes to curb her overactive imagination and found Luca's emerald-green eyes resting on her, accompanied by the merest hint of a smile.

"Are you feeling okay, Ari?" he asked.

"Yes, thank you. Just tired." *Dammit. Why did I admit that?*

He nodded and said, "Many of us are." Luca surveyed the room, pausing briefly on every person in the room as he spoke louder. "Can everyone hear me? I realize it can be difficult in an open space. Move closer if you need to."

Everyone in the room had their chairs facing him and indicated they could hear him. He continued, "Good. Enjoy the weather we have this morning but focus on the information shared during orientation. I want to briefly go over where we will be. On page seven is a map of Petén. Thank you for creating that on short notice, Joan. The site of Kanul is northwest of Flores and almost due west of Tikal. While at Kanul, the team will be about the same distance from our base here in Flores as we will be when we are visiting Tikal over the next two days. However, the roads are not as well traveled or maintained. The commute will take far longer.

"To capture information, the team will rotate among themselves. As of now, the plan is to come in once a week, with either Natasha or me. We will adjust that schedule as needed. Although Kanul is being excavated, most of it is still covered by vegetation and jungle. There is a biological station close by, where Meg and myself will spend some time. Anyone who is interested is welcome to join us. Please ask in advance so that excavation at Kanul does not slow or stall.

"Graduate students are assisting us. There are groups of them rotating in and out during our time here. They will move between the two sites of Kaq and Rax as needed. Some will be with us for a few weeks, others for longer, depending on their programs. They have a small gathering of tents between the two sister sites. We will join them or camp very close to them. We will see exactly what the situation is when we arrive and adapt as necessary. The work campsite is primitive, but the team will collaborate and make improvements while there.

"I am told we have a generator and that a supply truck will come every three days or so to refill our basics, such as food and beverages. Make sure you have all your medications and any antibiotics with you. Unfortunately, diarrhea is common. Zika occurs, as does malaria and dengue. Use your repellent and the supplied netting. Please. We have a first aid kit, and there is a more robust station at camp. I have training as an EMT, as does"—Luca nodded to the someone in the back of the room—"Natasha, and it is our hope our training will not be needed for anything serious.

"I wish to get this subject out of the way, because there was much concern over these two stipulations. The Global Heritage Organization underwrites our team and incurred expenses related to the site and project. The GHO mandated that everyone, including Natasha and myself, undergo an extensive exam, be current on vaccines, and pass with a clean bill of health, including communicable diseases. They also required menstruating women use medication to alleviate their periods, due to the inherent risks of working in the jungle for a sustained amount of time. These requirements were put in place for all our safety. I received everyone's signed health forms and contracts. Natasha has copies with her. If, for some reason, there is an issue, please speak with Natasha.

"I wish to share my disclaimer. All of us are adults and accountable for taking care of ourselves. That means each of you is responsible for attending to your needs. Eating well, hydrating with potable water, sleeping enough hours, and exercising outside of our work on-site. I caution you to observe your alcohol intake. Our work can be arduous and the days long. The jungle is hot, humid, and dangerous.

"Adhere to the safety procedures. Safety is covered in chapter two of your manual. It is more extensive than the email you received upon accepting a position. I will reiterate a few items covered in more detail in the chapter. Be aware of your surroundings and how you are feeling. Be sure to stay in groups when moving about, whether you are here in Flores or walking between the digs or the biological station.

"We will be working in a remote area. While Guatemala is beautiful, it has one of the highest incidences of violent crime. Narco trafficking and human trafficking are prevalent. Our base in Flores is considered reasonably safe. However, it is wise to keep your electronics and any other valuables in your rooms. Stay on alert even though we have police patrols transporting us back and forth to Kanul and while we are on-site. If you have questions or need clarification, ask Natasha or me. Additionally, if there is something we overlooked, please bring it to our attention.

"Most importantly, remember you are a guest here. We are visiting and working in an ancient and sacred location. Be especially mindful of the Maya and their firmly held beliefs and customs. Treat them with the utmost respect. Ari is happy to educate you further."

Pausing, Luca looked every single person in the eye before continuing. "I will not act as your nursemaid. However, I will ride your ass if you are not doing your work and doing it to your best ability. That means keeping all data and reporting current, and legible, for those of you who prefer to use notebooks. I will check from time to time. I will ask you to expand details or clarify if needed. I will also take you to task over safety, which is the biggest concern. You let me down, you let the team down. You fly home. Your expense. You were awarded a spot on this project because you are considered to be among the best of the best in your discipline for our focus here. You agreed to participate in this international interdisciplinary cooperative project. All of us will benefit immensely and find that we have expanded our knowledge outside our specific fields greatly."

Geesh, he's intense. Her up-front seat was not making being in Luca's presence any easier. While his eyes moved over the PhDs as he spoke, her eyes moved over him. His cargo shorts allowed her to appreciate his powerfully built legs. Ari's eyes drifted lower to his masculine feet, clad in simple leather sandals. Her eyes moved up, pausing on his zipper. Her body flushed with heat remembering his impressive arousal last night. She continued, taking in his lean hips and the ripped muscles of his torso, apparent under his soft, formfitting gray tee. Up and up her eyes traveled, taking in his broad shoulders, the sunglasses hanging from the front of his tee, the stubble on his chin and cheeks. She stopped on his lips. Her lips tingled, recalling his kisses and how their tongues had played. She sighed, apparently more loudly than she realized. Meg's elbow jabbed her in the ribs. Her perusing continued, right into the sexy green pools staring back at her. *Oh, shit. Shit!* The heat flushing her neck and face assured her that she was indeed blushing, and judging from its intensity, she was as red as a tomato.

Luca smiled crookedly, briefly, returning her gaze, and continued to speak as if nothing had happened. "Now that I have shared some of my expectations, I want to introduce Natasha Jordaan. She arrived last night, which is why I missed dinner." He motioned Natasha to the front of the room. "As you should know, Natasha is from South Africa. I believe we have every continent represented. She is my assistant on this project, my number one. Seek her out if you require something of me and I am not available. She suggested we have an icebreaker. Natasha? I ask that you begin."

Natasha came forward from the back of the veranda. Behind her rolled a small vermillion suitcase with an impenetrable-looking lock. She greeted Luca, kissing him on both his cheeks and hugging him, which he returned.

Once in front, she regarded the group, taking in each member of the team. She frowned slightly when her eyes passed over Ari.

What's with the bright red rolling case? Distaste for Natasha bubbled up in Ari before she could contain or question it. She felt like a small freckled freak in comparison to the South African's sultry dark beauty.

Natasha's megawatt smile matched her booming voice. "Good morning, everyone! I sat with some of you during breakfast. What marvelous food! So, I do feel I know a few of you somewhat. We have all read each other's CVs, so we are aware of our exceptional academic prowess." She nodded and raised her eyebrows. "In an effort to fast-track becoming acquainted, I'm asking each of you to share the following: a nonacademic trait you like about yourself and two things about yourself that we don't know. Think hobbies and interests. I'll go first." Natasha clapped her hands.

Ari inwardly rolled her eyes. She felt as though she were back in elementary school. Pressing her lips together to stifle laughter, she focused on the tall, stunning woman in front of her and the icebreaker.

"I have a photographic memory, so I don't forget anything." Her eyes dropped to her suitcase, and then she looked directly at Ari as she repeated, "Anything."

A chill raced over Ari.

"Whoa, there." Meg leaned closer to Ari and whispered, "She's sizing you up, mate. And what's with the red sidekick port? The serious lock is rather odd."

Natasha paused on Meg. "Did you want to share something?"

"No, Assistant Boss," Meg uttered, and everyone in the room tittered. Her response earned her a cool smile from the South African.

Natasha nodded and looked around the room, seeking to engage her colleagues. "Two things… Let's see. So, I collect antique coins from all over the world. I haven't been home, to South Africa, for over two years because I've been traveling the globe, moving from project to project, heading or assisting them. Recently I was—"

Ari stretched her back and rotated her shoulders while Natasha droned on.

"So, who would like to go next? Actually, stop." Natasha clapped again in delight. "We'll just go around the room." Her gaze landed on Meg. "So, you. You start."

Meg shared that she liked her trait of openness and enjoyed rock climbing and participating in triathlons. Joan went next, sharing that she was a nurturer, her husband of thirty years passed away last year, she used maps as backgrounds for her watercolor paintings, and she was a master gardener. She was disappointed to miss out on gardening this season, but her granddaughter was taking care of things.

As other members continued to share, Ari did feel as though she knew them better. Talk over dinners, breakfasts, and beers had been mostly academia focused. She also noted that Natasha was overly fond of the word *so*.

Matt stood up to share, and that in itself was adorable. He turned and waved to everyone around the room before he spoke. He stuttered a bit. "I'm a word geek. I'm thankful that language comes easily to me. Currently I speak"—he counted on his long fingers"—seven fluently. I have PhDs in linguistic anthropology and epigraphy. I've been studying

Mayan codices for years and can't wait to—"

Natasha cleared her throat.

"Sorry, Natasha. I rested on my expert laurels."

Soft laughter broke out in the room.

"Like Meg, I also climb. I love it. Something else…" He tapped his fingers on the temple area of his unruly mop of dark hair. "I used to build things, tinker. My father is a carpenter, and he taught me how to use his trade tools. I miss it. Building, tinkering—"

"So your skills may come in handy when we're out on-site or camping," Natasha said.

Matt pushed the bridge of his dark glasses up on his nose. "Yes. I expect so."

"Thank you, Matt."

Ari was next. She was surprised to find herself nervous.

Natasha's gray-blue eyes took Ari in, as if assessing her. "So, Red. Your turn."

Ari's temper went from zero to sixty in less than a quarter of a second. She detested the redhead nicknames that had plagued her most of her life. She wanted to spit. *Screw you, Natasha.* Was she imagining it, or were Natasha's eyes glittering, kinda witchlike? *Fine. I can meet your challenge and raise you.*

She lifted her chin in subtle defiance and stood. "Good morning, everyone." Although addressing Natasha directly, she looked around at those seated at the tables while speaking, smiling to soften her words. "While I love my hair, a gift from my remarkable and Irish mom, I do not appreciate anyone calling me Red, Ginger, Siren, Carrot-top, Strawberry, Cherry, or any other moniker. Not sure? Check with me first, and thank you. Let's see. A trait I like about myself? I'm direct. One thing about me that you may not know is that I swam competitively during college. Second, and in fairness, I play a mean game of poker, which might come in handy when it rains, which I understand is frequent during the summer months. I have a couple of packs of cards with me. Let me know." She faced Natasha, bathing her with a scathing look before her legs gave way from the anger rushing through her body.

Natasha's smile didn't reach her eyes. "Thank you. I didn't catch your name."

Before answering, she took a deep breath and counted to four. Her response was calm. "You didn't ask. It's Ari." She hadn't asked anyone. *Game on.*

Natasha pursed her lips, squinting as she sized her up further. She addressed Luca. "So, we've heard from everyone, which brings us to you, big guy."

Seriously? Big guy? What the hell?

Luca laughed, sending Ari's piss-o-meter through the roof. "I appreciate respect and best effort, in all aspects of my life and from others. I enjoy deep conversations. I run and swim to release tension and to stay in shape. I compete in triathlons, though not as many as I would like to."

There it is. Why Luca's physique is amazing. Ari took a deep, shivery breath.

"Thank you, Natasha." Luca picked up his binder, motioning for everyone to do the same. "Let's commence. We will break at ten thirty."

Natasha glided to the back of the veranda with her suitcase and sat down.

Ari's hand shook with anger as she put her pen to paper. *Dammit.* She rose from her seat and headed for the hall.

"Ari?"

She explained over her shoulder to Luca. "Excuse me. Lady's break. All that coffee."

"Anyone else need a break before we get started?" Luca asked.

Meg jumped up. "I do. All that coffee." She walked briskly to catch up with Ari.

Once in the bathroom, Meg placed her hand on Ari's wrist, causing her to look at her. "What was that?"

"What was what?" She leaned up against the sink edge to keep herself upright and rediscover the bones that had disappeared from her legs.

Meg nodded her head in the direction of the veranda. "Come on. Natasha. You. It was close to a catfight."

"It was nothing. I just don't like nicknames like Red. I overreacted. I guess I owe her an apology."

"It seemed like she was baiting you. I think she knows about you and Luca."

"Me and Luca? There is no me and Luca."

"Yeah, right-o. You two were playing intense tonsil hockey last night. His hands were all over you, one up your skirt, which was almost up to your waist. Nice blue lacies, by the way. You had one hand on his fly and another in his hair."

Ari was astonished. The heat flushing her cheeks told her she was bright red. "You saw all that?"

"Yep. Girl, that alcove wasn't as dark as the two of you thought. Matt and I were quiet, up to a point, and then when you didn't hear us, we made a ruckus. I can't blame you. Luca is gorgeous, not my type. But jeez, Ari, he's all man. And the way he looks at you, like he wants to eat you up. I want to give him a spoon. You two were great foreplay for Matt and me."

"Oh God…" Ari hugged herself with crossed arms. She pushed herself away from the sink and paced back and forth. "Oh God…"

"It's okay. I'm not going to tell you anything else about my amazing night."

"That's not what I meant."

"Oh. Right. No one has seen you with him, other than Matt and me. And we think it's great. You and Luca just need some sack time to work things out."

She whispered harshly, "Meg! Really!"

"Be honest with yourself."

"Ugh! Okay. Maybe." She faced the mirror and grimaced. Her hair resembled Medusa. *This humidity…* She braided her hair into one thick plait. She felt cooler. "Why do you think Natasha suspects something?"

"I think she knows. A person would have to be from another planet not to notice, not to feel it. There's so much heat. Whenever Luca looks at you, sexual tension sparks. It's like a force field. And face it, Ari. You are obviously attracted to him. Natasha is closer to his age, but she's not as hot as you. By a long shot."

"Thanks, but let's be real. You're biased, friend. Natasha is extremely attractive. And Luca and I aren't a thing."

"Okay, true. But she seems to know it, and it rolls off her in tidal waves. I find it off-putting. I think you're kidding yourself about Luca."

Ari shook her head. "I'm so in over my head. He's who I report to."

"No worries. We all report to him. Someone has to lead, right? Let's talk more during break, okay? Are you feeling better? We've gotta get back."

"Don't you have to go to the bathroom?"

Meg's eyes were gentle as she placed her hands on Ari's shoulders, her smile warm. "I'm good for now. I'm here for moral support, girlfriend. Come on. Get some cold water on that amazing face of yours."

She did as Meg bid. The water braced her but soothed her frazzled nerves, and her eyes looked less puffy. She patted her face dry with the paper towel Meg handed her.

"Okay, good. Look at me."

She looked into the shining sky-blue eyes of her friend.

"Got yourself together now? Because you look great, sexy brilliant you. And remind yourself about what you have going, Ari. If you don't, I will. You're the total package. Luca sees this. Actually, so does Natasha, and she doesn't like it. Ready?"

"Yes. Yes, I am. Thanks." She inhaled deeply, steeling herself.

"HI. CAN I JOIN YOU two?"

Ari opened her eyes to see Matt standing in front of her and Meg, a room towel draped over his pale wiry shoulders, looking like an expectant lost puppy. She came up on her elbows and nodded at the chaise between them, ladened with Meg's and her stuff. "Sure. Take this chair," she said, reaching over to clear it off.

Meg gave Matt a high-wattage smile and shifted her body. Patting the space she had made on the lounger, she said, "Sit here, Matty. I need some more sunscreen. I'm a fair one, you know. Blondes tend to burn easily, especially in midmorning sun."

He stammered, looking back and forth between Meg and Ari. "Okay…" His face pinked, but he sat and took the sunscreen Meg offered.

Ari found it amusing that Matt was uncomfortable with Meg's request. "It's okay, Matt. I know. I'm sure you are totally aware of just how nice of a base Meg has acquired on her fair skin." She winked at her friend. "You're naughty."

Laughing, Meg said, "I am. Matty, be a dear and put some sunscreen on my back. I'm happy to return the favor."

"You're lying on your back."

"Yep," she said, smiling coyly. "I am, but"—Meg rolled against Matt seductively as she turned onto her stomach—"will you untie my top?"

"Um…" His Adam's apple moved as he swallowed. He let out a visible breath and pushed the bridge of his sunglasses up, pausing to glance at

Ari before reaching to untie Meg's top.

As much as she was enjoying the spectacle, it was time to give them some space. Ari stood with her hands in surrender and announced, "I'm taking a swim. Matt, just rub it in for her. Maybe the two of you need a room?" She quickly pulled her cap over her damp hair, adjusted her goggles, and shook her head before diving into the pool.

The water was refreshing, surprising since the pool sat fully in the sun. Maybe the water circulating through the man-made waterfall along the east side of the rectangular pool had something to do with it. She surfaced and broke into a crawl, slicing effortlessly through the water. After a flip-turn, she swam another length, then several more. She was able to complete about ten strokes before changing direction. Her long-dormant swimming muscles began to fire. Swimming felt great. The last time she'd swum was late winter, in the university's indoor pool.

An unbidden image of Luca popped into her head, powering her dolphin kick, propelling her undulating body through the water. *Stop it, Ari.* Her chest rose, clearing the water, then her hands, cutting into the water with fierceness, then recovering for the next stroke. She came in for another turn.

"How's the water?"

That voice—it stopped her midstroke. In the deep end, she treaded water, squinting up. Luca smiled down at her appreciatively. Next to him stood the stunning, sleek Natasha. The high-cut coral one-piece she wore enhanced her deep russet skin, practically matching the stuccoed walls of the hotel. How long had they been standing there?

Although perturbed, she managed to keep her voice smooth and nonchalant. "You indicated you were going to be in meetings the rest of the day."

Luca's sunglasses made his eyes unreadable, but his blinding smile was impossible to miss. "Natasha and I decided we would hold our meeting here and enjoy the pool at the same time. We will sit in the shade." He pointed to a collection of tables with chairs under the pergola alongside the pool.

"Well, the water's great." She turned and kicked hard, moving back into her butterfly stroke, dousing Natasha and her ever-present rolling red suitcase.

"Oh!" Natasha jumped back.

Ari smiled just as her face entered the water. If Natasha hadn't wanted to get wet, she shouldn't have stood so close to the pool. She swam a few lengths each of back- and breaststroke before pulling herself out of the water to stand next to where Luca and Natasha sat in the shade, pulling off her cap and goggles in one easy movement and shook out her hair, spraying water onto Natasha again. "Oops, sorry. A bad habit I acquired during years of competition. You really should get in. The water is perfect."

Natasha's coral lips formed a firm line, the shade matching her suit perfectly. She was stiff with annoyance. "I prefer to dip. When I choose to do so."

"We've got a kayaking trip scheduled later in the summer. Are you going to more than dip then?" Ari asked, tilting her head, baiting her.

"So, this is your business how?" she asked testily, dismissing Ari by focusing on a page she had flipped to in her binder.

Luca watched the bickering in silence, a barely there smile evident.

Ari clenched her hands around her cap and goggles. "I need more sunscreen. See you later." She forced herself to appear calm as she walked over to Meg and Matt at the other end of the pool.

"Ari… Are you okay? Ari?" Meg pushed off Matt who was practically lying on her and stood. "Move over, lump." She nudged Ari and sat down next to her friend. "What happened?"

"Oh, Meg… I acted like I'm in high school. She brings out the worst in me."

"Come on." Meg grabbed Ari's hand. "Matty darlin', save our places, will you?"

Matt gave Meg a thumbs-up and a sweet smile.

"Let's walk," she said to Ari and ushered her from the pool area.

Luca watched Meg and Ari leave the pool area. He chided himself for not stopping Natasha and Ari's churlish banter, having experienced Natasha's bitchiness firsthand. While she had exhibited remarkable strength and control, this was the second time she had taken a break after tangling with Natasha.

He rubbed his hand along his jaw and then over his hair as he studied Natasha, who was fully absorbed in the binder and writing notes. Having her on the project was already proving difficult. How he wished she were not here, given his fascination with Ari, but Natasha was an excellent project manager. And of course, there was the directive from GHO that Natasha be his assistant. Luca could not possibly tell them no since the project was fully overseen and paid for by the GHO.

He was thankful to have spent time with her in Italy during the semester she was a visiting adjunct at the university. He had been a hollow shell of a man after Sofia's death and appreciated her stalwart support, but he was not interested in an intimate relationship with Natasha. He broached the subject with her over cappuccino one morning. It turned out that she felt the same. They laughed about it, hugged, and agreed to remain only friends and colleagues.

Natasha was a condition of this project. Luca could handle her. As academics, they were a great team, with well-matched skill sets. He liked Natasha as a friend and colleague, and although she could be temperamental, he respected the hell out of her. He still had no interest in pursuing more. He doubted Natasha did either. What had stirred his interest had just exited the pool area.

"Shit. Shit. Shit!" Ari grumbled as she walked back and forth in Meg's room. "Ugh! Why? Why do I let her get under my skin?"

"That's it. Let it out." Meg sat on her unmade bed, watching Ari pace.

Ari stopped and eyed her. "I'm getting your floor wet."

"I'm sure it will dry."

"I lost it. Again. In front of Luca. Dammit. Natasha makes me feel like a little girl. She puts me on edge." Ari resumed her pacing. "What is it about her? Shit."

"Sit," Meg said, pointing at her unmade bed.

"Your sheets are going to be wet. And actually, I don't want to sit on them. Weren't you and Matt rolling around in them last night?"

Meg burst out laughing. "Right. There's that. We sampled most of the real estate in my room."

Ari paused and rolled her eyes at her grinning friend. "Nice. I'll just continue pacing and take you up on your offer after maid service." She leaned against the door and raised her eyebrows. "Is this safe?"

"Affirmative."

"Hear me out. Okay? You're reminding me of my mom, Meg. In the spirit of friendship, I'll humor you."

"Good. I want to make sure you listen to my words. I've got a passel of siblings, and my mum has shared a lot of her wisdom over the years. Something she has told me time and again is no one can make you feel bad about yourself, unless you let them."

"I know. Sounds like my mom, another wise woman. Thanks for the reminder."

Meg nodded. "Do you want to share?"

"Natasha is a bitch."

"That's established." Meg laughed but immediately grew thoughtful and snapped her fingers. "But it's as if Natasha serves another purpose. I catch her observing a lot, particularly you. Did you ever run across her in the past?"

"No."

"Okay." Meg sprang from the bed. "So, what about the secret you have, the one that festers like a rock in your shoe."

Her eyes widened. Obviously she hadn't quite let go when she'd burned the letter. Ari shook her head in denial. "I don't—"

"It's just… Well, you started to allude to it when we were coming in from Lanquín. You said you signed on for this project in part to disappear. I thought maybe you might want to talk about it. Maybe you're still working through it. If and when you're ready, you can share. I'm a great confidant. I won't judge. I may even be able to help." Meg opened the door. "It's a beautiful day. Let's go enjoy the Mayan sun and the gorgeous men scenery." She waved Ari in front of her. "After you."

Ari smiled all the way back to the pool, buoyed by her new friend.

Luca sat facing the pool, paying scant attention to Natasha. Bothered by Ari's abrupt departure, he kept an eye out for her. It had been a while.

"Are you listening, Luca? You haven't made one comment, asked one question, or taken one note," Natasha said, throwing down her pen for emphasis.

His attention snapped back. "I apologize, Natasha. I did not sleep well."

Ari and Meg entered the pool, laughing as if they'd shared a joke. He was spellbound. Ari sparkled. Sunlight danced off her coppery tresses. The aqua bikini she wore accentuated the athlete she was, one of lithe grace and feminine power. She was toned without compromising her femininity. Her bright, infectious smile contrasted with her deepening tan, her freckles adding more interest. His blood quickened.

"Luca. Luca! Have you heard anything I've said?" Frustrated, Natasha turned in the direction of his focus, observing the young American stride across the pool deck with confidence.

Caught, Luca had the decency to look sheepish. He was silent.

"I see. Careful, Luca."

"*Zitta*, Nat," Luca said, standing and stretching. "I need a break. So do you."

Natasha stood as well, seething with anger, hastily piling her papers into a binder. She clasped the handle of her vermillion weekender, her words laced with heat. "Don't tell me to shut up. I'm going to my room."

"Perhaps you should," he called over his shoulder as he strode toward the pool.

LUCA SWAM UNDERWATER TO THE end of the pool. The water helped to allay his agitation with Natasha and dampen his desire. He swam a few more lengths and stood in the water at the other side where Meg, Matt, and Ari lounged.

"Ciao!"

"Hey, Boss," Matt said. "Natasha have an important phone call? She left in a hurry."

"Something like that," Luca said.

Ari stole a look at Luca as she popped open the cap of her sunscreen. Mistake. She connected with his green perusal. Fluttering erupted in her gut, up into her throat. She struggled to say something, and when it finally came out, it was raspy. "She didn't seem all that interested in hanging with us. Is she coming back?"

He turned, his mossy-green eyes looking deeply into hers. "I am not sure."

Meg stood, waving Matt to the poolside. "Come on, Matty. Come play with me." She jumped into the deep end; he cannonballed behind her, and they played gleefully, like young children before racing each other to the end of the pool.

Luca dropped his voice. "Do you wish for me to help with your lotion again?"

Wish. The way he said it was full of promise, making her body sing. He had to know he had this effect on her. She didn't answer but instead fumbled for her sunglasses, believing she could hide her feasting eyes behind the mirrored lenses. Her gaze moved leisurely from his slicked-back hair and handsome face, to his broad shoulders tapering into washboard abs and compact hips as he pushed himself out of the pool to stand on the deck, rivulets of water running over his body and puddling onto the deck. All of Luca was lean and unabashedly masculine. She was captivated and licked her lips at the idea of what it might be like to run her tongue over his skin and taste him. Ari's perusal continued to his full lips, which were smiling broadly at her. She slunk down in the lounge chair, mortified that he caught her ogling him.

She bit her lower lip, remembering all too well his touch on her skin, his kisses. She shook her head. "Uh, I've got it. Thanks."

His eyes crinkled, and his mouth quirked into a half smile. Disarming. Devastatingly sexy. "Let me know if you change your mind."

The sound of slapping wet feet announced Meg and Matt. "Are you guys going back in?" Matt asked, breathing hard.

"In a little while," Ari said breathlessly

"May I join all of you?" Luca asked.

"Sure!" Meg and Matt chorused.

"Ari?"

She nodded and swallowed, not trusting herself to speak. Inwardly, Ari sighed, wondering how on earth she was going to get through the afternoon.

"I will return." Luca walked briskly to the table he and Natasha had occupied.

Matt chuckled. "He's like the Terminator. 'I'll be back.'"

Meg joined in, giggling. She reached over and gave him a kiss.

"Not really. But that's funny, Matt." Ari watched Luca pick up his things through her mirrored sunglasses. The slow, incessant pulse of desire began to build low in her belly.

His graceful movements were becoming familiar and watching him a favorite pastime. He slipped his sunglasses on and pulled his hair into a knot with finesse that comes from much practice. He looked up, catching her once again. A smile broke across his face.

She dropped her gaze to the pool deck.

Meg leaned over and whispered, loudly enough for Matt to hear, "What an interesting game of cat and mouse you two are playing. You are in deep dookie, sweetie." Laughing, she added, "Oh, yeah."

Matt looked at his watch and stood, enthusiastically declaring, "It's five o'clock somewhere… How 'bout some *cervezas*?"

Both women nodded. Meg said, "Beer sounds perfect. I'm ready to bend the elbow."

"Huh?" Ari looked at her for translation.

"Aussie for drink. Just think, girlfriend, you're going to have an expanded vocabulary and"—she nodded at Luca walking toward them—"the hottest sex of your life, in this magical place."

"Meg!" Ari hissed.

"Hey, Luca, I'm getting us beers. Want one?"

Luca pulled a lounge chair next to Ari. "Yes. *Grazie*." He bent over, spreading out his towel, his lips subtly brushing Ari's ear as he sat down. His words were quiet, for her only. "I am thirsty. You appear to be as well."

Beside herself, Ari didn't respond. Instead, she regarded the pergola's shifting striped pattern over the chairs, tables, and cement created by the clouding sky, turning Meg's words and Luca's intimate innuendo over and over.

Matt arrived with the beers and passed them out, condensation indicating they were a great deal colder than the toasty temperatures. He looked up. "What do you think? Do we have time?"

Luca pushed his sunglasses up onto his head, perusing the skies. He sipped from the bottle before answering. "I believe so."

Ari raised her bottle to Matt. "Let's go for it."

"We can huddle under the brolly if it—"

"Clarification?" Ari asked. "Sorry to cut in."

"Umbrella," Meg corrected. "No worries, mate."

Matt took a big pull on the long neck. "Luca, fill us in. I read your paperwork, but I have a feeling it was terribly abbreviated."

Ari glanced to Luca, who was looking at her openly.

He smiled teasingly, then winked. "Perhaps that is a good idea. It is enlightening, possibly helpful, to know about your colleagues' backgrounds."

She wanted to die. He hadn't exactly thrown her under the table, but she was uncomfortable. And curious as hell.

Luca's voice vibrated with enthusiasm and reverence. "My work is in parasitic vectors. From a young age I have been driven by a powerful need to fully understand disease, how vector-borne pathogens migrate into populations. I hold degrees in molecular biology, entomology, and medical anthropology. The latest and most promising findings I have had are linked to a fly indigenous to the African continent."

Meg butted in when Luca paused. "You've been here in Guatemala before, right, Boss?"

"I have. I participated in a research project that studied the blood-meal sources of cave-dwelling Chagas vectors around the Belize–Guatemala border. I am here in part to follow up and add more data. I will work at the biological reserve where you will spend part of your time, Meg, in addition to leading the team's excavation."

"The research sounds fascinating and incredibly helpful to medicine and treatments, Luca."

"It is," he replied, nodding. "Discovery gets my blood pumping."

Ari didn't realize she had changed her posture while he talked. She leaned in, her elbows resting on her knees, her beer clasped in her two hands, between her knees. Nodding enthusiastically, she agreed, "Me too!"

"I met Carlos on that trip. He grew up in this area and will be assisting us on-site. His cultural perspectives will be invaluable."

"What do you think happened to the Maya, Ari?"

"No one really knows. There are theories about the seemingly sudden collapse of the Maya civilization from the eighth into the end of the ninth century, the Spanish conquest. Disease. Extreme drought. The collapse is an intriguing mystery. I wonder if we might discover any clues."

Luca lay back in his chaise and closed his eyes and put his sunglasses on. The sun broke through, bringing scorching heat with it. "It appears we are fortunate," he said, lifting his beer.

Ari squinted upward. The menacing clouds were all but gone. Her focus returned to Luca, entranced by the lips sealing the mouth of the bottle so that he could drain it. She remembered the soft feel of those lips and of his tongue as they explored each other. The taste of him. Yes, he was gorgeous. But his layers—Ari was deeply intrigued, beyond her physical pull to him. She yearned to spend more one-on-one time with him and discover more. She shifted on the chaise to quell her ache.

Matt rose and stretched. "I'm ready for a second. Looks like Luca needs another. Ladies?"

"Yes," they both responded.

Meg grabbed a book and flipped onto her stomach to read it.

Needing some distance from Luca, Ari offered, "I'll get it, Matt."

"You get the next round, Ari."

"Okay, thanks." She reclined against the angled chaise back. Her eyes unfocused and her heart hammered as she reflected.

Matt closed in. "I've got cold ones. Trade you, Luca."

"Thank you."

Ari heard a kiss, then Meg thanking Matt for her beer.

"Here you go, Ari." Matt slid another beer into her hand, taking the empty.

"Thanks," she said in a hushed voice. She returned to the thoughts, images, and emotions assailing her. Condensation from her beer made its way between her hand and the bottle, dripping onto her toasty stomach when she realized the truth. She was thinking "future" with Luca, and she had only just met him. Her parents often told her that the man she chose to spend her life with would probably be older and well educated, someone who challenged her in every way. Like Luca.

"Ari? Are you okay?" Luca's question pulled her from her musing.

Startled, she switched the bottle to her dry hand, shaking the moisture from the other, looking at him sideways, nodding. At this angle, she glimpsed his eyes through his dark shades. "Uh-huh. I just drifted off. Thinking about the Maya and that this is my last beer of the afternoon," she lied. She pulled deeply on her beer.

A knowing look covered his face. He finished his beer and leaned over, his words only for her ears. "Hm. I see."

Her sunglasses were proving ineffective. From his expression, Ari could tell he had read her mind, her body. He did see. Right through her flimsy fib. She bolted up and walked over to the rocks behind the lounges, preparing to dump her beer.

"Hold on there. What are you doing?" Luca had risen behind her, following.

"Said I was done. I'm going to"—she paused, her nerve endings tripping as Luca's hand lightly spanned most of the small of her back—"take a *siesta*."

He dropped it and reached around, gently taking her bottle, his voice low. "It is still cold. I will finish it. We have shared more than beer, yes?"

Her body pulsed like crazy. Luca had stepped closer, as close as he could without touching her again, yet she sensed every centimeter of his skin. He'd unleashed a desire that she had yet to fully acknowledge, but it was there, boiling under the surface. *He knows it too.* Being with him felt so right. His touches and kisses turned her to putty. "Yes," Ari whispered, swallowing.

Luca bent his head. "You smell of sunshine and spice. Delicious." His lips grazed her shoulder. "I will see you later."

Ari could only nod, missing his nearness immediately when he ambled back to his chaise. Turning slowly, she realized Meg and Matt had no idea the exchange had happened, so deep were they into their own private world. She glanced over at Luca while getting her stuff and slipping her sandals on. He was prone, eyes closed, a contented smile on his face, her bottle of beer clasped lightly in his extended hand.

FOURTEEN

A CHORUS OF GOOD-NIGHTS and see-you-tomorrows passed among team members as they emptied out of the *comedor*, moving through the open veranda to their respective rooms. Joan gave out big hugs with her wishes, her voice louder, standing out above the rest. Full from dinner and stoked with excitement about leaving for Tikal tomorrow, everyone was determined to get a good night's rest.

A large hand brushed Ari's wrist as she entered the stairs to her wing. Tingling nerve endings told her whose it was.

Somehow, they were alone. "Ari, please. *Un attimo?*" Luca's question softened his command.

Okay, a minute. I can do this. She steeled herself before facing him and caught her breath, wondering if she would ever not react to his raw sensuality. Luca's body was mere inches from hers. His heat and unique scent emanated from him. Without realizing it, she parted her lips. Her teeth softly bit her lower lip.

Luca emitted a soft growl. "You make me lose focus when you do that."

"Huh?" Heat flushed Ari's face. *What did I do?*

Luca cleared his throat and stepped back, but his eyes held hers. "I wish to talk to you."

"About what?" Although she immediately missed his closeness, the additional space was more productive if they were going to talk. She had trouble thinking when Luca was close, and when he touched her, all logic was overridden by her body's hunger.

"Last night. Today."

"I regret last night. I lost my head. It was unprofessional of me. I'm not looking for a colleague with benefits, especially my *boss*." The last word had some bite to it.

He frowned and slid his hands low to hold on to the front of his belt waistband of his shorts. "You should have read through the CVs. Then you would know I am more your colleague than your boss. Someone has to head the project and supervise reports and oversee findings, but I also work right alongside you. You would also know what specialties other team members have, their backgrounds, what they can contribute to this project while we are here."

Ari's eyes had followed his hands and rested there.

Luca cleared his throat, causing her eyes to fly back up and meet his, which alternated between looking stern and amused.

"Shit. Sorry." Her face was on fire. "My mind was somewhere else."

He wore a wicked smile. "Indeed."

Ari squirmed, not sure whether she should ask, but curiosity won. "What is Natasha's specialty? What else is she, besides your assistant? I feel like she took an immediate dislike to me."

He took some time before answering, then rubbed the bridge of his nose and ran his hand over his scruffy chin. "I have spoken to her about how she is around you. I believe things will improve. We met in university. Over the years Natasha has become a good friend and respected colleague. She was an adjunct for a semester, where I teach, three years ago. I have not seen her since then, but we have kept in touch. Aside from expertise in classical archaeology, Natasha is an adept archaeometrist and excellent project manager. Her analysis and skills will be welcome here.

"To address your comment about not looking for a colleague with benefits. I am not looking for that either, but I would be lying if I said you did not intrigue me. Very much." Opening his hands, he asked, "Can we sit by the promenade and talk? I wish to hear more about why you feel the way you do, and I am asking you to listen to what I have to say."

Ari wrung her hands together. "Okay. Just a little while. I should call it a night." Turning over what Luca had said, she kept her distance from him until they were outside and taking the stairs down to the promenade. Memories of last night were fresh in her mind. Gabbiness overtook her as they strolled onto the wide concrete skirt separating the hotel from Lake Petén Itzá. "Look, what woman wouldn't find you attractive? I apologize again for my part last night. I will admit that I really enjoyed our conversation at the pool this afternoon."

"I expect you did. I did as well. It was safe. Both of us were able to behave ourselves."

"Dammit, Luca. Don't say that. It pisses me off. I'm not some adolescent girl," Ari fired back.

He stopped and turned to face her, moving closer. "You swear a lot." Gently he took her hand and stroked her palm, softly with his thumb. "Why does what I said upset you? Because there is truth? Because you try to deny?"

She tried to ignore how his thumb sent currents of desire sparking through her body. *It's my palm for crying out loud.* "Yeah, I do swear like a sea captain sometimes. It lets the steam off."

He brushed back an errant curl from her face. "You are beautiful, Ari. I am drawn to you." He looked deeply into her eyes, his gentle smile made his eyes crinkle at their corners. "You are very much a woman. Steamy. I like your fire. It stirs me."

Ari found herself lost in his eyes, which had grown darker with emotion. He reached for her other hand, interlacing their fingers. Desire radiated through her body, making it difficult for her to breathe. She gasped for air, and her body began quivering from the intimacy of being entwined with a part of his body. It was too much.

"You are trembling."

"No," she croaked, her eyes shining. She shook her head and looked down. Maybe breaking eye contact would cool her jets. She inhaled a choppy breath—it wasn't working.

Luca put a finger under her chin and lifted it. "Yes. You are. Look at me." A slow smile erased his concerned expression. "I see. The truth is in your eyes. They are full of hunger, mirroring what I feel. Why are we fighting each other?"

"It's all wrong, Luca. This, us… It shouldn't happen."

He shrugged his shoulders and slowly released her other hand, finger by finger. "Perhaps not, but attraction does not always follow the logical. I know that. I suspect you have also learned that to be true."

"I report to you. My last relationship was with a man I reported to. He was the dean of my department. Eric and I ended very badly."

"Do you wish to tell me about it?" He ran a finger lightly down her arm.

"Not really. Let's just say he was a liar, a flaming asshole. I left it all behind when I came to Guatemala."

"I am sorry you were hurt, but I am not him. Not every man is deceitful or has an agenda. You fascinate me, very much. I find you to be a beautiful and desirable woman. We have a choice. Do we fight what pulls us together and be miserable for the duration of our time here? Or do we explore it?"

Uncertainty played over Ari's features.

Hopeful, he pushed a little more, gently asking, "Come with me?"

She bit her lower lip, then licked it and gave him her hand, wondering if she had made the right decision. While she fully felt safe with him physically, she was emotionally vulnerable.

He led her into a recessed alcove under the stairs off the promenade, where he encircled her with his arms and lifted her onto a waist-high cement ledge built into the wall.

"You are light. *Bellissima*," he whispered into her ear as he wove his fingers into her luxuriant curls, pulling out the hair clip. "I like it down." He ran the tip of his tongue over her earlobe and tenderly kissed and nibbled her neck, careful of her delicate necklace. "I love your freckles. There are so many paths for me to follow and explore." His finger stroked her skin softly. "Mm. I will take this one," he whispered. A trail of goose bumps rose behind his warm kisses.

Her heart knocked around in her chest. She writhed in his arms, wanting more, arching her neck to give him better access. So much for her indecision.

"Easy, *bella*," he breathed into her ear.

Ari swooned at Luca calling her beautiful and sweetheart, somehow more romantic in Italian. Her hands had a mind of their own. She threaded her fingers through his thick hair, pulling him closer, guiding him down her neck to her collarbone with gentle pressure. Her body hummed wildly as his kisses grew bolder.

He paused and looked at her, his eyes even darker with desire. He sought her sweet mouth, urging her to kiss him more deeply as his hands kneaded her breasts. His hands slipped under her tee and light cami to stroke her nipples, which immediately tightened. He sighed into her mouth.

Ari's hands moved under his tee to explore his muscled abs and chest. His heart beat wildly under her palm, like hers. *He feels so good.* Her breath was choppy and her clothing restrictive.

Luca's hands trailed down her back and cupped her firm ass. "I love that you wear skirts and no bras. Open your legs," he commanded gently.

She did as he bid, her skirt bunching up around her hips. She moaned as his fingers traced delicate patterns on her inner thighs, her head tilted back against the wall, her body boneless as a warm ache flooded her.

He pulled her head forward to taste her again and then gently released her. He traced her bottom lip with his forefinger, looking deeply into her eyes and then down to where his fingers worked under the lacy edge of her panties.

Her gaze followed his, hypnotized by what he was doing to her.

His quiet voice was thoughtful, thick with desire. "Copper. Blue last night. They blend in with your beautiful skin. I appreciate your taste in panties." He smiled to himself, immersed in what he was doing, whispering, "Open more."

She did as he commanded, and Luca stroked her core.

"Mm. Luca!" Ari cried. Her hands dropped to his waist, her fingers holding on to the front of his belt. She fell back and was supported by the stuccoed wall.

"You are very wet. Silky on my fingers." He kissed her deeply again, probing her rhythmically. Their tongues danced as she neared her breaking point in record time.

"Omigod! Luca!"

Satisfaction filled his features as she shuddered and then became limp. Her eyes were closed, a contented smile on her face, despite breathing heavily. He placed a hand over her galloping heart. She covered his hand with her shaky one.

Her eyes were heavy lidded. And they were still glazed as she opened them slowly. "Omigod," she said breathlessly. Her other hand caressed the enormous bulge straining against his zipper. *Damn.*

Smiling, Luca lightly covered her hand and lifted it, kissing her palm. "I will be fine. I wanted to give you pleasure tonight." He pulled Ari closer, kissing her tenderly. "Let us not fight our attraction any longer. Yes?"

She answered languidly, "That was a different conversation than you originally promised, and I agreed to."

"Perhaps. Perhaps not. You agreed to accompany me. We both talked, and we both listened."

"Our bodies had the conversation. We still need to talk. There are things left unsaid, questions unasked."

His amazing eyes glowed in response. "I like your forwardness." He caressed her cheek. "It is late. I will walk you to your room. You are unsteady."

"You think? You would be too."

"I look forward to being unsteady." He kissed her more deeply. "Soon."

EXPLORATION

Many years ago, all animals were great friends. Among the most admired was the b'alam, the jaguar. But he was also arrogant about his dazzling golden fur, often saying to other animals that none of them had as perfect skin as him.

One day he roamed too close to monkeys playing with an avocado. It landed on b'alam, staining his spine. Enraged, he took a monkey to his cave and ate it. The monkeys told Yum Kaax, the lord of the Mount, what had happened. Yum Kaax decided to help them punish the b'alam. They lured him from his cave and threw black zapote, ta'auch, a Mayan word that translates as monkey poop, at b'alam. That was how b'alam got his spots.

They were no longer friends, and b'alam hunted and ate the animals in the rainforest. Yum Kaax gave the animals gifts to protect themselves from the jaguar's attacks. Sharp fangs, thicker skin, and long tails.

B'alam hid among the plants, having to work harder to get food. He learned not to be so vain. He was still feared and admired for his ferocity, vision, and foresight. Our noble ancestors wore b'alam's lustrous fur because they wished to be as powerful and majestic as him.

—Tata
Mayan Shaman
Petén, Guatemala

VIVID DREAMS OF LUCA AND anticipation about exploring Tikal caused Ari to toss and turn throughout the night. She threw back the covers at five o'clock, seeking a bracing shower to fully wake her before heading down to a six o'clock breakfast alone. Absorbed in the team notes, she absently consumed her breakfast and coffee, trying to find out anything she might have missed in yesterday's meeting and commit the details to memory. Exiting the *comedor* at six thirty, she passed Matt and Meg giggling on their way in.

"Good morning! How'd you two sleep?"

Their goofy smiles spread from ear to ear, and they answered in unison, "Great!"

"How about you?" Meg asked.

"Not so good. Too excited. Tikal has been on my bucket list since I was a little girl. I've checked my camera batteries several times to make sure I don't run out of juice. Just know, I might take a thousand pics. And don't rib me about it, okay?" Ari raised her eyebrows in question. "I'm going to check over my packing one more time."

"Do you have plenty of memory?"

"I have an extra card, just in case."

"Don't forget your flashlight," Meg called behind her.

Ari stopped and turned. "Huh?"

"We're camping in the ruins! Did you forget?"

"Wh-wha-what? I didn't see that in the notes. Seriously?"

"Yup. It wasn't in the notes. Luca received approval late yesterday and surprised everyone at dinner. How did you miss that?"

Ari had been in another world during dinner. Quiet and reflective about the undercurrents between her and Luca, she had tuned out most of the dinner conversation. Specifically, she had focused on ignoring his deep voice—it turned her insides to hot liquid and made her unable to think. And she had to think. She was in a difficult situation. Had she created it? Encouraged it? Last night under the stairs came flooding back. She certainly hadn't stopped it. Her face flushed.

"How many nights?"

"Just tonight," Matt answered.

"But I'm sure it's going to be mind-blowing," Meg said. "Hey, why's your face all red?"

She ignored Meg's question. "Gotta go. I've got to redo my packing… What about tents?"

"I believe Luca gave that assignment to Natasha," Matt said.

Urgency threaded Meg's words. "Rattle your dags. You have, like, fifteen."

"Huh?"

"Aussie, for hurry!"

"Oh. Got it." Ari took off at a jog toward her room. Over her shoulder, she shouted, "I'll be back in a jiffy. Don't leave without me." Out of their sight and giddy, Ari jumped in the air and laughed. Then she skipped back toward her room with a smile so big it hurt. Tikal was at the top of her very long bucket list, and she was finally going to experience it.

"Good morning, happy one," Luca said, his eyes crinkling with amusement.

She stopped dead in her tracks. "Good morning," she said, faltering, heat flushing her face. "Um, I got a little carried away. I've wanted to explore Tikal forever. I'm kinda excited."

Luca's crooked grin made her stomach flip and release butterflies. Leaning over, he purred into her ear, "I like it when you are excited. It ex—"

"Morning, Boss! Morning, Ari! What a beautiful day! Can you believe we're going to see Tikal? I've got to pinch myself," Joan said, seemingly oblivious to the electricity pulsing between Luca and Ari. "I might have overpacked, but better than not enough. Glad I brought a ground roll for these nights out away from our hotel. A woman of a certain age like me, well, my bones and joints get rather stiff."

Luca's voice was warm and full of patience. "Good morning, Joan. Tikal is remarkable. We all will make sure you are as comfortable as you can be tonight. Fair?"

"Thank you, Luca," Joan said.

Looking at his watch, he said, "We leave in ten. Would you like help?"

"I'm good, kind sir. See you down at the shuttle." She waddled off, weighed down by multiple bags.

"What a fine woman, Joan. And where are you headed, Ari?"

Lost in Luca's mossy gaze, she scrambled to find an answer. "Um, forgot my flashlight."

Running a palm over his stubble, appearing to want to say something and then changing his mind, he said, "See you shortly."

Dense jungle shrouded early sunlight as the shuttle drove toward Tikal National Park. Despite her excitement, Ari blinked her bleary eyes repeatedly. The spotty night of sleep had caught up with her even though she'd downed four cups of coffee at breakfast. She grabbed the seat in front of her and unfolded, standing upright since she was petite. It felt great. Bracing her feet, she balanced as the shuttle swayed and bucked over the uneven road. Ari worked her shoulders, rotating them forward and then back, moving her head and stretching her neck while inhaling deeply to wake herself up. Better already. Still holding on with her right hand, Ari dropped her right shoulder and extended her left arm over her head, stretching as much as possible. She switched to the other side.

"Are you leading shuttle yoga, Ari?" Natasha called from a few rows in front of her.

Lost in focusing on stretching safely on a moving vehicle, Ari started. A derisive expression covered Natasha's face, aimed right at her.

Her words were out before she realized what they might infer. "Um. No. I have a crick in my shoulders. My body is wound kinda tight."

Natasha remained silent, continuing to stare at Ari through her shades, no smile.

God, she makes me so uncomfortable. She's always watching me, like I'm guilty of something or she expects me to be.

"I see," Luca said, seated next to Natasha, with a lazy, knowing smile.

The shuttle hit a dip. She thudded back into her seat, color flooding her body. A string of swear words flew through her mind, all aimed at Natasha. Ari busied herself with her camera, extracting it from its case, hands quivering as she pulled her lens cap off and pointed the lens out the open window, flustered and fully awake now.

Through her lens, she witnessed a Sunday morning in Petén. Reverence for the simplicity of Maya life filled her. Here, deep in the jungle and away from the bustle of more heavily populated areas, she had stepped backward in time. Mayan men led saddled horses along on the road's edge, where the rainforest had been forced to stop. Young children rode on top and, like their parents, were dressed in their finest Sunday dresses, pants, shirts, and shoes. Women walked closely, often carrying the littlest ones wrapped in colorfully woven slings.

The activity was riveting, and she longed to capture all of what she saw with her camera. However, she lowered it each time she was tempted to take a photo of a child, respectful of the Mayan belief that mirrors, even those within cameras, are portals to the otherworld, that taking photos of children would steal their souls. She watched the Maya until they were out of sight, hoping to burn the images into her memory. The lively conversation on the shuttle hushed as the team took in the beauty surrounding them. In short time, the team would arrive at the national park.

Luca stood suddenly and yelled, "*Para!*" Stepping to the door, he bounded out as soon as the shuttle slammed to a stop. The group emptied out behind him and stood in a half circle. Rife with impatience, Ari continued moving, curious why Luca had ordered the driver to stop when the park entry was another fifty meters ahead.

He braced his hand in front of her. "No! Wait! Do not move," he demanded, pointing just past the front of the shuttle.

In general, Ari hated it when people tried to order her around, but fear replaced her anger when she looked to where he pointed. She had seen tarantulas before—in pet stores and when Jimmy Robert brought his pet tarantula to school in sixth grade for show-and-tell. She had stayed as far away as possible. Had she known earlier, she wouldn't have gone to school that day.

Luca squatted. Gingerly he picked up the tarantula with his left forefinger and thumb and carefully flipped his hand so that its caramel-colored thorax rested against his large palm, filling it. Its hairy, segmented black-and-brown legs undulated, and retractable claws opened and shut, seeking escape.

Ari found it difficult to breathe. Profuse sweat—nothing to do with the days escalating temperature—broke out all over her.

Luca pushed his sunglasses onto the top of his head, where they nestled in the thick waves. Appreciation and wonder laced his words. "It looks to be a young mature male, harmless as I am holding him."

She stayed put, wrestling with the rising bile and light-headedness flooding her system. An unbidden memory surfaced.

Shafts of sunlight filtered through the planks of Aunt Nan and Uncle Pete's ancient barn, spotlighting particles of hay, straw dust, and the hard work of a barn spider that hung from the large truss above her. Flies buzzed to and fro in the morning light. She wanted to go home, but her parents weren't due back from their weekend trip for another day.

"Take off your sunglasses, Ari," Luca encouraged. "I have him. He cannot harm you."

She did as he bid but kept her eyes closed tightly. She swallowed convulsively and shook her head. That one memory, tucked deeply away from when she was ten years old, surfaced. She could smell the sawdust bedding and feel the straw poking through her soft flannel pajamas, making her itch. The crisp morning air chilled her exposed neck, hands, and feet.

The night was pitch-black when she ran into the old barn. She had climbed up into the loft after locking the barn door from the inside with the pitchfork. She had burrowed down into the dry straw of the loft, insulating herself from the chill of the autumn evening and her uncle's rage, desperate to get away from what she'd witnessed—her uncle pummeling her aunt with his fists and then kicking her as she lay on the floor screaming and crying, holding her pregnant belly, pleading for him to stop. She had shivered violently, crying and praying for her aunt, her unborn cousin, and herself until she fell asleep.

Through her flashback, Ari heard the oohing and aahing, talking, and questions from colleagues as they jockeyed to get a closer look.

"Wow, he's beautiful!"

"Aren't you nervous holding that thing, Luca?"

"Are you sure it's a young one? I've never seen that large a spider."

"Let me get a picture! How do you know it's a male?"

"I'd like to hold it," Natasha demanded.

Luca was brusque when he finally responded. "Not now. Just observe." Pointing to the deep indentions on the spider's underside, he said, "It is a male. See? It has epiandrous fusillae—an extra set of silk-spinning glands. All males have them." Ari sensed his shadow over her before he quietly said, "The spider will not hurt you. I have it. Trust me."

Ari drew her lips into a fine, tight line and shook her head again, more vehemently this time.

The itching moved along her right arm, a huge barn spider. It must have fallen as it was starting to take down its web above her this morning. Screaming, she swiped at the spider, causing it to land where she had slept, and vaulted upright and onto the ladder, racing down to the barn floor. Her heart threatened to burst out of her chest while she wrestled with opening the barn door.

Luca said, "Ari, open your eyes. Look. He is a fine specimen."

"Hey, Red. You've got to get yourself together. You're going to see bigger, badder things than a little spider in this place." Natasha sneered.

Ari barely opened one eye and then shut it again, tightly, and shuddered.

Something crawled over her bare foot. It was a wolf spider, almost two inches long. The hair on the robust hunter made it appear more menacing. Recalling her dad's suspected wolf spider bite from the spring and how the surrounding area had swelled and remained painful for a week, she screamed again and again, vigorously shaking her foot, flinging the spider against the barn wall where it scurried away.

"Ari…" Luca was gently insistent.

An engine started up. That meant it was six thirty and Uncle Pete would be driving away from the homestead to begin farming. He was punctual down to the second. She listened, waiting until it was safe to undo her makeshift latch on the barn door. Cautiously, she—

The shuttle engine became more pronounced. She opened her eyes and the memory faded, but she felt light-headed.

"Are you okay?" Joan asked.

Meg reached out to hold Ari and said, "I think she's going to faint!"

"Ari!" Luca's voice snapped with frustration, trying to reach her. He stepped in front of her, temporarily blocking her from seeing anyone else and holding the tarantula behind his back. His voice softened. "Look at me."

She looked for a place to anchor, finding it in the deep green pools of Luca's eyes, which held no ridicule, only kindness and concern.

"Good. Now breathe." He watched her carefully as she inhaled deeply, holding her breath for ten long counts before slowly exhaling, as her mom had taught her. "You are all right." Luca nodded and stepped away from her, vanishing into the dense vegetation. Quickly reappearing, he assured Ari and everyone else. "The tarantula is back off the road. He will not get squashed."

Embarrassed by her behavior, she took in the concern of her colleagues. Except for smug Natasha. Blushing hotly, she stared at the road in an attempt to get ahold of herself and her emotions.

His strong, lean hand extended low, offering her a lifeline. She took it. Tingling raced into her body, taking her by surprise. Even in fear, the deep hunger she had for him surfaced. Her eyes widened, and she raised her head.

Luca cast his eyes around at the rest of their group, seeking their attention and consensus. "Everyone, back on the shuttle. We have a long day."

He turned back to her. "Better?"

She looked up into his eyes and nodded. She saw questions flit through his emerald-green depths and something else. It hit her in the solar plexus. Ari inhaled deeply, held her breath, and then exhaled as slowly as possible to steady herself. What a hot mess she was.

Ari boarded the shuttle, guided by Luca's hand on her back. When seated, her body trembled from the stress of seeing the enormous tarantula and Luca's touch. She grasped her notebook and pen from her backpack after her hands stilled. A uniformed man came out of the little building at the entry gate and waved at their shuttle. It stopped, and Luca and Natasha hopped off.

Ari gave up on journaling and picked up her camera again, trying to capture everything she saw around her, not wanting to miss any of her experience in Tikal.

The shuttle swayed when Luca and Natasha stepped in and moved up the steps. They stood in front, holding on to a safety bar as the driver shut the doors and drove into the park.

"Everyone, eyes up front. Please," Luca directed. "We are checked in and have secured our campsite and guides for tomorrow morning's sunrise hike. We have roughly eighteen kilometers until we reach the area where we will camp. We will decide our course of action after we arrive. The gate said we are among the first in this morning." He spoke to the driver, who slowed down further. "I have asked our driver to drive more slowly than the posted forty-five-kilometer speed limit so that you can take in the majesty of Tikal. Most of you have not been here. It is a very special place. The park is expansive, five hundred seventy-five square kilometers.

"Laser technology has recently surveyed more than twenty-one hundred square kilometers of the Petén jungle. The tens of thousands of structures buried beneath the jungle foliage reveal the pre-Columbian Mayan civilization was much more complex and interconnected than originally believed. With this new information, the population estimate has been increased to between five and fifteen million. Causeways, defensive walls, fortresses, and ramparts indicate that warfare was rife. I remind you that Ari and Matt are our utmost experts on differing aspects of the Maya. We are fortunate to have them on our project."

Her eyes met Luca's, and she nodded. His smile was slow and reassuring.

"Ari?" he said.

She felt him studying her. She didn't dare look and gave him a thumbs-up instead.

"Why did we stop again?" Joan asked Luca.

"Ocellated turkeys and coatis are crossing the road."

Ari rose from her seat. "Can we get out again? I'd like to take some pictures."

"The park is full of them. You will see many more. I would prefer we continue on."

"Sure." Ari sat, scooting next to the window across from Luca, in front of Meg and Matt. Ebullient, she extended her lens out the opening, wanting to pinch herself. She was finally in the place that was at the top of her bucket list. She snapped away, capturing the turkeys and raccoon-like coatis before they disappeared into the dense green.

LUCA MOTIONED ARI ASIDE AFTER the group unloaded the tents and supplies from the shuttle. "Tell me."

"Tell you what?"

"About your arachnophobia."

Well, that is better than explaining why my finger ended up Natasha's nose. "I really don't want to discuss it." She looked past him, trying to see Tikal.

Luca waved his hand in her line of sight. "You cannot see much of Tikal until you walk in. The vegetation hides it."

She glared at him and batted his hand away. "Stop it. I can see a temple from here."

"You may not know this, but many, many people have a fear of spiders." He put his hands on his hips, his words taking on a lecture tone. "It is believed to result from evolutionary selection, because spiders are associated with disease and pain, especially the venomous varieties. They are very effective vectors. The fear is often inherited, but something tells me you may have had a negative experience that was traumatizing. You appeared terrified."

"Do we really need to have this talk now?" she asked, exasperated. "I want to see Tikal. I feel like I've waited my whole life to see this."

"Fine, I understand," he grumbled, throwing his hands up. "But it is difficult to absorb something fully when you have fear. It creates a wall, effectively diminishing the experience. I was under the impression that talking might help."

"I'll be fine. We can talk later, okay?" She found it difficult to pull her gaze from his.

"Promise?"

"Yes. Thanks for your concern. I kinda overreacted."

"If you say so. Until later then." He turned away, effectively dismissing her. "Everyone. Over here, please," Luca called, raising his arm overhead. Belting out over the symphony of animal and bird sounds, he laid out the day's plans. "First we will attend to our campsite—"

A chorus of disappointment met his words as the group stood in a haphazard circle.

"I realize you are eager to explore. We set up now while we can see and before it becomes too hot. You have until 1700 to walk the park, and then we meet at our campsite. Everyone is to explore in pairs or larger groups. Tikal is large and can be treacherous. Go slowly. Pay attention to the terrain and steps. Any questions?"

Natasha raised her hand. "I'd like to shadow you, Big Guy."

"That is fine, Natasha."

Big Guy. I'm going to puke. Ari walked to the edge of the group and studied the ruins in an attempt to block out Natasha and her annoyance. She couldn't see that much from the campsite.

Joan chimed in. "I'd like to go with you too. I understand you've been here several times before, Luca. You can provide me with some lovely insight, I'm sure."

"Why don't you keep Ari company, Joan? After all, this"—Natasha extended her hand and swept it in a wide arc toward the ruins—"is Ari's thing. She's an expert on Maya culture."

"Thanks, but I'll pass for now." Joan turned so that Natasha couldn't see her wink and winked at Ari, adding, "I'll pepper her with questions later, after I've walked the ruins."

A sour expression had replaced Natasha's smug one. Feeling much better, Ari smiled at the ground, appreciating Joan's purposeful and unwelcome intrusion. Other colleagues broke into groups, mostly threes and fours, and headed to get tent and camp supplies from the shuttle.

Meg came over and threw an arm around Ari's shoulders and giggled. She kept her voice low. "Hey, mate. Natasha looks mad as a cut snake. Why doncha come with Matty and me? We're both expert climbers." She nodded over at Luca, Joan, and Natasha. "And no dramas."

"I'd enjoy that," Ari said, warming to the idea of scaling a temple or two. She could use the support. The steep, uneven steps had looked challenging. Grabbing one end of a tent, she said, "Come on. Let's get our tent up first. You bunking with me tonight?"

"Where else would I be sleeping?"

"I thought—"

"Hey, we'll be out in the open. Matty and I should try to maintain a professional appearance." Meg grabbed the other end of the tent and put a bag of gear over her shoulder.

"Oh my word. Everyone has to know you're hooking up."

"Possibly. And I'm sure everyone is aware of the sizzle between you and our boss."

Ari groaned. "I hope not. He's just handsome and, okay, sexy…"

"Yeah, says you with your panties on fire and your tongue down his throat. All of us here are scientists. We study, question, observe. We research and look for the patterns and draw conclusions based on them. No one here is blind or stupid. We're also human and adults. Well, some of us more than others. I do think dear Natasha had her hopes dashed when Joan joined what she hoped would be a twosome. Gotta love Joan. She's cheering for you and Luca."

"Huh? What?" Surprise stopped Ari in her tracks. In the corner of her eye, she watched Matt and Luca pitch their tent. The two of them laughed and worked together as if they had known each other forever.

"Joan knows. Keaton told her."

"Keaton?"

"Crikey, it's close. Feel like I'm steaming in an oven." Meg cleared her throat, wiped her face, and retied the scarf around her hairline to catch any other sweat. "He saw you two walking the promenade. Before you disappeared for some time last night. Happened to look out his window. I guess it overlooks the water."

"Oh no—"

"Yep. He and Joan were examining maps and geology info."

"And you know this how?"

"Joan likes to share, but I asked her not to say anything to anyone else."

"Do you think Luca knows they suspect?"

"Come on, Ari. They don't suspect. They know. I have no idea if he knows they know. And what are you going to do about it if he does?"

"Hell, I don't know. I didn't come to Guatemala looking for this. I'm so overwhelmed with so many different feelings, confusion being one. I refuse to become his toy."

"There is no way you're a toy. Do you see the way he looks at you?"

Laughter burst from Ari. "Yeah. Pure lust."

"Don't be daft, girlfriend. There's more than lust. Granted, he looks like he wants to jump you half the time. Drag you off. Do something dirty in the bush."

Ari laughed harder and wiped her eyes. "You're so funny! Now he sounds like a caveman or some predatory animal."

"Well, you did point out he moves like a big cat."

"Guilty. He reminds me of a jagu—"

"And he watches you, a lot."

She remained silent, blushing and busying herself with organizing the tent poles.

Hands on her hips, Meg studied the ground sheet and tent she'd unfolded. "Hm. I think that we need an additional tent. This tent is supposed to be a four-man, but it's smaller. The three of us could squeeze in, but it would be really tight, especially with Joan being a bigger woman. In this heat, I really don't want to sleep any closer to someone than I have to, unless it's Matt, and that isn't an option tonight. I'll still share with Joan since he's bunking with Luca." She elbowed Ari. "You can have the single. You know, just in case."

"Knock it off. I am not sleeping with him or inviting him to sleep with me."

"Okay. Didn't mean to ruffle your feathers. Believe me, I'd sleep with Matt if Luca hadn't assigned him to his tent."

"I'll see if I can find a smaller tent."

Meg looked around, observing the tents in various stages of completion. She nodded at the diminishing pile of tents. "I think small is all that's left."

Ari left and returned with a smaller tent, dropping it to the ground. "This seems awfully small." She stared at it.

"It looks like a pup tent, maybe slightly bigger." Noticing that Ari wasn't moving, she asked, "What's wrong? Is it missing something?"

"Um"—her voice drifted off as she leaned all her weight to one foot and placed a hand on her hip—"I've never camped, Meg. I have no idea how to put a tent together."

"Pitch a tent," Meg corrected her gently.

"Yeah. See? I don't even know the correct jargon." She sighed deeply and offered in a loud whisper, "This is my first Indiana Jones adventure."

Meg bent over laughing. "Crikey, that's rich! Really? I thought you'd excavated before."

"I stayed in housing or large platform tents. This is"—she looked around, throwing her hands out from her sides—"very primitive. I assumed we'd be staying in something similar to what I had in the past. Guess not."

"Okay. Let's get your tent up first. I'll pitch it; you watch and see how easy it is, okay. Then you can help with Joan's and mine. Looks like our men are well into it. You good with that?"

"Absolutely," Ari assured her, nodding. Her focus drifted to where Luca and Matt worked, and she became so quickly engrossed she forgot to pay attention or listen to Meg's instruction.

Ari hugged herself, trying to contain her joy as she stood in the Great Plaza facing Temple I—the Temple of the Great Jaguar, which rose forty-seven meters. She felt like a giddy child before opening her birthday gifts, times one hundred.

Why had it taken her so long to get here? She acknowledged that if she'd visited at a younger age, she would have had a tenth of the perspective and appreciation for what she was now experiencing. Words failed to describe her depth of wonder as she stood within the Forest of Kings, surrounded by overgrown ruins and vine-shrouded bushes and trees, in once thriving, powerful Tikal—a Classic period Maya city-state. The surrounding jungle was a symphony of animal and bird chatter.

The Maya were geniuses. Awe and reverence filled Ari. Despite Tikal's location in a landlocked area, the Maya had built a massive reservoir to address its population's need for water. Walking through the ball court, seeing how the city had been laid out, and climbing the temples—it was surreal. The Maya were sturdy, shorter people. They had to be agile and athletic to manage the large steep, uneven steps of the temples without injuring themselves or falling to their deaths.

"Are you all right, mate?" Meg asked. "You're going to catch some of those big insects with your maw hanging open like that."

"I am so all right," she said, wiping away unshed tears. "I know I'm gaping. There are truly no words to describe it. It's just, well, I've dreamed of seeing this forever. The structural architecture and planning is astounding, similar to other sites I've explored or excavated in the Middle East, Africa, and Europe. Just feeling overwhelmed, emotional, in the best way. This place is part of the Maya mystery, you know? Like, how did they maintain an enormous city and grow enough food to support the population in a hilly territory like this?

"I mean, Meg, you're going to be looking at the *bajos*—the low-lying wetlands ringing our site, right? For long-lost technology that allowed the Maya to cultivate corn? Don't you ache to know? That's part of why you're on the project, right?"

"Seeing all this gets me jumping, and I can't wait to get on-site," Meg said. "Tikal is stunning. I've seen pictures, but they don't do it justice. You've got to experience it, get your feet on the ground, like our Outback. You should come visit sometime."

"I'd like to visit, see the Outback through your eyes." Ari continued, "We're in the middle of antiquity. Can you feel it? The energy? I swear, I close my eyes and Tikal comes alive."

A look of bemusement passed across Meg's features before she spoke. "No worries. Soak it all in, but keep us in your sights or stay out in the open. Remember what the boss said." Crooking her head in Matt's direction, she added, "I'm going to sit in the shade with Matty. Looks like he's studying some glyphs and taking notes. I might learn a thing or two." She wiped her forehead with the back of her hand, grumbling. "It's bloody miserable in the sun. I didn't think it would be this hot."

The majesty surrounding Ari was dazzling. She was aware of the scorching yellow disk in the sky and the sweltering air, but it wasn't really all that bad. She waved at Meg. "Joan did mention it's warmer than usual for this time of year, something to do with the trade winds. I'll be with you later."

"In thirty, okay?"

"Are you kidding? How about two hours?"

"Agreed. Set your watch, mate. You have that starry-eyed look, which makes me think you'll lose track of time and place." Meg stood next to

Ari, making sure she was setting her alarm. "We'll take a hike then. The Petén Basin is loaded with biodiversity. I'm chomping at the bit to see it. I can expand your scientific knowledge and appreciation for Mother Nature. Promise. And it's gotta be twenty degrees cooler out of this direct sun."

Ari lingered in the Central Acropolis in a dream state, taking pictures of the ruins, limestone stelae wiped mostly blank by centuries of erosion, and crumbling cartouches. She climbed the stairs to one of the nobility's palatial residences and sat on a stone platform off a hallway in a sliver of shade, allowing her an unobstructed view of the Ceremonial Court through the partially deteriorated wall. Tikal was magical. Ari drank from her bottle, having no trouble imagining what Tikal might have been like when sixty thousand people lived here. Or hearing the avid cheering as the bruising and bloody high-speed game of *pitz* was played between the men of Tikal and neighboring cities. She took another swig of her water and let the past slowly absorb her.

"Ari! Psst… Ari… Wake up!"

"What? Go away," Ari mumbled through the fog of sleep, wisps of her dreams of trekking through Tikal dissipating. There was the sound of a zipper, and then someone reached through the small opening and shook her by the shoulder.

"Come on, sloth. Your alarm is beeping. Didn't you hear it? I'm ready, except my bladder is full to burstin'. I certainly don't want to go to the loo myself. It's flipping black out."

Meg. Ari grunted. Her alarm was indeed beeping. She looked at her watch. *Two thirty. I've gotta move.* An urgency hit her. "Ooh. I've got to use the toilet too." Ari kicked off her top sheet, exposing the fact that she had slept in her panties and a cami. "Hold on. I'll go with you."

Joan popped her head into Ari's tent. "Come on, missy. We're cutting it close, and you know how Luca doesn't appreciate stragglers."

Ari sat up and opened her eyes, wincing in the light pooling over her. "Can you please turn those down or off. Hurts my eyes and attracts the insects."

"Okay, girlfriend. One is off and Joan, dim yours. Point it away from the tent, like that. Yup. Open your eyes and get moving. The boss is expecting us in"—Meg checked the glowing dial on her watch—"ten."

Ari huffed and groaned, falling back onto her bedroll. "It's too early," she whispered to herself, but even as the words left her lips, another thought, that of seeing the sunrise from Temple IV brought Ari to her unsteady feet. "Lead the way, girls."

"Dear, you need to change into something appropriate for hiking. Lace panties and a cami aren't going to do the job."

Ari looked down. Her face flushed with embarrassment at Joan's words. "I went to bed dressed so I could just pop out of bed ready this morning. I forgot I shed some clothes during the night. I was burning up."

Meg laughed. "You're right, Joan. Although I have to think there is a certain someone that might enjoy Ari's choice of sleepwear."

"Shut it, Meg."

"Oh, aren't we snarly in the morning? Come on. Grab your pants and shirt over there in the corner." Meg motioned with her flashlight, and Ari moved unsteadily to slip on her clothing. "Well done. I see some socks rolled up too." She motioned again with the flashlight. "Over there. Slip everything on. You can zip and button as we walk, and clean up after we get back."

"I need to brush my teeth."

"Fine. I could do with some of that too. Stick your finger out." Meg pulled a tube of toothpaste out of nowhere and squeezed a dab onto Ari's forefinger. "Want some, Joan?"

"Why not? I'm sure others will appreciate my fresh breath." She held her finger out.

"Probably. Right, Ari?"

"Meg…," Ari warned.

"Definitely snarly," Meg said, placing a dab on her tongue. "Ow! Forgot how it burns without water."

Ari ignored Meg and worked the paste around in her mouth. It stung like a bitch. But if she did get close enough to Luca…

The women passed around a bottle of water in the emerging moonlight, water-falling a mouthful each to avoid touching the lip of the bottle, swishing the toothpaste, before spitting onto the ground.

"Thanks, dear," Joan said. "Much better!"

Meg jumped. "Hey! You splashed some spit on my legs, Ari."

"I did? Sorry, Meg. You're wearing shorts? What are you thinking? Get some pants on. The mosquitoes will eat you alive." She looked around. "Wow! Look around. This is spectacular! You can see the silhouettes of some of the ruins." She took her lens cap off her camera, adjusted the aperture and speed. "I think I might be able to capture this. Remarkable…"

Meg slipped back through her tent flap. "Give me some extra light so I can find my pants, will you, Joanie? That's good—"

A deep, accented voice asked, "How much longer?"

Ari slapped her hand to her chest as she jumped. "Luca! You." Her heart skipped. "I didn't hear you come up."

"That is a problem. Be aware, always." Luca's tone was measured, but his expression softened when he saw the fear in her eyes. "I am sorry if I frightened you. Please be more aware."

Ari nodded, swallowing. Her heart hammered as she lost herself in his eyes. How did he look so sexy after just waking up? His hair was down. She remembered what it felt like when she wove her fingers through it, when he was kissing her, touching her.

Joan focused on holding the flap closed while sliding her flashlight under the flap to provide illumination for Meg.

Luca brushed his thumb across Ari's cheek. His eyes glowed and crinkled in a smile at her while he called, "Meg?"

Stepping out and wearing pants, she said, "Ready. Good morning, Boss."

"Yes, good morning, Luca," Joan said.

Luca nodded. "Meg, Joan. The others are up ahead with a guide. Stay close. Even though there is moonlight, it disappears frequently because of the fast-moving clouds. Use the flashlights to sweep the ground in front of us." He turned on his headlamp and walked swiftly, the women trotting behind him.

"Boss, we need to go to the loo," Meg said. "We'll be as quick as we can."

He pointed to a silhouetted group with flashlights. "We will wait."

The women walked silently to the circle of flashlights. Ari felt more awake now that she was moving. In her haste to get ready, she had forgotten her flashlight. She must have left it on top of her bedroll, hopefully off or the battery would run down. "Um, Luca, I forgot my flashlight."

Silence met her admission. She felt like a chastised child, and this early in the morning. "I'll partner with Joan."

He reached out, gently taking her by the wrist. "Why don't you partner with me?"

A few of the team cleared their throats softly behind Ari and Luca.

Ari trotted to keep up with Luca's quick, long strides. "Can you slow down just a bit?" she huffed.

"We are running late."

"My body isn't quite awake—" Ari stumbled into Luca when he stopped abruptly.

Colleagues stopped behind them. All talking ceased, and they held their collective breath, waiting for what would happen.

"We need to move at this pace or we will miss the sunrise. This is our only chance to see it, provided the clouds clear enough."

"I'll keep up with you, but I might bitch about it. Just letting you know. Nothing personal. I don't want to miss this."

He leaned forward. His loose hair brushed her face, his masculine scent washing over her, and his breath moist against her ear, whispering teasingly, "You do not want to miss anything with me, Ari."

Ari shivered involuntarily from his promise, squeaking, "Okay."

His smile was devilish, making her stomach flip. But it vanished before he turned and addressed the rest of the small group. "Stay close. Continue moving your flashlights around as we walk. There are animals about and others camouflaged but watching us. We will meet the other guides in about one hundred meters. You—"

An invisible menace thundered toward them, above the giant leaves of the canopy, drowning out his voice. He pulled Ari under his oversized poncho just before the heavy, hard rain pelted the group. So close, his masculinity was intoxicating. She wanted nothing more than to bury herself in it. He groaned as her body pressed up against his, then chuckled as the rain flattened the poncho around them, murmuring in her ear, "This is challenging."

Large drops of rain roared and spattered, drenching those who had forgotten their ponchos or umbrellas. They stood pressed together, backpacks overhead in an effort to stay dry. Others struggled to don ponchos and open umbrellas as the clouds unleashed their flood and then, just as quickly, stopped. The roar rapidly subsided into loud drip-drops as the clouds dashed past them.

Joan sputtered. "Oh my word. That was like, oh my, as though an enormous spigot of water was turned on full force. Amazing. And now, poof, the rain is gone. I'm soaked through. Except for my head. A lot of good my umbrella did me, that downpour came in so fast and furious."

"I realize many of you are good and wet; however, it is warm. You should not become chilled." He greeted the guides who appeared out of the dark, dry and smiling. *"Buenos días."*

Everyone else followed suit. Luca spoke with the guides and then introduced them, mentioning that one would be in front, one in the middle, and one would bring up the rear of the group. "Hopefully, your cameras made it through the onslaught of rain. Please, pay extra caution as we climb. The steps are steep and treacherous, even when they are dry," Luca said. "The clouds have blown over, and it looks as though there is no mist this morning, so we should see a stunning sun—"

Natasha said, "Sorry to interrupt, Luca. I'll walk with you, if you don't mind. You know how I am with heights."

Luca rested a hand on Ari's shoulder, stopping her from wanting to gnash her teeth. "Ari will stay in front of me. Matt and Meg, I would ask you to be on either end of our group to provide support for the guides." Addressing the guide closest to him, "Raul, can you please follow Dr. Jordaan, in case she requires assistance? Thank you. Let us head out."

Ari didn't dare glance back, but she was certain Natasha was practically spitting with fury.

The group stayed in single file, following the head guide on a path that appeared to glow slightly through the jungle. Occasionally Ari saw the outline of large shadowy hills. She knew those were more unexcavated ruins. Recently, lidar technology had made a major archaeological discovery, uncovering and mapping over sixty thousand structures obscured by Petén's dense vegetation, shaking up what experts and archaeologists knew about size and scope of Maya civilization. One of the structures was within Tikal, a pyramid over twenty-seven meters high, long been assumed to be a large hill.

From time to time, cedar and allspice bathed her in their aromatic scents. Before ascending, the head guide stopped close to a towering pale ceiba. He placed his hand on it reverently, sharing that it was not only the national tree of Guatemala but, more importantly, sacred to the Maya, connecting the underworld and sky with the terrestrial world. The group walked a little farther until they reached the base of the temple and then began climbing the long wooden stairs to the summit. The climb was slow and slippery. Several lost their footing or tripped more than once, Ari included. Finally, they made it to the top where their guides asked them to sit in silence.

Above them, voluminous clouds raced away, and the moon faded as persimmon orange and butter yellow tinged the predawn to the east. Below them, as far as they could see, the thick jungle canopy came awake—the birds, monkeys, and other animals taking up a full cacophonic melody. Ari sat serenely as the raindrops and dewdrops sparkled like diamonds in the rising morning sunlight. Luca's hand reached for hers under his poncho between them. He stroked her palm with his fingers and then squeezed her hand gently. Wings fluttered in Ari's stomach, and her heart glowed, grateful for his unspoken communication and beautiful moment.

AFTER RETURNING TO FLORES FROM the two days in Tikal, Luca and Natasha scheduled a team meeting before dinner. They planned to briefly go over the logistics of traveling the next day to Kanul—the location they would excavate and explore for the next ten weeks, into the second week of August.

"I need everyone's attention." Luca's voice boomed over the chatter. It died down quickly. "Thank you. I trust that all of you were impressed by Tikal?"

Nods and affirmative responses answered him.

"Good. We leave tomorrow morning at 0400."

Loud groans met Luca's announcement. Ari felt tired just thinking about getting up that early. Mornings were not her thing. But then breakfast didn't used to be either.

He held up his hand to settle everyone back down. "It is early. However, you can sleep on the shuttle. Or try to. You might pack something to rest your head on. The kitchen is supplying us with a light breakfast before we leave and snacks for the ride. Depending on how much you enjoy sleeping or how long it takes you to get ready, set yourself an appropriate wake-up call. I would suggest three o'clock since breakfast is at three thirty. I also suggest an early turn-in tonight. Please have your luggage ready tonight and on the shuttle before you go to breakfast tomorrow. Any questions?" Luca looked around the room. "No? Okay. We are done."

Three o'clock came too early for Ari. She had crawled into bed, frustrated, insatiable gnawing at her insides, night tossing and turning after saying good night to Luca, and that's all it was—a spoken good night between them. Bleary-eyed, she crawled into her seat for the trip to Kanul, using her more lightly packed duffel as a pillow, having left extra clothing, like her skirt, sundress, and some personal items back in her room. She was able to catnap.

After the shuttle exited the main road, travel through the jungle slowed considerably. The shuttle jolted over rutted earth, becoming smoother as they neared the excavation. Hired armed militia waved the shuttle to a halt. Luca and Natasha presented paperwork and identification to them, and the shuttle was ushered on, coming to a stop in a sizable clearing.

Luca rose from his seat. "Your attention up here please. A few things before we exit. Other teams of archaeologists, specialists, and graduate students are already at work, as should be the local Maya helping us. The majority of students working the summer session here are with the MRP, the Maya Research Program's field school out of the US. As I stated during orientation, some students will be here the duration, some for a few weeks. They will move between the excavations, as needed."

He pointed to the area behind him, which was littered with working students, academic leads, and tools. "This is Kaq. We will begin helping with excavation here today. For those of you who have not excavated or worked in the pits, the work is tedious. That said, finding your first artifact will connect you to humanity on a different level. What you know about your world is immediately broadened and deepened. Trust me when I say that discovering your first artifact is remarkable. I want you to experience this thrill and embrace the reverence of uncovering the past.

"As you can see, a grid system is in its infancy. Ari, Keaton, and Joan will oversee the gridding today. Several areas have been partially cleared, revealing the promise of structures. Ari is well versed in the methods of excavating. She has worked in sites throughout the Middle East, Africa, and Europe. She is our lone forensic anthropologist. Should you find any bone fragments or larger remains, stop working immediately and get her. Clear?"

The group was nodding and murmuring affirmative.

A Mayan man approached Luca and clasped his forearms. Both men broke out in large smiles. "Everyone, this is my friend and colleague, Carlos, whom I mentioned during orientation." He turned to Carlos. "I am glad you are here, *amigo*."

Carlos stepped forward to face the group after greeting Luca. They formed a loose circle around him. "Hello and welcome to Kanul. As Luca mentioned, I am Carlos Balam." He glanced at Ari upon hearing her audible intake of breath and smiled. "Yes, jaguar. You know your Maya. You are?"

Embarrassed, heated blushing colored Ari's face. "Ari Antony. I'm so sorry. Very little Mayan. Linguistics are Matt's department. I didn't mean to interrupt you, Carlos."

Luca broke in quietly, explaining to Carlos. "Ari is a PhD, our expert on Mayan culture, including the *Popol Vuh*. She has extensive excavation experience and is a forensic anthropologist, which will be very beneficial should we unearth human remains."

Carlos nodded to her, his smile making his eyes crinkle at their corners. "It is no problem. Nice to make your acquaintance, Dr. Antony."

"Ari, please."

"Dr. Ari," he deferred kindly. He returned to addressing the group, his voice rising above the generator humming in the background. "My English is learned from taking English-speaking tourists through the ruins of my ancestors, primarily Tikal. I grew up in a small community within Petén and still here."

His arms rose, sweeping the air around him. "Camp is set up as Luca requested. Behind me is your section of tents. Luca and Dr. Jordaan have cabin tents. The other tents sleep between two and four people each, which you are free to select. Mosquito netting has been placed inside the tents." Pointing to his left, he said, "Beyond the tents, down the hill, is the canteen area. For safety, it is a distance from all tents. I understand Luca has covered camp and site safety with you, but I want to stress again to not have food in or anywhere within the area of your tents." He pointed forward. "If you look behind you, past the field command center are the composting toilets, and farther away are the showers, indicated by the tanks sitting on top of the makeshift frames. Potable water is throughout the camps in jerry cans." He angled toward Luca and nodded.

"Thank you, Carlos, to you and your men, for setting up ahead of time and for this orientation."

"I will be around, amigo," said Carlos, leaving, walking the direction of the kitchen.

"Tomorrow we will head over to Rax, roughly a five-minute walk. Today we work at Kaq. Leave your bags in your tents, then check in at the field tent to familiarize yourselves with the schedule. Your tools and individual excavation and camp chores assignments for today are there as well. We have arrived after the midmorning break, so I will see many of you at lunch. We will have a short meeting after dinner, which will be early, and then turn in for the evening. I assure you that you will sleep well tonight and every night we are here. Our days begin at 0600."

Ari turned to go with the rest when Luca spoke, stopping her. "Ari?"

Before Ari could respond, Meg chirped behind her, "I've got you covered, mate." She picked up Ari's duffel and groaned. "Your pack is heavy."

"I ha—"

Meg waved her off. "I got it. Does she need her backpack, Luca?"

He nodded, looking serious, "Always."

Looking back and forth, a knowing smile crossed Meg's face. She said, "See you two later."

"I really should handle my own responsibilities," Ari said to Luca, uncomfortable as she watched Meg stumble between the two bags.

Luca's arms were crossed, his brow furrowed. "Your responsibility lies with something else right now. Do you have water?"

"A little. How much do I need?"

He stilled, and his lips formed a firm line. Displeasure rolled off him. "What are you to do about water?"

"Fine. I'll top it off. Where is the closest source?"

"Try a field tent behind you."

"Are you really going to wait? What's this all about, Luca?"

"Make it quick. Please."

Irritated, she huffed and turned her back on him, missing the smirk on his face. Her bottle was almost empty, so it was a good reminder that she needed to be more aware of when it was low, like refilling her tank when gas was at a third full.

He was right where she had left him. "Come with me." His light voice took the sting out of the command.

Ari followed along his side, miffed at being singled out when they had just arrived, peppering him with questions. "Why? Where are we going?"

The jungle erased their path quickly. "I am going to help you address a few things. We will take a short walk north to a large hill, due north, and rest where limestone juts out of the ground."

"How do you know this?"

"Carlos has told me. He knows where we have gone. If we do not return in the hour, they will track us."

The canopy and understory thinned out suddenly, revealing a large hill and evidence of a structure ahead of them.

"What things, Luca?"

He slowed and stopped, holding his arm out in front of her, signaling for her to do the same. "Look down."

A long trail of ants carrying bright green leaves moved on an unseen highway in front of her. She knelt and watched. "Wow! Are those leaf-cutters?"

"Yes. They work very hard, carrying up to twenty times their weight. They transport flowers also. Do not get too close," he said, gently stopping Ari, who had edged closer on her heels. "They will bite. It is nonvenomous, but I understand it hurts."

"How do they eat all these leaves?"

"They do not. They feed on the leaf sap. The leaves or flowers are chewed to a size they can carry and take to their underground nests."

"Fascinating. I can't even imagine lifting my own weight."

He could imagine lifting her petite lean body and having her toned legs wrapped around his waist. He cleared his throat and the image from his mind. "The ants grow a fungus by exuding a fluid from their bodies onto the leaves or flowers, contributing to an established fungus garden, which is food for their larvae. Their society is based on ant-fungus mutualism. The fungus needs the ants to stay alive, and the ants need the fungus to stay alive. Let's take a big step over and keep walking."

Ari and Luca reached the limestone. "You can sit here. There is enough shade to keep the direct sun off you." He placed his backpack at her feet. "I'll be back."

"Wait. Where are you going?"

Luca's answer was a quick smile at her before he stepped into the understory, disappearing.

"Luca?" she asked, her voice rising slightly.

"I am very close. Keep talking. I enjoy the sound of your voice."

"Why are we here?"

He came out of the leaves. "Do you trust me, Ari?" he asked quietly.

Speechless, she only stared back at him, on guard.

He opened his right hand. In it was a hairy spider, a tarantula much smaller than the one he had picked up on the way in to Tikal. Ari scooted back, her heart beating wildly against her ribs. "Shit, Luca. What the fuck?"

"I have it. Just breathe. I will hold it." He took his sunglasses off, allowing them to hang by his Chums. His eyes were calm yet full of concern. "Look at me, Ari." He placed his free hand on her wrist, encouraging her to move closer.

"If we are calm, it remains so. When threatened, its preference is to run and hide or rear up on its hind legs. Spiders are a bundle of nerves, much like you are now." He took off his safari hat and placed the tarantula on the wide brim. It just sat there.

"Tell me about what happened."

"Huh?"

"Take off your sunglasses and talk to me. Please."

She slipped them off, letting them hang from a cord around her neck, like his. Blinking, she tore her gaze from the tarantula.

"Just breathe. It will not harm you." He put his fingers out. The tarantula reached with one of its legs, testing Luca's finger. Finding it safe, the spider climbed into his palm and rested. Luca gently slipped it off his palm and back onto his safari hat.

Following the entire exchange, Ari's eyes were round with disbelief. She swallowed convulsively.

"Keep breathing, sweetheart."

That did her in, the sweetheart. Her heart slowed until he took both her hands in his, waiting patiently.

She swallowed again and took a deep breath. "My father… my father, he was bitten by a brown recluse." Ari shuddered at the memory of how his foot had looked—the large weeping, ulcerated sore that required hospitalization to stop the necrosis.

"I was in kindergarten. Papa was so sick. I thought he was going to die. All because of a little spider." She took another shaky breath. "I used to play with daddy longlegs. Can you imagine that? But after Papa was bitten, spiders, well, any spider, scared the shit out of me. My father took months to heal. He has a large permanent scar on his foot. It looks like a crater."

"Then there was the last time I stayed with my aunt and uncle. I was ten. My uncle was verbally and physically abusive to her. He came in from the field in the evening, pulling his work gloves off to wash up for dinner. He showed her a spider bite on his hand, claiming it was her fault for keeping a dirty, bug-infested house. She was pregnant." Her voice dropped into a whisper as she relived the horror. "He kicked her. In the stomach. I ran as she screamed, and I locked myself in their barn. I thought he might come after me."

Tears splashed down her face. "When I woke in the morning, a spider crawled up my arm. And then a wolf spider climbed over my foot by the barn door while I was peeking through the splintered door to see if it was safe. He passed me on his combine on the way to the fields. I ran to the house after I couldn't see him."

More tears poured forth. "Fuck." Shaking her head, she pulled the hem of her tank up and wiped the snot from her nose. "I found my aunt lying on the kitchen floor, the hardwoods covered in her blood. I called 911. Paramedics came and took her to the hospital. She was hemorrhaging and lost the baby. The police came. They drove their squad cars into the field and pulled my uncle off his tractor and handcuffed him. A woman detective took care of me until my parents came. I never went back. My parents never spoke to them again. In my world, spiders make bad things happen."

During her telling, Luca had pulled her into his arms, onto his lap. He stroked the top of her head gently and kissed it tenderly. "Sweetheart, I am so sorry you experienced those things. And I am a complete ass for trying to help you overcome your aversion to spiders. I believed I could help."

Ari looked deeply into his mesmerizing eyes. The green had changed color, resembling Lake Michigan during a great storm. Concern, not pity, flitted through their depths. She found such strength there and pulled away, sitting up straighter. "Sorry for all my tears. Thank you for just being there, Luca, and not judging."

He tucked a curl back that had escaped her braid, behind her ear. "I have no wish to judge you for your fears, only to help you face them, if you are all right with that."

Ari inhaled long and deep, gazing deeply into his eyes. "What do I do?"

"Do you want to help me release it back into the jungle?"

Her voice became choppy again. "Okay."

"I will be right with you, every step."

She nodded.

He extended his hand flat in front of the spider. It touched his fingers tentatively and climbed aboard. "Place your hand next to mine, Ari."

She did, sucking in her breath when the tarantula reached out and nimbly walked onto her palm. It tickled. She felt wonder when it calmly stayed put. "I'm sweating," she whispered. "Will that upset it?"

Luca smiled, brushing her ear with a kiss. "No, brave one. I will hold the back of your hand with mine. We will walk it back slowly together."

They rose and moved to where the jungle growth was denser and knelt together. The spider remained still.

"Lower your hand to the ground. Good," he said, sliding his palm from underneath the back of her hand. "You are doing great. Move your hand gently."

She mirrored his movement. After a minute, the tarantula walked off, stopping when only one of its legs touched her forefinger. It tapped her finger a few times and then moved into the undergrowth, disappearing immediately.

Ari was silent, stunned by what she had done.

Luca pulled her into his arms. "How did that feel?"

Her smile blinded him. "The best." She leaned forward, her hands framing his face with her hands, and kissed him fully. "Thank you," she murmured against his lips.

"You are welcome." His hand grazed her cheekbone, his eyes holding hers. "I would enjoy staying and kissing you more, but we should go." He stood up, offering his hand. She took it, and they walked back hand in hand until they saw the edge of their campsite. Luca pulled her back. His kiss was scorching, and she returned it. Both of them were breathing hard when they parted. He grinned and winked at her, squeezing her hand.

Freshly sponged off, Ari fell onto her sleeping bag. Joan snored softly, wrapped in a gauzy blanket of sorts. Meg's bedroll was empty, meaning she had bunked in with Matt. Which meant Keaton was where? *Where do Meg and Matt find the energy? I'm pooped.*

In her mind, Ari recapped her first day of working Kaq. It had been thrilling, yet squatting and bending over for hours strained her body. She came up empty during her time in the pit, but she, Keaton, and Joan made nice inroads on the grids. Seasoned from past digs, she was tasked with establishing the classification methodology. Ari corralled a few students and set about teaching them the system. During break, she chatted with Carlos, finding him warm and intelligent. Although she tried to get him to just call her by her name, he took to calling her "Dr. Ari" as a sign of respect.

Ari was also slated to work in the kitchen. Her job had been to cook the rice, which was an utter failure, rendered to a gluey substance. She overheard Natasha ask another lead archaeologist how someone could "totally fuck up rice." She felt even worse when Luca dumped his rice into the jungle, like just about everyone else. She had apologized, but Natasha had made her botched effort sting more by suggesting she be given KP duty. Natasha was a bitch. Given the opportunity, Ari was sure that, with time, she would master cooking rice over an open fire—and that was her last thought before falling into a deep sleep.

The weeks wore on, and the excavation at Kanul took on a rigid pattern—rising at five o'clock, breakfast, and excavating by six. There was a midmorning break, back to the pits or cataloging, lunch, a midday break, dinner, and lights-out. Ari thoroughly enjoyed digging next to the grad students and guiding them and sharing her knowledge about the Maya. It was if she were teaching a class in the jungle. She celebrated each find being unearthed from the jungle's shroud with them—clearly inscribed stelae, stone sculptures that merged human and animal characteristics, and architecture. Remains had been discovered a few times. Bones had elicited wonder until Ari determined they were musical instruments made from tapirs' jawbones and teeth. They all hoped to discover a big find—human remains, an overlooked codex, an important temple. It was possible; there was no tunneling evident, indicating looting of the site. They had just hit paved limestone floors.

Although her interactions with Luca were rare and too brief, Ari was able to watch him work. He had far more to manage than she did—overseeing the two excavations within Kanul and collaborating with the other lead archaeologists. There were evenings when she thought she might be able to talk with him, but he was pulled away into this or that conversation. She went back and forth—missing him, yet she was relieved their interactions were kept to a minimum. What occurred when they were by themselves could only be explained as combustion. She continued to wrestle with her intense fascination and growing emotions for him and the fact that he supervised her.

Having served their time, a number of grad students left, replaced by more grad students and archaeological leads. The tent community swelled into a small village as additional tents were erected and the pace of excavations progressed. The occasional and promised brief trips back to Flores became limited due to the volume of artifacts being excavated and structures exposed.

Finally, after seven weeks, Ari got the chance to commute back to Flores for two days with several colleagues, along with Natasha. The women spoke little to each other, immersing themselves in their extensive field notes and napping.

In Flores, Ari enjoyed her break, sleeping in, swimming, showering in her private room, and catching up on laundry. She called and updated her parents, and upon seeing Eric had called numerous times and left messages, she deleted them without listening. She also blocked any future calls and messages and deleted his contact information. Luca was ever present in her thoughts and dreams—which grew more graphic the longer she was apart from him.

The hair on the back of Ari's neck rose when she stepped into her room late in the second afternoon. She had spent hours at the pool, lounging and reading. Something was off. Her panic escalated when she noticed that her journal appeared to be at a slightly different angle on the desk. Her backpack was also hanging off the chair differently than she had left it. One of the shoulder straps was no longer hooked over the back of the chair. Someone had been in here since she had left, and it wasn't the maid. Ari had still been in the room when she came to tidy up in the late morning. She moved to the desk and picked up the journal. Her bookmark was under it, not inside as she had left it. Her hand flew to her chest and then to her pendant, where her throat pulsed hard and fast. She exited, making a beeline for the front desk, intent on an answer.

The desk clerk frantically waved an envelope at her. "Dr. Ari. *Buenas tardes.* This arrived while you were gone. Edgar forgot to give it to you, so excited was he about his daughter's wedding. It came in a stack of papers.

I am sorry for this."

"Good afternoon, Fredy! Don't worry about it. Thank you," she said, reaching for it, then yanking her hand back as if she'd been burned. The envelope fell to the ground.

He bent to retrieve it. "My sorry again. Here you are." Smiling, he placed it in her hand.

Fredy's apology and her surroundings faded as the uncomfortable feeling grew into anxiety. There was no mistaking the block print on the outside of the envelope; it was Eric's.

"Do you know when this arrived?"

He pointed to some numbers scribbled above her name. "See the date?"

"I do, thank you." The envelope had been delivered the day after they left for Kanul, seven weeks ago. There was no address under her name and no return address or postmark. *What the fuck? Is Eric here?* "Fredy, I came down to check on something. Do you know if someone has been in my room since the maid was there this morning?"

His face scrunched up before he responded, "I do not think so, but I will check." Please wait here, Dr. Ari." He disappeared through the door behind him.

She refilled her bottle with purified water from the large dispenser on the counter, her heart beating erratically.

Fredy reappeared. "No one of our staff has been in your room. Is everything well in your room?"

Her hands grew damp and her voice cracked. She was sure she had locked her door before going down to the pool. "Yes. Um... Um... Thank you for checking."

As Ari returned to her room to shower before dinner, she wondered who had access to it and why they had read her journal. She repacked her duffel with laundered clothes and other items, placing Eric's letter on top, planning on reading it over breakfast. She looked forward to returning to Kanul tomorrow and seeing everyone, particularly Luca. The shuttle was departing early. She put the chair in front of her door before climbing into bed.

The next morning, Ari walked to the *comedor* and sat in a corner for privacy, pulling Eric's letter from her front pocket, her buoyant mood sucked from her like quicksand.

"Buenos días, señorita. Café?"

"Sí, por favor." Ari rose to fill her plate from the buffet and then sat down. She took a deep breath to steady her nerves and opened the envelope.

> *Ariana,*
>
> *I remind you that I have your itinerary. I know where you're staying. I'm still waiting for your call and your apology.*
>
> *I believe I shared with you how much I enjoy Flores. Your hotel has a refreshing pool and nice view of the lake, don't you agree? It's a nice reprieve from the bugs and inhospitable climate.*
>
> *I am out of patience. I will not wait any longer. We must talk.*
>
> *ANSWER YOUR FUCKING PHONE!*
>
> *Eric*

Yeah, or else what Eric? Fuck you and your implied threat. I will never be under your control again.

Ari had been able to avoid him on campus and skirt the last two department meetings and year-end party. It was easier than she realized; she knew his schedule and his habits. She cut her semester weeks short, citing a family emergency, and graded her students' final papers via computer.

Why wasn't it obvious to him that she wanted nothing to do with him, ever again? Adding it all up together—the incident at her apartment, him tracking her down, the letter waiting for her in Antigua, the letter delivered here in Flores, the threatening tone of his words—she hadn't realized it until now that Eric was all about having power over her, controlling her. He was screwing with her. A chill ran through Ari. Had Eric been in her room? Someone had.

She tore his words into little pieces until they resembled confetti and dropped them bit by bit into her cooled coffee, turning it muddier as the ink released from the paper. The alarm on her watch went off, indicating it was time to board the shuttle. Perfect; she had lost her appetite anyway.

Luca was tired and cranky. Weeks without engaging with and touching Ari, all the while having her close by, were driving him crazy. When he could, he observed her work and enjoyed watching her interact with others. Her work on-site was professional and excellent—detailed and organized. She was kind, mentoring students on the importance of patience, technique, and about not compromising the integrity of their excavation skills. She listened to complaints and acknowledged the backbreaking work of moving rocks, roots, and dirt. She celebrated their finds with them, documenting them through photos.

One afternoon, last week, she had given the students working with her a concise and fascinating impromptu lecture on osteology and forensics after tapir bones had been unearthed. He wasn't the only one to pause and listen. Many had stopped to listen or come over to see why others took a break in their work. She had amassed a large captive audience that afternoon. Ari quickly became a student favorite with forensic knowledge coupled with Mayan cultural expertise and folklore. He missed her.

Even I underestimated the availability of my time. I need a break. Hell, the team needs one. They have worked practically nonstop for seven weeks. Ari, Natasha, and a few others are returning from their break in Flores. We are all going to take a break when they get back. Everyone has earned it. That decided, Luca fell asleep and dreamed of Ari.

"HAVE YOU CONSIDERED WHAT LUCA has been through? How it affected him? It's a wonder he isn't an empty man. Damn, I'm melting and slick with sweat. These damn bugs—"

"Hold on there." Ari dug in her bag and passed Meg some bug repellent. "Might help. What? What are you talking about?"

After pulling her paddles from the water, Meg laid them crosswise and sprayed each limb carefully, answering, "His wife."

Ari's heart plummeted to her feet. "He's married?" she spit out incredulously, her voice rising with each syllable. *Shit.* Not again. The memory of discovering Eric was a husband and father surfaced once again.

"Earth to Ari. Hello?" She snapped her fingers in her friend's face, laughing softly. "You're back. Good. Where did you go? You like, checked out. And look, you gotta keep your voice down. It'll carry over the water." The kayak rocked as Meg carefully turned, keeping her body low and centered. "Spritz my back, will you? This break was a great idea of Luca's, but I'm pooped. I really was up for sleeping and some bed gymnastics with Matt. How much farther do you think?"

"Sorry. I was revisiting something."

"Uh-huh. Your visit didn't appear to be a good one from my vantage point. Care to share?"

The effort to speak was like slogging through mud. "I was floored by what you said. Shit. I'll get over it." Ari changed the subject, opting not to bring her Eric into their wonderful day. "How can you be pooped, Miss

Expert Climber?" She handed the bottle back to Meg. "You'll have to get your face."

"Must be the climate draining me. It's bloomin' hot, then it rains outta nowhere. No, it's more like a monsoon outta nowhere. Crikey, being sticky all the time is wearing me down, girlfriend." She leaned in, wiping her face with the spritzed bandana. "Want some?"

Ari stared at her lap, staring at her hands and shaking her head. "I'm good, thanks," she croaked through the burning in her throat.

Speaking just loud enough for Ari to hear, Meg said, "The guys are behind us but not that far. Back to the subject." She squeezed Ari's shoulder. "I kinda left the tidbit hanging out there, didn't I? Damn, Ari. I'm so sorry. *Was* married. Luca's wife died in a car accident some years ago. Word is he was driving."

Astonished, Ari's head snapped up at that news. The bright sunlight dimmed, and the scenic cloud forest surrounding them faded as sadness for him bubbled up. She dropped her head again and whispered, "Oh, oh… How tragic."

Meg gently placed her hand on Ari's head. "I thought you knew. Try to cut him some slack."

"I will. Oh my God…" A bevy of emotions swirled in Ari, chief among them relief, guilt over the relief, and sympathy.

"Are you ladies okay?"

"Hey, Matty! We're fine. Hey, Luca. How's it goin'? Enjoying the kayaking?"

As surreptitiously as possible, Ari dabbed at her eyes before piggybacking onto Meg's response. "We're fine. Something flew into my eye. I think it's out now."

"Let me see," Luca insisted, steering their kayak right alongside the women's.

Ari blocked Luca from coming any closer with her hand. "I'm good. Really. Thanks."

His face was all seriousness, his voice insistent. "You need to flush your eye out. The jungle is full of pathogens and parasites your body is not familiar with. We have saline. Matt, get the first aid kit. It is in the orange dry bag."

The knowledge Meg had imparted altered Ari's go-to snarky response she used whenever she was told to do something she didn't want to.

Instead, she smiled. "I can wait. We're making camp around that bend up ahead, correct? It can wait until then."

"No, it cannot," he said, more sternly.

"Fine." Sighing, realizing she wasn't going to win this argument. *This is what I get for fibbing.* She accepted the saline, turning her back to him and the sun, pretending to dribble it into her eye. The saline ran down her cheek. She slipped her sunglasses on and handed the saline back. "All set. My eye does feel much better. Thanks, Doctor."

He nodded, then smiled back crookedly, his dimples creating creases in his ever-present salt-and-pepper scruff. "*Piacere mio.*"

She rounded her shoulders to hide her nipples standing at full attention under her bikini bra, but still, the telltale ache in the juncture of her thighs began to throb in response to his innuendo. *His pleasure indeed. Why does my body go stupid every time he's around? I am so in trouble.*

It had been close to eight weeks since those nights in Flores when they'd groped each other with unchecked urgency like two randy high school kids. Their heated kiss the first day they arrived at camp just hung out there—an invisible crackling energy whenever they were within range of or thought about one another. Long full days of working Kanul in the heat, humidity, and rain, along with keeping current notes on each day's exciting finds, didn't allow for much socializing or personal time. Everyone was exhausted and often a little crabby, especially Luca. He became more demanding as the weeks wore on, chewing out more than one colleague—for this or that, demanding the perfection he had outlined during their orientation.

As promised, Luca sent two graduate students home because they had not done their best. Several weeks later, he sent three more packing for taking off on a day adventure. They had not asked for the time off nor had they told anyone where they were going. Ari worked tirelessly and adhered to all the project rules, having no intention of meeting the same fate.

Regardless of the lack of contact with him, her desire for him hadn't abated. If anything, it had grown stronger. She watched him when no one was looking. The sound of his voice sent her heart racing. Every night, she fell asleep thinking of him, vivid dreams harassing her, sometimes two or three times nightly. Ari woke drained and wet, sure she had literally come as hard as she had dreamed. Having dream sex with Luca further wiped her out, causing her to often fall asleep during breaks. He was somewhere else during breaks, thank God, or he might have wondered why she napped almost every afternoon in the presence of Meg and Joan—who watched out for her and teased her mercilessly. Did he even care? Had she just been a good time? Maybe he was hooking up with Natasha, who seemed to be around him more often than not. Her flirty behavior and his responses were difficult to watch. The idea of them together alternately sickened Ari and made her blood boil.

He had checked through her work on several occasions, just as he had with everyone else. And he didn't notify her ahead of time, just as he hadn't with the rest of the team. One-on-one meetings with him were wholly professional, efficient, and direct. He asked probing questions and made remarkable observations, especially for not being an expert in every aspect of all the research going on. She couldn't help but be impressed. And, so far, she had come out unscathed, managing to stay current because she'd stayed up late. But every night, sleep overtook Ari the minute she crawled into bed naked and closed her eyes, never bothering to towel off from showering, despite sharing her tent with Joan and often-absent Meg, and the cycle began anew with dreams of soul-shattering sex with Luca.

The weather had, so far, been perfect during their break trip. The kayaking was pleasant given the abundance of cumulus clouds and their intermittent shade. Instead of disappearing, they began to morph into cumulonimbus, signaling severe weather.

Having just finished doing the dishes, Ari, Joan and Keaton joined the others silently around the campfire, so as to not interrupt Carlos who told the story of the hummingbird king—a legend passed down through the ages. Sheet lightning in the distance provided an interesting backdrop for his words.

Ari smiled and clasped the pendant at her throat, enthralled as she listened about how a baby Chirumà had been born to the ruling chief and his wife, on the thirteenth day of the month, a lucky day and a reminder of the Mayan's thirteen heavens.

A large, brightly colored hummingbird stayed throughout the long-awaited birth and left a red feather. The high priest determined that the feather was an omen from the gods, indicating Chirumà was extraordinary, just like the hummingbird. The community was happy except for the chief's brother. His chance to succeed his brother as ruler was now gone. Chirumà grew into a great warrior and a wise young man. No harm ever came to him, regardless of the risks he took.

One day, nomads attacked Chirumà and his uncle as they walked the perimeter of their village. He stayed close to his uncle. A shower of spears and arrows rained down on them but fell away. The uncle realized his nephew had a special charm that protected him and searched for it while he next slept. The uncle found the red feather and took it. After waking, Chirumà looked and looked, but he could not find it.

His father passed to the afterlife, and Chirumà became chief. He was compassionate, kind, and inventive. Under him, peace prevailed, crops were bountiful, and people were happy except for his uncle.

The young ruler was out hunting when the hummingbird present at his birth appeared. Before flying away, it said, "I am your guardian. Beware. Someone close to you means to kill you."

Chirumà walked back toward the village, pausing when he heard rustling in the grass. Watching, he saw nothing, but prepared his bow as a good warrior should. Then suddenly an arrow pierced his chest, turning it scarlet with blood. His strength ebbed away, and he fell into the sea of grass and died.

Something extraordinary happened to Chirumà. His body changed to the emerald-green color of the grass, his skin became feathers, and his hair a great crest of green and gold. His chest remained scarlet, and his arms became wings. His uncle watched as the glowing green bird with a bright red chest and long tail flew out from the grass and into the sky.

The people of the village mourned his passing. His uncle became chief. The village was plagued with famine and war. The uncle was captured, his body painted black and white, the colors of a slave. The enemies took him, and he was never heard from again.

The wise, peaceful bird and his ancestors perch high in the canopy, watching over the Maya. They are a symbol of freedom and hope, known as the quetzal.

Ari rubbed the goose bumps chasing along her arms. The sky flashed more often now. "I really love that legend, Carlos. Thanks for sharing it."

"You are most welcome, Dr. Ari."

"Hey," Matt piped. "I've got something to share. I was lunching with a few of the lead archaeologists yesterday and they mentioned the name, the American, a badass antiquities looter. The American stops at nothing to secure what he wants. They said the Maya have mentioned there is talk that he's in Guatemala." He looked from Carlos to Luca, asking, "Do you know anything about him?"

"Crikey. That's wild stuff and a little scary," Meg said. "I might not sleep well tonight, Matty."

Matt pulled her into the circle of his arm and said something in her ear, making her giggle.

A look passed between the two. Luca nodded at Carlos.

"I first heard of the American several months ago. The talk comes and goes," Carlos said in a hushed tone.

Luca added, "I have heard of the American over the years, and Carlos told me that there has been talk of him being in Guatemala, but no confirmation. This ebb and flow of talk has happened in the past. I believe it to be urban lore."

Ari leaned forward, resting her forearms on her knees, hands clasped in front. "I heard of him too. When I was working in North Africa. But as Carlos and Luca said, no confirmations of sightings. I think he's a figment of people's imaginations, created from their fear of confronting looters when working."

"So, Ari, you think he doesn't exist?" Natasha pointedly asked.

"We all know looting has been around as long as excavation. Hell, some archaeologists have been complicit in looting, fueling the illegal international antiquities trade. I tend to agree with Luca. I think the American is a great story for campfires and"—she smiled at Meg and Matt cuddled up across the fire from her—"late-night spooking. He's kinda like the boogeyman, holding all of us who recover historical and cultural treasures from the earth accountable."

Natasha's eyes narrowed on Ari. "I see. Interesting." She rose and stretched her arms up over her head. "I'm going to take advantage of an early bedtime. There's a storm on the horizon. See you all in the morning."

Within thirty minutes of Natasha leaving, the breeze strengthened, and the air turned noticeably cooler. Lightning and a crack of thunder announced the impending storm. Luca and Matt hurried to bank the fire while others sealed and covered supplies to keep them dry and secure. Everyone ran for their tents as the first fat raindrops hammered down.

Rain fell intermittently. Soft drizzle punctuated sporadic, roaring downpours, making it hard for Ari to hear anything. She slipped into a dry, clean sleeveless shirt and a pair of shorts after entering her tent, having learned that wearing anything damp brought on a chill, even when the temperatures were warm.

Ari had drawn the short twig earlier, giving her the single tent for the night. This was the first time she had pitched a tent all by herself. Any smugness with her success was checked by nagging concern. She had opted not to dig a trench around her tent. Hopefully, the weather would blow over quickly.

She had mixed feelings about sleeping by herself in the middle of nowhere, even though she was in a grouping of tents. It was only their team and Carlos. In Tikal, they had slept within the park boundaries. At Kanul, they were a much greater number—with armed security.

The rain paused, and she glanced at her watch. It was still early although dark. She grabbed her poncho, flashlight, and the deck of cards from her pack, deciding to visit Joan and Meg. Before leaving, she rolled all the flaps back and secured them, exposing as much of the screens as possible to encourage cross ventilation of the cooler air.

"Hello?" Ari rapped on the canvas, pressing her face against the mesh. The tent was empty. She ran the short distance and tried another. "Meg?" Ari called, spotting her through the screen. No answer. Louder, she said, "Hey, Meg!"

Meg looked up from writing in her journal. "Oh, sorry." She sat in her bikini and motioned to Ari. "Come on in, mate."

Ari nodded and stepped in, leaving her sandals outside. She dropped her poncho next to the screen. "Where's Joan?" She laughed at Meg. "You're back in your bikini. It certainly doesn't take much to sweat in Guatemala, does it?"

"Nope. It's so humid I can lick moisture off my arms. Joan is probably in Keaton's tent. Working even though the boss gave all of us a few days' respite. They were in a deep convo when the sky opened up."

"It's cooler outside now. I vented my tent."

Meg stood. "Maybe we can get some cross ventilation going. Lemme check. This side vent is closed. The vents are easy to miss if you don't camp. No worries." She motioned Ari to the back of the tent. "Tie those flaps back tight, please. I had to shut them when the last monsoon blew through." She placed her hands on her hips, surveying the tent. "Okay, they're all open. I think that's the best we can do." She pointed to her bedroll. "Sit."

"Ugh. It started again. The rain is misting in. Do you have something to put down that can absorb the moisture? Your floor is going to get wet." Ari glanced at Meg. "I thought you changed."

Meg threw a shirt to Ari. "Try this. It's not clean, but it'll do. I did change, but I was melting, so I put my suit back on. Much cooler. I'll probably sleep in it. Or naked, if Joan doesn't care. Shouldn't bother her since you slept in the buff every night at Kanul."

"It was hot."

"Uh-huh. Hot was in another tent."

"You mean Matt's?"

"Luca's. You think he slept naked?" Meg laughed, slapping her knees. "Guilty! Oh, girlfriend, you are blushing like a bride. Obviously you wondered. I bet he's magnificent."

She wiped some of the moisture from her face with the hem of her shirt. "Let's change the subject."

"Okay. Sorry, girlfriend. I wish we had thought to put our awning up. It might help keep some of the misting out but allow the breeze. Does your little tent have an awning? We should have brought the tent from our site. It's roomier and you're a great tent mate, although you talk and moan a lot in your sleep."

"Um, you never slept in our tent."

"Oh, right. According to Joan. Hey, I think the rain stopped. Help me with the awning?"

Ari looked through the front screen, her face quickly getting drenched. "I don't think so. It's a heavy mist, like we're in a cloud." Thunder boomed again, and lightning crackled. The rain followed, slapping the ground hard. "What do you mean I talk and moan a lot in my sleep? I had no idea rain could be this loud. It's like being in a waterfall."

Meg yelled over the rain and winked at Ari. "I think you dream about Luca. Sounds like it anyway. Did you by chance bring your cards?"

"How utterly embarrassing." Lying, she said, "I have no idea what I dream about." Ari retrieved the cards from her coat pocket, waving them with a smile. She recalled her day as she sat, her muscles aching pleasantly from hours of kayaking. "I'll help you with your awning if the rain stops before I leave. Fair? Jacks Back?"

"Um, have we played that before?"

"Yep." She shuffled and dealt each of them five cards.

"Okay, but let's do a practice round first. How do you remember all these games, Ari?"

"Years of playing."

Meg organized her hand. "You start. You should just sleep with him."

She looked at her cards and placed them in front of her on the bedroll. "Jeez. We're here to work. What do you have?"

Meg showed her cards and laid them opposite of Ari's. "Not as strong as you. I can't open. Yeah, we're working, but there's ample time for other interests. Matt and I find the time. You and Luca are so"—she added air quotes—"disciplined. All work and no play. That makes for imbalance."

"Discipline isn't a bad thing. And Luca really bothers me," she said, gathering the cards, shuffling, and dealing again.

"How so?"

"He's so watchful, like earlier today. Remember? When we were kayaking. He and Matt stayed behind our kayak the entire time. Can you open?"

"Do I really need to state that we are in the jungle? That we are in a place where something, anything can go suddenly and horribly wrong?" Meg looked at her cards. "Yep."

Ari rolled her eyes and sighed. "I never forget that. It's just… Well, I don't need a keeper. I feel like he's always watching me. It feels presumptive and irritates the snot out of me. Does he treat you like that?"

"You certainly haven't seemed irritated. Granted, none of us has had much time for anything except work. I think back to Tikal, when you were practically in his lap during that astounding sunrise. Or when he was teaching you about tarantulas, leaf-cutters, and jungle insects. The way you explained it, you hung on his every word. Nor did you seem irritated when we were in Semuc Champey. You stripped him naked with your eyes. You ate lunch with him. You went caving with him. Do I have to bring up our hotel? You were humping him in the hallway!"

Ari blushed. "Okay. But you don't realize he disappears afterward, in a flash. Each time. And now Natasha is a revolving moon around him."

"Natasha is his assistant. That's it. She's gotta be at his beck and call. Remember who you are talking to. It's me. Come on. Be truthful. What happens? Is there a pattern?"

Ari leaned in so she wouldn't have to speak so loudly and chance being overheard when the rain slowed or stopped. "He and Natasha have a history."

"You assume it was intimate."

"I do, even though he cautioned me not to assume. They're comfortable with each other, in sync. She just seems to know him really, really well. You've seen how she is with him. 'Big Guy.'" She sneered. "I'm an emotional yo-yo. He flirts with me, and then he's distant."

"Hm. Me thinks you are attracted to one another beyond the physical."

Ari's stomach clenched, worried others might see she was attracted to him, that she might have feelings for him. She firmly denied Meg's assumption. "That idea is just too… just too crazy."

"What? Really? Who do you think you're kidding? He's gorgeous! And you're adorable. Together, you're a stunning couple."

"We are not a couple. I'm not looking for a relationship. Becoming involved with the de facto leader of our group would be a poor decision on my part."

"Sometimes the relationship comes looking for you. It just happens." Meg leaned forward. "Circle back to your history comment."

"Luca and Natasha met in Italy, when they were in college. After his wife died, she came in as an adjunct at the university he teaches, for a semester. That's all he said."

"I see. And all the more interesting that he shared that with you. Maybe they had a brief fling, maybe not. He told you not to assume. Maybe she is still interested in him, or maybe she has some twisted agenda because of you. Have you thought of that? Natasha comes off as kinda calculating and cold. I just don't envision them together. I think Luca likes spicy and hot. Which you are. Sometimes you have to follow your heart."

"You are very funny. I'm not hot, and you have me in love with him. I merely find him physically attractive. There are aspects of him I find galling."

"How so? He's charming, funny, considerate, kind, detailed—"

"Yes. I see all that, but he is a perfectionist and has a short fuse. And he has no patience. He can be inflexible and demanding, and there is this alpha male energy to him. How many cards do you want?"

Meg looked over her cards again, brow furrowed. "Two, I think. As your friend, might I point out that you are throwing up roadblocks where none are necessary, and you are also a perfectionist, who also happens to have a have short fuse." She chuckled to herself. "Alpha male… Crikey. How yummy is that? The sexual tension between you is off the charts. You need to have sex with him."

Ari dealt Meg two more cards. "I don't want to talk about that."

"That doesn't help me." Meg gathered her cards together and handed them to Ari facedown. "Can we play something else, like Old Maid?"

Luca lay on his bedroll and listened to the rain, his arms folded and cradling the back of his damp head. The break from Kanul had been the right decision. The team already seemed revived. Kayaking the river was meditative and beautiful. Dinner was full of laughter and genuine camaraderie. He had a great team, people who appreciated and supported each other.

Thoughts and images of Ari had taken up permanent residence in his mind. He envisioned running his fingers through that silky cascade of hair. The desire to feel and taste her again made his body ache and stir. Luca was wound tight with need and short on patience. The evocative woman was in his blood, and it was driving him crazy. It had been over two months since that evening in Flores and close to that since they shared that sizzling kiss after she had bravely handled the tarantula at Kanul.

He watched her when no one was looking, mesmerized by her freckled, tawny skin and her graceful, lithe form. The sound of her voice and her laughter took the monotony out of his work and made his heart race. They needed to explore their escalating desire for one another before time ran out.

NINETEEN

SNUG AND DRY IN HER small tent, Ari drifted off to the chatter of howler monkeys and the *slap, slap, slap* of water on the leaves in the canopy above. Sometime during her deep sleep, she had rolled into the side of the tent, her body encouraged by the natural slope of where she'd pitched it.

A dream of floating in water woke her. She lay in a shallow pool, her bedding and clothes saturated. Turning on the flashlight and moving its beam around her tent showed water covered most of the entire floor. Her backpack was on slightly higher ground than where she lay. It was dry but only because it rested on her now-wet clothes for tomorrow. She cursed herself for not digging a trench.

Ari shivered. *Shit. I can't sleep in water.* A glance at her watch told her it was only just after midnight. The jungle was eerily silent except for the occasional patter of rain falling among the leaves or onto the ground. She unzipped her tent screen and poked her head out. It was blacker than black since lightning no longer zinged across the sky. She moved her flashlight around, surveying a number of tents. Things looked different in the pitch black. Per usual, and in a hurry to clean up, she had not paid all that much attention to who was where when pitching tents after kayaking. And now, disoriented from sleep and with the anxiety of needing to leave her tent, she struggled to remember. Her beam raked the jungle edge, looking for reflections that would indicate animals were near. Nothing. Driven by discomfort, she stepped out, panic lurching in her throat, on the hunt for Meg and Joan's tent.

She scampered to the tent she believed was Meg and Joan's, calling their names in a loud whisper. It had to be theirs. It was the only one without the awning up. She and Meg hadn't gotten it up because it had been raining when she'd left.

Her call was met with silence. She unzipped the flap and stuck her flashlight in, pointing it at the dry floor. Loudly whispering again, she called, "Meg! Joan! It's me. My tent is waterlogged. Do you have room, a dry shirt, and a spare blanket?" Watching what she was doing so as not to trip and fall into the tent and on one of the women, Ari shed her sandals before stepping over the canvas threshold and securing the flap behind her. Despite the warmth, she shivered. She heard movement and then a deep grumble. *Shit. Whose tent is this?* She raised her flashlight. A just-woken Luca sat on his bedroll, a sheet rumpled around his hips. His chest was bare, and she glimpsed untanned lower skin before dropping the flashlight. It turned off on impact.

"*Merda!* What the hell?" Luca's sheet rustled as he searched for his lantern. He switched it on, catching her like a deer in headlights. Confusion covered his face. "Ari. What are you doing in my *tenda*?" Sleepily, he presented his backside as he rolled over.

"No! No!" Ari hissed. "I thought this was Joan and Meg's tent." She put her hand out in a motion to stay him. "Don't move. You're naked!"

He shook his mane and sighed. "You are in my *tenda*, in the middle of the night, and you are telling me what to do. I know I am naked. This is how I sleep." He repeated his question again. "Why are you in my *tenda*?"

Feeling humiliated, she cast her eyes downward. "My tent is wet. I woke up in a pool of water. I'm wet and cold and tired. It's black outside. I was just looking for a place to sleep. I thought I was in Meg and Joan's tent. I'm sorry." She started to back away.

Luca's expression softened. He ran his hand through his hair and then over his face. "Let me guess. You forwent digging a trench."

"Um. Yes," Ari admitted, wringing her hands together in embarrassment. "Not the best decision."

"Indeed. However, that is a discussion for another time. I am tired. I have an extra sheet." He pointed to the corner next to her.

Ari shivered as she reached for it. "Thank you."

"I have dry clothes you can sleep in. Avert your eyes if you do not want to see my ass." He rolled over again. She started to look away, but curiosity stopped her. She stared, transfixed. His ass was just as nice as the rest of him. *God, he is beautiful.*

His eyes sparked with amusement as he rolled back to face her, with something bunched in his right hand. "Did you enjoy looking?" He raised his eyebrows.

Ari wished the earth would open up and swallow her. She stayed silent.

"Here," he said, tossing the clothing to her. "The shirt should cover you up well. You are *così minuta*." He stared at her, as if waiting for her to change in front of him.

She caught the shirt. "Aren't you going to turn around?"

Smirking, Luca shut off the lantern and lay down.

"I can't see!"

"You need *la luce* to get dressed?"

"Yes, I need light. I like to be able to see what I'm doing. And I don't know where to put the blanket or where to sleep."

Luca turned the lantern on again. With his back to her, he said more gruffly, "Put your wet clothes outside the *tenda*. You can hang them on the clothesline in the morning. Lie down where there is space. Do it quickly. You are wetting my floor, and I wish to go back to sleep."

Ari slipped out of her wet clothes quickly and into the soft tee, sneering, "I'm so damned sorry." Luca's tee fell midthigh, enveloping her in his scent.

Under his breath, he muttered, "Not as much as I will be."

Feeling contrite, she lowered herself to the floor. "I really am sorry, Luca. I didn't mean to wake you. Thank you." She rolled herself into the sheet—a close but safe distance to the side of the tent, attempting to chase the chills from her body and the image of Luca naked from her thoughts.

"Sleep well, Ari." He dimmed the lantern.

Ari swore she was in her bed back home. She was toasty warm, especially her backside. The realization that she was not home jolted her fully awake. Ari tried to roll over onto her back, but Luca's long body blocked her. She started and immediately chastised herself. He was asleep. She had rolled into him at some point during the night. *How utterly embarrassing.* In the low lantern light, he slept on his back, his mouth soft in repose. She sat up slowly, careful to not disturb him. His left arm extended past his ear, and his right dropped dangerously low over the crumpled sheet barely covering his hips.

Rain whispered against the tent. Ari grew braver in her observations as her eyes adjusted to the faint lantern light. Luca embodied lazy, catlike grace, even as he slept. His thick, loose hair fell in waves around his chiseled face. The generous lashes she had noticed every time she looked at him appeared even more lush with his eyes closed. They almost brushed his cheekbones. His eyebrows were dark and heavy, balancing the masculine planes of his face. Her tongue darted off her top lip as her gaze paused on his full masculine lips, remembering the scorching kisses they last shared by the promenade, before leaving for Kanul eight weeks ago. A longing sigh escaped her.

Ari studied his well-formed broad shoulders and muscled chest, arms, and ripped abs. Her eyes moved lower, pausing on a flat scar that ran from the inside of his right hip. Her brow puckered, wondering how he got it. The scar disappeared under the sheet, along with the downy black hair trailing from his navel. She was helpless in her physical attraction. He was beautiful. Her hand had a mind of its own and reached out, lightly caressing his scar. His evidence of arousal was immediate. Alarmed, Ari whipped her head around.

His eyes locked with hers. They were dark and full of desire. "Mm. You look like you want to eat me. What a nice way to wake up," he purred. He sat up, the sheet bunching over his arousal, entwining his fingers in her tresses. His eyes were hungry as he looked into hers. "Soft. Beautiful." Chemistry crackled between them. He ran the tips of his fingers over her jaw and then pulled her hair back gently, urging her face to tip up toward him. He pulled her closer, smiling his tender, sexy smile. His fingers brushed her necklace, gently holding the hummingbird pendant between his thumb and forefinger, the corner of his mouth turned upward, creating one of the dimples she adored. "Lovely. *Colibrí.* Do you know the folklore?"

His smile made her stomach flip. Ari's eyelashes fluttered as she fought to stay grounded, her voice breathy when she answered, "Yes, safe passage."

"Where did you get it?"

"My father, prior to this trip."

"A very good talisman. Safety of heart and soul." His other hand came up and tenderly cupped her chin. He stared deeply into her eyes and lowered his lips to hers, taking her bottom lip between his teeth, sucking softly. He let go to kiss her gently.

Her heart jumped erratically. She wanted to devour him, but she kissed him back tentatively.

Luca kissed her more deeply, his tongue demanding. Seeking, asking. He broke long enough to whisper, "It is okay, *piccolo mia*?"

Little one. I like that. Ari surrendered. She opened her mouth wider in answer. Their kiss grew fierce and unrestrained as they explored each other's mouths.

Panting, he pulled away. His hands framed both sides of her face.

She looked into his eyes, fearless and brimming with trust. Her breathing matched his.

His hands slid to the bottom of the shirt she wore, impatiently slipping it over her head. Her skin was exposed and flushed as she filled with warmth. Luca's green gaze was full of appreciation as he drank her in. His long, tapered fingers traced where his eyes traveled, setting off wave after wave of yearning pulsing through her body.

"*Perfecto.* I wish to touch all of you. Lie still." He laid her back, following her down. His fingertips grazed her skin, but his touch was so soft that it felt as if currents sparked between them. He took his time kissing, nipping, and licking, moving from her neck to outline her collarbone, kissing her again and then drawing her back, brushing his fingers over her breasts, painfully erect nipples, ribs, and down to her taut quivering abdomen. He splayed his hand out, fingers resting on both her hip bones. She was so small compared to him. His brow creased with concern, his voice thick with desire. "Tiny. Do you have room for me, Ari?"

"Yes," she whispered, arching up as his hands moved lower and to the outside of her hips, cupping her ass.

"I want to bury myself in you," he murmured as he nibbled her exposed neck.

She shivered involuntarily at his admission. Her breathing became shallow.

He smiled and gazed into her eyes, purring, "Turn over."

Her eyes rounded.

"I said I wish to touch all of you." He looked deeply into her eyes, challenging her.

She saw that he battled with patience. She turned over carefully, keeping her knees together, aware that her panties were soaked.

His voice choked as he ran his palm over each of her cheeks. "White tonight. Your lace excites me." He slipped his fingers under the lace at her lower back, slowly and softly stroking the cleft between them. He groaned, drawing them back out and gently stroking the back of her legs.

She groaned and shuddered as he drew serpentines behind her knees.

Luca chuckled. "You enjoy?"

"Yes," she sighed, her body writhing under his touches.

He traced his fingers back up to the tops of her thighs. "Open, sweetheart."

She parted her legs.

"More, much more."

Heat rushed to her face. She felt vulnerable, yet she was so aroused her legs opened without another thought. She heard his sharp intake of breath.

"You are"—he rubbed his fingers over the crotch of her panties—"so wet."

Her panting grew heavier as he stroked. Her body was electrically charged, tingling and tightening in response to his touch. The desire in his voice made her blood rush and pool in her core. She ached worse than she could ever remember.

He slid his fingers up over her panties and traced her spine upward. His fingers were moist and slick. From her.

Desire wracked her body. She writhed and clamped her legs to control the thrumming in her pelvis.

"No. Keep them open," he commanded quietly. Soft kisses followed his leisurely, tender tracings back down her spine.

She shivered again. "Please, Luca," she said, losing control. *Damn.* He was going to take her over the edge, and he hadn't really touched her yet, not like she craved to be touched.

"These have served their purpose." She felt his hot breath as he tugged at her lace bikini panties with his teeth. *Omigod.* She swooned from the unleashed heat and moisture building between her thighs. "Lift up, or I will tear them," he growled.

She lifted. The air felt cool in comparison to her feverish body.

His warm hands caressed and kneaded her naked cheeks as he kissed and nibbled her.

She was coming undone. Her juices dripped onto Luca's sheet and bedroll.

"Beautiful." His fingers slid between her toned thighs, teasing, bringing her to a fever pitch. "Flip back over."

She snapped her legs together.

His eyes glowed with desire. "No, *bella.* Keep them apart." He slid two fingers into her again, deeper, and massaged her nub. "You are close. Look at me." The sky crackled above them, and rain drummed on the tent as the sweet ache grew fiercer.

"Luca…" She gasped. She was so close.

"I want to watch your face. Look at me."

She looked into his eyes, returning his intense gaze with her own. Ari found trust and the desire to please her in those dark green depths. She allowed herself to fall, achieving a release like nothing she had ever experienced.

He kicked the sheet out of the way. Her breath hitched at the sight of his full length, swollen and thick with need. She placed her palm over his heart. It galloped like hers. Luca's mouth covered hers once again, their tongues dancing as he moved over her, his knee sliding between hers, opening her. Ari's body rose, welcoming him as he pushed into her body and rocked in its wetness.

She fell asleep after Luca pulled her next him, spooning her from behind. Fully sated, she slumbered like the dead until the insistent feather-like stroking of her body woke her, fluttering want unfurling in her belly.

He teased her, brushing his lips against hers, and pulling back when she kissed him more forcefully. His gaze scanned her naked body lazily, then lingered on her lips. "I want you slow and deep," he said huskily, drawing each word out. He entwined his fingers with hers and pulled her arms above her head, looking deeply into her eyes. "Lie still."

"Luca, please. I need—"

"I know. You need. I need too." She squirmed as one hand continued to hold her wrists while his fingers traced around one breast and then the other, returning to pull her nipples. His hands ran over her hips. The ember of desire caught, arousing her like wildfire. She brought her hands to his shoulders.

He shook his head, a smile tugging at his mouth. "No. Leave your hands where I put them." He licked one of her nipples and then sucked deeply, teething gently while his hands explored her hips.

A groan escaped Ari as pleasure ripped through her. Her hips bucked up, seeking him.

"Lie still or I will stop. It would be a shame to try to sleep in your state of arousal—granted you are not quite where I want you."

She stilled, as much as she could. It was delicious torture. Through his curtain of hair, Ari watched him smile before he moved to her belly, his fingers and mouth continuing their sweet assault on her body, bringing her to the brink of losing it again. She gritted her teeth in an effort to remain motionless as his smooth muscles bunched and glided with his movements.

His hands slid over her hips, exploring the bones that framed her concave stomach and reaching under her to knead her cheeks. "You are so beautiful," he murmured into the velvety skin of her thighs as he coaxed them apart, his fingers and tongue slowing, languidly stroking her core.

His pleasurable torment made her toes curl. She gulped for air. "Omigod, Luca. More." Ari panted as her sweet ache intensified, rocketing toward ecstasy. "I want more. You. Please."

There was no hiding Luca's desire as he raised his head from her apex. His green gaze had darkened, turning malachite, pinning her with its intensity. He moved over her, his thick rigidness stroking her thigh, leaving a moist trail.

Face-to-face, Ari met Luca's hungry, demanding eyes with her own. Her body was on fire, and she opened her legs wide in urgency.

He waited outside the entry, giving her full control. "Take me in slowly," he hissed through his clenched teeth. "Yes, nice and slow, like that."

She stopped, enjoying the sensations, the thick hardness of him. She pushed toward him.

He pulled back, his breathing harsh. "Slowly, sweetheart," he said, answering Ari's whimper.

A few more slow strokes and she upped the pace. "I understood you were giving me control," she said through her hard, labored breathing in answer to Luca's surprised expression. She caressed his stubbled jaw, enjoying its rough texture in contrast to the slickness their bodies created. Ari pitched her hips forward, her feverish eyes searching his, begging him, as she careened over the edge. Luca right behind her.

Unlike the aftermath of their first time together, Ari was wide-awake and chatty afterward. She broke from being spooned by him and sat up, crossing her legs and pulling the sheet onto her lap.

"Tell me about him. The man you had a relationship with." Luca rubbed her back, his touch feather soft. "You said it ended badly."

"Eric was the dean of my department. I became involved with him, and he turned out to be a liar and an asshole." She twisted to look directly at him. Her eyes were full of anguish. "He was married and a father. I had no idea until I saw him with his wife and daughters at an ice-cream shop close to the university. I was so ashamed of myself. I never would have become involved with him had I known." She took a deep breath before continuing. "I left as soon as I found out, staying with my parents that weekend. I applied for this project that weekend, just made the deadline."

"Ah, that is why you submitted a concise CV."

"Concise is a nice way of putting it." She smiled at him, then twisted back to hug her knees. "That feels so nice, Luca."

"The concise part or my fingers on your lovely naked back?" He smiled at her, his head resting on his forearm.

"Your touch."

He purred, then said, "No headshot."

"Um, yes. I forgot that. Not on purpose. I wasn't functioning on all cylinders. I didn't realize it until I met Joan in Semuc Champey." She looked over her shoulder at him. "And no one let me know. I guess my face wasn't as important as my creds, huh?"

"An oversight by you that turned out for the best. I would not have brought you on."

Ari changed position and faced him, her voice rising as she asked, "What do you mean by that?"

"You are far too alluring. I would have decided you were too tempting and have passed on you." He laced his fingers through hers and kissed them.

"And now?"

"There is no going back," he whispered.

Ari nodded in agreement.

"What is it, *bella*? Something else gnaws at you."

"He's contacted me twice since I've been here."

"What do you mean, contacted you?" He sat up abruptly. "Why? How does he know where you are?"

"His secretary tracked me down. She was able to dig up everything. My new phone number. My itinerary. He stated it in the letter."

"What?"

"I spent two weeks in Antigua before traveling north. There was a letter waiting for me at my hostel when I first arrived. He knew about the project." She left out the part about Luca. "And when I was on respite in Flores with Natasha, there was a letter waiting for me again, a lot nastier. It came right after we left for Kanul, and it wasn't postmarked."

Luca pinched the top of his nose, as anger and fear mushroomed. He kept his voice even. "Can I see the letters?"

She shook her head. "I burned the first and washed it down the shower. I made confetti out of the second and added it to my coffee."

He pulled her into his arms and kissed the top of her head, murmuring into her hair. "Sweetheart, I do not like this. He is stalking you."

"I'm fine. We're in a place he can't contact me. I figure I continue the radio silence, and he'll just give up. Maybe he already has."

He put a finger on her chin, gently turning her to look at him, and kissed her forehead. "His actions deeply disturb me. You are a brave one. Thank you for sharing with me." He lay back, pulling her on top of him, stroking her cheek and then kissing her deeply.

She broke free of the kiss, smiling into eyes fixated on her. "Again?"

"Mm. I believe so," he said, running his hands over her ass, pressing her against him.

Her fingertips lightly traced the scar that ran the length of his hip bone and disappeared into his groin. "Does this have a story?"

Luca rolled to his side, propping himself up on one elbow, cheek cradled in his hand. His other hand reached out, playing with some of Ari's curls, his eyes darkened as he spoke. "It does. Not a happy one. A car accident."

"I see. I'm so thankful you came out of it okay. Sometimes…" She didn't know where to go with her words. Meg had shared what she knew, but it was bare bones. Her hope was that Luca would confide in her.

He sat up and covered both Ari's hands with his. Anguish etched his eyes in the soft light. The evening from eight years earlier came rushing back to him.

He was pinned in his crumpled car. Sofia, eyes closed and pale, slumped motionless in the other seat. He called her name, becoming louder and more frantic when she did not respond. Her loose blouse made it impossible to see if she was breathing. Smoke from the blue and orange flames licked the twisted metal in front of his shattered windshield, mixing with a fog of chemicals released by the airbags, burning his throat. It was difficult to breathe. His legs, chest, forehead, and hand burned, and his ribs felt as though someone had kicked him. Something metal pierced the windshield and Luca, pinning him to his seat. His gut and hip were numb, and a dark stain spread over his shirt and pants. Blood. Weak and shaking, he attempted to open the door, but it would not budge. Sirens screamed as they got closer. Then someone pounded on his door and asked if he could roll down his window.

"My wife," he said. Others in uniform were at her door. It groaned and snapped as they broke it open. "My wife," he cried weakly. The rescuers leaned in, anxiously checking her vitals. The men were silent; their grim expressions told him the truth before they said the words. "Sir, she is gone. We're sorry." Their words barely registered with him. "Sir, you are burned and bleeding. We need to saw the post to move you." His door was wrenched open with the Jaws of Life and his seat belt cut in several places. He passed out as they extracted him from the car. The next thing he remembered was the cold too-white lights in the trauma center and deep sorrow. Sofia was gone. Guilt engulfed him. He was at fault.

She scooted closer to Luca as he relived the accident. Her eyes were dark with emotion. "I'm so sorry, Luca. I'm so sorry. I brought this on by asking." She stroked his forearm and then reached to cup his face tenderly, coming up on her knees to kiss him. "A very wise man I know told me that fear diminishes the ability to experience something fully."

His eyes came back into focus, and he ran his hand over his face with a groan. His expression was earnest, assuring her. "You have no reason to be sorry." Smiling ruefully, his eyes crinkled at the corners. "My words. Touché." Unrelenting rain pummeled the tent as Luca gathered her into his arms. "You and I cannot be truly intimate if we hide and do not share. You have trusted me with your fears and pain. It is time I do, as well." He swallowed, quietly admitting, "I rarely speak of it. Still, after eight years, it is painful."

He began haltingly. "I was married. Her name was Sofia. When dating, we discussed having a large family. But ten years into our marriage, we were still not parents. She became pregnant soon after we married, but several months later, she miscarried. She was inconsolable, wanting to be by herself. I gave her the space, and when she was ready, when we were ready, we tried again.

"After the second miscarriage, we grieved harder. We became anxious as well as excited with each ensuing pregnancy, and pregnancy after pregnancy ended in miscarriage. Our emotions escalated. She withdrew, as did I, not knowing how to comfort her or how to process the grief I felt. It is so difficult to lose a child, the dream of having a child. I threw myself into research and teaching.

"On the morning of the accident, Sofia was running late for work. She left her diary on our bed. It was open. I have never been a person who snoops. However, when I went to close it and put it back in the nightstand drawer where she kept it, I saw another man's name on the pages.

"I read every last page of her diary. What she wrote told a different story, exposing all her lies and deceit. She never planned to have a child. Sofia had no desire to ruin her body. And on the days she was supposed to be grieving, she shopped or met up with her lover."

Luca rubbed the bridge of his nose, then shook his head. "How did I not see that? How had I not known what kind of a person she was?

"I called in sick and cancelled my lab for the day. I had no plans when she called later that day, asking me if we could meet our friends for dinner. I was stunned and numb, but I agreed.

"We had known this couple for years. We had regular dinners with them, out and at our homes. All of us had gone to Capri for a long weekend the summer before. Like me, the husband competed in triathlons. I ran with him on occasion, never realizing he and my wife were fucking each other and had been for years.

"Normally, she took the train to and from home and work, but the restaurant was in the opposite direction, so I said I would pick her up at the end of her day. I confronted Sofia soon after she got into the car. My anger escalated as I drove. We were screaming at one another when I exited from the *superstrada.* I was livid. I must have had my eyes off the road. I missed the sharp turn. The car went airborne.

"The metal fence post that punctured the windshield on impact sliced into my abdomen, just missing my internal organs and femoral artery. Sofia died of a broken neck on impact."

Ari gathered Luca to her, trying to absorb the demonic guilt he carried, kissing his shoulder, realizing there were no words she could use to express her empathy for him. She looked in his eyes and could see that he understood her silent response.

They held each other in silence until he relaxed and fell back to sleep. She ran her fingers over his warm, damp flesh, still absorbing the awfulness of what had happened, attempting to soothe any remaining remorse and unease he had. After wiping away the last tears of compassion, she laid her hand over his heart and then adjusted so she could rest her head on his chest, her body pressed to his side, arm slung over his abs. Kissing him once more, she closed her eyes, whispering, "I love you, Luca."

Ari pulled back the flap Luca had hastily dropped sometime during their lovemaking last night and looked through his tent screen. The coast was clear, or seemed to be, as much as she could tell in the velvet black. She made one more pass with the arc of light from her flashlight. No one. The early morning was still quiet. Luca purred in his sleep, the picture of contentment. She smiled to herself and slowly unzipped the screen and stepped out, turning to zip it back up, keeping her flashlight pointed downward so not to disturb him. She stretched and yawned. She was going to need a nap later.

"Good morning, Red. I see you kept Luca company last night."

Ari jumped, dropping the flashlight. Its beam underlit Natasha's face, giving her an evil look. She shushed her and whispered angrily, "Lower your voice. I told you not to call me that. I was clear about that during orientation. And what I was doing in Luca's tent does not concern you."

"It's five thirty in the morning. You are supposed to be in your tent, not moving about our camp. It is dangerous to be out here by yourself."

"Well, thanks for having my best interest in mind. My tent floor got soaked by the rain, and I needed a dry place to sleep."

Natasha's words were coated with malice. "Did you? Sleep?"

"I did, thank you for asking. Why are you up at this hour?"

"I couldn't sleep. After all the ruckus last night, it's too quiet. Then I heard a zipper and wondered why. So here you are, sneaking out of Luca's tent."

"She's not sneaking, Nat." Luca stood bare-chested, in hastily donned and not fully fastened cargo pants. He looked feral and so damn sexy with his hair spilling over his broad shoulders. Annoyance registered on his sleepy face. "You two woke me with your squabbling." He extended his arms upward, stretching, and added, "Ari's tent was wet. She was in need of a dry spot to sleep and thought my tent was Joan and Meg's. It was a downpour, and I asked her to stay."

"How convenient. And the reason she's sporting one of your shirts?"

"None of your fucking business, Nat. Go back to bed."

Putting her hands on her hips, she leaned toward him, pissed. "I'm up now."

"I am too." He pulled on the shirt he had been holding, buttoning it. "I will start a fire. Daybreak is soon, and it looks to be beautiful. Ari, you can help me with coffee after you slip on something that covers your legs."

"Sure, but before I change"—she swatted her calf as she gathered her wet clothes she left under the awning last night—"look, Natasha. I realize we got off to a less than ideal start, but I thought things were smoothed over with… with all our teamwork"—Ari swept her extended hand in a half circle, then fanned something away from her face—"out here. I don't want to ruin my, or anyone's, and that includes you, experience. Our excavation and related scientific discoveries are events we should be proud of and be celebrating." She slapped her thigh, coming away with a small dark mess, likely a dead mosquito. "Damn mosquitoes." She took the repellent Luca handed her and sprayed herself liberally as she continued. "I apologize for whatever I've done wrong or you presume I've done wrong. Can we let bygones be bygones?"

"What the hell does that mean?"

"Jeez. Call a truce is what I'm asking for, although I have no idea why."

Silence came from Natasha as she considered Ari's offer, staring at Luca, a myriad of expressions passing over her face.

Omigod, she still has a thing for him. What woman wouldn't? How naïve am I? Ari watched him. His face remained impassive under Natasha's scrutiny.

"Fine, Ari. Truce."

"Let's shake on…" Her words faded as Natasha walked away. To Luca, she said, "I'm going to find my repellent and get a layer of clothing on. These mosquitoes are eating me ali—"

The hunger in Luca's expression stopped her. His voice was husky from sleep and sex, caressing her, reigniting her flame. "Get yourself covered." He kissed her softly and took her wet clothes.

"More clothes, yes. On it." She took off toward her wet tent at a jog.

He called to her, "Bring some of your things that are wet. They can dry by the fire with these while we have an early breakfast. I worked up quite an appetite."

EXCAVATION

Our ancient rulers and nobles practiced auto-sacrifice. Both men and women engaged in the bloodletting of their own bodies, using stingray spines marked with sacred glyphs. Women ran thorned ropes through their tongues, and men cut the head of their penises.

These rituals created great quantities of blood. After the blood dripped onto the bark paper and soaked in, it was set on fire and offered for purification.

The smoke coiled upward toward the sky, enabling them to communicate with divinities and their forebears. Our ancestors often asked for advice or help or requested that the gods or their ancestors once again enter the earthly sphere.

—Tata
Mayan Shaman
Petén, Guatemala

TERRIFYING, OTHERWORLDLY SOUNDS EXPLODED IN the black dawn, something like out of a horror movie. After two months of sleeping in the Petén jungle, the roaring and barking still made Ari break out in a sweat and her heart gallop. Gradually her brain woke and, with it, awareness.

"Damn monkeys! Can't you just shut the hell up?" she yelled before burying her face in her camp pillow and pulling her discarded shirt around her ears to muffle the howling. "I'm never going to sleep through the night again."

In a beat of silence, soft laughter bubbled up on the other side of the tent. "Oh, girlfriend. The jungle is their home. They're loud, but crikey, you've got to admit, bloody amazing. Like King Kong-sized roaring lions, yep?"

Sitting up, Ari rubbed at her sleep-encrusted eyes in an effort to open them. She could just make out Meg's form on top of her bedding in the dim lantern light. "Meg! You were with Matt. I didn't expect you, didn't hear you. When did you come in?"

Meg cheerily responded, "G'day, mate!" Winking, she added, "I'm an ace with zippers."

Ari glanced at her watch and grimaced. Four thirty. She had to rise in thirty minutes for the day and could have used the extra sleep. "Not quite day. But I'm awake now. Do you mind if I turn the lantern up?"

"No worries. Just know I may fall back to sleep. I'm bushed. We were going off—"

"Um, more than I care to know, okay?" She could just make out the satisfied expression on her friend's face. "Meg?"

No response. Meg was fast asleep.

Ari lay back and closed her eyes, willing herself to slip back into the dream. She and Luca had been in the middle of intense sex, well, pre-sex. She was slick from the all-too-real images. The dream images of Luca's mouth all over her and her responses made her groan. *Omigod. I want him so much.*

Meg's loud snoring, similar to a chainsaw, quickly ensued, sometimes in sync with the raucous howling of the monkeys. Ari focused on her deep breathing, but after five cycles, she was more awake than ever. It was not working, and she used to be able to sleep anywhere, anytime.

The last vestiges of her dream disappeared. The combination of howler monkeys and deep snores was distracting. She gave up, envying her friend's easygoing ways. Meg always upbeat, positive, relaxed, and interested.

She checked her watch again. Five o'clock. Maybe writing would help. Pulling her journal from her pack and opening it to a blank page with the intention of writing, she moved the lantern closer and turned it up. Her pen stilled on the paper, mind blanking. How could anyone sleep or function through this racket?

Meg snuggled deeper into her bedding and sighed.

Ari's thoughts shifted. She had slept great the other night with Luca—worn out and sated from their passionate lovemaking. Was he sleeping now? Her body flushed and heated.

Soft rapping on the tent startled her, accelerating her heart to a point where it was suddenly difficult to breath. The jungle quieted, as if it was waiting to know too.

"I hear you stirring. I have made a fire. Come sit with me," Luca's melodic deep voice encouraged.

Ari chastised herself. This is what she got for wondering. Of course he knew she was up. She rose and unzipped the screen, not bothering to try to muffle her efforts, and poked her head out, almost bumping into Luca's solid, sculpted chest. "Oops. Sorry."

His eyebrows rose, and amusement lit his eyes and mouth. "Good morning. Are you always so loud?"

She looked up into those spectacular eyes of his and smiled a smile just for him. "Good morning. Meg won't hear me. She sleeps like the dead."

"Mm." Luca's smile grew. "I suspect she and Matt had an active night."

She wasn't about to take that bait. "Did the monkeys wake you too? I'm still not used to them. They're howling less, now that morning is coming."

He leaned in, his hair brushing her neck, sending shivers through her body, which was now permanently imprinted with all his touches and kisses. His lips grazed her ear. "No. A shouting petite redhead woke me. Then I began to think about her more. I became—how shall I put it?—more awake." His meaning clear, Luca stepped back and looked deeply into Ari's eyes, allowing her to see his hunger.

A zipper sounded on the edge of the campsite. Luca shuttered his expression, and the sensual teasing lilt of his voice vanished. "Coffee is brewing, and the others are rising. The sky softens. Slip into some clothes and come greet the morning with me."

Twenty One

TWO NIGHTS LATER, ARI TOSSED and turned, unable to sleep. The teams had worked longer hours than usual. An opening to what looked to be a significant temple was revealed in Rax, and only when the jungle's shadows made it impossible to see without lanterns and headlights did they stop, disappointed to be so close to discovering more. Ari had choked down her food and taken a quick shower, falling into bed, sure she would crash early.

That was not to be. Hunger for Luca gnawed at her. It grew and grew as the hours passed. Decision made, she grabbed her flashlight and exited her tent quietly. She was sure of where Luca's tent was this time, and that was where she intended to go. Her heart jumped around in her throat as she approached. Coming closer, she was able to discern the soft glow of a lantern light. Quiet talking and a woman's voice stopped her in her tracks. His laughter carried through the screen, and then the sound of the screen's zipper sliding had her turning off her flashlight. The night was moonless night. She was cloaked in darkness.

Natasha stepped out. Behind her was Luca, his camp shirt hanging open, exposing his beautiful chest and abs. His hair was slightly wild. She was familiar with the look. It was how he looked when waking up. Natasha turned to him, her hand going to his chest. She leaned in and spoke so low that Ari couldn't hear her. Then she embraced him, and he returned it, his murmured words carrying clearly to where Ari stood. "I am glad you are here. Sleep well, Nat."

"I will, Luca. Thanks."

A broad smile accompanied his words as Natasha turned on her lantern before walking away. "My pleasure."

Pleasure, my fucking ass.

Luca watched, waiting until Natasha's lantern disappeared into a tent. He started to slip back into his.

"I don't know what to say." Ari turned on her flashlight.

He stumbled back out, closing the screen behind him, swatting at the air around him. "Ari?"

"Yeah. It's me." She laughed, not kindly. "Surprise."

"Come inside. The insects are thick." He walked to her, gently taking her hand, guiding her to his tent. "You are shaking."

She wrenched her hand from his, furious. She enunciated every word. "Do not touch me."

"Lower your voice. You will wake everyone and everything."

"I doubt it."

"We can talk in my *tenda*. Please."

"Fine." She walked stiffly behind him, shedding her sandals and passing inside as he held the flap open. He zipped it closed behind her.

Luca's tent was large. A divider made it multiroom and multiuse. The room they currently stood in was neatly organized as an office, outfitted with a table and several chairs, where he had gone over her paperwork. The zipped screen door in the divider led to his sleeping quarters.

He checked his watch. "What are you doing here? It is late. You will be up in a few hours."

"As will you." She angrily wiped at the unwelcome tears wetting her cheeks and dripping off her chin, her voice rising with each word. "What the fuck do you think I'm doing here? I haven't been with you since the kayak trip. I… Finding you… Goddammit. I… goddammit…"

He held his hands up, as if to ward off blows. "Ari, wh—"

She held her hand out, palm facing him. "Stop! Not another word!"

His voice grew serious. "Please lower your voice."

Sniffling, then taking a deep breath, her words came out in a rush. "I came to see you because I couldn't sleep. I believed we had something special. You led me to believe that. I took the chance. I let you in." She was crying hard now, no longer yelling at him.

He ran his hand over his face as he looked at her, a myriad of emotions jostling around in him like bumper cars. "Neither of us was looking for something to happen, but it did. We have undeniable chemistry. However, I must be honest with you. I have no idea what might happen after our time here ends. It is easy to leave a passionate relationship when you leave a beautiful, timeless place."

"Chemistry? It's more than that."

Silence filled the room, like a great white elephant.

"You and Nat—"

"Do not accuse me of things you assume." Irritated, his voice snapped. Now he was yelling. "I care about you. You need to calm down and lis— "

"Care for me. I care for my plants at home." She unzipped the flap, choking on her tears. "You're just like him, like Er—" The last of her yelling was swallowed up as she ran from the tent.

Ari heard him calling her name, but she kept going until she was in her tent. Joan snored away, and Meg was MIA. She scrunched her camp pillow around her ears and silently cried herself to sleep, her heart shattered.

"We've got something! We've got something! Dr. Antony, follow me!" A grime-covered, deeply tanned young woman waved her hands in the air, literally jumping up and down with excitement. A black baseball hat capped chin-length, wavy black hair that framed a flushed walnut-hued face.

The student's enthusiasm was contagious, and the familiar rush of discovery filled Ari. She moved forward and then paused, holding up her hand and calling, "Where?"

"It just off-site, up ahead," she answered. "We thought you might like to see it before you tell the others."

"Hold on, let me grab my pack." Luca's constant harping about always having water on hand had made an impact during her time here. He was the ultimate worrywart, but Ari appreciated it. From experience, she knew even seasoned archaeologists and anthropologists occasionally forgot to replenish the necessary items, like that fellow outside of Rabat two summers back.

Although frazzled from not sleeping well, Ari smiled and extended her hand, deferring to the student, who was a few inches shy of her own five foot three, and stockier. "Okay, lead the way. Show me what you've found."

Like Ari, the student wore long pants, a long-sleeved shirt with her cuffs rolled up, and sturdy hiking boots. She also wore a yellow scarf tied around her neck. A bottle of water hung from her belt, and a machete, which was odd. For safety, machetes were to only be handled by team members and leads or used under their guidance. She ignored her niggling concern.

The student wasn't familiar to her, but then so many had come and gone during the past weeks, and there were some she never did get to work alongside. Ari trailed the student and quickly became lost in her thoughts. She sniffed and wiped at her nose. Admittedly, she suffered from her own unique form of tunnel vision when she was focused on something, like now. She struggled to make sense of the blowup she had with Luca. Last night complicated things. It was a stark contrast to the exquisite thrills she experienced by literally unearthing the past in Kanul.

Ari was pissed and tired from crying and a lack of sleep. She was mortified. She had had amazing, mind-blowing sex with him and, feeling certain she was in love with him, spoken the words. What the fuck? Thank God he had been asleep. Right now all she wanted was to escape. Maybe she could finagle some time in Flores again. She tripped and almost fell. It jarred her back to the present. "I'm awful with names. Can you remind me?"

Flashing a smile, the student turned and started moving. Calling over her shoulder, she said, "Inés."

Ari picked up her pace as Inés moved forward, talking faster and louder, taking care to step over exposed, tangled roots under the thickening understory. The sounds from the excavation site had become muffled by dense foliage. "How far have we walked? I didn't check my watch before leaving."

"A few of us had an idea to go look for a cave, um, a cenote. We found one. This is so cool! Don't you think it's cool, Doctor?"

Ari tried to break in and respond, but the overzealous woman didn't pause. She wanted to ask why they decided to search for a cenote and if they were coring; the teams had their hands full with the two excavations. They couldn't spare workers to begin an excavation in another area. Surely one or two of the lead archaeologists accompanied the students.

Inés changed direction, heading left with confidence. Ari mulled over the claim that a cenote had been found while increasing her pace to keep up with Inés. Well, it certainly was possible. Caves were sacred to the Maya. Portals to Xibalba—the underworld. There were thousands of caves and cenotes—natural water-filled sinkholes—throughout the Yucatan.

"So you all have been coring?"

Inés ignored her questions, answering. "This whole thing is so cool! I never dreamed that digging could be so exciting when I volunteered to do this. It sounded boring. Digging in the dirt like when I was a little kid, getting all gross and sweaty every day." She bent slightly forward as they pushed uphill. "God, I hate this heat and humidity. I mean, look at my hair! And my nails! Even though I wear those nasty gloves, the dirt gets under my nails. I have to pick them out every night. It takes hours. But now..."

Although Inés appeared to be around Ari's age, she sounded younger. The terrain flattened out. Inés turned right, and the terrain dipped. She kept her pace up. No path was evident, but she seemed to know where she was going. Dark green leaves slapped Ari in the face and brushed over her covered arms and legs. Occasional rocks and the slick plant-covered jungle floor caused her to almost fall a number of times. She stayed as close as possible because the jungle swallowed Inés up quickly.

Insects flitted all over, some landing on Ari and then taking off just as quickly. Mosquitoes hummed around her face and exposed hands but kept a distance, sensing the chemical barrier emanating from her body. Her calves burned from the pace and changing terrain. She dodged a large spider and its web. *Shit. Breathe. You held a tarantula.* They were definitely heading away from Kanul. She was certain of it. Invisible tendrils of fear rose as Ari's system went on full alert. Restricted by the pounding of her heart in her throat, she gasped for air. "Inés?"

No answer. Inés kept moving.

Ari stopped, fought for her breath, and shouted, "Inés? Stop!"

Inés stopped, stumbling backward toward Ari and falling to her butt. She rose and brushed herself off. "What?" She sounded annoyed.

"Is it much farther? Where are we going? Kanul is over there." Ari pointed behind her and to her right. "You know the excavation rules. We need to return."

Inés's hand struck out like a rattlesnake, turning Ari around and closing the distance between them in a heartbeat. Her hold was like a vise. The young woman's demeanor changed abruptly. She lifted her black baseball cap and smoothed her hair with a practiced wrist. Then she put the cap back on, turning it around into a snapback, all with the same hand while holding on to Ari. "No. We're not going back."

The chatty, scatterbrained student disappeared. Cold, black eyes, one with a large black mole above the heavy brow, moved over Ari. She hooked her thumb into the waistband of her pants and sneered, speaking slowly and quietly. "Dr. Antony, so many questions. There has been a change in plans." Inés stepped back with an ugly smile before placing her free hand to her mouth to make a loud birdcall.

Ari's eyes widened as Inés patted the machete hanging from her belt, running her finger over it, almost lovingly. She put her finger to her lips and narrowed her eyes in warning. "Shh," she demanded harshly, pulling a small clear bottle from her pocket and opening it, then liberally dousing part of the yellow bandana she had pulled from her neck.

Bile rose, and Ari's breathing became more labored as the cold fingers of realization dawned. *What in fucking hell?* Ari started to yell and jerked in the iron grip, but she couldn't free herself. Inés wrenched Ari's wrist painfully, causing her to cry out. "Stop struggling. I promise I will break it," she said, clapping the fabric over Ari's nose and mouth.

Ari fought to hold her breath. She grew dizzy, needing to take a breath.

"There is no point in fighting it, Doctor. Breathe or I'll knock you out myself," Inés said, sounding bored.

Fear rendered Ari complacent. The pungent, sweet-smelling scent was the last thing Ari remembered before black spots expanded and the jungle floor rose up to meet her.

LUCA SWATTED AT THE INSECT buzzing in front of him. Sweat trickled into his eyes, stinging and blurring his vision. The sun was not at its zenith yet, and he was roasting. He took the bandana tied around his water bottle, pulled his sunglasses off, wiped his eyes and the nosepiece, and then replaced them, tying the scarf around his hairline. Its coolness dissipated quickly. He placed his hat back on top and scanned the activity around him, observing his colleagues and their assigned students working diligently at their tasks with a myriad of tools to expose what had been buried for centuries. Large piles of sifted earth buttressed many grids. Artifacts lay on drop cloths, and several students worked with professors to catalog the findings electronically. Backpacks were scattered in the shade, keeping charged electronics, batteries, and water cool. The students, professors, and leads worked well together, and enthusiastically.

Where was Ari? His attention was interrupted by the arrival of the resupply truck that came every Monday and Thursday. A few students waited to help unload it and to get dibs on the fresh fruit and cheese. They whooped as they saw the cases of beer, calling to him, "Dr. Fierro, thanks!"

"See if there is extra cold storage or float it in the river so you can enjoy it at the end of the workday," he responded. Luca returned to perusing the excavation again, going slower this pass, grid by grid, making sure to carefully look over each person. His eyebrows knitted together. That luscious hair of hers must be tucked under a hat since he was unable to spot her immediately. But still, he would know her anywhere, dressed in any way, hair up or down. His brain and senses had memorized every centimeter of her skin, her movement, her taste, her smell.

She was not present. Maybe she had walked back to camp for something.

"Morning, Big Guy. You look distracted. Everything okay?"

He nodded as Natasha stopped and stood almost shoulder to shoulder next to him. *"Ciao."* He sometimes forgot how tall she was. He surveyed the work in front of him. "We are making a lot of progress. Have you seen Ari?"

"I'm not her keeper."

His anger flashed, causing each of his words to be clipped. "A reminder to you. We are all each other's keepers out here."

She paused before answering, contrite. "You're so right. I'm sorry. So, when is the last time you saw her?"

"Breakfast. However, I did not talk to her."

"So why don't you ask Meg? Or Matt? They're such a tight little group."

Luca fully faced Natasha and bared his teeth. "Goddammit. This is beneath even you, Nat. What is up your ass? Check your dislike of her or whatever is driving your comments. I was there when you agreed to a truce with her. Honor it, please." He inhaled deeply to dissipate his outburst. "Meg is on the botany project with Joan, Rhys, and another team. You know how it works. The teams and projects are fluid. That is the beauty of this organization. Matt is not needed here yet, nor is Joan. They can assist Meg. We all benefit. Ari is supposed to be here, and she is not. You did not answer me. Did you see her?"

Natasha stared at her sandaled feet.

His gaze followed. "Where are your boots? They are mandatory."

"So… What shall I answer first? Your question about Ari or my choice of footwear?"

"You are sorely trying my patience." He pulled off his broad-rimmed field hat and crushed it to half its size. "As you are aware, things can go bad in an instant when we are out working. Ari first, then address your boots." His eyes passed slowly over the vast gridded excavation area in the distance, searching again.

"Fine." Natasha pointed to a grid farthest from them. "I saw her arrive. She gave instructions to that group of grad students and worked with them for a half an hour or so until she seemed comfortable with how they processed the soil." The pace with which she spoke picked up. "You might check with them."

"Thank you, Nat," he said dismissively and walking briskly to where the students worked. He moved among the grids, methodically, checking in with each group of students. No one had seen her. He was on his way to Rax when he passed another grad student coming in late, his head down, trying to avoid Luca. "Good morning."

"Good morning, Dr. Fierro. I realize I'm late. I overslept. The kitchen gave me a late breakfast." He held out his hand, full of tortilla covered in beans and cheese.

Natasha joined Luca. "Good morning, Dr. Jordaan."

"Good morning, Elliott. So, I see you're running a little behind?"

"I am. It won't happen again."

"Elliott, have you seen Dr. Antony this morning?"

"Yes. She had her pack."

"What do you mean?"

"I think she went to get water. It's miserable out here today. I saw her glance over there." Elliott took a bite of his sandwich and looked north to the encroaching jungle, talking with a full mouth. "Like someone hailed her. A woman, a student I think, stepped out briefly. Dark complexion, short black hair, maybe a dark cap, or both, dressed like many of us. You know, long pants, shirt, boots. Oh, and a yellow scarf around her neck. Dr. Antony left with her, I guess."

Luca's stomach burned at the possibility that he might be forced to send her home; it was impossible to imagine not having her around. That Ari might have deliberately put him in this situation after their blowup last night pissed him off. He followed Elliott's gaze, frowning. "Did you recognize the woman?"

"A new group of students came in a few days ago." The grad student's voice grew quieter. "I couldn't see her clearly, though nothing about her was familiar, but then I haven't been able to spend a lot of time with them. Um. Can I go work?"

"Of course. Thank you."

The student hoofed it to a grid and pulled his gloves on.

Turning to Natasha, Luca frowned and said, "We are not exploring anything in that direction." He pivoted and took a step. "I need to check at Rax."

Natasha placed her hand on Luca's arm, stopping him. "She's not there. I checked, Luca. Another student confirmed the same details Elliott just shared, almost verbatim. I touched base with the lead that received the new students. She didn't have anyone matching the woman's description. Oh Jesus, Luca—"

Luca's face had gone white.

TWENTY THREE

TWO MEN AND A WOMAN trudged through the jungle with a hostage. "Can we stop?" one of the men asked. "How much of that crap did you hold over her nose and mouth? She's still out and getting heavier with each step. I need to rest." He rolled the tied-up woman off his shoulder and massaged his knee. She plopped to the ground in a heap.

Inés snarled. "Dammit, Beto. You might have hurt her. Then we've got more issues. I did as I was told. She was the one who fainted and hit her head. Chloroforming her was easier then. It should be wearing off very soon. Try waking her up." She breathed audibly and spoke more gently. "I understand you're tired. You carried her most of the past thirty minutes."

"She's already hurt. Look at that gash. She cracked her head good on that gamba root. You carry her next time. Or Harry. Have you forgotten? One of my legs is shorter than the other. My body isn't meant for carrying."

Dappled sunlight moved across Ari's face. She struggled to open her eyes as searing pain shot through her head.

A booted foot nudged Ari at her hip, rocking her. "Wake up, Dr. Antony. Time for you to carry your own weight. Your beauty nap is over," Beto said.

Feeling battered, Ari mumbled. Opening her eyes was impossible. Nausea swirled in her stomach after each try.

"Give her water. I think she needs some," the second man said.

"We took her after breakfast. She doesn't need water. She hasn't done anything, other than be carried." Inés responded.

"Come on…" Frustration edged his voice.

"Fine, Harry," Inés said. "Give her some water. But use it sparingly. We still have some distance to travel."

Water dribbled down Ari's forehead. It burned along her hairline. Droplets seeped into her eyes and mouth.

"Not her face, stupid. Her mouth—"

"Shut up, Nes." Dirty fingers pried Ari's lips apart. "Drink. Slowly, Doctor."

Her throat was on fire, but Ari gulped the water. She had never been so thirsty. Her heart beat erratically. She was dizzy, even with her eyes closed. The sharp pain in her head ricocheted, like an errant pinball.

"We should have forced water down her before now," said Beto. "She's no good to us if she can't function."

Inés said, "You're a bright one. Whatever would we do without your astute observations?"

"Shut up. Give me the bottle." He put the bottle up to Ari's mouth, encouraging her. "Drink more. Sip slowly."

Ari sipped, but gagged. Whatever had made her pass out also made her feel sick.

Harry laughed spitefully when Ari spewed water all over Beto's boots. "Man, there's other stuff in there besides water. Like, her breakfast maybe." He laughed harder. "Gross. You can wash them off later—"

"And you can carry her the rest of the way to camp," Inés said.

"Aw, come on. You've got to admit it's funny, the good doctor puking all over his boots."

"We don't have time for this. We've got to make camp. The sun will set soon. I'm hungry, and we need more water."

"Just give her a few more minutes to absorb any water she didn't toss," Harry said.

"Give her some of your zapote. It might help."

"She just puked!"

Beto said, "Just a few nibbles. It might settle her stomach."

"Can you chew?" Harry asked Ari.

"Yes." She grunted. Her stomach felt better since she threw up.

"Don't bite my fingers, or I'll knock you out. Okay? Don't think you want another lump on your head after hitting that gamba root."

"Okay," Ari said, slowly opening her eyes, needles of pain racing through them. Her vision was blurry. Nausea threatened again. She breathed slowly and deeply. *Better.* Pain and fear continued to make her heart knock wildly within her chest.

"Open," Harry ordered.

She was barely able to make out the details of Harry, other than he was lanky, sunburned, and had long, dishwater-blond dreadlocks, tied with a grimy bandana. It hurt, but she opened her mouth. He shoved the fruit in with dirt-encrusted fingers. She chewed slowly and swallowed carefully. "More, please," she said, coughing.

Inés laughed mirthlessly. "So polite, Doctor. Give her another small bite."

"Why don't you give her some of yours?"

"Finished mine." She glanced up at the sky. "Let's get going. I think the doctor can walk now."

Ari tried to push herself up, but her hands were tied behind her. Confusion etched her expression.

"Oh, there's that," Inés said. "Help her up."

Beto hoisted her to standing. Ari swayed; nausea bubbled in her belly. She willed it down.

"You fall over, you'll have to get yourself up," Inés said.

Ari held her head up and stared into Inés's black eyes unblinking, fighting for balance and to not get sick. Her vision cleared, but a jackhammer pounded in her head.

Inés squinted at her. "Also, you yell, we leave you. In the jungle, hands tied. No way to fend for yourself. Got it, Doctor?"

Tears pricked Ari's eyes. "Yes." She could barely breathe or move without the overpowering urge to vomit. How in the hell could she get free?

Harry's expression was curious. "This is the renowned expert? She looks like some random grad student."

He was almost as tall as Luca. *Luca…*

"Trust me," Inés said. "This is her."

"Are you a real redhead?"

"Harry," Inés said.

"Dr. Antony—"

"Shut it."

Beto interjected, "This isn't your rodeo, sister. We're equals. Let him talk."

Inés whipped around, looking at each of the men pointedly. "Listen, you two idiots. The less you say, the better. The good doctor is going to help us. Afterward… That's to be determined."

"Why have you taken me? What the hell do you want?" Ari asked forcefully, the effort depleting her immediately.

"So many questions. You will have the answers soon." Inés's smile did not reach her eyes. "Ready, Doctor?"

She sensed there was far more to Inés's question, but asking now would give her nothing. Ari nodded. At this time, she had no other option.

"Let's go. I want to make camp as soon as possible. Beto, get the doctor's backpack. Harry, check the compass again. I'm tired and hungry." Inés looked up at the canopy and then at each of them, clearly unhappy. "This has taken longer than planned. Dr. Antony, you cook?"

"Some. I don't feel good."

"Tough shit. Muddle through it. You're making dinner tonight in return for us putting you up. Beto, you lead. Doctor, fall in behind him. You bring up the rear, Harry."

Short, dark Beto turned on his heel and moved forward. His awkward gait was just shy of a jog. Ari's head and stomach screamed in protest as she followed, stumbling, hands bound together at her wrists, captive.

"I thought you said you could cook, Doctor," Inés spit from the other side of the campfire. The machete at her hip gleamed in the firelight, making it appear more menacing.

Ari took a deep breath, speaking in a monotone. "I did. You just didn't ask what."

"The beans are burned."

She hung her head. She hadn't burned them on purpose. The beans tasted like the ashes from the fire she'd cooked them over. Her stomach cramped with hunger and intermittent nausea. Ari suspected she suffered a concussion. Her head still pounded, and she was relieved to feel a huge knot on her forehead—a good sign that her brain wasn't swelling. Her hand came away with a lot of blood. She had opened her head; without a mirror, she was unable to see how bad it was or clean it.

Her calves ached. They must have hiked another couple of miles through dense jungle growth and over large hills after she'd come to. Ari had staggered more than walked, tripping and falling a few times, only to be roughly jerked up by Harry and pulled to her feet. Occasionally one of them wiped the oozing blood from her burning forehead. Attracted to her blood, the mosquitoes and other insects swarmed her forehead. Harry tied a soiled bandana over the wound to keep the bugs from biting or laying eggs. She needed to get repellent on it.

Inés, Beto, and Harry hacked away the jungle growth with their machetes, but she still suffered scrapes and cuts, and her pants and shirt snagged repeatedly and tore from the trees and bushes that grabbed at her. The sturdy hiking boots she wore kept her feet from harm. She was dizzy and bone tired—other indicators of a concussion, wanting to collapse where she stood and sleep forever. She needed to stay awake as long as possible tonight. She was the only person looking out for herself. The erratic pounding of her heart continued. Based on the information Luca and Natasha had shared during orientation, Ari suspected she was also dehydrated, probably from vomiting so much.

A primal need to survive suddenly surged forward. *Don't give up, Ari. You are stronger than this. Look for the opportunity. It will come.* "Can I please have a little more water? I've kept it all down since we arrived here."

Inés brought Ari's bottle over. "Last bit of yours. And we're low, only a few sips each for the three of us."

Alarm filled her. She took only one sip even though she wanted all of it.

"Don't worry, Doctor. We have a filter system at our permanent camp. It does us no good if any of us are sick. We'll fill up tomorrow."

Ari had an orange and a few snack bars in her pack but eating now was out of the question. Maybe after everyone fell asleep she could try to, hopefully, keep down anything she ate. Her pack was on the other side of the campfire, next to where Harry sat looking smug. He creeped her out, staring at her for long periods of time, occasionally winking at her or licking his thin lips when he knew the others weren't watching.

Inés caught Harry staring at Ari before dinner and slapped him hard.

A red impression of her hand was still visible in the flickering firelight, where his sorry excuse for a beard did not cover his cheek. Apparently they had a thing going; however, she wore the pants in the relationship.

Deepening nightfall cocooned the jungle. Although she was chilled from sweat, full of fear, and endured a sore throat and a massive headache, Ari began to nod off.

Harry called quietly, “Hey, Red.”

Ari bristled but swallowed her anger. She was in no position to respond.

“Hey, Red. I’m talking to you.”

“Leave her alone, Harry,” Beto said.

She watched and listened. Animosity crackled between the two.

“I want to know where she’s going to sleep.”

“Not with you. Time to turn in.” Inés offered her hand to Harry.

“My cheek still hurts, woman.” His eyes glittered, but he stood up and meekly took her hand.

“Good. It will serve as a reminder.”

They walked over to the small tent with their arms around each other’s waist. Harry ducked in behind Inés. The flap zipped, and the lantern turned off.

Beto said, “Well. That leaves you and me, Doc. You can sleep next to the fire or with me.” He leered and pointed to the lean-to.

Ari’s muscles tensed, and her heartrate flew. She’d have more protection out in the open, next to the fire. “I’ll sleep here. Can you add wood, please?”

“So polite.” Beto added wood to the fire and made a small stack close to Ari. He motioned to her to bring her hands forward. “Wrists together.”

“I don’t understand,” Ari whimpered.

“You think I’m leaving you untied?” He efficiently wound the rope around her wrists and tested his knot. He pointed. “Feet.”

“Please, no—”

“Want to sleep with me? I’ll keep you nice and warm.”

She snapped her feet together and stared at the roaring fire.

After hobbling her ankles, Beto left. He returned with a thin blanket and draped it around her shoulders.

"Is there mosquito netting?"

"What the fuck do think this is? No. You are at their mercy, just like you're at ours. Add the wood as you need. You're welcome for my thoughtfulness. Sleep tight." Laughing, he added, "Don't let the jungle bugs bite."

He crawled into the lean-to and pulled the mosquito netting down. Snoring started almost immediately.

She rolled onto her feet and shuffled over to her pack. Everything she had packed was still there, including her knife, which she pocketed immediately. Her fingers grazed her compass. She pocketed it too.

Discomfort washed over her as she overheard grunting and giggling coming from the small tent. The repellent was in the front pocket of her pack. She focused on removing and spraying it liberally where she could, then wiping her neck, ears and face with the back of her tied hands, preparing herself for how much it was going to hurt her gash. It stung like a bitch. She sprayed some above her and hobbled under it, trying to get as much coverage as possible. Nocturnal noise obscured the misting sound.

She pulled the orange out, indecisive about eating it. Convinced the zest would be snuffed out by the repellent, she peeled it, her mouth salivating. Inés yelled out, apparently at the culmination of coupling with Harry, startling Ari. She dropped the sections to the ground and hurried to retrieve them and clean the debris off as best she could. Ari shoved two sections into her mouth. She was so hungry.

She dug for her phone, having taken it because her camera battery needed charging. She had been recording the project's progress with photos and video as well as her notes. It was still fully charged. No service of course. *Shit.* She shut it back down, closing its waterproof, protective bag and placing it under the false bottom of her pack, just in case the opportunity arose where she could use it.

Feeling dizzy from her exertion, she hobbled back to the fire pit with one of her water bottles and pulled the peels from her pocket, flinging them into the dancing flames. She lowered herself to the ground, where Beto had left her, carefully so she wouldn't jar herself and cause her head to pound harder, and pulled the blanket around her—more for the comfort than the need to be warm. It was plenty warm. Her stomach wasn't rebelling. She sipped a little bit of her water, rationing it until they gave her more.

Luca had to know she was gone. She gazed at the stars sparkling in the inky night. *Was he searching? Would he be able to find her?*

The temperature dropped noticeably as a breeze picked up. Ari moved the small stack piece by piece, even closer to where she would sleep, realizing she might need to stoke the fire through the night. She added one more log, the fire growing as it caught, and added another. Satisfied, Ari moved as close as she dared, lying down on her side and curling into a fetal position, feeling safer; granted, that was relative to her predicament. Tears ran from her eyes and dripped onto the rough blanket. *Why won't they tell me why they have taken me?*

Giant trees to the west creaked and rustled, yet they were unable to block out the beacons of hope shimmering in the juniper-purple night above her. Water gurgled soothingly behind her as it glided rapidly over moss-slicked rocks and rainforest detritus. Frogs serenaded her while she ate the bar in three bites. Ari's stomach relaxed completely. She stared at the molten-gold flames in front of her. The damp, hard ground was unforgiving on her sore joints and muscles, but it was also wonderfully pungent—and her last thought before she drifted off.

TWENTY FOUR

NATASHA GRABBED LUCA'S FOREARM. "THIS could become our worst nightmare."

He ran his hand over the back of his neck in thought. "I will talk to Carlos." Looking around, he struggled to comprehend what they could be facing. "He grew up here. He knows the terrain well. We will assemble a search team immediately." He broke eye contact with her, his attention diverted by someone in the distance. "Good. He is here. Walk with me."

Luca strode quickly toward Carlos. "*Uno momento, por favor.*" To Natasha, he commanded, "Prepare for travel. Medical supplies. Pack tents, nets. Lanterns, water, compasses, and… Go off the emergency list. We leave as soon as we can."

Natasha moved fast and blocked Luca, facing him, making him sidestep her. She jogged at his side to keep up with his pace. "Luca. Think. If she has been taken, they are way ahead of us. We're best to leave in the morning. We only have, what, seven hours of daylight? Who oversees Kanul while we're gone looking for your girlfriend?"

He gritted his teeth. "Natasha—"

"Amigo, what is happening?" Carlos asked, looking from Luca to Natasha.

"Carlos." Luca motioned for him to walk with them. They stopped at the far edge of the excavated site. His jaw tightened, and a muscle worked in his cheek. "We have a problem. Dr. Ari is missing." He turned to Natasha for confirmation. "About two hours?"

She nodded.

"A young woman, not with our project, according to Dr. Jordaan, convinced her to leave."

Carlos's brown face paled. "This is not good, amigo."

"I know. I need a tracker. Do you track?"

"*Sí*, but my cousin is better. I will run and get him. My village is an hour. We will return within four hours, ready to—"

"It's nearing noon, Carlos. Don't you feel it makes more sense that we leave at dawn?" Natasha said.

Luca turned to her, answering slowly, emphasizing each word. "*We* are not going. *You* are staying here. You will continue to manage our team and their finds and fill in for me while I am away, overseeing the Kanul site. The other leads will fill in as needed, as they have since we have been here. Excavating Rax and Kaq are collaborative."

She returned his frostiness. "Luca. I need to be involved. I need to help search. I have skills."

"You are involved and will be, just from here. I know you have skills, but I have the relationship with her. You do not. Set me up so that I can communicate with you."

"Understood. But what do I tell the others if they ask?"

He paused before answering. "What do you tell them the other times I am not here?"

She nodded. "Right. That's fair. But Meg and Matt—Luca, they're close. They are together often. They are going to know something is up, especially if she chose not to go off on her own."

"Initiate the protocol immediately. I suggest you stick to the premise that Ari became lost. As of now, we are not certain she was abducted. We surmise. What we do not want to spark is panic. You can share that a team of trackers is searching for her and that I am with them. Is that clear?"

"I'm not happy about it, but I will do as you request. It appears to be the best course of action right now."

"Excuse me. Dr. Jordaan, we do need to leave soon to find as much as we can, before any tracks disappear. Animals and heavy rain can erase signs. Rain is coming."

She sniffed the air, a quizzical expression on her face. "I don't smell rain."

As if he didn't hear her, Carlos continued, "Luca, pardon to your doctor knowledge, but I think it would be a good idea to bring my grandfather. Tata is shaman."

"Thank you, Carlos," he said, exhaling. "We can use all help."

"I will assemble what you need," Natasha said and headed toward the campsite with purpose.

"Double-check everything. And be sure to add two of our radios and a charger so we can communicate."

She responded to Luca without turning to face him, with arms raised, two thumbs up.

Carlos took off at a run in the direction of his village.

Luca's steps grew heavier as he distanced himself from Kanul's center. When he was sure that no one could see him, he let the emotion come and surrendered to the pain. Gasping for air, his heart thrashing in his ears, he dropped to his knees and prayed.

THE BANGING OF UTENSILS DREW Ari from her dream state and added to her raging headache. Sharp needles of pain throbbed in her eyes as she cracked them open. Lush hues of green surrounded her, patches of sunlight mixed with shade. Her head and body hurt more than last night. She shivered. All of her was soaked. It must have rained while she'd slept like the dead.

"Well, look here," Inés said in a snotty voice. "The doctor is awake. Harry, help her up. I'm hungry."

Fear churned through her system. Ari swallowed convulsively, pushing it down, down, down. She had to find a way to escape.

Harry grabbed her roughly and held on to her while she got to her feet. "Good morning! Up you go, Doc. How did you sleep?"

"Untie her so she can cook," Inés ordered. "We don't want her to burn the beans again or fall into the fire."

"I don't know." He laughed, leering, purposely twisting the rope securing Ari's wrists, causing her to yield to the pain. "She might be tasty. I'm famished. I really worked up an—"

Inés's voice was full of acid. "Harry…"

"Okay. I'm just funning. You're so damned serious all the time, Nes."

She walked over to him, fists on hips. Her fury belied her small size. "Enough."

"Guess you didn't give it to her as good as you assumed last night, huh?" Beto chortled.

Harry pushed Ari away roughly and stepped over to Beto. He punched him hard in his soft stomach, sending him sprawling. "Shut up, asshole."

"Knock it off, you two." Inés seethed. "Beans, Doctor. Now."

Feverish and fighting nausea and dizziness, she moved to do as ordered.

Ari felt much better after eating. She did not burn the beans this time, but she did undercook them. No matter that they were bland and the texture was what she imagined chewing cardboard would be, she was full. They broke camp quickly after breakfast and hiked for several hours.

She was less sore now that they were moving. The nausea was gone, and her headache had dulled considerably, but she continued to experience bouts of light-headedness, along with the low-grade fever. Determined to escape, Ari focused on opportunity, recalling the map Joan had shared of the area. One larger river with numerous tributaries ran through this part of Petén. Ari believed she was on one of the two western tributaries. But then again, Kanul was just off the southwestern part of the river. Maybe she was closer to the excavation than she had first thought. Maybe her abductors had walked in circles to throw her bearings off. Maybe. The trouble was that all the rainforest looked the same to her. It was so dense it swallowed them up as they moved through it.

The sun rose higher in the sky. About two hours out of camp, they topped off water bottles after finding a small stream. Ari drained one bottle within minutes of filling it and refilled it again before they resumed. They trekked for hours over the uneven and rugged rainforest terrain and had not seen any other water source.

For the first time in over twenty-four hours, she had to pee. "Can we stop?" she asked. "I need to go."

"Potty break," Harry called to Beto and Inés ahead of them. They all stopped.

Off to her left was denser underbrush that would offer her some privacy, but still… "I need privacy. Please."

Harry continued to stare. "So polite. Points for that, but nope. Just go."

Humiliated, Ari turned her back to him and unzipped her fly, challenged by her tied wrists. There was a slap and a yowl behind her.

"Knock it off. No more," Inés barked. "Go up with Beto and wait."

Footsteps receded behind Ari's back. "I can't possibly drop my pants or pull them up when I'm tied."

Inés patted the machete hanging from her belt and glared, sending her a silent message. "Fine. Then I retie them. No trouble. Don't try to run." As she untied her, she added, "You are a real pain in the ass sometimes."

Ari glared at her and quickly stepped off into the underbrush and peed, then readjusted her pants behind Inés's turned back. "I'm ready." She held her arms out, wrists together. The skin was starting to bleed where the rope had chafed.

Inés wrapped the rope roughly around her wrists and knotted it, then pulled hard to check that the knots held. "Catch up."

She blinked back tears from the pain. Her wrists burned more with every step. She walked as quickly as she could with Inés trailing her. Beto and Harry weren't too far ahead. When they were together again, Inés scampered ahead of Ari, inserting herself between the men. "Get back in formation." She fell in behind her. Harry was again at her back.

"Up ahead, Nes!" Harry yelled.

The sound of rushing water grew louder. The small group trotted down a short steep hill and turned to the left where the jungle stopped at the river's edge. Sunlight sparkled on the water rushing over towering rocks scattered among vines and trees. It was beautiful and wet.

Ari edged closer to the bank. A refreshing spray coated her face and scraped arms. She could dolphin kick across. She dug deep into her energy stores and stepped forward.

"No you don't," Inés said, jerking her back roughly.

Ari fell to the ground. "I only wanted to rinse off."

"Bullshit," Inés ground out. "You think we're stupid?"

Harry roughly pulled her to standing. "I'm game but only if you strip down, Doc," Harry whispered in her ear. "I'm curious if the curtains match the carpet."

She shivered with revulsion and stepped away from him.

Inés moved in, angrily poking Harry in the chest with each word, her back to Ari. "Harry, do you think I'm deaf? Knock it the fuck off."

Beto's back was also to her, so absorbed was he in Inés's dressing down of Harry. Ari slipped her knife out, cut the rope, and dove into the water. The current was faster than she had realized. She gave up swimming and allowed the current to pull her downstream, hoping, praying it would slow somewhere and she could climb out and find her way back to Kanul. It was a long shot, but it was the only one she had.

Ari had no idea how far she had traveled when the river slowed into an eddy. She used the last of her energy, managing to swim to shallower water and crawl onto the bank and into the understory to be shielded from the sun.

The exertion had taken its toll. Her stomach heaved. She rolled away from her vomited beans, took a great shuddering breath, and faded.

"I found her," Beto hollered. "Over here. Inés, I'm gonna puke. There're flies all over her face. Maybe she's dead."

Ari sensed more people gathering close.

"Naw. Look at her chest, Beto. It's moving," Inés said.

Ari felt a whiff of air, then a cool hand touched her head.

"Aw, fuck. She's burning up. Those flies were in her wound. Goddammit, he's gonna be pissed. We gotta put something on it.

"Here, tie this so it covers it," Harry offered.

Ari's head was lifted, her neck bent at an uncomfortable angle. She felt a scratchy fabric being wrapped around her head, which was ready to shatter from the pain.

Needles stabbed at Ari's eyes as she struggled to open them. She croaked, "Water."

"Get her pack. She had a bottle on either side."

"Got it. Hey, she has some ibuprofen."

"Smart doctor. Get a few of those too," Inés ordered.

Her head was lifted again.

"Open, Doctor. Sip slowly. You have a fever."

Her throat raw, Ari drank slowly. She swallowed the two pills dropped into her mouth with more water, choking some as they passed through her throat. She fell back asleep.

Ari woke, shivering. Her wrists were tied with fresh rope; she had been moved and lay under mosquito netting. The needlelike pain in her eyes was gone, but they still burned. Someone had taken the extra bandana from her backpack and torn it, using it as a barrier between the rope and her raw, seeping skin on each wrist. What else had they taken from her pack? The sun was still high, meaning she had slept more than a day or for not very long.

"Well, look who's up," said Harry.

Ari pulled back as Inés reached toward her.

"Stop it, Doctor," she said, laying her palm on Ari's forehead. "I'm checking your fever. You're cool. Appears it broke. Beto, get her some more water."

Sipping the water was easier this time. She finished the bottle and then fell back to sleep again—dreaming about fleeing and making her way back to Kanul.

The next time she woke was to their conversation. Carefully she shifted closer, hidden by the netting, focusing intently on every word.

"We're really late bringing the doctor back. He's going to kill us. You know how pissed he gets. He goes from zero to sixty before I can blink. Remember when he hacked the finger off that woman? Mira. All because she spilled his water? He's fucking nuts," Beto said, his voice filled with fear.

"The doctor is still weak. I think she had a concussion, and the cut on her head is filled with pus. I hate to bring her to him in that condition. He'll eat her alive or hurt her or—"

A slap filled the air. "Ow! Don't hit me again, Inés. She was burning with fever."

"She isn't any longer. What do we care what he does with her, Harry? You're an idiot. It's not my fault she hit her fucking head and did that to herself. He'll probably have the medic look at her. He needs her."

"What if she tries to escape again? It took us hours to find her. If we hadn't seen her hair—"

Inés's tone was mocking. "Yeah, and if she hadn't been on our side of the river, we never would have found her if she had. Such a smart doctor."

Ari heard movement and held her breath. It sounded as if all of them had stood up.

Inés continued. "The doctor was carrying a knife on her. That's how she cut the ropes. She also had a compass. I took them both. Top quality. She's not going anywhere, except with us, and we've got to get going. We'll keep her hobbled, giving her enough rope to walk. We need to get her up and go, get as far as we can while we still have light. She's had enough of a beauty sleep."

"You're a bitch."

"No, I'm just being realistic. We're forced to camp again tonight because of her stunt. The later we are, the more danger we face. We work for a dangerous, unstable man. I'm tired of babysitting her. He can have some of his other minions watch her or whatever the hell he has planned for her. She goes to work tomorrow. That's it."

Ari made a loud rustling noise as she rolled onto her back, her anxiety mushrooming into fear as she watched the insects flitting outside the netting above her. Their conversation ceased. Her pulse jumped erratically in her throat, and she broke into a cold sweat. Who was their employer, and what the hell was work?

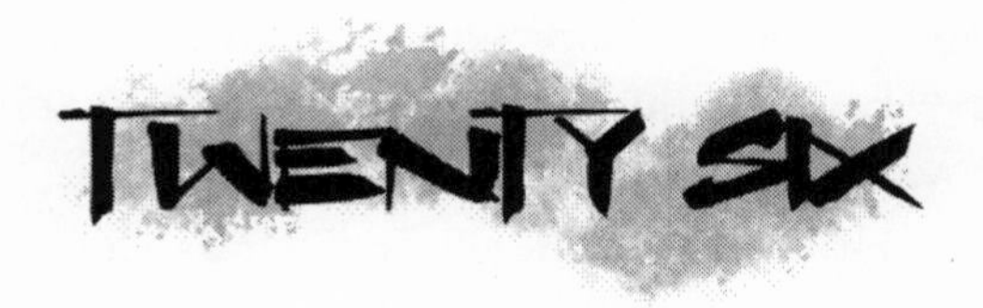

LUCA PACED. SLEEP HAD ELUDED him last night, so he read and wrote by lantern light instead. His prayers for Ari's safety quelled his fear. He spoke to her in his mind, encouraging her to have courage. He packed his bag, stoked the fire, and started coffee.

Pink fingers of dawn were visible above the treetops along where the river ran to the east. The birds sang loudly as the sky lightened. Luca was draining his third cup when he heard movement in the other lean-tos around the makeshift camp. Good. They would set out soon. He heated more water for coffee.

"*Hola!*" Carlos said, rubbing his eyes. "Did you sleep?"

"*Buenos días.* No." He rose and poked at the fire with a stick, then picked up the pot. "Coffee? Did you?"

"*Sí, y sí.*" Carlos watched Luca pace. "I'll wake the others. We need to go." He placed his hand on Luca's arm. "We made a lot of progress yesterday." His almost-black eyes held Luca's green ones. "We will find her, amigo." He left to wake the men.

Luca stared at his boots and ran his fingers through his hair, pulling it up into a ponytail. Inhaling deeply, he nodded to himself, putting all his faith in Carlos's certainty. He was pulled from his reverie by the groggy men who smiled and rubbed their eyes as they stumbled toward him and the fire. He nodded to the men. *"Buenos días! El café esta listo?"*

"*Gracias*, amigo," they answered in unison, helping themselves to the steaming brew.

Carlos addressed the circle of Maya in Spanish. "Attend to your needs and pack. We leave immediately."

A chorus of agreement acknowledged his orders.

Luca brushed the sweat seeping into his eyes without thought, intent on not twisting an ankle as he followed Carlos and the other men through the dense understory of the jungle. Already—even in the deep shade—the temperature was uncomfortably warm.

They cleared a path with machetes, but it was slow going. Gus, the tracker and Carlos's cousin, watched for clues—torn leaves, trampled low vegetation, broken branches.

Luca bit back his anxiety and annoyance over their slow pace. Because they had left early afternoon yesterday, the search party was at least a day behind Ari and the kidnappers; they needed to make it up. Her safety weighed heavily upon him. Working in Guatemala was not without safety issues, among them trafficking of drugs, people, and antiquities. And people lived in abject poverty—many seduced into the low trades and trafficking for the money or silenced by those who were involved. It could be dangerous, deadly. Everyone on Luca's team knew this. Everyone was well versed and trained in safety protocol, but knowledge and training were not fail-safes. What had enticed Ari to go with the woman?

At the outset, Gus had picked up the tracks of three people, one female and two males where the sapodilla tree stood, only meters away from where Natasha had seen Ari and the woman vanish. He believed the men had been waiting just past the ceiba tree for the woman to lure Ari. Gus had also discovered blood on one of the gambas—the prominent buttress roots of the sapodilla.

Tata had stepped forward and knelt. He dipped his fingers into the coagulated blood and lifted them to his lips. In Q'eqchi', their Mayan tongue, he told Carlos the blood was from a head wound from a woman and it tasted of fear. Carlos translated his grandfather's discovery to Luca, who went pale.

Luca rubbed at his scruffy face and then forced himself to say, "Ask him. Please. Is it a bad wound?"

Carlos turned to Tata and asked in his tongue of origin. His grandfather shook his head and spoke in Q'eqchi'.

Carlos translated. "No, but she will have a big head pain."

Signs that three, sometimes four people were moving through the jungle became easier for Gus to find. Yesterday the men's footprints had changed every thousand meters or so, indicating they had taken turns carrying something heavy, possibly a person. Possibly Ari. Gus had not seen any more blood—another good sign. The group was headed northeast. The route and their pace indicated that whoever had her knew this area well.

Like yesterday, Luca was thoroughly soaked within minutes of hiking. Gus assured him that they were on the right path and that they were closing in on the group they tracked. Late in the afternoon, Gus called, "Up ahead. Do you smell it?"

"*Sí, sí,*" the men answered excitedly.

Luca turned to Carlos. "What?"

"Inhale, amigo. It is light but hangs around, a stranger to this forest."

He caught the scent. "Woodsmoke. A campfire."

"Yes! This is good. It rained last night, and still we smell it. They are not so far."

Gus led, motioning to the men to pick up their pace. Soon they were in a small clearing, with a creek to the east and the jungle canopy to the west. He walked to a pile of ashes and poked carefully with a stick. "Someone ate fruit with a peel." He pointed his stick at the fragile form of ash.

"Ari has a habit of keeping food in her backpack, often an orange or avocado," Luca said.

"This is good information." Carlos pulled up a peel, some of which wasn't charred, and held it to his nose. "Orange peel."

"They slept here," Gus said. He walked over to a small tree and knelt down. "A lean-to here. One person." Then he walked to the other side of the clearing, kneeling and inspecting the ground lightly with his hands. "A tent here. Two people. Active."

What the hell? Where did the other person sleep? Fear churned in Luca's stomach as he absorbed the guide's words.

Gus moved back to where the fire had burned, walking slowly around the ashes, then moving out farther and circling again. He scrunched down, palms brushing the earth. "A smaller person slept here, by the fire."

Ari. Irritated by their slow pace, Luca gritted his teeth and kicked at the ground.

Noticing Luca heading out of the clearing, Gus asked, "Where are you going?"

"After her."

Gus pulled himself up to his full brawny five feet and bellowed, "No."

Luca halted, throwing up his arms. "What do you mean, no?" He was incredulous.

Carlos put his hand on Luca's arm. "Amigo, my cousin is correct." Luca pulled away, but Carlos grabbed him more firmly and said, "We need a plan. We know they have machetes and knives, but not whether they have other weapons. They are adept at moving through the jungle. It appears they planned to take her, but we do not know why. We have no idea who we are dealing with."

"I am sorry," Luca said, placing his hand on his friend's shoulder. "You are, of course, correct."

"You are a very smart man, but you must think with your head. Not your heart."

"I am; however, I am worried. She is my colleague, my responsibility."

Carlos nodded, looking deeply at Luca. "Tonight we will camp next to where they camped, and make plans. We will examine their campsite more thoroughly in the daylight. You asked me—us—to help you. Allow us to do so, amigo. I care about Dr. Ari. She is a nice lady. Why don't you gather some wood? Gus will help you. I will make the lean-tos and organize cooking."

"Thanks, Carlos," Luca said.

"Be sure to take a light. And your knife and machete. The light fades. It will become dark quickly."

Luca and Gus went in search of firewood. Luca put his headlamp on over his hat and turned it on. It was as dark as night where the fading sunlight could not penetrate. He turned back toward the clearing, his arms full of kindling. His headlight caught a flash of a small object in the distance. That was odd. He moved his head slowly in an attempt to locate it again. There it was, where the ceiba grew at the north edge of the clearing. He moved toward the immense tree.

"Where do you go?" Gus asked.

"Here," Luca said, dumping the kindling into Gus's already-full arms. "I will be right back."

Luca jogged in the direction of the tree. What was it? Nothing natural.

About three meters away, he lost sight of the object again. He stopped, his breathing heavy in the oppressive humidity. The wind cooled his damp skin, causing him to shiver. He moved his head slowly, bathing the dark green leaves in the headlight beam, scanning each leaf carefully. A small object reflected back at him. He walked forward steadily, keeping his eyes glued to the object, then reached and closed his hand over it, gently lifting it from the bark where it had been tucked into a fissure. The hair on his neck rose, and his heart stuttered in his chest as he opened his hand. Ari's delicate hummingbird necklace reflected back at him.

REVELATIONS

The first calendar was used to make predictions and calculate festival days. It was called tzolkin. The second calendar was agricultural, dictated by how long it took Earth to travel around the sun. Both calendars were only known and understood by the priests, who were great students of Heaven and its bodies.

They charted and recorded the courses of stars, planets, predicted eclipses, and observed the solstices and equinoxes.

The calendars were combined into what is known as the calendar wheel. It repeats every fifty-two years. To adjust for differences in time and space, our ancestral priests grouped years in multiples of twenty, allowing them to perform very large calculations accurately thousands of years into the past and the future.

The codices chronicle the Mayan accuracy of time and astronomy. The basic units of Mayan measurement are: kin (day), uinal (20-day month), tun (a year of 18 uinales, 360 days), katun (20 tunes, 7,200 days), and baktun (20 katunes, 144,000 days).

—Tata
Mayan Shaman
Petén, Guatemala

TWENTY SEVEN

SHE HAD SAT IN SILENCE, watching as Inés, Beto, and Harry worked efficiently to break down the camp after eating.

Inés snapped her fingers. "Up you go, Doctor. We have a half-day's hike. You can carry your backpack again."

She waved Ari's knife and compass in front of her face. "I'll hold on to these."

"Those are mine," Ari spat out.

"On second thought, I'll keep them as your personal thank-you for escorting you safely through to your destination." Inés looked at Beto and Harry. "Move it."

Ari and her captors had been walking for over four hours, pausing twice to rest and relieve themselves. Her breathing was heavy, and she plopped onto the ground once, when she glanced up at movement in the treetops; her equilibrium was off. She righted herself under Inés's pinched expression.

The jungle-camouflaged river burbled and splashed to their right as the group pushed north. Colorful birds chased each other and flew around the small group, as if to accompany them to their destination. Once, Ari thought she heard the telltale thrumming of a hummingbird, but she hadn't spotted one. With that thought, her tied hands migrated to her throat. Empty. None of them had noticed that she tucked her necklace into the bark of the ceiba tree after they'd set forth from the makeshift camp days back. She prayed it remained caught in the bark. It was a long shot, but with any luck, Luca might see it. If he was looking for her. *Please, Luca, find me.*

It was difficult to see under the dense canopy, and the ground was sometimes treacherous and slick in places where the sun was unable to shine. After falling, she kept her eyes on the uneven ground, looking for roots and vines.

"Pay more attention. We don't need you hurting further." Inés turned and resumed walking behind Beto. Ari followed, and Harry brought up the rear. Suddenly they were walking a well-trodden and swiftly widening path.

Ari slowed. "Do you hear that? Talking? Metal clanging? There are people up ahead." Could they help her, or would they be dangerous? The ground ahead of her was deeply rutted, like from a heavy truck. Rainwater partially filled the deepest ruts. *Why are there tire tracks in the middle of the jungle?* Uncertainty rooted her to the spot, preventing her from taking another step.

"Doctor," Inés said, facing her. "Remember when we first met? When I told you there had been a change in plans?"

Ari blinked rapidly, speechless, her eyes unable to look away from Inés.

"I take your response as a yes," Inés said coldly. "We are arriving at"—she used air quotes—"the change in plans."

Ari's breath whooshed out. Her mouth opened and closed over and over.

"Don't worry, Doctor. And stop looking like a fish gasping for air. No one is going to hurt you or off you. Not yet anyway, that I know of." Inés's eyes gleamed maliciously. "Let's not keep him waiting. He expected us before now, but you slowed us down."

Harry asked quietly, "You going to explain that to the American, Nes?"

"The American?" Ari asked. "Who…"

Beto shook his head. "I imagine he's super pissed. Probably needed the doc before now."

"She would have been useless, puking and fainting. I'll explain to him, and he'll just have to understand. Let's go."

"You do that. He scares the hell out of me." Beto's voice dropped lower. "Those eyes…"

Inés placed her hand between Ari's shoulders and pushed her forward. "Move."

They climbed another steep hill and walked out into a clearing bathed in sunlight. The heat soared, the air rivaling a sauna.

"We're here," Harry said.

Inés laughed derisively. "Astute as always."

Harry dropped his backpack stuff with his blanket and netting on the ground and stretched and groaned. "Goddamn. That feels better. My back can breathe. Too damned hot." He grabbed his bottle and drained it, and turning to Inés, he said, "Maybe you can give me a nice rubdown later?"

She hit him hard on the arm. "Seriously? That's what is on your mind at this moment? Jesus."

Ari began to sweat profusely from the sudden exposure and increase in temperature. She lowered her pack to the ground and was rewarded with immediate respite from a gentle breeze caressing her soaked back. Her eyes blinked rapidly to adjust to the change in light. Blindly, she bent over and reached for her bottle in the side pocket. Standing and drinking slowly, she lifted her sunglasses hanging from the cord around her neck and slipped them on. *Omigod.*

WHAT ARI VIEWED STAGGERED THE imagination. The ground in front of her had been cleared of all organic matter, exposing part of a massive site—the biggest active site she'd ever seen. Numerous excavations were happening at once, versus the two at Kanul.

She appraised the closest excavation with an experienced eye. Cord lines were strung out to mark the site, forming five-by-five-metered squares. Excavation units. Multiple transits were spaced around the site, accurately measuring the horizontal and vertical angles and distances. Precisely aligned one-meter-wide balks bordered adjoining trenches to aid stratigraphic analysis. More cord lines climbed upward on the clearing's perimeter, disappearing into the deep, densely forested shade. They were way ahead of the work at Kanul.

Excavation tools and supplies littered the balks and the edges of the site. Dozens of volunteers and students, joined by local Maya, worked arduously in the white sunlit day, many under shade provided by pole-mounted tarpaulins over the trenches. The sharp pinging of picks and thudding sounds of trowels digging in the earth was familiar, reminiscent of her time spent digging as a graduate student volunteer in Morocco and as a doctoral supervisor in Italy.

Analyzed dirt was removed by buckets and poured into the waiting wheelbarrows spaced at intervals throughout the site. The dirt, which no longer held any archaeological significance, would be used as back dirt to refill test pits and depleted excavated units.

Multiple immense canvas awnings provided shelter for the large paper-laden tables. From her past work as a field director, she knew the papers were survey maps and diagrams indicating the topography of the surveyed site and where to trench. Additional transits lay heaped under the tables.

Whoever was responsible for overseeing this project was seasoned and meticulous. She counted a dozen tables dedicated to processing artifacts. Small groups of people quietly focused on their tasks of cleaning, sorting, and inventorying. After the artifacts were assigned an object type, year, and running number, she expected that they were placed in open bins with secure lids behind the tables. She watched a man fill out an inventory card about the artifact in front of him. From where Ari stood, it looked like a shard of some type. The man placed the card in a shoebox-shaped container behind him. It was stacked on top of other similar boxes. The methodology appeared efficient.

Two storage buildings, built from durable fiberglass-reinforced plastic, were stationed just past the tables. They resembled trailer-sized Porta Potties but with windows and reinforced screened doors. A larger building, likely a field laboratory, had been built from wood, the roof corrugated metal. Through the door and multiple windows, she glimpsed people inside working.

Loud, steady buzzing drew Ari's attention overhead. Two drones. One hovered, panning the dig. The domed lens underneath protected the camera taking aerial photographs. The other drone flew north, soaring higher and higher, disappearing above the trees. Based on the size of the excavation, she suspected the second drone was being used to search for any other patterns and changes in the soil and vegetation that were impossible to see on foot. But for what exactly?

Inés broke into her reverie. "Let's walk, Doc. You can check out your new digs." She laughed derisively. "Digs. Get it?" She forcefully poked Ari in the back. "Move."

The excavation was exceptionally well funded. More rainforest had been cleared to the west of the dig. A large RV camper skirted the perimeter of the beige tent village and was hooked up to a generator. Additional generators could be seen behind the RV. To have air-conditioning in this heat and humidity. How fortunate.

Three military-style Jeeps and a small, unmarked white van were parked down a sloped hill to the right. One hundred meters past the vehicles, four mammoth tents with front-zip screens had been combined to create an enormous kitchen. A water-filtration system was stationed just outside the kitchen flaps.

"Pretty nice, huh, Doc?" asked Inés. "Of course, you won't be spending any time in here since you can't cook."

Folding tables had been placed end to end in a *U* shape, close to but not touching the walls. Most were neatly piled high with food and kitchen items. Jumbo coolers bookended the tables. Additional coolers and plastic bins were stored under the tables.

"It's very nice, unexpected," Ari said coolly.

An outdoor kitchen was set up another fifty meters away. Multiple grills were arranged in a crescent shape. Buckets for collecting grease and waste were placed between the grills. Another water-filtration system had been placed here as well. Dozens of picnic tables sat within several immense white tents with roll-down screen walls, providing archaeologists and volunteers with shelter from sun, rain, and insects. This setup was far more extensive than any expedition she had participated in. *What organization is underwriting this?* Most archaeology exploration and excavation, like Kanul, operated on bare-bones budgets.

Where the hell were they? Mentally she flipped through a file folder of archaeological sites in this area. Images flew through her mind. This site was not one of them.

She played devil's advocate. Maybe she wasn't where she originally thought. There were roughly three thousand archaeological sites in Petén. Maybe her spot-on internal navigation system had failed because of her concussion as well as the stress she had been under the past days.

She closed her eyes and opened them again. Forgetting about her vertigo issues, Ari stumbled backward and caught herself just in time as she looked skyward. The sun was where it should be at this hour. The river's tributary was to the east of where she stood. "Where are we exactly? I don't recall this site, Inés, and I've studied all of them extensively. My postgraduate specialty is Mayan archaeology and culture. All periods and—"

A man appeared out of nowhere, the glaring sunlight keeping her from seeing him clearly. "It's rather difficult to consider yourself a true Mayan expert if you have only studied. Places and people have more profound impacts when you experience them firsthand. They come alive. Don't you agree?" He stepped closer.

What the hell? No, it couldn't be. Ari lowered her head, shaking it to clear any remaining cobwebs that still might be affecting her from the concussion.

"I'm pleased you have arrived. Granted, it was later than I expected. Welcome to Ajal."

Ari's head snapped up. Her mouth flew open, and the breath whooshed out of her, like someone had gut-punched her. "No...," she managed to whisper.

Eric stood before her. Real as rain. Burnished a deep red-gold from the pounding, relentless Petén sun. His closely clipped flattop had bleached almost white in the sun. His square body had lost its softness. He wore a khaki short-sleeved shirt and shorts, as though he was on safari. Brown leather boots, caked in layers of dried mud, covered his feet. A wide-brimmed sun hat hung down his back from its knotted cord. Menacing energy rolled off him.

He took off his mirrored sunglasses. "Hello, Ariana." His eyes had an eerie otherworld appearance against his deeply tanned skin.

The effect was downright creepy, and although she knew him, fear snaked its way through her.

Inés barked with laughter. "Doctor, I understand you know each other quite well."

"That's enough, Inés," he said sharply. "Take your brother and lover and make yourselves useful. I will find you when I have need of you. Plan on helping with lunch." He addressed Ari, his ice-blue eyes brooking no argument. "Come with me."

She had to jog to keep up with Eric's clipped pace as he moved across the open space. He stopped when they were off by themselves.

"You... You...," she sputtered, her head spinning from the exertion and his sudden appearance, her arms pressed into her ribs and fists clenched.

"Come now, Ariana. You never were one to be at a loss for words."

She drew a deep breath and let it out slowly, absorbing the fact that Eric stood with unwavering confidence in front of her, in a locale unknown to her, somewhere within the Petén jungle. That he may have orchestrated her abduction, that he may have been responsible for putting her at risk these past days enraged her. Adrenaline exploded in her and she erupted, charging furiously at Eric. Ari launched herself, ready to pummel him with her fists.

He turned and punched out while she was in midair, hitting her in the face and knocking her to the ground. She sprawled on the trampled earth and drew herself up onto her hands and knees, preparing to attack him again.

He looked down at her and shook his head. With calm disdain, he said, "Tsk, tsk. No, you don't. Behave yourself, Ariana. I recall that you're good at that and following rules and instructions. You will do as I say."

Pain slammed through her head. The light faded in and out, and her mouth tasted metallic. Blood.

"Get up. I don't do drama, and from what I remember, neither do you."

Every ounce of hatred she felt for him poured through her eyes. Heart pounding, vision blurry, she panted. "You hit me! You bastard."

Eric sneered, and his almost-white blue eyes glittered ominously. "You charged me. I merely defended myself." His voice dropped as he squatted. Face-to-face with her, his voice grew deadly. "Do not do it again. You're a mess, Ariana. You smell." He slipped his sunglasses back on and stood. Over his shoulder, he yelled for water and raised his hand high, fingers spread.

Ari spit blood out onto the ground. There was plenty. She had bit her tongue when he punched her. *Shit.* She gagged from the vomit burning her throat. No one had ever raised a hand to her. She spit again and started crying. Her blood, mixed with saliva and tears, drooled down her chin.

Scornfully, Eric said, "That's attractive."

"Fu—"

Water hit Ari forcefully, drenching her. She choked as it cut off her breath and filled her mouth. While it refreshed her, being doused with water made her livid. She spit out more blood and glared at him with hatred, stumbling to stand.

"Thank you," he said, handing the bucket back to the Mayan man standing next to him. "I believe that will do. You can go." His nostrils flared, and his voice was full of poison as he said, "Come see me after you have cleaned up and cooled off. You are to stay in the cleared areas only. My men are armed." He pivoted and strode away.

Twenty Nine

"YOU KNOW MANY DETAILS ABOUT your doctor, amigo," Carlos said.

Luca's expression was evident in the ribbons of moonlight coming through the clouds above and in the glow of the fire's dancing flames. "She likes to share."

"I see," Carlos said. "We have known each other for some time. I recognize your feelings."

"Hell, Carlos. I am unsure of my feelings. I do know I like her. I like her heart. I am very concerned."

Carlos nodded and smiled to himself. "I see."

Luca raked his hand through his hair and pulled it back into a ponytail, understanding his friend did not believe him.

"Dr. Ari is fiery."

Luca smiled wistfully to himself. "That she is."

Carlos wasn't ready to give in just yet. He pushed some more. "There is passion between you. I see it, and more. It is new, like the first sparks of intense fire. *Sí*?"

He shook his head and chuckled. "You are observant. What we have… I do not know. I care for her deeply. We are like magnets. We are pulled together strongly, and we repel just as strongly. Sometimes she holds back, as do I. I enjoy the back and forth."

"I do not see much repelling, except when she left your tent in the early hours during the kayak trip, before the Sun God woke."

"You spied on us?"

"No, amigo." He chuckled. "You know in your heart that is not true. That hour is my shift. Dr. Meg moves back and forth nightly. There is a lot of, um, what Americans say, musical tents, going on."

"Musical tents…" Luca smiled. "Yes. Dr. Matt and Dr. Meg. Dr. Ari is special. Please keep us to yourself."

"I see how you look at her, watch her when you think others are not paying attention. She does the same with you. It's an interesting game you two play. My silence is my gift, but others know. You are like *colibrís*, drawn to the sweet nectar of each other."

Colibrí. He patted the secured front pocket of his shirt where he carried Ari's hummingbird necklace. The first time he had noticed the necklace was in Cobán, when she dropped her duffel on his foot. Her liquid-brown eyes had sucked him in, and then her vile temper had burst forth. While she told him off, his eyes traveled over her supple, freckled neck, stopping at the necklace. An unusual choice, he thought. It was on their kayaking break and the first time they were truly together that she told him about the necklace's significance. They bared their souls that night. *That was when I realized I am in love with her.*

He unzipped the pocket, carefully pulling out the necklace. The sterling was cool to his touch. He stroked the delicate hummingbird between his thumb and forefinger, recalling that night. He hardened as he remembered the sinewy, dewy softness of her body, how she arched up to him as he explored her, and how she kissed him and welcomed him into her succulent heat. He had moved inside her for some time, learning what she wanted and what she needed. She had sought to please him, a willing partner. He took his pleasure only after she had hers, draining him, and every time thereafter. His body and heart ached for her. It had been far too long since they had been together. His mind weighed heavy with worry over her health and safety. Where was she?

He looked to the twinkling heavens and full moon that were slowly disappearing behind thick clouds. Silently he spoke to her. *Hear me, Ari. I am coming for you. Observe. Leave clues. Use your survival skills. Be strong and safe.*

Tata came out of his tent. He addressed Carlos in Q'eqchi', all the while looking at Luca.

"Tata asks if you believe," Carlos said.

"Believe what?"

"In the magic and the supernatural."

Luca sat up taller and inclined his head. "I am not sure how to answer that. I am open. Is that acceptable?"

"Tata wishes to perform a ceremony to protect Dr. Ari and to bring us to her safely."

"I cannot argue with that, but we need to devise a plan to extract her, along with several options."

Carlos placed his hand on his shoulder. "We will. Tomorrow morning."

He leaned forward and nodded at Tata. "What do I do?"

Tata spoke again to Carlos, who translated for Luca. "Sit here and open your mind. Its power is limitless. I am to get something for Tata."

Luca slipped the necklace back into his pocket and zipped it. While he waited for Carlos, Tata dug out the ash from the campfire. Luca motioned he would help, but Tata waved him away, motioning for him to remain seated.

Once cleaned, Tata placed twigs and branches in a small pile. He stood and spoke loudly, turning to each of the cardinal directions—north, south, east, and west—before pulling six tapered candles from the small bag Carlos had retrieved. Tata dug four holes within the pit in the four cardinal directions but outside the piled wood. He placed a covered candle in each. Chanting, he secured a royal-blue and a purple candle in the center of the small mound of wood he had built in the very center of the piled twigs and branches.

Luca was so engrossed in watching Tata that he did not realize the other men had joined. They sat on blankets, watching silently, their lips moving soundlessly while Tata murmured and prepared for the ceremony.

Carlos sat next to Luca, leaning over and quietly explaining the ceremony. "Tata asks for assistance. The blue candle represents the sky. The purple is for all our ancestors, including Dr. Ari's. Tata will call each of the directions into the circle and light them. Red is the energy of the East, of the sun, our father, who illuminates our path. Our father helps determine what our course of action should be. Black is the energy of the West. It is the energy of Grandmother Moon, who shows us the way of the teacher. Yellow is the energy of our Mother Earth, the South. This energy absorbs what no longer serves us. It also provides us with what will serve us. Mother Earth energy nurtures and helps to sustain us, especially important in this situation. The white candle is the energy of the north, Father Sky. This energy reveals our authenticity, what we stand for, and whom we should stand with. All these energies will help to balance our bodies, souls, and bring about a peaceful, healthy recovery of Dr. Ari."

Tata's voice became more impassioned. He reached into his bag again, his hands overflowing with crushed pine needles. Blowing on his hands, he dropped the needles onto the pile of wood. He flicked his wrists, and the candles and fire lit. Luca blinked, stunned by what he had just witnessed. He had heard that the great shamans had this gift of lighting fire, but he had believed it to be an embellished story.

Tata sang in his ancient tongue, then quieted. He sat on his blanket staring mutely into the fire, reading the flaming licks and glimmering embers.

"We will stay until the fire is out. If you pray, amigo, now is a good time," Carlos whispered.

Luca experienced a shift after the ceremony, as if an enormous weight had been lifted. Hope buoyed him. As directed by Tata, he went to his tent in silence. He placed Ari's necklace under the shirt he used for a pillow, and for the first time since her abduction, peace filled him. She had slept at this camp only last night. Thunder boomed in the distance, and lightning hurtled through the black night. He slept soundly while huge raindrops splattered his tent.

"*BUENOS DÍAS*," CARLOS SAID TO Luca, handing him a steaming cup of coffee. "How did you sleep?"

"Good morning. I slept remarkably well." Luca yawned and ran a hand over his hair and scratched the lengthening beard on his face. He smiled. "As though I was drugged."

"Shaman magic is just that." Carlos chuckled. "Tata probably put a little extra something in the ceremony for you and your worry." He took two blankets from the vibrantly colored pile and handed one to Luca. "The ground is wet from the rain. Sit, amigo. We will drink our coffee and talk while we wait for the others to rise. We need to plan carefully."

"A few of us should hike ahead and investigate," Luca said. He drank a few more sips of the strong, hot brew and then stood. "I volunteer."

Carlos stood as well, reaching out and placing his dark brown hand on Luca's forearm. "Gus says we are very close to rescuing Dr. Ari, less than a day." He looked at him deeply. "You have emotional investment, amigo. Perhaps you should stay here while I go with one or two of the other men. Split our numbers. We can decide the plan once we return with what we know."

Luca walked away from the fire to the edge of the clearing and tossed his remaining coffee in frustration. "What you say makes sense, but I should go. She is most familiar with me. We have no idea who has taken Ari or for what purpose." He looked over at Carlos. "You say we are close. What has Gus shared?"

"He says four sets of tracks are fresh. Two women, one with more weight, and two men, one larger with very big feet, and one smaller. There are many tracks. And we know that the four of them spent a night here."

Luca leaned forward, listening intently. "Right. What else?"

"There are footprints in the moist ground. Branches and leaves are torn in multiple areas. They went into the perimeter of the jungle to relieve themselves. If we walked in past the branches and leaves, we would likely find more proof. Understand?"

"Gus knows all this?"

"*Sí*, and there is more." Carlos walked back closer to the abductors' campsite, motioning for Luca to follow. "The person who made the lean-to was not kind to the young trees he used. He scarred them with his impatience." He stroked his palm over the gouges in the trees, closing his eyes and mumbling something in Q'eqchi', then reopened them. He walked to the fire and squatted. "There is evidence of two fires. You saw the peel ashes in the pit. They were from the first fire and were placed under the coals on purpose. You said Dr. Ari had fruit with her. They ate beans." Carlos pointed to his left, into the jungle. "Burned beans are over there, close to where you threw your coffee. Someone is not a good cook." He shook his head in disgust. "How do you mess up beans?"

Luca threw his head back and laughed.

"What makes you laugh?"

"Burned beans. The lovely doctor does many things exceptionally well. Cooking is not one of them. I suspect she may have been the cook." Feeling some relief, Luca grinned and asked, "These are promising signs, *sí*?"

Carlos's smile twinkled in his dark eyes. "*Sí*. Very promising."

Luca pointed to the north end of the clearing while he dug in the pocket of his shirt. "I found this the other night hanging from that ceiba tree." He opened his hand.

"*Colibrí. Muy bueno.*" Carlos stood, his eyes big. "Do you recognize it?"

"Yes. It is Ari's. It is a very special necklace to her."

"*Sí. Colibrí*, a favorite bird of the Great God."

"I saw it reflect in my headlight. I believe she left it on the ceiba to let us know we are on the right path, to not give up." Luca put it back into his pocket and zipped it.

"The *colibrí* symbolizes safe passage. Dr. Ari is telling you, us, that she is safe. For now. Another promising sign." Carlos broke his contact with Luca. "It appears breakfast is ready." Stepping forward, he patted each of the men on their backs. "*Buenos días*, amigos." The men sat on blankets around the dwindling fire, enjoying a breakfast of beans and fresh zapote, the fig-flavored fruit of the sapodilla tree.

"Now to the business at hand...," Luca said, taking another sip of just-brewed coffee and looking to Carlos. "Finding Dr. Antony. I understand we are closing in on her and her abductors."

The men nodded enthusiastically.

"I will go," Gus said, standing and folding his blanket, "and take Tomás, Pablo, and Carlos. Jorge and Dante, you remain here with Tata and Luca."

All the men nodded, except Luca. Tracking ability and survival skills were fairly even should the groups become separated. Tomás ran like the wind with great endurance and could return to this campsite quickly if necessary. Pablo had shamanic training, which might be needed.

Luca could not stay. He cleared his throat. "Gus, I appreciate the thought you have put into grouping us, but I feel strongly about going with you. Dr. Antony does not know anyone else here, except Carlos, and not that well. We suspect she has been abducted. I can safely assume she has been through a lot. Additional people she does not know may stress her more. She is most familiar with me. I ask that someone switch places with me."

"You make good sense. I will stay," said Carlos.

"*Gracias*, Carlos." To the rest of the men, Luca said, "We should check reserves before we separate."

The men left the fire circle and returned with their packs. They spent the next hour divvying up food, tarps, equipment, tools, and medical supplies.

Tata spoke, and Carlos translated. "Tata will share his herbs, Pablo."

Luca pulled his hair into a ponytail and added a bandana, then his hat. His sunglasses hung from the cord around his neck. He slipped his pack over his shoulders and looked around at the men. "Ready?"

The men kept the tributary to the right as they trekked north, following the plentiful signs left by Ari and her abductors. At midmorning, the group took a break.

"The tracks are more recent," Gus said excitedly. "We are very close."

"Good, then let us go," Luca said.

Gus stayed him with his hand. "Patience is needed. We must be more careful the closer we get. We must be quieter. Do you have binoculars?"

"Yes." Luca pulled them out of his pack.

"May I look?"

Luca handed them to him. "Of course."

"Mm. *Sí*, good," Gus said, peering through them. "We have many companions."

"Following us?" Luca looked around, not seeing anything but shades of green and dappled sunshine where the rays were able to break through the canopy.

"Maybe. Look into the trees. What do you see?"

Luca slowly fanned the area with his binoculars Gus had returned to him. "Ah… nothing."

"Look, Doctor."

"Birds of different sizes and colors," Luca said. His voice dripped with sarcasm. "Why are we looking at birds when we should be looking for Dr. Antony?"

Gus ignored his question. "What else?"

"What else, what?" Luca ground out through his teeth.

"What else do you see? This is important, Dr. Fierro."

Luca inhaled and let out an exasperated long breath. "Monkeys. Happy? Can we go now?"

"No. We cannot go now. Tell me everything you see."

Luca's voice was rife with impatience. He rubbed the back of his neck. "Seriously? I see red-breasted birds and larger brown ones with speckled heads. I see zapote hanging from that tree over there."

"Doctor."

"Fine. There is a highway of leaf-cutters crossing where we will next walk," he continued, moving with the binoculars.

"And?"

Luca scrubbed at his hand over his face in frustration. "Palms over there." He pointed. "The trunks are covered in skinny thorns."

"Root spines. *Sí*. What else?"

"The leaves are large. They resemble deeply split fans."

"What do you notice about them?" Gus prodded.

Inwardly, Luca rolled his eyes. "About the leaves?"

"Yes. Look carefully," Gus said, his voice rising.

"One is torn. In half."

"*Sí!* Does the tear look accidental?"

Understanding dawned on Luca. "No! It appears it has been deliberately torn."

"What else?"

Luca pulled the binoculars from his eyes. A sad expression covered his face as failure overwhelmed him. "I see nothing more."

"Look again, Doctor. Travel each of the palms, slowly, with your eyes."

Impatiently Luca looked again. He was about to quit when he saw the edge of something orange and blue peeking out from one of the lowest root spines of a palm farthest from them. He tossed the binoculars to Gus and ran toward it.

Gus, Pablo, and Tomás puffed in exertion after sprinting to catch Luca, who stood holding a colorful headscarf. Luca put it to his face, inhaling its scent. *Ari.* His voice quaked with emotion. "This is Ar— Dr. Antony's. She often wears it."

Gus said, "An odd place for a scarf to be. Either it fell off Dr. Antony or she left it here as a clue."

Luca folded the scarf and put it in the cargo pocket of his pants.

"You carry much," Gus said. Then softly so that only Luca could hear, he asked, "Is it too heavy?"

Luca responded, "No, amigo. I will be fine. *Gracias.*"

"Let's keep moving."

THIRTY ONE

THE CLANGING OF PICKAXES HITTING rock and thudding into softer vegetation and earth brought Luca, Gus, Tomás, and Pablo to a halt. They dropped into crouches, scuttling close to one another to speak. Gus put his finger to his lips. They remained silent and were able to hear voices carried on the wavering breeze.

"American and—" Luca spoke loud enough to be heard over the occasional squawking of parrots.

"Maya also. And I don't know…," Gus said, closing his eyes to listen harder. "A large number. Stay here quietly. I will look and return." He made no sound as he left.

The men sat in the night-like shade to wait, Tomás and Pablo on either side of Luca. His sentinels. The two men had their backs to him, watching the jungle for predators and visitors. Luca reached into his pocket and withdrew Ari's scarf. He held it to his nose and inhaled her familiar scent. He closed his eyes, retreating into his own private sanctum. Inhaling again, his body responded as images of her came to mind—shining earth-brown eyes when she was happy or angry as a hellcat or deepening to a rich cognac when they made love.

She had been furious with him the night before she was taken, misinterpreting Natasha's presence in his tent. He had been overwhelmed by Ari's explosive and emotional outburst and unfounded accusations, allowing his temper to get the best of him, deciding not to go after her, let her cool off. Hell, he had just stood there—mostly mute except for when he had wondered aloud whether the passion they had would last outside of this summer-work bubble. That was fucking brilliant.

To see her so distraught and angry hurt him, but his protective shield, honed from Sofia's deceit, resurrected itself. He had been imprisoned within it, unable to free himself as Ari broke apart.

What had he done? Ari was not Sofia. His decision to remain professional, forego intimacy with her, was epic stupidity.

That he had crushed her ate at him. Luca had tossed and turned the rest of the night, planning to speak to her in the morning, but she buffered herself from him within their circle of close colleagues. She went to the Kaq dig. He began his day restructuring the schedule for Rax. By the time he arrived at Kaq, she was gone.

Luca craved her. He needed her like he needed oxygen, water, food, and perhaps, even more than sleep. He thirsted for her smile and laughter. He hungered to watch her eyes spark when he challenged and teased her. He appreciated her intelligence, dry wit, and ethics. He yearned to hold her. She felt so right in his arms, especially when she slept, purring contentedly. He ached to be buried and moving inside her, as close as he could possibly be with another person, as close as he could be with the one he loved.

He had to fix it, fix them. If he was fortunate enough to get the chance. When he got her back, Luca would rectify everything. *Merda.* He was tired of sitting on the ground, tired of doing nothing. He was starting to stand when Gus appeared.

"Amigo! You gave me a fright. I did not hear you," Luca whispered loudly.

"*Gracias* for your compliment, Doctor." Gus chuckled. "I have not lost my ability. We can speak normally; we are enough of a distance."

Luca stretched his back and shoulders and rubbed his neck. "Tell us. What did you find?"

"There is a very, very large excavation. Many people dig and do other tasks. Many tents and Jeeps. A building. A sleep-in trailer and generators. Backhoes."

A helicopter flew overhead. All four men watched it through the treetops. It appeared to be landing and dropped out of sight.

"They may have a small airstrip," Luca said in disbelief.

Gus scratched his chin. "I do not have the knowledge, but I think it is secret and illegal."

"An operation such as this requires a hell of a lot of money," he said thoughtfully. "It must be privately funded. What can this be?"

"*Sí*, Doctor. We need to talk more before we go to get Dr. Antony."

"You saw her?"

"*Sí*. She was arguing with a man with flat white hair. I overheard a few Maya passing in front of me call him the Americano."

"What?" Luca shook his head. He had to have misheard Gus.

"The Americano."

"He's real…," he said, feeling sucker punched. Matt had brought up the American during the kayak trip, around the campfire. They dismissed him as fictitious, archaeological lore. Luca rubbed fiercely at his beard. "Goddammit." Of all places… And Ari was with him. "Does Dr. Antony appear to be healthy and moving freely?"

"*Sí*. I saw her from a distance. I heard her angry words and gestures. She was not happy with the man. She does not like him. She screamed at him. He hit her, and she went to the ground. He laughed at her and then walked away."

"He hit her?" Luca's voice rose in fury.

"I did not see it well. It happened fast. The doctor did get up. She held her hand to her face."

Angry, Luca paced. "What did she scream?"

Gus looked down, thinking, then looked Luca directly in the eye. "I'm sorry, Doctor. I did not hear it clearly. Aaron? Abram? It was difficult over tools and equipment. He had a bucket of water thrown on her after she was on the ground. They are clearing more jungle on a large hill near the river, with the backhoes. Probably a temple swallowed by the jungle."

"That is not the proper way to prepare a site. They could be destroying priceless history and artifacts," Luca said. He was perplexed. Who was the American? Did Ari know him? It seemed as though she might since she had called the man by a name.

"One more thing." Gus paused before speaking. "When the Americano walked away, she did also, but in the opposite direction. They passed in front of where I hid. A woman with short black hair and dark skin led her away. I believe she may be the woman that Dr. Jordaan described. I could see that Dr. Antony's mouth was red and her cheek purple. She was crying."

Luca clenched and unclenched his fists repeatedly. His blood boiled. *What the hell? Merda.* He turned toward the site with intent, his anger evident in his brisk pace.

Gus jogged alongside him and stepped in front of Luca, blocking him from going farther. "I understand how you might feel, Dr. Luca. But it is not good to go yet. We should walk back a mile or so and camp tonight. We need to think this through. I will go watch again in the morning. We will be patient, like stealth cats with mice."

"I disagree. I think we should walk in now and get her."

"And then what, amigo? What if they do not want her to go? They took her for a reason. We need to talk extraction strategy."

"I hear the guerrilla in you, Gus."

"*Sí*. I still have those skills. But remember that many, many Maya were guerrilla. There are many Maya on this site helping the Americano. They have similar skills, and many of them have guns. I do not have a gun. None of us do. That could make rescuing her very dangerous."

Guns? What in hell was going on? Luca massaged his temples, wanting to yell, scream, roar. But to do so could put Ari, and all of them, at risk. "Is there nothing we can do tonight? I am deeply worried about her."

"I believe she is safe. They need something from her." Gus began walking in the direction where they would make camp. "Come. Tomás has the radio. We will call Dr. Jordaan. Maybe she can help in some way."

Luca followed, his mind turning over what Gus shared earlier. He swore under his breath, his thoughts churning. Was there any way he could reach her and let her know he was so close?

Gus addressed the rest of the group. "Dusk is coming. The jungle will be black soon. We need to pick up our pace so that we can set up camp before sunset."

The men walked briskly. Despair cloaked Luca. He would report back to Natasha tonight with the additional information that Ari had been spotted and that she was with the American. He really existed. What would Natasha think of that?

He wanted this entire ordeal to be over, safely. In all the years he had done fieldwork, nothing like this had happened. Sure, colleagues and students became sick, and they were bitten and stung by insects and animals. However, no one had been abducted, until now. And apparently by the American's organization. A part of him had believed the American was lore—a great story created among archaeologists and anthropologists when they suffered boredom on a dig—like stories around campfires, embellished in the retelling, making the lore legendary. But another part of him had felt the rumors were too prevailing and proved the existence of a ruthless, heartless antiquities criminal. Recently, precious archaeological artifacts from Turkey and Peru had shown up in a European millionaire's estate sale after he died. All the items were traced to several excavations the American was rumored to have looted. Yet his existence had never been proven or his identity uncovered.

Goddammit. He closed his eyes and repeated the words Tata had given him last night. Peace moved in, like a soft blanket, helping to chase away the shadows of despair. He focused on the task at hand—getting Ari safely away from the American. After dinner, they would make a new plan with the information Gus had shared.

An engine grew louder. The same helicopter flew overhead, back in the direction from which it had come, gaining altitude as it moved farther into the distance. He wondered who was onboard or who had been dropped off. What was the American doing in this location, excavating a site of this magnitude, possibly without consent from the Guatemalan government? Why had he kidnapped Ari? He would soon have answers to his many questions.

ARI OPENED THE FLAPS FARTHER to help circulate the stale air in the stifling tent that Inés had yanked her to after her clash with Eric. It did nothing. Feeling faint, she unzipped the front screen flap and stepped out and under an attached awning. Her swollen tongue and lip throbbed with pain, and she could barely move her jaw. Every time she moved her mouth, the split in her lip reopened and bled. A camp chair and an accompanying table with a lantern sitting on top sat in the awning's shade. This was somewhat better than steaming inside. A battery-operated fan was clipped to the edge of the awning. Ari reached and unclipped it. She turned it on and moved it slowly over her face and body. Much better.

"Does the fan help?"

She whipped around to face Eric. He had snuck up on her again. She sneered at him.

"It's nice to see you too, honey. I'm sorry about earlier, but you, like everyone else here, need to understand that what I say goes. You will not receive special treatment even though you are my guest. Inés is bringing you water to drink and to cool off with. Looks like you might need some ice for that lip and jaw." He tipped his face up, sniffing loudly. "You stink. And you always smelled so nice, Ariana. Inés will accompany you to the shower, and you can then change into something less offensive."

Her voice was thick with anger and from biting her tongue. "Change into what exactly, Eric?" She rubbed her cheek where he had punched her and spit out the rest of her response. "I am hardly your guest. I was taken, not asked. And certainly not given time to pack. You had me drugged."

"Yes. Sorry about that," he said almost cheerfully, hands on hips, a large sheathed machete hanging from his belt. "We'll discuss those details later. I've got to get back to work. In the meantime, you will clean up. She'll find other clothes for you to wear, and you will wait here for me. We'll eat dinner together. Here, by lantern light."

Ari enunciated every word. "I will not eat with you."

Eric calmly took off his sunglasses. His light eyes flashed dangerously. "You will do as I say. All this could have been avoided had you not run off. I'm unhappy with you for leaving me, Ariana."

"I couldn't leave you fast enough. You're a man-whore. A real son of a bitch."

"I suspected you had a potty mouth."

"You are the shit of shits. Take me back to my colleagues."

"Any other insults? You are in no position to make demands. You are my guest, whether you believe that or not. You will conduct yourself within the confines of my rules. You do as I say, and you will be returned to your colleagues safe and sound within a few weeks."

"A few weeks? Are you fucking crazy?" Yelling made her mouth bleed more. She spit blood onto his boots.

"Nice," he said, stepping closer and drawing back his hand.

Ari jumped back, finding the tent against her back.

His arm struck out, his hand closing around her wrist to right her, squeezing it painfully. "Careful, Ariana. You destroy this tent, you'll be sleeping with me."

"Over my dead body."

"That can be arranged." Eric laughed and put his sunglasses back on. He turned on his heel and walked away.

His threat made her shiver. Her mind was bombarded with thoughts. What the hell had she ever seen in him? How was she going to get out of this predicament? She was ashamed of turning her back on Luca and running off, like a child, the night before she was taken, regretting not talking things out with him. She had a difficult time reconciling the man who flirted with and made love to her with the man she'd found saying good night to Natasha at his tent. Was a search party out for her? She had put all of them at risk by going with Inés. Colossal stupidity.

In the distance, Inés walked toward her with a water bottle and a towel. Eric stopped her and spoke. Ari couldn't hear the conversation, but she did see Inés nod, turn, and walk away in another direction. Eric made a beeline for her.

Ari slumped in the camp chair, moving the fan over her face, watching Eric come. She lowered her head, determined to fight the powerlessness she felt. What was she going to do? She couldn't show weakness. His letters and her interaction with him demonstrated he would only get off on it. She pushed herself upright, forcing herself to look straight at him. "What do you need of me? Why the kidnapping?" She waved her hands around her. "What's your connection to this excavation?"

Eric regarded Ari silently, his fingers steepled under his nose. "Do not give Inés any trouble. Afterward she will take you to our medic. You have injured yourself, several times, and you may have a concussion. I need you as healthy as possible."

"Doctor," Inés called gruffly, her expression resolute. Her demeanor was different in front of Eric. "Come. You will bathe. I have clothes for you to wear."

Ari eyed Inés with resignation. Right now there was no escaping. Armed men walked the perimeter of the large camp, and she suspected there were sentries strategically placed around the excavation. Security at Kanul was a priority, but this was an entirely different magnitude. "Where?"

"The showers. Follow me."

She followed Inés across the clearing and down a hill, closer to the river. "Soap?"

"Of course."

"Do you do everything he says? He's such a son of a bitch."

"The Americano is a good man. He works hard and works us hard. He pays us well, with bonuses based on production. He is tough because he must be, but he is consistent. We know what to expect."

Ari tripped on a root snaking through the ground and went down on all fours, blindsided by Inés's revelation. Eric was the American?

FOR YEARS SHE HAD HEARD rumors about the American—a ruthless looter and thief of priceless antiquities. She had never met anyone who'd run into him though, so she'd dismissed the rumors.

As she walked behind Inés, Ari integrated the man she had known before arriving in Guatemala with the archaeological urban legend. The signs had been there all along, she just wasn't looking for them—occasional secrecy, edginess, and disengagement. There was also the downright iciness directed at her when she had seen him with his family on that spring day, the ensuing violence at her apartment afterward, and his nasty letters. Her eyes now open, she realized he had been stalking her and that his interest in her was tied to what he wanted her here for. Which was what? She gently rubbed her hands over her pounding skull. It was all just too much to wrap her head around, but she had to. Her safe release depended on it.

She had to find a way out of here. Get more information, which required that she be a diligent observer and listener and also strategic. Eric had his opinion of her. However, she had grown tremendously while in Guatemala, and he didn't know that. She had discovered her spine of steel, which was encouraged and celebrated by Luca.

"Doctor…" Inés held the rusting door of the shower stall. "Pull the latch over there," she said, indicating a molding rope in the corner. "Hang your sunglasses over the ledge." She stared at Ari with open malice now that Eric was not around.

The shower consisted of corrugated metal walls on three sides and a door that could be locked from the inside. A small but functional showerhead extended up from one corner of the stall. Ari had privacy, yet she could see three hundred and sixty degrees around her, since the walls only came up to her chin. The lukewarm water, a good distance from the river source, came out in a trickle, and it felt great. Sweat and grime seemed to have embedded in all the layers of her skin. She moved to wash her hair. It was difficult because her hair was knotted and matted in places. And it was painful. She still had a significant headache, and the wound at her hairline began to bleed again.

Most of the activity was concentrated on the large hill. Limestone had been exposed by backhoes since she had been brought here, and now men were frantically digging with shovels. What did they think they might find? They worked fast but not carefully. The energy was manic.

Luca popped into her thoughts again. Fresh tears mingled with the water. She admonished herself to toughen up. Tears weren't going to do her any good. The image of him disheveled, his camp shirt open, and he and Natasha embracing that night, flashed. Was there another reason he had his shirt open and she was there? He had tried to talk to her, warn her about assumptions. "Shit." Ari winced after ripping off a thick scab from scrubbing roughly at her arm. The blood from it and her head added to the thickening muck under her feet. Her body wracked with silent sobs. God, it hurt.

"Hurry up, Doc. This isn't a spa."

"No shit, Sherlock," Ari lobbed back. She was only able to see the top of the woman's dark head.

Inés's voice was sharp. She asked loudly, "What?"

"Was I talking to you?" Ari's voice rose in anger. She was pissed to be reminded that she was Eric's prisoner.

Inés sounded unsure. "Weren't you?"

"Is your name Sherlock?"

"No."

Ari turned the water off and grabbed the towel draped over one of the walls. She squeezed the excess water out of her hair before patting herself dry. "Do you have lotion?"

"Are you kidding me?"

"Well, you have soap. It makes sense that I would ask the question. I didn't pack my wash kit because I had no idea I was being kidnapped."

"No." Inés sneered. "The Americano only asked me to get you soap.

He said you smelled like shit."

"Can you please ask the American asshole? I'm sure he has lotion. I recall he likes to primp. Enjoys the scented stuff, although out here anything scented is an insect magnet."

"You are disrespectful. Watch your mouth. And no, I will not ask him."

"Where are the clothes I'm to wear?"

Inés threw them over the partition. They landed in the rapidly disappearing muddy water.

"Thanks. So considerate of you," Ari said hatefully as she put her arms through the sleeves of a lightweight shirt and began buttoning it. No undergarments. *Shit.* She would go commando. She splayed her legs to keep the oversized pants from falling back down her trim legs and onto the mud floor, struggling with the long belt, now slick from landing in the draining soapy water.

"You take too much time. I'm needed for lunch."

Her voice full of anger, Ari shot back, "Am I a magician? You just threw them over the wall. You could do with some patience. I need my sandals. Please." The last words came as an order. She ducked as her sandals sailed over the partition, only able to catch one as the other thudded to the shower floor, spraying muddy soap onto the borrowed pants. "Nice, Inés. You could have handed them to me."

Mean laughter erupted from the other side. "Let's go." The shower creaked and snapped as Inés banged on it. "Now, Doctor. You are to see the medic."

Ari took a deep breath, steeling herself for lunch and what might follow, and unlocked the door, pushing past Inés and toward the kitchen area.

"What do you think, Ariana?" Eric shook out his paper napkin, as if he were at some nice restaurant, and placed it on his lap.

"What do I think of what? Dinner? Looks better than the beans I've been eating for days, but I lost my appetite when I knew I'd be eating with you."

Eric's fork paused midway to his mouth, his face taking on a deeper shade of color in the flickering lantern light. Annoyance sparked in his eyes, but it was gone just as quickly, as if she'd imagined it. "My discovery. It was quite a surprising find."

"Your discovery? All by yourself? Really? And just what is this discovery? Why am I here? Answer me!" Fury seethed through her. "How did you finance this operation? I have an idea what you're paid by the university. What the hell are you involved in, Eric?"

He leaned in. His heated words were measured as he spoke. "You'd be best advised to lower your voice and not bait me. My fuse with you is short, compounded by this fucking miserable weather."

"Your bravado doesn't impress or frighten me. Even if you are hell-bent on hitting and abusing me to convince yourself that you control me. I doubt you discovered the site by yourself." Ari's rage made her brave. She leaned in, almost nose to nose with him. "Because you just aren't that smart. But if you did, it was just dumb luck. And God help you, you're looting it!" She sat back, her heart pounding. "What the fuck is wrong with you? You consider yourself an archaeologist and anthropologist? What well-respected archaeologist and anthropologist loots? You know antiquity is reverent. You're an embarrassment." She snapped her fingers in the air. "Jesus, you had me abducted to figure out just what it was you discovered. You don't have the expertise, and I do. You need me to explain just what it is you"—her hands swept the space around her in a circle—"have here. I'll give it to you though. Apparently you have the muscle and the connections. What is it?"

"Shut up, Ariana. You always had a bitchy quality to you." He lunged at her, spilling her untouched dinner.

She shot up from her camp chair and out of his reach, yelling, "Stay the hell away from me, you fucking prick." She seethed at Eric. "Take me back. I will not help you."

"You are not going anywhere until I determine you may do so. Is that clear? This is my operation. You will do as I say, when I say," Eric said, glaring at her, and threw his napkin down onto his empty plate. "I will see you at 0700. Do not keep me waiting."

"I won't, only because I have no choice. But keep your distance, or else…"

He stepped close to her, standing mere inches from her face, dropping his voice, yet it was full of warning. "Or else what, Ariana?"

"I responded to your letters. Or should I say, I responded to your wife."

He flinched and stepped back. "You're full of shit. You wouldn't do something like that."

"Wouldn't I? Have you ever known me to lie? Pull your leg?"

"Explain yourself."

"Sir, yes sir." Ari saluted, her anger quelling the fear biting at her ankles. "I wrote your wife."

"You're lying. You don't know her name."

"Am I? Have I ever lied, Eric? That's your forte. You know the answer to that as sure as you stand before me. I addressed it to *my ex-lover's wife*. How do you like them apples? I told her that was why I had to address her in that way because you conveniently left out the facts that you were married and the father of two beautiful teen girls. I explained how we met. How you pursued me. When we were first intimate and that I broke it off immediately upon seeing you all at the ice-cream shop. I even sent her a few selfies of us in our favorite Japanese restaurant—you know, the one where you were nuzzling my neck. Oh, and one of you sleeping in my bed." She snapped her fingers as if to recall something elusive. "Oh, and that one of you and me after the first time, me in that navy-and-white-striped button-down you are so fond of. Remember that one?"

Eric's face paled beneath his tan. "What? You're lying! You deleted those pictures."

"You really are an imbecile. There's a file for deleted images on phones. You didn't know that? And guess what? I uploaded them to my computer for safekeeping, and a flash drive, which is with a trusted friend." She extended her arm, palm up, as he moved even closer. "Step back, you bastard. I apologized to her for my part, but I wanted her to know what an asshole she is married to. And now I see you're even more. A criminal, the scourge of the earth. You steal, lie, cheat, and hurt people. You get off on it."

He grabbed her by the wrist and bent it, forcing her to her knees. She cried out in pain. "I like you on your knees, Ariana. We never got to do this, did we?"

"Fuck you."

He pinched both sides of her face between her jaws as he held her there. The pain was excruciating. Her mouth began to bleed again. He let go and grabbed her by the throat.

"Do you want to?" His breathing was rapid, unsteady. Eric reached to his zipper, before dropping his hand to his side. His voice shook with fury as he spoke. "You little bitch." He applied more pressure, forcing her to a prone position. "You're a liar. People who lie to me don't fare well."

She struggled onto her hands and knees, wiping at the dirt and blood on her face, shaking with fear as much as from anger. Her wrist throbbed in pain where he had grabbed her, and her throat was raw from the pressure of his choke. She looked up at him through her tears, her voice scratchy. "Try it. It's stamped and ready to be mailed from Flores if I am out of contact longer than two days. It's been longer than that. How many days, Eric?" she taunted. "When's the last time you spoke with your wife?"

He laughed and shook his head. "You really are good, Ariana. You had me going. But there is a big hole in your story. You had no idea I would be here." He threw his hands out, palms up, and shrugged his shoulders, laughing again, harder.

"But I did. You said you would see me, in your letter, not the one that waited for me when I arrived in Antigua, but the one in Flores, somehow delivered to me without a postmark. It got me thinking, and I acted." She righted herself onto her knees and struggled up to her feet. "I wanted nothing to do with you ever again. I felt guilty for my part in our relationship. To forgive myself, I told the truth. I wrote it in Antigua, and I did feel better. I thought about the letter all the way up to Flores, and I read it to several of my women colleagues to see if they felt the tone was correct."

"You what?" Eric exploded, slapping his forehead. "You told others about us?"

"Imagine my guilt. Oh, I'm sorry. You couldn't possibly—"

"Shut up! Shut the fuck up! You will keep your mouth shut. These are my people, and they follow my orders. Take your walk and don't be late tomorrow morning."

"And then what?"

"That remains to be seen."

She flipped him a bird with both hands and turned on her heel, her head pounding again. She ran to the kitchen, now vacant. Everyone else had eaten before she and Eric. The humming generator kept it softly lit. She put a hand to her hairline, then looked at it. No blood. The glue the medic applied earlier still held. The acetaminophen was wearing off; she had more in her tent. Her body quaked from what it had taken to spin a story of lies. She prayed that her courage and her fibs held together.

"Are you okay, Doctor?"

Ari jumped. Harry and Beto appeared out of nowhere, looking genuinely concerned. Harry said, "Your mouth is bleeding."

"Where did you come from?" She wiped her mouth on the sleeve of her borrowed shirt. "I will be."

"The American sent us. You are to be walked back, but Nes is waiting for me. Beto will take you."

"I'm not going back to my tent. I can't leave here, but I can refuse to be in his presence."

"He left, super pissed," Beto said. "You shouldn't make him angry, Doc. He does bad things to people when they get him as mad as you made him."

"I just want to get out of here. I didn't ask to be here. I was kidnapped. What the hell is wrong with all of you?"

"He employs us. We do as he says. No questions. The American didn't tell us anything other than to get you and bring you back, pronto."

"How did he know where I was?"

The men exchanged a look between them. Finally, Harry spoke. "I gotta go." He left and quickly vanished in the dark.

"The word is he initially planned on heading your project but pulled out of it after this discovery happened last summer," Beto shared.

"He said it was his discovery."

"Did he? Interesting."

"It wasn't?"

He slowed, stopping and turning, wrestling with his conscience. "Doctor, there was a group of people who made this discovery last summer. The American was part of it. The others… the others vanished."

"Wh—"

He shook his head, his eyes turning hard. "No more talk. There are many ears in this camp. Come on. Let's go."

Night came early in the jungle. Before joining the men around the fire,

Tomás walked the perimeter of their small campsite, asking the gods for safety and guidance.

Luca held out a steaming dish of beans, plantains, and zapote upon his return. "Are you hungry, Tomás?"

"*Gracias*, Doctor. Where did you find the zapote?" He lowered himself to his blanket and balanced the plate on his knees.

"Next to the river. I am not sure if it is fully ripe. It looked like it and peeled easily but…"

"I will eat it and not complain. *Gracias*."

"Gus?" Luca spooned food onto the camp plate.

"Coming. I added more to the fire. It should be good for a while." He rubbed his hands together in an effort to rid them of excess dirt and wood fibers before taking his plate. "*Gracias*, amigo."

Luca filled a plate and sat down with the three men around the fire. After several bites, he said, "Let us plan. What ideas do we have to rescue Dr. Antony?"

"Tasty." Gus licked his fingers and smacked his lips. Nodding, he said, "This is what I think. We need to observe for a day or two, and then we make a plan. We only arrived late afternoon. We do not know the routines they have in place. We need to note them and plan accordingly. I want to count people and have a better idea of the scope of their organization and the site and tent village."

"No. Tomorrow. Reconnaissance early in the morning, plan, rescue. We need to get her out and away as soon as possible. And we need to talk to Dr. Jordaan ASAP." Luca said.

"*Sí*, amigo. But we must think with our heads and not our hearts."

THIRTY FOUR

THROUGH THE PARTIALLY DESTROYED ROOF, the sky was a beautiful robin's-egg blue. Ari removed her sunglasses and slicked the water from her nose and under her eyes. Perspiration mixed with her wet clothing, plastering it to her skin, resulting from the sudden monsoon shower that began as soon as she'd left her tent and subsided when she was twenty meters from where she now stood. She was miserable, hot, and steaming like some fish being cooked in parchment paper. Steam was literally rising from her clothes.

It was hard to believe that Eric's people had opened the temple. They had razed the ground, ripping trees, vines, and other vegetation to reveal the impressive building. Who knows what they might have destroyed in the process. She looked down, following the steps until they were engulfed by the murky shadows, and closed her eyes to adjust to the darkness, wondering again why she was kidnapped to be here. He had yet to reveal exactly. Her eyes had adjusted when she reopened them. Eric was some distance below her. Every once in a while, she glimpsed a glow of light from his headlamp.

His voice boomed, echoing off the ancient pocked walls on either side of her. "Ariana, I'm waiting!"

The steps were scarred, uneven, and huge. Her heart jackhammered in her ears, and fear made her cautious. One misstep and who knew how far she would tumble before landing. Or breaking her neck. She ached to place a hand on one of the ancient walls to steady herself, but disturbing the past went against everything she believed.

She wanted only to spend time here to study the temple and uncover its mysteries. Once-vibrant paintings and numbers in Mayan were evident from paint fading and flaking on the building's plastered walls. Reverence filled her. To her right and left was history she had never seen in her studies and research of the Maya—damaged yet detailed and extensive Mayan glyphs for as far as she could see. Ari knew that Franciscan missionaries had destroyed most of the Mayan codices during the mid-sixteenth century, yet she was sure that these glyphs were indeed part of a codex. A new codex but on the walls instead of bark-paper books. If Matt were here he would know and could translate it, explaining what deities and astrological events it chronicled.

Eric bellowed again.

Annoyed that she had been pulled from her musing, Ari yelled back, "I'm not coming down without a flashlight or headlamp, you asshole!"

Fast, closing steps indicated Eric was coming back up, returning to where she stood. He arrived, huffing and puffing in her face. Two Maya accompanied him. She glared into his pale-blue eyes. How had she ever found them remarkable? Now she agreed with the Ajal's gossip. His eyes were glacial, ghostly. She shivered.

"Afraid?" he asked.

"Of course not, you pig," she retorted, stepping back, wiping the sweat and rain from her face with her forearm. "Your breath leaves something to be desired."

He laughed and leaned forward. "Interesting since you used to practically drool when I kissed you, if I remember correctly. And pant, like a bitch in heat."

"You're foul. I never drooled, and I certainly never panted. Your kissing was elementary at best."

Fear lurched into her throat as rage filled his expression. He spoke to the Maya in Spanish, telling them to wait below. They switched their headlamps back on before descending.

"You are to stay with one of the Maya or me. That way you have plenty of light and supervision." Eric grabbed her by the forearm, squeezing hard to make his point, his tone venomous. "There won't be a next time. You disrespect me in front of others, you suffer the consequences. Understood? You will watch your mouth and your tone. This is your last warning."

"Ow! Eric, stop!" Tears sprang to her eyes. "You're going to give me more bruises." She pulled away. "Does hurting me make you feel like a big man? Because you aren't. Catch my meaning?"

Eric's hand shot up, ready to strike. A throat cleared behind Ari. Eric lowered his hand so fast it was as if she had imagined it.

A deeply accented voice said, "Doctor. We should go down."

"Right." Surprise registered on Eric's face, and his eyes warned Ari once again. To the man behind her, he said, "You need your headlamp. Dr. Antony can walk between us. What is your name again? I forget."

"Carlos, sir."

"Oh, yes. I have trouble with names sometimes. We have so many Maya here assisting," he said, turning on his headlamp.

Carlos's voice sounded familiar. Was it possible? She didn't dare turn around.

"Stay between us, Ariana. You don't have a headlamp," he said over his shoulder. "Carlos, watch that Dr. Antony doesn't slip or fall. We need her expertise down here." He led the way, disappearing down the steep steps into the black void.

"*Sí*," Carlos said to the space vacated by Eric.

She turned to look at the man behind her. Her eyes grew huge, and a big smile wreathed her face. He smiled back but kept his mouth closed, his dark eyes pleading for her not to give him away. He nodded and extended his closed hand over hers, depositing something that felt cool and delicate. It couldn't be. But it was. She held her necklace. Tears pricked her eyes and hope of being rescued soared. Her message had been found.

"Where the hell are you?" Eric yelled from below. "Hurry up."

She yelled back, "I had something in my sandal, cutting into my toe. I'm putting it back on now. Be patient." Heeding Eric's earlier warning, she added in a softer tone, "Please."

With shaking hands, she undid the clasp, bringing the necklace up to her neck and fastening it, pulling gently to make sure it was secure. Her hand closed around the hummingbird. She prayed for safe passage and slipped it underneath the generous shirt. Taking a steadying breath, she stepped off the uneven large step, fear bubbling in her belly about what might be in the dark farther on.

Carlos moved closer, his headlight illuminating a few steps ahead of them. "Slow and steady. This is dangerous." He placed his hand on her shoulder and said, "We must be patient."

"Thank you. My equilibrium is off."

What little daylight came through the ceiling disappeared into blackness, lowering the temperature considerably. Ari rolled down the long sleeves of her shirt. The going was slow. The light from Carlos's headlamp illuminated the walls, revealing various characters and mythical fearsome lords of the underworld. She paused when she realized that the stairs led to Xibalba, what the Maya called the underworld. Carlos was silent behind her. Typically, Xibalba was entered through a cave or quiet water. Obviously, this was neither, which meant Ari, Carlos, and Eric were inside a temple created to entomb a Mayan king. And there was the possibility of human remains. Now she was sure why she had been kidnapped. Eric needed knowledge of Xibalba and forensic expertise. This discovery was going to rock the annals of archaeology, anthropology, and Mayan culture.

On approach, she had only glimpsed a decimated ruin tucked into the large hill through the roaring rain; the temple had been swallowed up by centuries of earth and creeping jungle. During dinner last night and prior to their blowup, Eric boasted that the temple and extended site had been discovered through camera-equipped drones, to create a 3-D map of this area. Furthermore, data from satellites and the lidar technique were used to detect and measure changes in the terrain. She had remained quiet and pushed the food around her plate, floored by what he'd shared with her.

He had completed the survey of this site in mere hours, whereas several members of the teams working Kaq and Rax were assigned to continue surveying the areas throughout the excavation. Ari had shaken her head, dumbfounded. *Who is underwriting this?* A purist, she preferred to learn and discover by immersing herself in the environment, just like she preferred real sugar to substitutes. Nothing compared. But she also knew that lidar's data points were far more accurate and cost-effective when compared to hours collecting measurements and profiles.

Eric and the two Maya waited on a landing. "Keep up with me and pay attention. The steps are uneven and much larger than you are used to. Some have chipped and crumbled. One slip could take you to the bottom." He stepped down.

He sounds like he cares, when he really only cares about what I can tell him. "Eric, please. Wait. Can we, um, Carlos and I, hang here for a while? I would appreciate taking some time to study what covers these walls."

Eric didn't look as though he was convinced.

"This is why you sent your thugs to get me—because of my expertise in the *Popol Vuh* and Mayan mythology, correct? The paintings tell that this is the temple of the king. This architecture represents the nine levels of Xibalba." Pointing to the wall, she added, "Look. See what the art portrays?"

Dismissive in tone, he came back to face her. "Not much of anything. Looks like disintegrated fragmented paintings."

"Well, I see souls from the underworld. See? Here and"—her hands moved expressively—"here. See? The flesh is depicted as separating from the body." He looked where her hands guided him. "And look at the eyes. They hang from their sockets." She turned to the wall on her right, pointing again. "This person—the king, I believe—is falling backward. And these? These are the gaping centipede jaws of Xibalba. The king is falling into the underworld. This here"—she pointed to another part of the painting—"this is one of the massive underworld rivers. It is blood, filled with scorpions." She snapped her fingers by her temple, trying to recall more about Xibalba. "The names escape me right now."

She looked upward thoughtfully, carefully so that she didn't fall. "I believe we are in the second tier. Have you seen a door or an opening where a door might have been?"

He paused, then said, "Don't leave her side, Carlos. If she disappears, you will be held accountable." His expression of annoyance changed to interest. "You're Maya. Do you think what Dr. Antony says is true? Might this be a portal to the underworld?"

Ari noticed Carlos was frowning but not because of Eric's threats. He appeared worried. His breath was shaky as he answered quietly, "*Sí.* This is a king's tomb." He pointed to where the stairs disappeared behind Eric. "And the stairs lead to Xibalba." He shuddered. "We should not be here long. I will stay up here with the doctor."

"Did you see a door or a door opening?" Eric looked around. "I don't see one."

"We'll look." She reached out her hand to Eric, feeling he was capitulating. "Can I use your notebook to make notes and drawings?"

"It's your lucky day. I'm feeling generous, Ariana. I happen to have an extra." He knelt down and pulled his pack from his shoulder. Withdrawing the notebook, he said, "And here is a pen. You have fifteen minutes." He made a show of setting the timer on his watch.

"I need more time."

"No. If I remember, you're pretty good at the glyphs. I also want you to determine which king. I need you farther down. There are remains."

She didn't want to be down there with him. Something felt off, and it wasn't Eric. Carlos was nervous. "I'm not that good. Not my specialty. I have a better chance if you give me more time. The paintings are in pretty bad shape—"

"Twenty minutes. That's it. It's unfortunate we couldn't snag the epigrapher traveling with you. He's got to be the best. We'll find a way to bring him in later." Eric reset his watch, his eyes ghostly as he ordered, "Don't try my patience."

She blanched. Eric had considered taking Matt. She set her watch. He turned and descended, disappearing quickly, his headlight beam ricocheting off the walls below and then vanishing completely as his steps became silent. Carlos squeezed her shoulder—reminding Ari that he had her back. She took another deep breath and opened the notebook, hope sparking.

"I don't know much about the glyphs. Do you?"

"No, Doctor. Tata does and Dr. Matt, but…" He opened his hands and shrugged. "I do know these things. This temple connects to Xibalba. The Americano should not be here. He does not respect it. Bad things happen to those who don't respect the past."

His warning filled her with foreboding. "I wish Matt were here, of his own free will. Between us, we might be able to figure out what we are looking at, what this represents." She knelt, placing the notebook on her thighs as a writing surface. "This temple is astounding, and it has been untouched for centuries. I feel it here." She placed her palm over her heart. "Do you feel it, Carlos? We are moving toward the sacred."

"*Sí*, Doctor. There is ancient energy here. Because you feel it and believe it, you will be protected. The same is true for me. Xibalba is alive."

She set to work, doing the best she could to copy glyphs and paintings into the notebook. Every time Ari filled a page, she tore it out, folding it and putting it in the inside hidden pocket of her pants, thankful she drew fast. She drew something basic to give to Eric later. Ari glanced at her watch; she had only minutes left. "Can you follow me down one more tier? Your light is glancing off another painting. I think I have just enough time to capture—"

Screaming erupted below them. It sounded far away. A man keened, his cries carrying up the stairs and echoing off the walls. "Help me! Help me!"

Eric. Omigod. Ari shot to standing so abruptly she tottered. Carlos grabbed her forearm, keeping her from plunging down the steps.

The keening and calls for help continued.

"What do we do? Someone is hurt." She began to shake.

Someone was running. One of the Maya who had accompanied Eric was suddenly in front of them, breathing heavily. He spoke to Carlos in Q'eqchi', and Carlos translated to her. The Americano had slipped on crumbling rock, falling into a ravine-like place below the last level. From what the Maya could tell, both arms and legs were broken. He lay partially submerged in water. He appeared to be in a lot of pain.

Several more Maya joined them on the landing.

"He will quickly go into shock, Carlos. We need to keep him warm. He needs blankets, quickly. Shit. How do we bring him up?"

He directed the men to get blankets, potable water, and ropes, and to rally more help. They turned, taking the steps at a pace bordering on a run.

"They will be back as soon as possible," he said. "It will be a long, tricky rescue. We may hurt him more as we bring him out, or it could finish him."

"What do you mean finish him?"

He was silent, but the expression on his face relayed his thoughts.

Ari felt sick to her stomach. Despite how Eric had treated her, despite the asshole he was and the fact that he looted antiquity, she could not leave him below. "How far are the other men?"

"They are close. Let me help you out to safety, then I will go get them."

"No, I want to stay. I know some basic first aid. I can help somehow. I'll go down and talk to him, keep him awake, while you—"

"Not right now. You need to go out of the temple. You need to focus on your footing so that you don't end up like him. Dr. Ari, Luca is with them. He needs you to be okay." He shook his head, looked around at the crumbling walls, then up to the partially caved-in ceiling. "Perhaps…"

Luca was close. She smiled, blinking through her tears. Goose bumps covered her arms as cool air raced up from below. The back of her neck prickled as she asked, "Perhaps what?"

"Maybe the gods had enough of his pillaging and his black soul."

ARI SAT WRINGING HER HANDS under the awning of her tent. She looked at her watch. An hour had passed since Carlos had escorted her out of the temple. He had described what he had seen—Eric lying in the shallow, murky water, his arm and legs bent at inconceivable angles, labored breathing, his skin gray under his deep tan. He alternately moaned, pleading for one of them to end the pain, or closed his eyes and gritted his teeth, his face drenched in perspiration. Carlos had covered him with a blanket and said a silent prayer, then radioed for help from the command center.

Tired of sitting, she stepped out into the stifling afternoon and paced back and forth until the first fat raindrops caused her to retreat back under the awning. Loud rumbling signaled that the rain was about to grow worse. She moved closer to the tent flap in an effort to stay dry. A torrential downpour and spectacular light show erupted and then disappeared just as fast as it had started. The sun came out, but the air was like breathing water.

The unmistakable chopping sound of a helicopter grew louder. The percussion from the blades and the rotor reverberated in her body. Ari walked toward it to observe. Branches and leaves whipped as it hovered briefly over the open area by the kitchen, in preparation to land. It was larger and sleeker than the others she'd seen since being brought to Ajal, resembling the medevac helicopters back in the US.

The door opened after the blades slowed to a stop. Natasha jumped out. She wore a dark Kevlar vest emblazoned with white letters on its back. Ari had no trouble reading INTERPOL from where she was. She unzipped the screen and stepped inside and watched in disbelief, her heart ricocheting against her rib cage and sweating bullets in the stifling tent. What the hell? What in fuck was going on? What was Natasha doing here?

Natasha's back was to Ari as she yelled to the Maya who had been with Eric in the temple. "Where is he?" She switched to Spanish, asking again. Nodding, Natasha spoke into a handheld radio, then motioned to the medics who had climbed out behind her, yelling, "We need the basket, blankets, and bags. Bring all the ropes. We'll try to fashion some type of winch. He's at the bottom of a temple. Stat!"

Natasha and the medics moved out at a jog behind the Maya, with their equipment, quickly disappearing over the rise in front of the temple. Ari stepped out of the tent and switched on the portable fan. She sat in one of the camp chairs, feeling it was the safest place for her.

Percussive whirring indicated another chopper was coming in. It slowed and hovered, landing farther away. Guatemalan militia, and men wearing bulletproof vests with INTERPOL on them, exited and fanned out over the Ajal site, which was now surprisingly sparse of humans. They worked together, herding Eric's remaining associates to the clearing. Mindful of the guns, his associates followed directions, kneeling and bringing their hands behind them to be cuffed.

Activity broke out on the other side of camp. What now? It seemed there were more visitors. She rose, her heart skittering. There was no mistaking it. Luca stood with a small group of Mayan men. He hadn't spotted her.

Oh yes, he had. An enormous smile lit his handsome face. He said something to the men—some of whom Ari recognized from the Kanul project—and strode rapidly toward her. She ran as fast as her wobbly legs could carry her, launching into Luca, crying uncontrollably.

His strong arms circled her, pulling her closer and back into the shelter of the jungle shade, one hand stroking her back as he kissed the top of her head, murmuring, "Thank God you are okay." He gently moved her away from him but continued to hold on to her. Pushing his sunglasses up to rest on top of his hat, his voice dropped as he asked, "You are okay?"

She nodded, noticing how tired he looked. Dark shadows were evident under his beautiful green eyes. "For the most part. I'm tired. Sometimes I'm light-headed or have a headache, but maybe I'm dehydrated."

"And what about these?" His thumb gently brushed the thick scabs on her forearms. "And this?" His eyes took on an angry glint as his fingertips grazed the fading purple of her cheek. "I heard about this."

Her eyes opened wide with disbelief. "How?"

"We have been taking turns watching, planning on when to strike. I understand you also hit your head. Show me where."

Ari's hand drifted to the area above her temple. She grimaced as Luca gently pulled the dressing off and examined her wound, palpating it gently. It still hurt.

"This dressing is fresh, as is the glue. Was it infected?" He pressed the dressing back onto her skin.

"Yes. The medic debrided and cleaned it of infection and gave me an antibiotic. He also gave me something for my headaches. How—" She shook her head, tears spilling down her face. "How did you know about my head?"

Luca turned to the older Maya standing behind the others, a man Ari did not know. Gesturing and smiling warmly, he explained, "Tata, this is Dr. Ariana Antony, Ari, the woman we have been tracking. Ari, Tata is Carlos's grandfather and a shaman. He has been instrumental in our effort to find you. He determined you sustained a head wound very close to the area where you were kidnapped. That is how I knew."

Ari stepped forward and extended her arms. "May I?" she pleaded.

Tata nodded and gave her a beaming smile.

She threw her arms around the small man, squeezing him tightly. Her voice quaked with emotion. "*Gracias!* Thank you!"

Tata's wise eyes held Ari's gaze. He spoke slowly in Q'eqchi'. Carlos stepped in as translator. "Tata says he is happy, Dr. Ari. He says you give good hug."

Tata placed his hands on her shoulders, as if reading her, and spoke again.

"He says you are healing. Allow Luca to help you. In time, you will be whole." Carlos mirrored his grandfather's movements, touching his head and heart. "Here and here. Tata says he should go to the temple. There are unhappy gods, and he wishes everyone to be safe."

"I feel better that Tata has determined you will be all right, but I will go over you thoroughly." A dangerously sexy smile broke over Luca's face. "Come here. God, how I have missed you." He pulled her into his arms, speaking into her hair. "I am so sorry that I hurt you. Please forgive me. There was and never has been anything between Nat and me."

Ari returned Luca's kiss with everything she felt. Smiling coyly, she said, "I look forward to your medical opinion, Doctor." She sighed into his broad chest. "I've missed you too, Luca. More than I can tell you. I'm sorry I ran off and you were trying to talk to me. It was wrong of me not to listen." She tightened her arms around his waist.

"Get a room, you two!" a voice behind them said.

"Matt!" Luca said. Confusion covered his face. "I do not understand. You flew on this?" He indicated the helicopter. "With Natasha?"

Matt rocked up on his toes in excitement. "Yup, what a surprise, huh? She asked me to stay put until things settled down. You can't see this site from the air. It's camouflaged."

"Indeed," Luca said.

Ari looked from Luca to Matt and then back to Luca. "What am I missing?"

"Natasha has been secretly working with Interpol's Heritage Crime Division, or something like that, helping to expose looters plundering antiquity. Cool how you knew and kept it quiet, Luca. Super slick."

Luca remained silent.

"I overheard one of your radio calls with Natasha. Of course I told— "

"Me!" Meg bounded out of the helicopter behind Matt. "Girlfriend, you look worse for wear. Come here. I was so worried about you," she said, yanking Ari out of Luca's arms and into hers and about squeezing her in two. "Hi, Boss. You look bushed." Meg gave Luca a kiss on the cheek.

"We're here to help get the American out. We'll be back." Matt grabbed Meg's hand. "Come on, sweetie."

"Luca," Ari said as she watched the two go. "Matt is going to shit when he sees what's in that temple. If I'm right, it's a new codex. There are crumbling paintings and walls and walls of glyphs, depicting, from what very little time I had to study them, a massive story."

"Seriously? Is that what—" He threw his hands out. "You are saying this site is—"

"Significant. The temple is a portal to Xibalba. It's the temple of a king. I want to go back in and study the temple. Not now but soon, before I return back to the States. And I'd feel better with Carlos. Thank God he showed up when he did. And Tata too. Does anyone have a camera in your group? Mine died, so I brought… Oh, my phone. It may still have power since I turned it off."

He kissed her deeply, murmuring against her mouth, "You are talking too much." Breaking the kiss, he looked into her eyes. "Easy, sweetheart. You have been through quite an ordeal."

"Come with me to see it. As soon as they get Eric out, of course."

"Eric?" His voice turned deadly. "As in the Eric you told me about?"

"Yes. Turns out he's the American. Can you believe it? He orchestrated my kidnapping because he needed my expertise."

"Stay here." Luca gently pushed her away and strode toward the temple, fury evident in every step he took.

Ari stayed put, unsure what to do during Eric's extraction. She mulled over Natasha's unexpected appearance and her role in all this and that Luca had known she was with Interpol. Something just didn't add up.

She wandered down to the kitchen to eat since she had nothing to do but wait while Eric was extracted. Ari surveyed the mess. Food, plates, and utensils that hadn't been taken were strewn all over the area, along with trash. Insects coated the discarded and half-eaten food, and small rodents scurried away when she approached. A few bins remained. All perishable food was gone, as were the coolers. Two grills were stripped bare, and it looked as though someone had tried to dismantle the filtration system. Bags of rice and beans shared a shelf with a large pot. Ari laughed to herself. The Maya left, but they made sure they were paid. She wandered over to the remaining bins and opened them. They were empty.

"How's the grub?"

"Meg! Did they get him out? There isn't any, except rice and beans, which need to be cooked. This place has been tossed."

"We're pulling out as soon as they load the American and the other bad men." She hung her arm loosely around Ari's shoulders. "We have food on the helicopter. We can eat and talk while the pilot flies us back."

"You, Matt, Luca, and me?"

"Yup. Natasha and her Interpol associates are taking the American to a hospital to address his injuries. They will be escorted by a few Guatemalan military coppers. The rest of the coppers are taking the arrested men somewhere to await charges and whatever follows from there."

She held up her finger. "Just clarifying. When you say coppers, you mean police, not helicopters?"

"Yup, as in the Guatemalan special operations, the Kaibiles."

"Whoa. Those guys have a scary reputation. I wouldn't want them taking me anywhere. Natasha is brave to ride with them."

"She holds her own, let me tell you," Meg said, sitting. "She has a whole different vibe when she steps into the Interpol identity. The bitchiness disappears, but she has a don't-fuck-with-me thing going. I think the Guatemalans didn't know what to think of her, especially because she was giving the orders to the other Interpol agents, who happened to be men."

Ari was dumbfounded by everything being revealed. She sat across from Meg at the long table, elbows resting on the table, knuckles supporting her chin. "A lot has happened. I need time to process all this."

"We all do. This summer will go down in excavation history. Let me briefly bring you up-to-date. It was a treacherous walk down to where Eric was. Did you go down there, girlfriend?"

Ari shook her head. "I was going to. He demanded that I go down there. I was on the second tier with Carlos, looking over wall paintings and what I believe is an undiscovered codex, when we heard his screaming." She wiped at the tears wetting her cheeks. "Oh my God, Meg. It was awful. Carlos took me out, tended to Eric, and radioed for help. Then you all showed up, suspiciously fast."

"We were in the vicinity. Luca radioed earlier, saying they had found you." She reached across the table and held Ari's hands in hers. "Matt and I helped with the ropes. I couldn't see much. It was black as hell, except where the lights lit the walls and water." She paused, tapping the table in front of her. "Otherworldly… Yeah, that's the perfect word to describe it. Luca had to be held back when he got down there. Looked like he wanted to tear Eric apart. It took, like, five men to hold him back. What a miserable scene. I think we almost lost the bastard, but Natasha's and Luca's training kicked in. They were amazing, along with the medics. Got him stabilized. We did our best not to cause damage. Tata… You met him, right?"

Ari nodded.

"He has this amazing presence. The Maya were so reverent with him. He also tended to the American and said a bunch of words in some Mayan language. Carlos said he was talking to the lords of Xibalba so that we all could exit safely. Omigod. That's why they took you! To help explain all this!"

"Yeah, and examine any remains. The temple is that of a king. It's been sealed for centuries from what we can tell. It's very likely that the king is entombed. There are probably others as well."

"Wow. That's unbelievable." Meg swatted at a passing fly and scratched her nose. "Matt wants to come back. He was over the moon with excitement, said you were right, there's a new codex within the temple." She stopped talking, looking past Ari. "They're coming out now. I guess he's okay to fly for further treatment."

Ari rose and walked toward the ambulatory basket, meeting Natasha, who blocked her access. Eric moaned loudly behind her.

"You don't want to see him. He's been given pain meds and is delirious, raving about being marked by Xquic. He has a tattoo of a serpent extending down one side of his face. It's the oddest thing. Carlos said his face was unmarked before he descended," Natasha said.

Xquic. The Blood Maiden. The Hero Twins' mother. Ari shivered, and the hair stood up on the back of her neck. Her voice was full of disbelief. "Carlos is right. Eric's face was unmarked. I don't understand all this, Natasha. But… thank you."

Natasha slipped her sunglasses off. Compassion filled Natasha's eyes, turning them to slate. "I have to accompany him, Ari. We've been looking for the American a long time. Eric Schaus did a great job covering his tracks and hiding in plain sight. I have mounds of paperwork to fill out, so I doubt I'll be back before the project closes for the summer. You've been through a traumatic experience. I understand he is a horrible, violent man. I wish you the best, truly. And I wish you the best with Luca. He deserves to be happy, and you make him happy."

"I thought you disliked me, as well as the idea of him and me. I was certain of it. Why the change of heart?"

Natasha's warm smile was tinged with sadness. "We discovered Eric was the American before he took his position as dean at your university. Interpol was delving into all his relationships. You were under suspicion due to your affair with him. His wife and daughters were also under surveillance. I kept an eye on both of you all year and was added as Luca's assistant after you agreed to participate.

"Luca knew why I was here, to track down and apprehend the American. However, he had no idea Eric was the American or that you were also under suspicion. I apologize for the subterfuge. I hope you can forgive me, Ari. Rumors were that Eric might surface in Guatemala. He had been here before. People disappeared. It's awful you were sucked into all this, how Eric involved you in all this. I have some"—she held her hand up, her thumb and forefinger just a breadth apart, and smiled again—"regret how well I played my part. From how you reacted, I was very convincing. It was all part of my cover. Most importantly, I want to clarify something. Luca and I were talking about the project the night before you were abducted. We had some project issues to deal with. When I think back, I realize it appeared otherwise. I did not mean for our discussion and friendship to be misconstrued. I'm sorry if you thought differently. I think you're remarkable, Ari, and I think the world of him. I believe you are who Luca needs."

She totally fooled me. Wow. Her voice broke with emotion. "Thank you, from the bottom of my heart. Take care of yourself." She reached up and hugged Natasha. "Be safe."

Ari stepped back as the blades and tail rotor roared to life, glancing at Eric, whose eyes were closed in pain. She glimpsed the tattoo on his face as they loaded him. She shuddered. A strong arm encircled her waist. *Luca.*

Natasha disappeared into the helicopter and came back out, carrying her vermillion suitcase by its handle. "Come with me, Luca. Ari, you can come as well."

They accompanied Natasha back to the kitchen where she lifted the suitcase onto one of the tables and opened the lock. She extracted a red accordion folder and handed it to Luca. "I was legally bound to confidentiality by Interpol. I only shared with you what I was allowed. I have things to tie up with the American, so I'll call you in the next day or two, get you current. Until then, read what is in the file." Her eyes swept her surroundings. "This site will be secured by Interpol, working in tandem with Guatemala's Bureau of Educational and Cultural Affairs until someone reputable can take over. The infrastructure and supplies will remain. This is an exceptional find."

She nodded at Luca and Ari and Meg, and Matt, who had joined them. "Can I clarify anything else before I leave?"

Meg spoke. "We, myself and Ari, have been dying to know. What's with your red sidekick port?"

Natasha laughed. "So I don't misplace it. I carry important and confidential reports and information. So, logistics… Two more helicopters are en route and will arrive shortly. One will fly you all back to Kanul. The other will escort the American's unsavory comrades to Guatemala City for processing. Interpol agents will accompany you and stay at Kanul, escorting you safely back to Flores when you and the team are ready. John Robert is the lead agent. He has a remedial understanding and appreciation for archaeology, so he won't drive you too crazy." Her voice grew more serious. "Luca, it's likely there will be unrest and a possible uptick in crime due to this site being shut down. I suspect the American promised the Maya payment and hasn't followed through." She squeezed his bicep, emotion filling her eyes. "So stay alert, Big Guy. Keep Carlos and his friends and family close, especially Tata. Having a powerful shaman such as him can help."

Luca pulled Natasha into his arms, giving her a hug, then releasing her. "Thank you, Nat." He smiled warmly, his eyes crinkling with humor. "And sorry that I was so tough on you, my far-more-accomplished-assistant-than-I-realized."

Natasha entered the helicopter after the medics secured Eric. She waved at Ari, Luca, Matt, and Meg, yelling over the thumping and winding of the craft. "You all take care. Keep in touch. I look forward to hearing about everything." The door closed and locked behind her, and the helicopter rose, quickly disappearing over the jungle canopy.

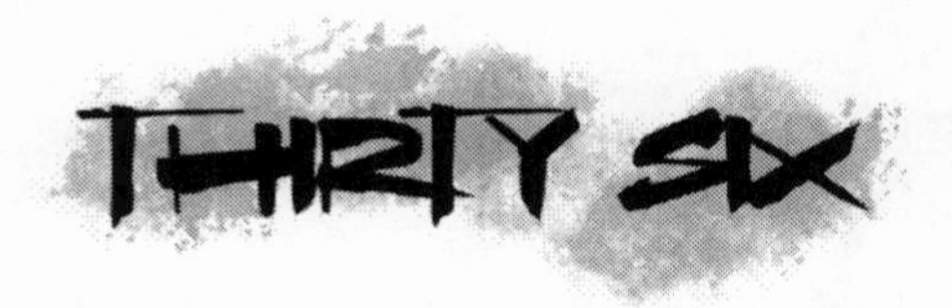

ARI SLOWED AND STARED, A stupefied smile lighting her face, and she squealed with glee. "Luca! How? It's safe, right?"

"It is," he said with satisfaction. "You have been talking about little other than a good bath since you woke from your very long sleep. I asked our Mayan friends where you could bathe. They showed me this place." He paused, enjoying her giddy reaction. The timbre of his voice changed. "You had me scared, Ari."

"I guess I was incredibly tired," she replied, spellbound by the river gently lapping at the green bank in front of her. It was clearer than any water she had seen over the past weeks. No churning. No muddy eddies. No white water. Instead, it was calm, beckoning. The sun sparkled off the surface, creating a magical scene as water bugs and dragonflies played on its surface.

"You were recovering from injuries." He stepped in front of her, cutting off the view. "You are still weak, even after two days of sleep. I see it in your movements. Your face is drawn, and there is paleness under your freckles. You appear to have lost some weight too."

"Maybe just a teensy." She began to argue but then amended her statement under his intense look. "Okay. Maybe my strength is not my usual."

"And?"

"And my clothes are looser. I'm sure I'll fill back out. I mean, I eat like a horse. You know that. Hell, you've commented on it more than a few times, to the point I was getting embarrassed…" She looked at her sandal-clad feet, feeling uncertain. "Are you worried I won't?"

"There is not so much to you. I just want you to be healthy." He slid his thumb under Ari's chin, gently lifting her face, encouraging her to look him in the eye. He pushed away stray curling tendrils that had escaped her french braid. "Are you worried I have lost interest?" His expression flickered, moving from concern to a crooked, sexy smile. "That has not happened," he said, enclosing her hand.

Ari's breath quickened, and her stomach flipped.

"Come with me."

They set out, meandering away from the river and walking farther from camp. "Where are we going? What all is in that bag? I thought I was going to get to dip in the water. I want to wash," she said, whining like a child.

"So many questions."

Frustrated, she stopped, yanking her hand from his. "Where are we going?" she demanded. "I just want to get clean." She spoke louder and faster, her hands clenched at her sides. "I want to wash the dirt of Eric, Inés, Beto, and Harry off me. The taint of being kidnapped. I feel so… so dirty—" Sobbing washed out her words.

"Ari." He gathered her to him, stroking her back softly while she let it all out.

She snuggled in deep, drawing strength from his silence and solid presence, finally crying herself out. The sure beating of his heart and his gentle touch calmed her.

"Better?" he asked.

She nodded into his chest.

He placed his hands on her shoulders, gently pushing her back from him. "Walk with me? I have a surprise for you," Luca said, smiling, offering his hand to her. Although pleasant, holding hands was not enough for him, so he gathered her to his side and slipped his thumb into the belt loop of her pants, pulling her alongside him. His body stirred from the multiple points of contact. She fit perfectly under his arm—granted she had definitely lost weight. And although he towered over her, they walked comfortably in lockstep. "Not too much farther." He ached to extract his thumb from her belt loop and run his palm over her ass. *How I have missed her, worried about her.*

"I hear humming. No, like"—she cocked her head, listening—"like loud rumbling. Rapids? I don't know if I have the strength to bathe in those. Let's go back to where we were."

"We could, but I believe you would be disappointed." Luca pushed through dense vegetation, pulling her behind him. A few more steps and they were again at the riverbank. On the other side of the river was a waterfall. He dropped the bag and released her hand, his green eyes glowing with a mischievous glint, daring her. "I wanted to grant your wish. Want to get wet?"

"A waterfall! It's perfect, better than a shower!" Ari threw her arms around his neck and squeezed, peppering him with tiny kisses all over his face.

He kissed the top of her head, then wrinkled his nose. "Ah, you are a little ripe. Do you have enough energy? Maybe we should walk back." Luca teased her.

"No! I'm fine, really." She blushed, stammering, "Is this, like, private?"

"Yes. I have asked that you not be disturbed. And that if we do not return by"—he looked at his watch—"sixteen thirty, some of our colleagues will come looking for us. It is thirteen twenty now." He smiled wickedly, reaching down to the bottom of his tee to strip it from his body. "I propose to hold you and wash you since you are weak," he said through the shirt sliding over his face. Free of it, he winked, his hands moving to his buckle. "Are you bathing in your clothes?"

It was impossible to tear her eyes from his broad shoulders, leanly muscled chest, and washboard abs. Her heart raced, and her breathing hitched as understanding dawned. Over three hours of privacy to bathe with him, be with him, in the afternoon of what should be a workday. "Um, no. But what I wouldn't do for—"

"Soap?" Luca asked, extracting an unopened bar of soap from the bag he had dropped.

"Hey, that looks like my camp soap!"

"It is. Forgive her, but Meg went through your kit at my request. I thought you might appreciate yours over mine." Unwrapping the soap and lifting it to his nose, Luca inhaled. "It smells like you—cinnamon and honey. You can be upset with me." He dropped the wrapper and soap back into the bag.

"Are you kidding? You're so thoughtful. I feel totally unkempt." Ari began unbuttoning her shirt, then hesitated. "Aren't you going to turn around?"

"I would prefer not to. May I remind you that I have seen you? All of you?"

"It was dark."

He smiled slyly. "We had a lantern, remember? I assure you, I saw my fill." Huskily, he said, "You are beautiful."

He thinks I'm beautiful. A broad smile blanketed her face. "Fine then." Playfully she turned her backside to him and shed her clothes, wading into the knee-deep, refreshing water and moving toward the waterfall. It looked perfect, not too big or powerful yet strong enough to satisfy her need to slough off her kidnapping. "Omigod." She sighed to herself. "The water is heavenly."

Ari reached the waterfall and paused, transfixed by its music and beauty. An iridescent sheet of water rushed out of thick foliage covering the jutting rock wall some twenty meters above her, plinking onto rocks and into the river. Nestled back and under the waterfall was a shallow tranquil pool of water and a flat green expanse of earth, dappled by moving sunshine. Large leafy plants bobbed gently along the pool's edges, hiding a grotto beyond. She took an eager step forward, giggling as the sparkling mist covered her skin, cooling it in the midafternoon heat and humidity. Ari felt the filth from her ordeal wash away. Reaching up, she pulled the elastic band from her hair and loosened the braid.

Luca splashed in, following in her wake. His eyes scanned the surrounding jungle and the water for any trouble while appreciating his delicious view of the petite woman he was crazy about. Her beauty took his breath away. She resembled a river nymph. Her wet titian hair hung past her shoulder blades, and freckles chased over her body. Water sluiced over her lean legs, mesmerizing him. He remembered all too well what they felt like wrapped tightly around him when he pumped into her. He shook his head, gently stroking her shoulder, then trailing down her arm to clasp her fingers. Speaking into her ear, just before pulling her under the waterfall, he asked, "Enticing, yes?"

"Yes." Ari shivered from his touch. The desire in his eyes had her full attention. "It's perfect. How on earth did you find it?" Pointing, she said, "Look. There's even a grotto back there, behind those large leaves. See it?"

"I do," he said, smiling lazily. He pulled her forward to stand with him under the cascading water, soaking them. "Bath, my lady?" Luca extracted the soap before tossing the bag into a drier area of the grotto. Teasingly, he pulled the soap away from her reaching hand, smirking. "I will wash you."

Ari's eyes grew big. Her heart galloped in her chest, making it hard for her to breathe, to speak. She took a deep breath to try to slow her heart, exhaling. "Okay."

"Head first." He quickly worked the bar into a lather. "Get your hair good and wet."

She stepped closer to allow him to work the suds in more easily. His strong fingers massaged, working in circles all over her scalp—the crown of her head and methodically down to her front hairline, becoming very gentle when he neared her wound. He paid particular attention to the area around her ears and above the nape of her neck. The only people who had ever washed Ari's hair were her mother when she was young and her hairdresser—and that was pleasant but nothing close to what she was experiencing now. Luca washing her hair bordered on orgasmic. She closed her eyes, attempting to still the sensations wreaking havoc in her body. A moan escaped her.

He worked the soap lower—over her neck, shoulders, reaching behind to her upper back. Ari was silky, smooth, and his erection throbbed in appreciation. Her tight nipples were evident under the suds sliding over her body. Luca's awareness of how he affected Ari excited him. His hands bracketed her waist and slid down her hips. As much as he wanted to touch her, he wanted to build the sexual tension between them. He yearned to taste her parted lips. But not yet. Instead, he stepped back slightly and laughed, teasing her. "Am I washing too hard?"

She shook her head in response.

"Why are your eyes closed?"

She responded by opening her eyes. They were dilated, and her face flushed as she took in the glory of him. Her mouth formed a silent *O*.

"Wash me," he said thickly, handing her the soap. His hair hung loose, falling just below his massive shoulders. He bent over so she could lather his head. Her movements mirrored his. She felt as though she would faint from wanting him as her hands worked into his hair and scalp and then traveled over his neck and shoulders.

"Turn," she said, her voice cracking. She breathed deeply before soaping his sculpted back, working lower as she admired his body. Suds and bubbles ran down his muscular legs, into the river, dissipating in the moving water. Her hands moved more slowly as she washed him. Every part of Luca was lean, wiry muscle. His ass was no different. She stilled.

"Why did you stop? My ass would like a bath as well. I could do it, but I much prefer your hands on me." He growled. "Relaxing and exciting at the same time."

Her heart drummed in her ears. She lathered the soap again and did as he asked, losing herself in the tingling rioting through her body. Since when had a man's backside turned her on?

He groaned as she left electrically charged tracks on his skin.

She shook her head ruefully, turning him gently to face her. His heart cartwheeled under her hands as she massaged his chest, his heart galloping in concert with hers. His skin was warm under the crisp water. Memories assailed her—of touching him, tasting him, and dare she admit—she blushed again—biting him. She worked in larger and larger circles, dropping lower and lower to his narrow hips. He was so beautiful. She bent and kissed the scar running inside his hip—remembering why he had it, sadness welling up in her, and then, with a will of its own, her hand moved slowly over his smooth, thick rigid length. It had been far too long.

Luca inhaled sharply. His palms slid over her breasts and down her flat belly. He stroked her hips and then cupped her ass, massaging it with more ardor.

"Maybe I wasn't done," she said.

"We have only begun," he said softly as his fingers played in the cleft of her cheeks and moved underneath to caress her sleek thighs, probing inside her core and then moving rhythmically with sureness.

Ari bucked in Luca's arms. "Yes," she whispered into his mouth.

He sucked and then gently bit her lower lip. Her body pulsed in response, pressing against him, aching to be filled. His body's insistence firmly prodded her belly.

He pulled back, eyes searching with an intensity that made her melt. "Come with me," he said, pulling her through the rainbow of spray into the grotto tucked away. Once there, he pulled her against him, his mouth seeking, covering hers. His unbridled hunger erupted. Luca devoured her with his mouth, tongue, teeth, and hands.

Ari arched against him returning all his touches, kisses, and soft bites.

He slipped his hands beneath her cheeks. "Jump as I lift you." Hoarsely he said, "Wrap your legs around me."

She did as Luca asked, moaning loudly as he thrust into her. Their mouths and bodies fused, and they took turns without speaking, playing with their pace, stretching out the edges and absorbing the reeling sensations behind the fall of water at the grotto's opening, delirious with passion as they sought to wring each other and themselves out.

TOMORROW WAS IT. WHERE IN hell did her summer go? And what a summer! A knock on her door pulled Ari from her thoughts. "Hi!" was all Ari could muster, lost as she was in Luca's green depths. When would she stop feeling giddy and shy around him?

"Good evening, sweetheart." Luca kissed her deeply and then took his time admiring her. "I really like you in that yellow sundress." Grinning, he added, "If you have to wear something."

His words and sexy smile almost had her pulling him into her room and stripping him. But tonight was the party, the breaking up of the team. That's what it felt like anyway. "Thank you. I like you in that green tee. Brings out those amazing eyes of yours."

"Amazing, huh?" He kissed her leisurely and fully. His thumb under her chin lifted her gaze, allowing him to look deeply into her eyes. "Ready?"

Her voice trembled with emotion as he took her hand. They walked toward the *comedor*—where the team gathered for their last time together before departing to their homes and places of work scattered all over the globe. "As ready as I can be. I hate to see everyone go. I will miss them terribly. I feel adrift, Luca."

He stroked Ari's hand with his thumb in silent answer.

Dinner was rowdy, quite a change from when they had all met over three months ago. There was an abundance of laughter and a few tears as people jockeyed to talk to each other.

"Can I have your attention, please?" Joan stood and tapped her beer with a knife. "Hello? Hello?" she called over the loud talk. She tapped louder, and the room finally quieted. "Thank you, friends. I want to say a few things." Her voice cracked with emotion. "I'll try to make this short and sweet."

Some soft laughter broke out, and then the room was silent.

"I know. I'm not one to be succinct. Well, except for my mapping. I arrived lost in Guatemala, a lost, lonely widow. I have had the time of my life, and I wish to thank Luca for making me—I believe the oldest by far—part of the research project. I have a renewed sense of purpose and a spring in my step. Each of you is remarkable, and I hope that I, in some small way, contributed to helping with and documenting the excavation and ensuing discoveries. I hope to see each of you again and to support you with my work. I will miss you dearly. Please stay in touch."

The room erupted in applause, and more than a few were wiping at their eyes. Luca appeared next to Joan, wrapping his arms around her shoulders and giving her a big side hug. She beamed up at him, said something, and then left. The room quieted again.

Surveying his colleagues in the room, Luca spoke slowly, his voice full of emotion. "As you know, I have participated in many projects and headed more than a few. This project was one of the most fulfilling and definitely the most harrowing." He paused before continuing. "The synergy among you is outstanding, given your unique focuses. When I was asked to oversee an interdisciplinary team, well, I almost passed. I could not conceive how it would work. Think about it. The primary objective was archaeological and anthropological exploration. Sure, I built the team as requested—inviting linguistic anthropologists, epigraphers, biological anthropologists, ornithologists, botanists, and entomologists to ap—"

Slightly in his cups, Matt boisterously interrupted, standing and raising his beer. "Hey, Boss, you're a molecular biologist, entomologist, and a medical anthropologist. Quite an interdisciplinary package. Works for you."

Laughter erupted around the room. Meg took that opportunity to reach out and guide Matt back to his seat, kissing him quiet.

"You have me there, Matt. Thank you." Luca grinned at Matt to assure him his interruption caused no ill feelings. "Have another beer." He continued after the laughter died down, conviction fortifying his words.

"As I was saying, I had my doubts regarding assembling the different disciplines. I could not have been more wrong. In the future, I wish to model more teams such as ours. I expect others will as well. As you now know, besides being a standout anthropologist, Natasha moonlights for Interpol. I have been in continual contact with her since she took the American—Eric Schaus—into custody. He is recovering from his injuries, if any of you are curious. He will never walk quite the same though, and he will be prosecuted.

"The site of Ajal is now officially renamed as Xquic, in honor of the mother of the Hero Twins. If you have any questions regarding the significance, read *Popol Vuh* or ask Ari." Luca winked at her. "Her knowledge is encyclopedic. Xquic has been offered to me, to oversee. I accepted."

Chaos erupted. Luca waited patiently for the talk to die down. His gaze rested on Ari, pleading for her to remain calm.

Meg elbowed her, speaking into her ear. "Did you know, girlfriend? We've simply got to talk. Your Eric is the American! Omigod, Ari. I never put it together. The guy we pulled up was such a flipping mess, like something trampled him. Unrecognizable, other than being a human."

Ari shuddered at Meg's mention of the trampling, remembering what Carlos said in the temple. She spoke out of the side of her mouth, her eyes riveted on Luca and what he was going to share next. "I had no idea. And he is not my Eric. Only Eric. The biggest fucking asshole to ever live. I'll fill you in, I promise."

"All right. Thank you for your support and attention. I have one more item. I welcome the chance to work with you again. There will be an application process for permanent and rotating positions. I expect that I will be inundated with requests after the news gets out about the site. Funding is already coming in. Any of you applying will receive priority consideration. The site has particular significance and is currently secured by Guatemala's Bureau of Educational and Cultural Affairs and Interpol. I am going home to tidy up my affairs and put in a request for a sabbatical, then return." Luca raised his beer. "Thank you all, and safe travels. *Salute.*" He made his way toward Ari, extending his hand, he asked, "Accompany me outside?"

She reeled from Luca's news and checked her emotions as they walked hand in hand, understanding he had been bound by confidentiality. They had avoided talking about the future. Her stomach, head, and heart were a mess. Ari bowed her head, blinking back tears and struggling to calm the fear making her heart to beat erratically. She sat on a concrete bench in the moonlight on the promenade, facing the water. Her arms were drawn in stiffly against her ribs and crossed in her lap, legs crossed at the knees, clenching and unclenching her hands—to the point of pain.

He sighed deeply, sitting down next to her. "Look at me, Ari."

She turned slightly, gazing into the thickly fringed bright green eyes of the man she loved, the man she trusted with her life and wanted to trust with her heart.

"Sweetheart. I am sorry you are so distressed, and I am also sorry you had to find out in this manner, in front of the team. I was bound by confidentiality." He drew her closer to him, kissing her softly and taking her hands in his. "I wanted to ask you to stay, but I feel like it is a lot. You and I have happened quickly, unexpectedly. I went crazy when you were kidnapped, and what you meant to me became very clear. That night we argued, before you were taken, Nat and I were discussing some serious issues with the project. You did not allow me to explain."

"I know, and I'm sorry for that. Natasha told me the same thing before she left Ajal with Eric. I've let it go, Luca."

"There are things I said that I should not have said, and there is something I should have. I love you, Ari. I heard you that night of the kayak trip. I pretended to be asleep. After loving and marrying the wrong woman, I was scared. I was scared to hear it from you and to say it, to trust what we both feel for each other. I want you with me, but you have a life back in America. I am torn."

Ari went slack-jawed. Deep within herself, she had buried the hope that Luca might feel about her as she did him. But hell, who falls in love in a span of mere months? It was the thing of fairy tales, something she had desperately clung to for so long. Could she trust that it was real? Her eyes widened and filled with fresh tears. She was giddy with joy. "I love you too. I meant it when I said it the first time."

He grinned, his eyes glowing. He let out a long breath he'd been holding. "Thank God. Come here." He pulled her into his arms.

She resisted, standing up and stepping away, fiddling with the *colibrí* hanging from her necklace. "I love you, but I'm afraid."

"Of me?" he asked earnestly.

"I'm afraid of falling, Luca."

"What do you mean, falling?"

"Falling in love. Falling for the wrong man again. Falling out of love."

He gathered her to him, holding her close, running his hand over her back. "I'm not him, Ari." He felt her stiffen.

"How does this work? You and me?" she asked into his chest, into the very place his heart beat erratically, just like hers.

He set her away from him, looking into the earthy brown eyes that felt like home, his mischievous glint challenging her. He continued to hold on to her upper arms. "Would you consider coming back here with me? Working side by side, permanently? The funding coming in can more than support us, and we can stay in the large RV that the American was forced to vacate. Our work is not glamorous, but it is a passion we share and it is important. What do you think about flying to the States first and then to Italy, to get our affairs in order? I want to meet your parents, and I wish for you to meet my family."

Ari was totally overwhelmed. She was at a loss for words, soaking in what he had said. What if it didn't work out? She placed her hand on Luca's forearms and looked into his eyes, pleading. "I need some time to think, Luca. I need to go back home and see if I feel the same about you, about us. We've been in our own world this summer."

"Ari," he said in anguish, running his hands through his hair. "I can go with you, then you will be sure how we fit into the everyday world."

"Please, Luca. I need time by myself. I really think this is the right thing for me to do."

Breathless, Ari wriggled free and stepped back. "I need to pack." She choked through her tears and turned, running up the steps.

He fell back onto the cement ledge, remembering the much better memory of their hot passion and driving Ari wild. *Merda.* What should he do now?

The Guatemala City airport was busy; however, the check-in moved efficiently. Ari was bleary-eyed, having not slept well. She had cried herself to sleep and most of the way into Guatemala City. Hours early before she needed to check in, she plopped onto the linoleum floor, using her duffel as a back cushion against the wall. She set an alarm on her phone, then pulled her knees up and wrapped her arms around her ribs, taking a deep breath, attempting to clear Luca from her thoughts and silence the mishmash of emotions jostling inside her like bumper cars. Her gritty eyes stung as she closed them.

It was of no use. She couldn't stop thinking about him. A lone tear trailed down her cheek; then another chased it. More threatened to follow. She scrubbed at her face with the heels of her hands, not wanting to call any more attention to herself than her hair already did—granted, her Cubs hat concealed most of it. She needed to get ahold of herself. She'd feel better when she got on the plane. But another voice niggled inside her. But what if she didn't? What if she was making the biggest mistake of her life? She took a shuddering breath and put her earbuds in, nodding off, transported by soothing music, waking to her alarm two hours later, having dreamed of him, of them.

Her steps were leaden, full of the sadness permeating her soul, as she stepped up to the counter. Nausea swirled in her stomach as she placed her duffel to be weighed. "I'd like to purchase a ticket, *por favor*," she said, handing her passport to the ticket agent.

A familiar voice spoke up behind her as the agent reached to take it from her. "What is your final destination?"

Ari whipped around. She knew she looked a mess with her swollen eyes and blotchy face. He didn't look a whole lot better. Purple smudges lay under tired eyes. Her heart rocketed to life. "Luca," she said breathlessly. "I… I… don't need to think us over. I know."

He smiled a sexy dimpled smile, and his eyes glowed. "I know too." He pulled her into his arms. His heart raced like hers. "I began to fall in love with you in Cobán, at the bus stop. I was tantalized by your short fuse, that gorgeous hair of yours, and those bright pink panties. *Merda.* My love for you has only grown. I only want more, *bella.* More time. More conversation. More laughter and sharing. More going to bed and waking up to a new day with you. More loving you."

Tears coursed down Ari's checks and dripped off her chin. A blazing smile lit her face and eyes. "I want that too, Luca."

"Then where to, *bella*?"

"How about Italy with a long layover in the States?"

Luca stepped up to the counter next to her and handed his passport to the agent. "We are traveling together. Two tickets, please." His arm snaked around her waist, pulling her next to him, where she fit perfectly, kissing her deeply.

ACKNOWLEDGMENTS

Afraid to Fall is my first work of fiction, inspired by numerous trips to Belize, Guatemala, Mexico, and Nicaragua. Creating the story, allowing my characters, observations, and passion for those cultures to steer the arcs and substories was unbelievably fun. I hope you enjoyed it.

I want to thank my editors Anne Victory and Starr Waddell for their meticulous work. Your questions, comments, insights, patience, and humor were monumental.

Cupcakes for my writing colleagues: Enid, Kassie, and Marjie. You've been with me every step of the way, and I love you all for it. Celebrating with me upon finishing the manuscript was delicious. Thanks for pushing me and encouraging me, especially when my brain stalled. Your support and ability to make me laugh so hard that I snorted was invaluable.

You are my muse, Karen. Your insight, questions, and ideas challenged me. I so appreciate your patience and enthusiasm when helping me work out the kinks and problems, and your uncanny ability of seeing the forest through the trees when I could not.

To my four kids and husband, I love you more than I can ever tell you. For the many times I called you by one of the characters' names or started to, so deep was I into writing in those moments and transported into the story, I'm sorry. Thanks for giving me space to dream and create, for placing meals in front of me when I forgot to eat, and for being the best cheerleaders a blossoming fiction writer could ask for. Thanks too, for patiently waiting until the blank expression faded from my face and I returned to the real world to be present with you. Always you.

GLOSSARY

For interested readers, I've included a glossary of Mayan words used in *Afraid to Fall* and their English translations. An asterisk denotes the Mayan words that were used fictitiously.

Guatemala recognizes twenty-one Mayan languages. I opted to use Q'eqchi' due to its prevalence in the Petén Department of Guatemala, where the majority of *Afraid to Fall* occurs.

Semuc Champey: "where the river hides beneath the earth" is located in the Alta Verapaz Department, near the Q'eqchi' Maya town of Lanquín. The karst formation consists of tiered, turquoise pools atop a three-hundred-meter bridge naturally created from limestone. The Cahabón River flows beneath it.

**Kanul*: "abundance of serpents" is the archaeological site housing the excavations of Kaq and Rax.

**Kaq*: "red" is an excavation area within the Kanul site. The Mayan color for the cardinal direction of East, where the Father Sun was born, who illuminates a person's path and shows them the correct course of decision or action. *Kaq* is always at the top of Mayan maps.

**Rax*: "blue" or "green" is an excavation area within the Kanul site.

**Ajal*: "awakening" is the previous name of the *Xquic* site.

Xibalba: "place of fear" is the Mayan underworld in *Popol Vuh*.

Xquic: "Blood Maiden" is a mythological figure of Xibalba, from the *Popol Vuh* and the goddess of the waning moon. The Hero Twins' mother. The new name of the Ajal site.

Sutton Bishop enjoys having a foot in both worlds—real and make-believe. She has degrees in forensics and anthropology and a minor in world history. Her writing is inspired by her travels and life experiences. She lives in the Midwest with her husband, their four kids, and a passel of pets.

Afraid to Fall is Sutton's debut romance.

Find Sutton online at:

Website: www.authorsuttonbishop.com
Facebook: www.facebook.com/Author-Sutton-Bishop-268554723644909/
Twitter: www.twitter.com/SuttonBishop2 (@suttonbishop2)
Instagram: www.instagram..com/authorsuttonbishop/